Mermaid Hair
and I Don't Care

CJ MORROW

Tamarillas Press

Cover image: ©Jenny Tiley
Design: © CJ Morrow

ISBN: 978-1-913807-09-2

For my family.

Books by CJ MORROW

Romantic Comedy:
Escape to Christmas Cottage
It's PAMELA Rigby Actually
Sooo Not Looking For a Man
We Can work it out
Little Mishaps and Big Surprises
Mermaid Hair and I Don't Care
Blame it on the Onesie
A Onesie is not just for Christmas

Psychological Thriller:
Never Leaves Me

Fantasy:
The Finder
The Illusionist
The Sister

One

'How's it going, Lil?' Oliver Banstead breathed fag breath and stale *Old Spice* aftershave over Lily as she approached.

'Great.' She pushed past him on her way to the stairwell – the best place for a private phone call at Bensons Wholesale Electricals.

'Heard anything about the job yet?'

'What job?' Lily could hear her own indignation. How did he know?

He tapped his nose, gave her breasts a lecherous grin. 'Don't worry, you'll get it; you've got all the right *credentials*.'

'I beg your pardon.' She was giving him a chance to apologise.

'Just joshing, just joking.' He winked and waddled off.

'Disgusting fat toad,' Lily said under her breath. He got away with murder because he was the company's most successful salesman though Lily didn't think that was justification for some of his behaviour.

Once in the seclusion of the draughty stairwell she

rang her best friend.

'Hi Tess. How are you?' Lily began before she continued without waiting for the answer. 'Can I borrow your navy and pink shoes? I need them tonight.' Lily waited on her mobile while Tess considered her answer.

'Yeeesss,' she said, but it was a drawn out yes, a hesitant yes.

'I promise I won't damage them. Anyway, I got them repaired last time. No harm done.'

'Mmm,' Tess still sounded unsure. 'Okay.'

'Great, I'll pick them up on the way home from work. Got to go. See you later.' Lily ended the call and left the cold, echoey stairwell.

Lily had worked at Bensons for six years and, despite the creep that was Oliver Banstead, it had always been a great place to work. Until lately. As she made her way back to her desk she wondered how long the company would still be called Bensons, wondered if it would even exist in a year's time.

'Sorted?' Damon asked as Lily sat down. He spun his chair round and, still sitting on it, walked it over to her desk. He rested his chin on his hand and waited.

'Yeah. No problem.' Lily gave an involuntary shudder at the memory of the last time she'd borrowed Tess's shoes – the repair had probably cost more than the shoes were worth.

'So you're all set for tonight?' Damon giggled, then clamped his mouth shut to suppress it.

'Yes. Definitely.' Lily shook her head and swung her hair back behind her shoulders. It was long, dark, glossy and curling in all the right places thanks to the last-minute super blow-dry she had managed to squeeze in at lunchtime.

'Looks fab,' Damon said, taking the cue.

'Thanks. Feels a bit odd having it like this. At work.' She gave a half-embarrassed laugh. Lily never wore her hair down for work; it was far too unruly. She had a hair-dress code just as she had a work-dress code – serious, smart, business-like, hair pinned up and sprayed into place until rigid. Completely under control. It ensured that on first impressions you were taken seriously. You could impress with your excellent work once you were in the job. That was how she had come to be joint-head of finance at Bensons Wholesale Electricals at the age of thirty-one. Joint-head with Damon, who at forty-seven said he had no ambitions to climb any higher but was being very supportive of Lily's aspirations.

'Do you think you'll hear anything before your two weeks off?' Damon whispered so no one else would hear. Sound carried in Bensons, which was why you had to make private calls in the draughty stairwell.

'Probably not.' Lily sighed. But it would be a great start to her annual leave if she heard she'd been appointed finance director before five pm.

'Did they say they'd let you know before your holiday?'

'No. But Oily Bastard just asked me about it. Does everyone know I've gone for it?'

'I don't know. I certainly haven't told anyone. Not even The Europeans.' He glanced over at his hardworking team, Urve from Estonia and Beata from Poland, their heads down as usual, quiet and studious; Damon frequently congratulated himself on choosing such excellent staff.

'He gave me one of his special leers, peered right down my cleavage. I should report him; he's disgusting,'

Lily continued. 'Then he passes it off as a joke.'

'Were there any witnesses?'

'No.'

'Never are. He's clever like that. Anyway, he's top salesman again this month…' Damon's voice trailed away.

'It's a disgrace that he gets away with his behaviour just because of that. I can't believe no one ever complains; this is the twenty-first century for God's sake.'

'He's harmless really, just from another era. It's all talk. He stares at my cleavage.'

'You haven't got a cleavage,' Lily said.

'*Moobage*, then,' Damon said, crossing his arms, hunching his shoulders and squeezing, just to prove the point. 'But he still stares. Dirty leche. Anyway, never mind about Oily Bastard, you've got tonight to look forward to.' Damon gave Lily a wink.

'Yes. I have, haven't I?' She sat up straight and breathed in deeply. Tonight's the night, she thought to herself. Definitely tonight.

'We had a bit of bad news while you were away,' Damon said, his shoulders dropping. 'Josh is going. Leaving today.'

'What? How? I was only away a few minutes. Poor Josh.'

'He's all right about it. He's well past retirement age. Apparently, they've been very generous. A good redundancy package, he said. And he can claim his state pension now; he's been deferring it. Says it's good all round.' Damon looked pleased with himself, he was such a hub of gossip, or as Damon like to call it, essential information.

'Poor Josh,' Lily said again. 'I'll go and wish him

good luck before he goes.'

Poor Josh who worked in the post room, who'd worked there, so the story went, since his wife had run off with his best friend twenty-five years ago, leaving Josh with two stroppy teenagers and the need for a less stressful job. Various stories circulated that he'd been an astronaut or a city banker – neither rang true; Josh had a rotund body and a jolly face with a matching personality. No one could imagine him athletic enough to go into space or mean enough to be a banker. He looked much more the part he played at the company's annual summer fete – a fortune teller, complete with crystal ball and gold earring.

Poor Josh. Was he the first of many? Nobody knew. If Lily didn't get the finance director job she didn't know whether she would still be at Bensons herself. It had been made clear to everyone that Bensons didn't need two heads of finance; it needed one, and a director. Damon was as keen for Lily to get the job as Lily was, otherwise they'd both be applying for one job – each pitted against the other.

Ever since Bensons had been subject to a hostile takeover nothing had been the same. Rumours abounded, people had left – not made redundant it was emphasised – without so much as a goodbye, processes had changed, everyone felt nervous, jumpy.

'I'm so sorry you're leaving, Josh,' Lily said as she entered the post room.

Josh was leaning against the counter top; surveying his domain. He had a wistful look on his face. 'Probably the best time. I'm not getting any younger,' he said, turning and smiling at Lily. 'They're outsourcing. Much cheaper, they say. Not sure how that's going to work, but what do I know?'

'I'm sorry, Josh. I had no idea.'

'No?'

'No. Really. I know everyone thinks Finance knows everything, but we really didn't know about this.'

Josh shrugged. 'Would have made no difference. Don't worry about it.'

'What will you do?' Lily was beginning to wish she hadn't come to see him. Was she making him feel worse?

'Well, I think I might go and stay with my sons for a while.'

'Your sons?' Lily said, thinking of the stroppy teenagers. Of course they weren't stroppy teenagers anymore; they would be older than her now.

'I might even move down near them. They both live near the coast with their families – I've got seven grandchildren now. They're always asking me to go down there, stay longer than just a holiday. Nothing to stop me now. Devon awaits.'

'Sounds really great,' Lily said, sounding horribly false and overly cheerful.

'And what about you?'

'Me?'

'Have you heard about the job?'

Lily's eyes widened in alarm. 'What job?'

'Finance Director. You went for it. How did it go?'

'How do you know?'

Josh laughed. 'Everyone knows. We're all backing you.'

'Thanks,' Lily said, thinking how humiliating it would be if she didn't get it. 'Well, good luck Josh. I hope you have a great time with your sons.' She held her hand out.

Josh took her hand, shook it, then holding onto it, placed his other hand on top. 'Ooh,' he said. 'It's a big night for you tonight.'

'What?' Did everyone know her business?

'Life changing,' he said, letting her hand go. 'You do the right thing, Lily.'

'What do you mean?'

Josh picked up his bag, tapped his nose and left, leaving Lily standing in the post room alone.

What the hell was that about?

Lily knocked on Tess's door and waited. Then knocked again when Tess didn't answer.

'Just coming,' Tess's voice called from an open window upstairs.

'Hi,' Lily said when Tess finally came to the door.

'Come in, come in. Sorry. I couldn't find them, I was hunting for ages.' Tess went through into her kitchen. She handed the shoes over; they were still in the bag from the shoe menders. 'I haven't worn them. To be honest I never felt safe in them after what happened.'

Lily winced but said nothing. They'd been friends since they'd met in the reception class at school and that friendship had never failed, but sometimes Lily knew that she pushed her luck – especially when it came to borrowing shoes, these ones in particular. Lily and Tess were like chalk and cheese, Lily was loud and a little brash, Tess was sweet and gentle. Physically they couldn't be more different too, where Lily was sturdy – a word her mother often used to describe her – Tess was delicate; often hiding behind her fine, fair hair. Fortunately, they wore the same size shoes.

'In fact, why don't you have them? Keep them. I think you've worn them more than I have anyway.'

'Let me give you something for them.' Lily thought about how much they had already cost; she should have just bought a pair herself to begin with.

'No. No. I don't want anything for them. They're a gift.' Tess leaned in and hugged Lily.

'Thank you, hun,' Lily said into Tess's hair.

'So, what's the big occasion? Why do you need the shoes?'

'I think tonight's the night.'

Tess's eyes narrowed. 'Meaning?'

'I think Will's finally going to do it. Finally going to ask me to move in with him.'

'Okay,' Tess's voice had that hesitant tone again. Lily hated that. 'Why tonight?'

'Because he messaged me at six this morning and he'd written 'URGENT' in block capitals, several times. Said he'd booked a table at Fabio's and had something important to ask me.'

Tess's mouth dropped a little. She nodded. 'Oh.'

'And, and, it's our ten-year anniversary. That was a Friday too. Well, nearly. The actual date is tomorrow, but you know what I mean. I remember it like it was yesterday.' She remembered parts of it anyway. The less drunken parts, but wasn't everyone drunk at uni? Wasn't that why you went?

'Okay.' There was that annoying hesitation yet again.

'What?' Lily snapped.

'It's not as if you've actually been together all that time, is it? It's only really been about two years, hasn't it?' Tess paused. 'And you thought he was going to ask you on Valentine's Day, the last time you wore the shoes. Are you sure you want to wear them again tonight? Not worried they're unlucky or jinxed?'

'No. And yes, I do want to wear them; they go with my dress. Anyway, I think he was going to ask me then. It was just when I got stuck in the drain it sort of killed the moment.'

'Like an omen,' Tess said, half to herself.

'No. No. Why are you being mean? I know you and Will don't get on but really...'

'We get on fine,' Tess said, patting Lily's arm. 'I like Will, I really do. It's just that you were so upset when he didn't ask you last time, I don't want...' Her voice trailed away. 'Look, I don't want to spoil it. You go and have a great time. Tell me all about it tomorrow.' Tess's big, false smile was just too bright.

'Yes, but you've pooped all over it now.'

'I'm sorry.'

'Mmm. You're forgiven, but only because of the shoes. I love these shoes.' Lily held the bag up and grinned.

'They always looked better on you anyway,' Tess said; but Lily knew that wasn't actually true.

'I'd better go.' Lily headed for the front door.

'Have an amazing evening,' Tess called as Lily got into her car. 'Hair looks fab, by the way.'

'Thanks.'

'And, Lily.'

'Yes?'

'If he doesn't ask you, you can always invite him to live at your place.'

Lily considered for a moment. 'No,' she said. 'His place is much bigger. And better.'

♥ ♥ ♥

Lily spent the next two hours plucking, waxing, shaving, tweezing, exfoliating and buffing. By the time she zipped up her dress and stepped into the shoes she was exhausted and hungry, but she looked and smelled delicious. She was ready and waiting to be picked up; in fact she still had fifteen minutes until Will's arrival.

'Just enough time,' Lily said out loud, 'to paint my nails. Yes.' She pulled out the drawer of nail varnishes, sifted through the bottles looking for the right colour. She wanted something elegant and alluring and sexy – and something quick drying, very quick drying.

She found the dry-in-sixty-seconds maroon polish, shook it, and began to paint her nails. Wow, it was just the right look – elegant, classy, and definitely alluring. One coat was fine but two would look just perfect, even if it might take longer to dry.

She wandered around the house flapping her perfect nails in the air to ensure they dried. The wander also helped her get used to the shoes –she'd forgotten quite how high they were and that they pinched a little. She was determined that there wouldn't be a repeat of the last time when she'd got her heel stuck in the drain. She'd felt such a fool as her foot dropped five inches and her ankle went over onto the filthy drain cover. She'd felt an even bigger fool when Will had prised the shoe out of the drain and been livid that he'd dirtied the knees of his new trousers. She remembered only too well the horror of wearing the shoe as she clip-clopped into a restaurant full of gawping Valentine diners and the heel flapping behind her like a giant dog's tongue.

Lily was determined nothing was going to go wrong tonight. Nothing. She imagined the surprise she would feign when Will suggested she move in with him. She could move in immediately – they'd both already agreed to take the next two weeks off work but not go away, just spend some quality time together doing anything they liked, spontaneously. Perfect timing.

She ran to open the door when Will knocked. He beamed at her, his lop-sided grin, his head of thick, floppy hair making him the most gorgeous boyfriend ever. Soon they would be proper live-in lovers. She could refer to him as her partner, instead of her boyfriend.

Lily grinned back and stepped forward to hug him, then stopped.

'You're wearing your biking leathers,' she said, blinking in disbelief. She'd hoped for flowers but all he carried under his arms were helmets. 'I thought we were going to Fabio's.'

'We are. I thought we could go on the bike. I've got the spare helmet with me.'

'But…' Lily waved her hands at her clothes. 'I'm not dressed for biking.'

'That's okay, just get changed, babe.' He stepped inside, dropped the helmets and began to unwrap the hideous old wool scarf he wore for biking. 'Hold that,' he said, thrusting it into her hands. 'I need to use your toilet.'

Lily stood still and, stunned, waited for him. She could feel her mouth setting into a hard, straight line and the scratchy wool scarf was making her hands itch.

'Get ready,' he said when he returned and grabbed the scarf from her. It pulled on her nails.

'Argh. Look what you've done.' Instead of the elegant maroon talons she now sported white fluffy paws.

'Sorry. Oh God you've got those damn shoes on.' He glowered at her feet. 'You can't wear them on the bike.'

Lily breathed in slowly. 'I'm not going on the bike. And neither are you.'

Will glanced at her, opened his mouth to speak then changed his mind. He threw the scarf on the sofa and began unbuttoning his leathers.

'Okay,' he said. 'You win.' Then under his breath, 'as usual.' He was, at least, wearing a decent shirt and smart jeans under the leathers. 'You'd better call a taxi,' he said as he smoothed his jeans out over his biker boots. 'Unless you want to drive.'

'No.' Lily said, envisaging champagne as she picked up her phone. She glanced at the fingernails and sighed.

'Make it quick too; I had to grovel for the table and we can't be late.'

So there'd be no time to redo the nails then. Lily's heart began to sink. Maybe Tess had been right about the shoes, maybe they did bring bad luck.

They stood in line at the restaurant, waiting for the waiter to seat them. That was the trouble with Fabio's, it was everyone's favourite Italian at the moment and they were capitalising on it, turning people away, or making them wait out on the pavement. From her place in the queue she could see a table with an ice bucket, a bottle of champagne peaking from beneath a folded white cloth. She examined the smooth couple in front of them, her so slender and with perfect nails, him so suave and much older than his companion – it was definitely for them.

'You have booked?' the waiter asked in heavily accented English.

Will leaned in and answered. Lily didn't even try to hear what he said just watched mesmerised as the smooth couple were shown to their table, one that didn't contain the champagne. Maybe Lily had been right; maybe Will had ordered champagne.

'Err please. This way.'

They followed the waiter.

'For us?' Lily said, realising that the champagne *was* for them. 'You did this?' She leaned over and kissed Will full on the lips.

'*Bellisimo,*' simpered the waiter as he pulled out Lily's chair.

Things were looking up.

'I'm so glad you could make it tonight,' Will began. 'I know it was short notice and that we hadn't planned on seeing each other tonight.' That wasn't strictly true; Will had said he was busy.

'How could I refuse when you put urgent in your message?' Lily beamed. 'What's the champagne for?'

Will beamed back. 'You. Me. Us.' He laughed and nodded to the waiter to pour. 'What are you having? I might go for the steak. I expect you'll be choosing your favourite pasta.'

Lily laughed. He knew her too well. She took a sip of champagne and felt the bubbles glide down her throat. Champagne. Will never bought champagne. It must be a special occasion; she could barely contain her excitement.

'I love this restaurant,' Lily said, after her second glass of bubbly on an empty stomach; it was already going to her head.

'I know you do,' Will smiled and Lily's stomach did a

quick little flip; he was so devastatingly good looking, a gym-buff body and thick, dark hair. 'That's why I chose it.' He winked.

They shared oysters as a starter, Lily's idea. Will didn't particularly like oysters but he agreed without hesitation. That was a good sign, wasn't it?

'How was your day?' Will asked. 'How's work?'

'Not good. People are twitchy. Someone got made redundant today. Josh. Remember him? He was the fortune teller at the summer fete.'

'Old chap? Dressed as a woman?'

'Yes.'

'He probably should have retired years ago.'

'That's not the point,' Lily said as the waiter laid their main courses down in front of them.

'Prego,' the waiter said.

'Thank you,' Lily and Will chorused.

'Prego,' the waiter said again.

'Thank you,' Lily said again.

'Prego.'

This could go on all night. Lily watched Will scowl and the waiter melted away.

Will was scrutinising his food, separating the vegetables from the meat, he didn't like the two to touch. When Lily cooked for him at her place she served his food on a special large plate she'd bought at a flea market. That way there was never any chance of contamination. When he cooked for himself in his own home, he often served vegetables in a bowl, separate from the meat – if he bothered with the veg at all.

Lily smiled secretly to herself; she'd soon get into the swing of these cute little quirks when they lived together, or maybe train him out of them.

'What was so urgent that you had to message me at

six this morning?' she asked, feeling excited. It was the first time she'd felt brave enough and mellow enough to ask; the furry nail varnish didn't matter now.

'Ah, yes. That's what I wanted to talk to you about.' Will gave a nervous little smile.

Bless him. Lily beamed encouragement back at him. He cut a piece of steak and popped it into his mouth. Lily watched and waited as he chewed and chewed. Finally, he swallowed.

He opened his mouth to speak, 'Well…' he said but was cut short by three men bursting into Fabio's. A murmur went through the restaurant as first Will's, then Lily's, attention was caught by the trio.

They had violins.

They were pushing their way in between the tables and heading straight for Lily and Will.

Lily put her hand to her mouth.

How romantic. How thoughtful of Will.

She couldn't wait to tell her friends. She couldn't wait to tell her parents. She pictured the drive up to see them, Will at her side and the whole family planning for the future.

The violin trio reached Lily and Will's table. Lily let out a little contented sigh as they paused and readied themselves to play.

The music struck up, Lily didn't know what it was, some cheesy *romantica* song. It didn't matter; it was the thought that counted.

Then they walked past Lily, past Will and stopped at the smooth couple's table. The man nodded and the trio focused their attention on his lucky companion.

The song went on for ages. Lily felt sick. Every note stung. She wanted to stand up, call them back, tell them they had got the wrong table, the wrong couple.

Will cut in to his steak; Lily watched him pop another chunk into his mouth. He caught her eye and winked.

Oh well, all wasn't completely lost. It didn't matter; it was still their special night.

'I wonder how much that cost?' Will rolled his eyes and began chasing peas around his plate carefully manoeuvring them away from the steak.

Lily shrugged and stabbed at a pasta shell; she really wasn't hungry anymore.

When the music stopped all the diners clapped. Lily joined in. Will stuffed another chunk of steak into his mouth and carried on chewing.

'Oh,' Lily said as she watched the man get down on one knee. She heard the words, "Will you marry me".

From across the table Will grimaced at Lily.

After the new fiancée had said yes, the diners clapped again. Even Will stopped eating and put his hands together, rolling his eyes again. The violin trio started playing 'Congratulations'; people sang along.

'That was a bit much,' Will whispered, when it was over.

'Shush,' Lily said, as the violin trio left and everything returned to normal. 'It was romantic.'

'Bit too showy for me,' he said.

'Really. How would you do it?'

He shrugged and laughed, pushed his empty plate away and called the waiter over. 'Can I get a beer?' He raised his eyebrows in question at Lily; she shook her head; the champagne was more than enough alcohol for her.

'So what was it that was so urgent?' she said, giving him another opportunity.

'Oh yeah, about that.' He looked shy and bashful,

embarrassed even.

Lily leaned forward and smiled encouragement.

'I wanted to ask you…,' he stalled.

How sweet. Lily felt warm and soft.

'I wanted to ask you…Well it's about our holiday….'
His voice trailed away again.

Bless him.

'We're not having a holiday,' Lily said, helping him
out.

'Yeah, that's what we agreed, but…'

Oh my God. Oh my God. He'd booked a surprise
holiday. Had he? A surprise holiday to celebrate their
ten-year anniversary. Could that be possible? Lily's little
heart fluttered in her chest.

Calm down, he hadn't said anything of the sort.

Yet.

'I just need to use the facilities,' he said, standing up.

'But…' Lily said to his retreating back. Had he
actually said anything about a holiday? Had Lily got so
excited, so carried away that she'd missed what he was
saying?

She tapped her furry nails on the table as she waited
for him to come back. He was gone an awful long time.

'Sorry about that,' Will said, sitting back down. He
belched loudly. Lily could smell it. She turned away.
'Sorry,' he said and then sniggered.

Lily jumped straight in. 'You were saying about our
holiday, or rather, our time off work.'

'Yeah. That.' Will picked up his beer and took a long
swig before putting his glass back down on the table.

Lily waited. The shoes were starting to really pinch
now; she'd forgotten how much they did that. She tried
to flex her toes.

'You know how we said we weren't planning

anything these two weeks, just being spontaneous, take it as it comes?' He reached for his beer again.

'Yes,' Lily said. Did she sound too eager?

'Well, bit of a change of plan.'

'Yes.' Lily leaned forward. She was definitely sounding too eager now.

'You know Jed, my mate?'

'No.'

'You do. He's Big Lee's younger brother. You know Big Lee.'

'Yeah.' Will worked with Big Lee and Lily began to wonder what his younger brother had to do with their surprise romantic holiday.

'Well, he's booked a holiday biking across America, right across from New York to LA, through all the states in between. Sounds cool, doesn't it?'

'That would take ages.'

'Yeah, about four weeks. With stops. Of course.'

'Yeah. I can imagine.' Could she? Did she really care?

'Jed is going with a bunch of mates, four of them. Only one of them broke his leg last week playing football – how stupid is that? Means he can't go. So Jed's invited me along instead. Everything is booked and planned. Now I just turn up and go. How cool is that?'

Lily's heart sunk. 'But it's our ten-year anniversary.'

'What is?'

'Tonight. It's ten years since we got together.'

'Is it? But we haven't been together for all those ten years, have we? More like two. It's not like a real anniversary, is it?'

'Apparently not.' Lily sighed. Underneath the table she kicked the shoes hard against each other until they came off; no point in suffering the pinching now.

'When is it?'

'What?' Will finished his beer and plonked the empty glass on the table.

'This biking thing?'

'Tomorrow.'

'What? Tomorrow, tomorrow?'

'Yeah. That's why it was so urgent.'

'But you said you wanted to ask me something?'

'Did I?'

'Yes.' Lily pulled her phone from her bag and flicked through her messages. 'Here,' she said, flashing the phone in Will's face. 'I'll read it out, shall I? *URGENT, URGENT. Booked a table at Fabio's. Something important to ask you.* So what did you want to ask me?' There was still a chance Will could redeem himself. There was still time. Wasn't there?

But Will's blank expression told Lily that there wasn't. 'Um,' he said. 'I suppose I just wanted to check it was okay with you.'

'Why? Why bother with all this?' Lily waved her arms around her head. 'All this wining and dining. Why bother? You're going anyway, aren't you?'

Will didn't answer, just looked into his empty glass. 'Do you want another drink?' he asked.

'No. I. Bloody. Don't.' Lily said, grabbing her handbag and feeling for the shoes under the table with her feet. She found one and pushed her foot into it – the pinching was worse than ever; she shouldn't have taken them off. She found the other shoe just as Will shuffled in his seat which meant he moved his feet which sent the shoe flying across the restaurant floor, skittering along the gap between the tables.

'Idiot,' Lily hissed, getting up with as much dignity as

she could, given that she had one foot several inches higher than the other. She limped between the tables, stooped to pick up the shoe and stomped out.

She stood in the street inhaling deeply, holding back tears of frustration and anger. She flicked through her phone for a taxi number.

'What was that about?' Will's voice said from behind her.

'Are you joking?'

'Look, I'm sorry I spoiled our holiday, but we didn't have anything booked, so it's not like we've lost any money or anything, is it? No real harm done. You could go and do that spa thing you suggested we did. You'll have plenty of time for all that now. You know, hair and nails and all that stuff. You'll enjoy it more without me.'

Lily glared at him. Glanced down at the nails he had spoiled, realised that he hadn't even commented on her super smooth blow dry, never mind admired it. 'I can't spend two weeks doing that. When I suggested it for us it was for one day, a couples' day. You know, massages, that sort of thing.' She sniffed hard, fighting back the tears.

'What?' he said. 'What now?'

'Those ten years we've been together, or not, according to you,' Lily said, her voice breaking, her head wobbling with fury. 'Consider them over. Forever.'

'Come on, babe, you don't mean that.'

'It's finished. Enjoy your bloody biking holiday. I never, ever want to see you again. Do you understand?' She didn't wait for him to answer because the taxi arrived and she jumped straight into it, slammed the door behind her and told the driver to go. She didn't look back, she didn't wave.

Will could go and rot in hell.

Lily hobbled from the taxi to her front door, slammed it shut behind her and kicked off the cursed shoes – maybe Tess was right. She caught sight of herself in the hall mirror, her face streaked with tears, red-rimmed, mascara panda eyes staring back at her. That's what Will had done. Selfish toad.

His biking leathers were still spread across the back of her sofa where he'd left them; his helmets took pride of place on her dining room table. She took everything outside, lifted the lid of her wheelie-bin and dropped them into it. They hit the rubbish festering in the bottom with a reassuring thud. She hoped they were soaking up the fetid bin juice.

Two

'What you need is a holiday. Right now.' Tess picked up Lily's iPad and started searching for holidays.

Lily felt numb. They were sitting among the debris of a takeaway pizza that Tess had brought with her and eaten most of – Lily seemed to have lost her appetite.

'Where do you fancy?'

'Nowhere on my own.' Lily inhaled through her nose, filling her lungs, determined that she wasn't going to cry again. 'I can't believe he's done that to me. Just buggered off like that. He's already gone. He messaged me from the airport. He's even changed his WhatsApp photo to a map of the US.'

'Yeah,' Tess said her tone suggesting that she didn't mean yes at all. 'Here's one, Cornwall. Beautiful quaint village just five minutes' walk from blue flag beach. That sounds nice.'

'Will and I went to Cornwall once. It rained the whole time.'

'Not Cornwall,' Tess said, swiping the page away. 'Devon. Ever been there?'

'No.' Lily shook her head slowly. 'He must have

booked extra annual leave; he only had two weeks booked and he's away for four. But he said he only knew about it the day before.'

'Never mind, sweetie,' Tess muttered, stroking Lily's hand and pushing the iPad at her. 'Look at this one. It looks nice.'

'Yeah. It does.'

Tess grabbed the iPad back and began to read out the description. 'Idyllic, one-bedroom character cottage, modern bathroom, country kitchen. Just ten minutes hike from excellent surfing beach. Available now due to cancellation. There's a phone number. Sounds good. Shall I ring?'

'I don't really want to go away on my own,' Lily whined.

'You won't be on your own. Weren't you listening to me last night when you rung me at midnight? I said I'd get some time off and I have.'

What a kind, loyal friend Tess was. Even after the long sobbing phone call she hadn't even uttered one single "I told you so". Not one. And she would have had every right to say it, because Tess had warned Lily not to expect too much from Will.

'Oh. Okay. Yeah. Good. Thank you.'

'So, shall I ring them?' Tess sounded as though she was irritated with Lily now, which wasn't normal for sweet natured Tess.

Lily supposed she'd even exhausted Tess's patience. 'Yes please,' she said, pulling herself up on the sofa and straightening her shoulders. 'Sod him.'

Ten minutes later the deed was done, credit cards had been flashed and two weeks in Devon beckoned.

'Better start packing,' Tess said, laughing. 'We're going tomorrow. I'll drive so you don't even have to worry about that.'

'Great. Thank you.'

'Try to sound a bit more enthusiastic.' Tess leaned over and patted her friend's knee. 'Come on, it'll be fun. Just you and me, doing girly things like we used to. Remember that holiday we went on with your parents when we were thirteen? Remember the giggling after lights out?'

'My parents were pretty strict, weren't they? We had a nine pm curfew.'

'I thought your parents were cool. If it had been my mum it would have been eight pm. Remember the pool and the water slides? That was great fun. And fish and chips most evenings and popcorn in that funny little cinema with the threadbare, sticky seats.'

'I think they might have been leather.' Lily smiled at the memory.

'Maybe, but still sticky.'

'Urgh,' they chorused together.

'I remember that summer because at the beginning of it I was taller than you and by the end you had overtaken me.'

'Oh yes, I remember.' Tess smiled.

'I also remember you saying I'd catch up, but I never did.'

'No. Well, a bit.'

'Not at all,' Lily said, but didn't laugh. 'That's why I wanted to wear your shoes last night; because Will is so much taller than me and I wanted to match up to him.'

Tess smiled again but didn't say anything.

'Doesn't matter now,' Lily sighed. 'I can't believe that the last ten years meant so little to him. He hadn't even realised it was our anniversary. I really thought he was going to make some sort of commitment; I've dropped enough hints. I told him last year I was looking for something more… permanent. He agreed it was a good idea then turned up with that bloody pet rat with its scary little hands and giant front teeth. Said it would be great company for me.'

'Oh. So that's where it came from. You never said.'

'Would you? I was so horrified that he'd do that and too embarrassed to tell anyone, even you.'

'Well it went to a good home. My nephew, Rafe absolutely loves it, he's taught it tricks and everything. They're quite intelligent you know.' Tess was doing her best to jolly Lily along.

'At the very least I thought he would ask me to move in with him,' Lily said, sick of even thinking about the rat. 'He's got that lovely big house.'

'It's not *that* lovely…' Tess's voice trailed away.

'No. Well he's got that big house that could be lovely.' All it needed was a damn good sort out, redecorating and all the man-cave crap dumping. 'Doesn't matter now. It's over. It's finished. I'm not going to waste any more of my life on him. Loser. Waster. Arsehole. He can swan around America on a bloody stupid motorbike in sweaty leathers, getting chafed thighs and a greasy neck. I don't care. I don't want him. I don't need him. I'll get over him. I've got better things to do. I've got my career.'

Tess's head, which had dropped a little during Lily's ranting monologue jerked up. 'Have you heard something?'

'No.'

'I'm sure you'll get it. You're brilliant at your job. They'd be stupid not to give it to you.'

'Bit of big step up though, 'head of' to 'director'. I think my age might go against me.'

'No, no. You said that about the 'head of' job.'

'I want it more than ever now. I want to prove to myself, and that bloody bastard, that I don't need him. Rumour has it only two were interviewed – me and an external.'

'You're a shoo-in. They always give it to the internal candidate.'

Lily sighed. 'I hope you're right, it would take my mind off this Will rubbish.'

'What you need is a holiday romance.'

'Urgh, no.' Lily's nose went up as her mouth went down. 'I'm off men. Completely.'

'There's nothing like a rebound to perk you up. A holiday romance is perfect. No strings. No chance of bumping into them in the middle of Sainsbury's on a Saturday morning when you've just popped in for a pint of milk and you've come from the gym and you're still in your gym gear and you reek a bit.'

'What?'

'No chance of them being your mum's best friend's cousin.'

'What?'

'Well, you know what I mean.'

But Lily didn't. Was Tess speaking from experience? It sounded like it.

'I don't know what to take with me. What are you taking?' Lily screwed up her eyes. 'What's the weather like there?'

Tess laughed. 'Same as here probably – all weathers. Take warm clothes and cool clothes and swimming gear. We can go in the sea.'

'Yeah, I have always wanted to learn to surf. Sort of had the chance that week in Cornwall with Will, but he worries about the pollution in the sea so won't go in the water. He wouldn't, so I couldn't. The sea will be freezing though.'

'No. It's summer.' Tess laughed as she picked up her handbag. 'I need to get off now. All this talk about clothes has made me realise I might have to do some emergency tumble-drying and now I think about it, emergency waxing too. Oh God.'

'I'm covered on that,' Lily said with a bitter laugh. 'Spent quite a bit of time last night defuzzing. Waste of time as it turned out.'

'Well now it won't be; you're beach ready. I'll pick you up about eight.'

'Eight? That's early. It's Sunday. I usually have a lie in.'

'Plenty of time for that on holiday. We've got two whole weeks, and I want to miss the traffic.' Tess gave Lily a quick hug. 'Eight. Okay.'

Lily stood on the doorstep and watched Tess drive away and eyed the ugly wheelie-bin. She really needed to drag it round to the back garden, especially if she was going to be away for two weeks. She grabbed it and began to trundle it down the side of the house. Then she remembered Will's leathers and helmets.

She stopped, lifted the lid and peered in. They were gone. The cheeky bastard had been round and retrieved them and not even knocked on the door, not even put a note through the letterbox. Had he followed her home and watched her dump them in the bin? Now she thought about it she was sure that's exactly what he'd done; he'd definitely have come round to retrieve the biking leathers, he needed them for his holiday. If she'd been in any doubt, or having any regrets about dumping him, she wasn't now.

On the plus side they must have stunk to high

heaven; that bin had never been cleaned out ever and the stench made her gag.

Last night's dress and the infamous, ill-fated shoes were still on her bedroom floor. She dropped the dress into the laundry basket then fished it out and wondered if she would need it in Devon. She sniffed it, the aroma of Italian restaurant – lovely when you're there, not so lovely when you're not – drifted up her nose. Maybe not. She dropped it back in the laundry and kicked the shoes under her bed. She'd never wear them again.

Two hours later Lily lay on her bed exhausted from the effort of thinking about packing, actually packing, and kneeling on the suitcase and fighting with the zip to get it done up. She thought about Tess's car, which wasn't big, realised that her suitcase wouldn't fit in the boot and decided it would have to go on the backseat. But that was okay; Tess would probably bring enough luggage to fill the boot anyway.

After tidying up and showering, Lily set the alarm on her phone – seven am, urgh – and climbed into bed. Will's face drifted into her consciousness, his beautiful brown eyes, his thick wavy hair that was always in his eyes, always being swiped aside. He had the most infectious smile, he laughed easily. What a shame the outside didn't match the inside – selfish, immature Will.

She closed her eyes and waited for sleep to come and when it didn't she picked up her phone. Why? Why?

There it was, a message from Will: *Just to let you know I arrived safe and sound. Suffering a bit from jet lag but okay otherwise. Hope we can still be friends?*

Friends? Friends? Was he mad? What a stupid question. Of course he was mad. Mad, selfish and stupid. She deleted the message then flicked through all of his messages intent on deleting them too. What a fatal mistake; she'd never realised how many photos he sent her. Endless selfies of the pair of them together. There must have been ten of them taken on the London Eye.

She remembered that day with fondness – her birthday – a special treat he'd arranged in secret. It had been followed by dinner and a show, Les Misérables, her favourite. Even though Will hated musicals, and that one especially, he'd sat through it and almost enjoyed it, just for her. She remembered them running down platform three at Paddington Station just managing to get the last train home, him berating himself for not booking a hotel, her telling him she preferred her own bed anyway. And they'd spent most of the next day in it too.

Maybe he wasn't so selfish.

Not all the time anyway.

She fell asleep and dreamt of Will. In the dream he asked her to marry him and in the dream she said no. There was no likelihood of either ever happening now.

The alarm went off and shocked her awake. Was it really seven already? She allowed herself a little doze and woke again thirty minutes later, it was all hell let loose then to make sure she was ready when Tess arrived. Tess didn't do late, didn't understand late and had no tolerance for those who embraced tardiness, even if she did smile sweetly to cover her exasperation.

But this time it *was* Tess who was late, by a whole ten minutes. She arrived breathless and pink-faced at Lily's door.

'Hi.' Lily cast her eyes over Tess's face looking for a sign. 'Everything okay?'

'Kind of. Sorry about being late. *Not* my fault. My God is that your case? What have you got in it?' Tess's eyes dropped to Lily's bulging luggage. 'It won't fit in the boot.'

'Yeah, really wasn't sure what to bring. It can go on the back seat, can't it?'

'Umm. Yeah. Err…'

'What? It's not dirty or anything. Or have you already filled the back seat up with your stuff?'

'No, no. It's fine. Shall we go?' Tess leaned in and grabbed Lily's case and trundled it to the car while Lily locked up. When she reached the car she could see the suitcase already filling most of the rear seat and Tess was fiddling about in the boot. Lily headed for the front passenger seat, grabbed the door and yanked it open.

'Oh!' she screeched. 'You nearly gave me a heart attack.'

'You know Gemma, my sister-in-law.' Tess was standing next to Lily with a pained look on her face. 'Back in a minute, Gem,' she said and closed the car door, pulling Lily away. 'Sorry about this. Bit of a family crisis. Kicked off last night. Gemma and Joe had a big fight so Gemma's coming with us until things cool down. It could be make or break for their marriage and there's my niece and nephew to consider. Anything we can do to help… well… you don't mind, do you?'

'Doesn't sound like I've got a choice. But is there room? At the cottage, I mean?'

'It's okay. I've rung them. They're going to put

another bed in the bedroom. It'll still be fun.'

Lily shrugged and sighed. She already had misgivings about this holiday. 'I'm guessing I'm in the back.'

Tess nodded slowly and led her friend round to the driver's side, opened the door, leaned in and pulled the driver's seat forward so that Lily could clamber in behind it.

'Hello, Lily.'

'Hi, Gemma.'

'I hope you don't mind me gate-crashing your little holiday.' She paused before continuing in a whisper, 'Need to get away.'

'Course not,' Lily said as Tess got into the car, pushed her seat back and rammed it into Lily's legs. Between the front seat crushing her legs and her own suitcase pressing into her ribs and chin she felt as though she were in the coils of a boa constrictor.

She winced silently.

'Sorry I have to sit in the front but since I had to have that emergency caesarean with Pixie-Bella, I've never been right.'

'Mmm,' Lily said to the back of Gemma's perfect blow-dry.

'That and I get car sick; never was before I had that wretched epidural.'

Lily didn't respond. Pixie-Bella must be six years old by now and didn't everyone use the car sick excuse to sit in the front. Gemma picked up a Massimo Costa coffee and sipped it through her immaculate lipstick. The car filled with the aroma of coffee, it made Lily feel light-headed especially as she hadn't had time for breakfast.

This was going to be a long journey.

Three

'I hear you've finally dumped that loser Will,' Gemma said, half turning to Lily.

Lily watched Tess's shoulders go up and tense.

'I'd rather not talk about it and don't call him that.' Lily turned away and looked out of the window.

'Take it from me; you're better off without him,' Gemma continued, undeterred. 'Don't get yourself saddled with a loser who tells you what to do then wants you to keep on having babies even though you nearly died with the last one.'

'You didn't nearly die,' Tess said quietly.

'Well. Felt like it at the time. They're all pains in the arse, Lily. They can't help themselves, it's all part of being a man.'

'Gem,' Tess said, dragging out the word. 'Lily doesn't want to hear this.'

'Why not? It's the truth. You're a bright girl, Lily, you've got a good job, you concentrate on that and don't rely on anyone; least of all a man.' Gemma stopped to draw breath before continuing. 'I hear he's buggered off to America for a sad-sack jaunt on a motorbike.'

Lily didn't answer but Tess did. 'That's enough now, Gemma. Just leave it there.'

Gemma clamped her mouth shut and Lily could tell even from the back that the effort not to speak was painful for her.

For the next hour and a half, Lily sat in the back and seethed. More than once she considered asking Tess to turn around and take her home. The holiday was supposed to be about forgetting Will, not having him rammed down her throat. She laughed out loud at the irony of that thought.

'That's the spirit. Sod him,' said Gemma taking her cue to start talking again.

Lily threw Gemma a dirty look but it bounced back off her perfect, cast iron hairstyle. It was one hell of a bob, incredibly dense and not a hair out of place, sleek and blue-black it had a personality all of its own: defiant. Perhaps feeling Lily's eyes on it, Gemma reached up with her perfectly manicured hand and smoothed it flat. Lily was sure she heard it crackle.

'Do you have extensions?' The words popped out of Lily's mouth before she could stop herself.

'Certainly not.' Gemma's voice filled the car with indignation.

'Oh.' Lily sat back and thought, serves you right for sticking your conk in my business. 'It's just that your hair is so thick and so perfect.'

'Yes. It just goes like this, so easily. I like to look groomed and while perfect grooming is never too much trouble, my hair is just so easy to manage.'

'Lucky you,' Lily said, pushing her own, now unruly mane back behind her ears.

As they arrived at Taunton Dean services a dog ran

out in front of the car, Tess executed a nifty swerve and an emergency stop.

'Tess, don't do that. Do you want me to be sick?' Gemma waved her hand in front of her face, fanning herself.

'Did you want me to kill the dog instead?'

'Too late,' Gemma said, fumbling in the foot-well until she found her discarded Costa cup. She peeled the lid back and vomited profusely into it.

The stench of coffee flavoured vomit made Lily and Tess gag simultaneously. Tess wound the window down at the same time as manoeuvring into a parking space.

'Sorry about that, but I did say, didn't I? People are supposed to keep their dogs on a lead when they exercise here.' Gemma huffed as she popped the lid back onto the Costa cup. She still looked immaculate, even her lipstick remained perfectly intact.

Lily could hardly stand up and held onto the door after hauling herself out of the car. She wriggled her legs to get the circulation going.

'That,' said Gemma, pointing at Lily, 'is what my legs were like after I had Pixie-Bella. Lasted weeks.'

Lily sighed, Tess rolled her eyes and Gemma strutted off in search of the toilets carrying her vomit cup.

When Lily and Tess caught up with her she was at the sinks, she whipped a toothbrush complete with case out of her capacious designer handbag, produced some toothpaste from a separate front pocket and cleaned her teeth. Lily spotted what looked like a tooth whitening gel in that pocket too.

'That's better,' she said after the final rinse. 'I cannot stand the taste of vomit. Tess, no more swerving.'

Tess shook her head.

'I'm starving; shall we get a little snackette?' Gemma

led the way to the restaurant while Lily and Tess trotted obediently behind her.

It didn't take long for Gemma to nibble around the edges of a croissant before suggesting it was time to get back on the road.

'I'll have a word with her later,' Tess said to Lily as they followed Gemma to the car. 'She's so used to being in charge and telling her children what to do; she forgets how to behave when she's with adults.'

Lily climbed into the back of the car and folded herself into the seat. Before the vomiting incident she had planned to ask Gemma to swap seats; that was out of the question now. She rearranged her suitcase, pushing it away from her and pressing into Gemma's seat. Gemma twitched but had the good sense not to comment.

They set off and had barely covered five miles when Gemma turned around and strained her neck.

'What?' Lily snapped.

'Can you hear that noise?'

'What noise?' Tess said, alarmed.

'A tapping and buzzing. Can't you hear it?'

'No,' Lily said.

'Don't, Gem, you know I've just got this car back from the garage.'

'Sorry, Tess, but I can definitely hear something. Turn the music off and listen.' Gemma flicked the button on the radio and waited.

'I can hear something now,' Lily said, wearily. 'Sorry, Tess.'

'I can't,' Tess said. 'Are you sure? What is it?'

'It is tapping and buzzing. But it's only faint.'

'Where's it coming from?'

'The back,' Gemma said, sounding a bit too triumphant.

'Oh no,' Tess whined. 'That's the same noise the front axle thing made and that cost me a fortune. I hope it's not the back one now.' She began decelerating and indicated to pull over onto the hard shoulder.

The car crawled along the gritty tarmac.

'Can you still hear it?'

'Yes. Sorry, Tess, I can.' Lily patted her friend on the shoulder as Tess switched the engine off and pulled the handbrake up.

'I wish this had happened at the services,' Gemma said as they stood on the windy embankment watching cars hurtling past. 'This is playing havoc with my hair and at least we'd have been able to coffee ourselves up to cope with it.'

To Lily's eye Gemma's hair was still rock solid. Her own hair, however, was not. She cursed herself for not having her work hair – that would have withstood a hurricane. Friday's beautiful blow dry was now a distant memory, not helped by having to hurriedly wash her hair and not dry it this morning. She fished in her handbag for a hair-scrunchie while Gemma fished in hers for a cashmere shawl which she draped elegantly around herself while Lily and Tess shivered.

'The AA said an hour max,' Lily said, grateful that she had her card with her.

'I should join,' Tess said, half-heartedly. 'Especially now I officially have a crappy breaking-down car.'

'I leave that to Joseph. Thank God, your brother has some uses.'

But it was another two and a half hours before the

AA man arrived – they'd been informed via two phone calls that a lone female took priority – and they weren't alone so they would have to wait. During that time they had been beeped and waved at numerous times, offered a lift by a car full of teenage boys – even though they had no space - and by a car transporter. When the AA man did turn up it was Gemma who marched straight over to him and began talking the instant he opened his door.

'I've told him what the problem is,' Gemma said, hustling Tess and Lily away. 'Give the man the keys, Tess.'

'I can hear it,' he said, five minutes later. 'But I don't think it's anything serious.'

'Oh good. Thank you. Thank you.' Tess looked as though she might kiss him.

'Well, what is it? We need it sorting out. We're on holiday, you know. We can't spend two weeks wondering. You need to sort it out now.'

'Don't be so rude, Gem.' Tess smiled at the AA man but he didn't smile back.

'You'll need to empty the boot,' he said, heading for his van.

'And what will you be doing?' Gemma called after him.

'Paperwork,' he shouted back without even turning around.

Tess opened the boot and Lily helped her pull out the assorted bags and stack them on the verge while Gemma stood and watched.

'Aren't any of these yours?' Lily asked. 'Because I know none of them are mine.'

Gemma forced a straight-line smile at Lily but said nothing.

'There's the noise,' the AA man said, he was back clutching a clipboard.

Lily leaned in and picked up a cerise leather holdall. It buzzed as the contents knocked together. She put it down and began to unzip it. God only knew what was inside.

'That one's mine,' Gemma said, snatching the bag. 'And it's private.'

'And it's buzzing,' Lily said while Tess winced.

'I think that's the cause of your problems.' The AA man didn't bother to hide his amusement. 'Shall we check?'

'There's no need. Thank you very much, patrolman,' Gemma said, snatching the bag and getting into the front seat again.

Patrolman? Who the hell calls anyone patrolman? Lily laughed out loud when she heard it. Tess started to load the boot back up while Lily signed the paperwork. It appeared that Gemma was not going to help with the luggage. Again.

'I don't know if I can get on with your sister-in-law,' Lily whispered as they slammed the boot down together. 'She's a bit lady muck from turd hall. Maybe if we stop at the next services I could hitch a lift home.'

'Please don't. Please. I know it wasn't what we planned but I was put on such a spot. She was on my doorstep at one in the morning, wailing and performing like only Gemma can. But I was already awake and expecting her because my brother had rung. I hate it when they fight; I always seem to be in the middle of it. I don't know why.'

'Because you're too nice. But why did she have to come with us?'

'I offered her my place while I was away.' Tess

shook her head slowly. 'But she wasn't having any of it. You've seen what's she like. My mum calls her *Madame* in a French accent.'

'Why French?'

'I don't know, but it always makes us laugh.'

'I want to know what's in that bag.'

'I dread to think.' Tess shuddered.

They clambered back into the car. Gemma acknowledged their presence with a quick nod while staring straight ahead and clutching the offending bag tightly to her chest. Tess's seat pushed up against Lily's legs again, causing immediate pain.

'Before we go anywhere I want to know what's in that bag,' Lily said.

'It's private.'

'We have a right to know.'

'No, you don't.'

'Yes, we do. We stood on that windy embankment for hours and I'll probably never get a brush through my hair again, so I want to know why we had to suffer that.'

Tess started the car.

'Don't drive off yet, Tess,' Lily snapped quickly followed by, 'sorry.' She placed a hand on her friend's shoulder; it was both conciliatory and restraining. 'Give me the bag,' Lily said. She leant forward and pushed her arm between the front seats.

'It's not what you think,' Gemma hissed.

'Give it.'

'Have it.' Gemma flipped the bag at Lily and it hit her full on the nose.

'Ouch.' But Lily had her prize; she pulled it back into the rear seat and began rifling through the contents.

'Tongs and heated hair rollers and straighteners and

a hairdryer and brushes and serums. How the hell did you get all this in this bag? No wonder it was clanking and buzzing.' Lily eyed Gemma's rigid bob again – low maintenance? 'Oh, is this the culprit?' From the bag Lily pulled out a long plastic handle with a bobbly pink roller-ball on the end and flicked the on switch. It immediately started vibrating. Lily laughed. Tess sniggered.

'Don't be so smutty.' Gemma's voice was high and loud. 'It's a cellulite massager.'

'Of course it is.' Lily switched if off, stuffed it in the bag and pushed the bag back at Gemma as Tess put the car in gear.

Lily sucked her lips together and tried not to snort as Tess drove off.

Gemma never said another word for the rest of the journey. Even when, despite the satnav, they got lost and stopped twice to ask for directions, she sat silent, tight-lipped and stoic, her hands clasped on the bag on her lap.

They arrived at the cottage just after five and it was raining heavily, the clouds so low and thick that it felt like night. They sat and stared at the front door through high-speed windscreen wipers; none of them relished the prospect of getting out.

'Shall we wait until it eases off?' Tess said, turning the engine, and with it the wipers, off.

'Yeah. I hope it won't be too long; I'm dying for the loo and all this running water is making it worse. And I'm starving.' Lily flumped back in her seat just as Gemma's stomach growled its agreement.

'Excuse me,' she whispered.

'Don't worry, Gem,' Tess said. 'We all feel like that.'

Gemma turned her head away but not quickly enough for Lily to miss that she looked as though she might cry.

'Do you think it's going to let up?' Lily asked. 'What do you think, Gem?'

Gemma shrugged her shoulders but continued to look away.

Lily stared at the cottage; it was pretty; white walls under a dark grey slate roof, a neat little window on each side of a green door. But it looked tiny. It was enclosed on all sides by tall trees in full foliage that together with the rain turned daylight into twilight.

They waited another fifteen minutes during which time the rain got heavier and the windows misted over completely. Lily drew a smiley face in the condensation and Gemma neither moved, nor spoke.

Suddenly, when no one expected it, the rain stopped and the sun came out, filtering through the leaves and dappling the car in sunlight. Tess turned around and beamed at Lily before opening the door. Lily needed help getting out once Tess had pulled the driver seat forward. She stood in the fresh air shaking her legs, urging the blood back into them. By the time they reached the front door Gemma was already waiting, silent and sentinel and still clutching the buzzy bag.

Tess pulled her phone out and flicked through her messages. 'The key is on the upper right-hand window ledge,' she read out.

Finally, Gemma spoke. 'There is no upper right-hand window.' She sounded so damned imperious. 'Do they mean the upper right-hand ledge of the right-hand window?'

Lily and Tess exchanged silent glances.

Tess ran her fingers along the top of the window. 'Urgh, here it is,' she said, waving a dripping key about.

They fell through the front door into the kitchen, which opened out across the back to a dining and sitting area. The floors were slate and the walls were white, colourful rugs hugged the floor, colourful furniture spread around the room. The bedroom was the first door to the right of the front door, and the bathroom was at the end. They all ran towards the bathroom but it was Lily who won the race. Gemma's face was crestfallen and for one mad moment Lily almost offered Gemma the chance to go first. Then stopped herself.

When she came out of the bathroom Gemma darted straight in.

'I suppose we'd better get the cases in,' Lily said, feeling sick with hunger now.

'Done.'

'Oh you didn't do that on your own. You should have waited. I would have helped.'

'I helped,' said Gemma, fresh from the bathroom and smelling divine.

'Great,' Lily said as Tess darted into the bathroom. 'Nice perfume.'

'I saw a pub at the end of the lane, it does food too. Shall we go and eat now? I'm beginning to feel faint for lack of food and I'm getting a migraine.' Gemma patted her long, elegant fingers over her brow.

'Yeah, let's leave the unpacking 'til we come back,' Tess said, returning from the bathroom.

♥ ♥ ♥

The end of the lane was a soggy fifteen-minute walk,

but at least it wasn't actually raining and only the ground was wet from the occasional heavy drip from the trees above. The pub was as old as the cottage with a giant oak door that, judging by how hard they had to push it, had swollen in the rain. But once inside they were thrilled; the place was busy but not heaving, the aroma of hot food was alluring and the cheery welcome they received from a waitress already clearing a table for them was so inviting.

They flopped down into their seats at the same time pulling off their jackets.

Tess studied the blackboard specials while Gemma perused the main menu, but Lily just sat and took in the ambience – it was lovely. The walls were old stone, the tables and chairs were oak and tapestry, there was a real fire and, even though it was summer, the way it was smoking suggested it had just been lit.

The waitress took their drinks order – Lily and Tess had the recommended local cider and Gemma chose tonic water – while they deliberated over their food choice; although they were all so hungry that they could have eaten anything and everything from the menu.

'That's good,' Lily said, after drinking half her cider down in one go. 'What are you having?'

'Haddock from the specials menu,' Gemma said.

'Me too,' laughed Tess.

'That'll be three then,' Lily laughed. Whether it was the prospect of food, the comfort of the pub or the potency of the cider, she didn't know, but for the first time since Friday evening she was beginning to relax.

They followed their excellent fish dish with a sticky meringue, strawberries and clotted Devon cream.

'I love Eton Mess.' Tess licked her spoon.

'I love pub grub,' Lily said, finishing off her fourth

cider. 'It's so satisfying.'

'And calorie laden,' Gemma said, pushing her barely touched meringue around the plate before giving up and moving it to the side. 'I wish I could be like you, Lily, and eat whatever I want without caring about weight gain.'

Tess shuddered.

'Are you implying I'm fat?' Lily, subdued by the cider, was not as insulted as she should have been.

'No. No.' Gemma actually sounded flustered.

'Good. Because I'm not. I'm sturdy. You can ask my mum.' Lily burst out laughing and Tess joined in, a look of relief on her face.

The plates were cleared away, more drinks were bought and a pub quiz started.

'What shall we call ourselves? What's our team name?' Tess asked, wielding a pencil.

'Escapologists,' Gemma said. 'Because we're escaping.' She laughed rather too loudly and several people stared at her.

'I'm not escaping anything,' Tess said, softly.

'No, of course you're not. You're our…' Gemma fumbled for the right word. 'Carer,' she said, finally.

'Ooh, thanks.'

'I'm making up for you, Tess because I'm escaping two things; Will and my work situation.'

'They'll both work out,' Tess said, patting Lily's arm.

The quiz was a riotous mix of general knowledge, which Gemma seemed to have an abundance of, and local knowledge which none of the girls had. But they laughed and enjoyed themselves, clapped vigorously when the prize money went to a local and Gemma declared herself migraine free.

They stumbled out of the pub into a pitch black,

cool, damp night.

'Which way?' Lily said before giggling.

'That way,' Tess said, pointing up to a clear sky where stars blinked at them. 'Twinkle, twinkle.'

'Shush,' Gemma said. 'We should have brought torches.'

'Phones,' Lily and Tess chorused.

'What?'

'Torch app.'

They tottered down the lane by the light of their phones, Lily and Tess giggling, Gemma expressing concern about her shoes and potholes.

'It's very secluded down here,' Tess said, giggling again.

'Good. Makes it harder for anyone to find us.' Gemma's response was quick and snappy.

'Well, I don't have anyone looking for me,' Lily giggled.

'Shush, don't speak too loudly. Someone might be listening.'

'Who? We just said it was secluded.'

'Well, someone might be following. Or waiting. Come on.' Gemma stood between them and grabbed first Lily's and then Tess's arm and quickened the pace until they were almost running.

They fell through the front door, still laughing and giggling, kicked off their shoes and queued for the bathroom.

'It's nearly midnight,' Gemma said when she came out of the bathroom. She was the only one who had changed for bed, removed her makeup and cleaned her teeth.

'I'm sorry about the bag, Gem,' Lily said, feeling warmer towards Gemma now. The effects of the cider?

'Forget it.'

'No, I was mean. But I was annoyed after we stood on that motorway getting blown about.'

'And ogled,' Tess added.

'And beeped,' Lily said.

'Well, it's over now. I'm ready for bed.' Gemma gave a curt smile.

'Me too. And I can't be arsed to find my PJs.' Lily kicked her shoes out of the way and started pulling her jeans and top off. Gemma looked away and Tess giggled.

Lily threw her clothes on the kitchen floor and padded towards the bedroom in her underwear, but Gemma had beaten her to it. Their cases were stacked neatly in the corner and Lily looked around the room and frowned.

'There are only two beds,' she whined.

'No, there are three.' Gemma pulled back the duvet of the bed furthest from the window. 'I'll have this one.'

'I can only see one more bed,' Lily said, frowned.

'It's here.' Tess sounded forlorn. 'I'll take it.'

Lily padded round to Tess's side and tucked in between the second bed and the window was a low put-you-up bed. There was no space to walk down either side of it and it was at least a foot shorter and lower than the other beds.

'It's too short for you,' Lily said, looking up to Tess who was at least four inches taller.

'Yes, I thought so too,' Gemma said from beneath the covers which she'd already pulled up around her as she nestled down into her bed.

'Well you're not that much taller than me,' Lily said. She didn't feel quite so disposed towards Gemma now.

'And you're the gate crasher, after all.' Lily watched Tess's face screw up in what looked like pain.

'Yes, that's true.' Gemma paused. 'But I'm the one who paid for the petrol, didn't I, Tess?'

Tess nodded slowly.

'*And* I paid for tonight's dinner and plentiful drinks, in case you hadn't noticed.'

Lily thought about it for a moment then realised that she'd been quite oblivious when the time came to pay the bill. She hadn't even thought about who paid for it, or how. That cider must have been very strong.

'And I'm a little older than you. And I do have a bad back as I said in the car; I've never been the same since Pixie-Bella.' Gemma sighed.

'Fine, I'll sleep in the camp bed. Don't you worry about it.' Lily climbed onto the bed from the foot end and tottered along its length until she reached the pillow, then wriggled her way in under the duvet.

'I don't mind taking it, Lily,' Tess said.

'It's fine. It's not your fault.'

'Maybe we could take turns,' Tess offered.

'Yes, maybe we could. All three of us.' Lily hoped that Gemma was getting the message, but the gentle, rhythmic breathing that came from Gemma's bed suggested she was already asleep.

Lucky Gemma.

Four

Lily slept the longest and the deepest, and had the worst hangover.

'Urgh,' she groaned, peering up at the curtains dangling just six inches above her head. The sunlight sneaked its way beneath them and hurt her eyes. 'What time is it?'

No one answered.

Lily closed her eyes and groaned again. Her tongue felt like a dry sponge and was sticking to the roof of her mouth. Someone in the room stunk; it made Lily gag.

She could smell bacon. Bacon? And she was actually hungry even after last night's large dinner. She sat up slowly, her head thumping, her body aching. No more cider. Ever again.

She shimmied down to the end of the bed, her knickers riding up and giving her a wedgie as she did so. She wriggled to unravel them, then placed her feet on the floor. The carpet felt cold and rough. The stench was even stronger now; she looked around for the culprit.

'Oh,' she said, finding herself alone. The other two

beds were neatly made. When did that happen? She cupped her hand over her nose and mouth and sniffed.

'Urgh.' She found herself gagging again.

She stood up and felt the room sway, grabbed hold of the end of Tess's bed and manoeuvred herself along the floor to her suitcase. There was no sign of any of the other bags that had been piled there the night before. Unzipping a corner, she reached in, fished around and pulled out a pair of socks and a long cardigan.

'Morning Lily,' Tess said, smiling when Lily entered the kitchen. 'Coffee?' Tess waved a cup at her.

'Yes please. Where did that come from?'

'I brought supplies,' Gemma called from the other end of the room. She was sitting at the dining table in front of expansive bi-fold windows. Behind her the vista was bright blue.

'What's that?'

'Breakfast,' Gemma answered.

'No. I mean that blue.' Lily pointed beyond Gemma. 'It's sky.'

'What? Really?' Lily padded down to the table but before she could look outside she had to sit down quickly.

'Hanging?' Gemma laughed.

'Mmm. Weren't you two?'

'Yes,' Tess called over. 'A bit. That local cider is strong stuff. We'll have to be careful.'

'Not me.' Gemma's voice was smug and superior. 'I stuck to tonic water all evening.'

'Did you?' Had she really?

'Here, drink these.' Tess put the coffee and a glass of water in front of Lily.

'That smells nice,' Lily said, eyeing Gemma's empty

plate.

'Which is more than can be said for some of us.' Gemma arched a perfect eyebrow. She wore full make-up including lipstick which hadn't been dislodged by her breakfast.

'Is that smell me?' Lily asked, sniffing. Of course it was; who else could it be? And it really wasn't pleasant.

Gemma picked her plate up and took it to the kitchen. 'Would you like a bacon sandwich,' she called back.

'Love one. Thank you.' Then she turned her head to look outside. All she could see was blue; the sky seemed to go on forever (either that or the cider had affected her eyesight). She squinted looking for a horizon.

'We're up high,' Tess said by way of an explanation. 'We're on a hill. If you go outside you can see the sea.'

'There you go,' Gemma said, putting the bacon sandwich on the table. 'I knew you'd need one so I already had the bacon waiting.'

Lily's mouth salivated before she even began to eat, she'd have to be careful not to dribble.

The restorative qualities of greasy food is well known and not exaggerated. After eating the sandwich and drinking the water and coffee, Lily felt almost normal. She ran her hand through her hair, it was matted following the wind tunnel experience on the motorway and the frizzing effects of the late-night damp walk back from the pub.

'I think I'll take that shower that I obviously need,' Lily laughed, taking her plate to the kitchen and dropping it in the sink of hot, soapy water.

Gemma and Tess exchanged a furtive look.

'What? Sorry. I know, I know I honk a bit, but... well.' Lily shrugged.

'Yeah,' Tess began. 'Might be a problem with the water…' Tess's voice tailed off.

Lily waited, looking between Tess and Gemma.

'Yes,' Gemma added. 'I had to wash my hair,' she nodded her head around implying that it didn't look that good by accident despite her previously saying it was no trouble. 'And Tess had a shower and there doesn't seem to be any hot water left.'

'Sink's full,' Lily said, staring accusingly at the washing up.

'Boiled a kettle for that.'

'Well, can't we just put the hot water back on?'

'We could, if we could find it.'

Lily stomped into the bathroom and looked for a switch, a cupboard, anything. Finding nothing, she came out and stomped around the cottage, opening doors and starting to cuss.

'We've done that,' Gemma said.

'So what am I going to do? How will I have a shower? Can't you ring someone Tess?'

'Rang and left a voicemail and sent a message. No reply so far.'

'Great. What can I do? I stink. As you've made very clear, Gemma.'

'You could boil a kettle. Have a strip wash in the bathroom sink. My granny used to call it a cat's lick, swore by them.' Gemma turned away and started filling the kettle.

'Great. What about my hair? I can hardly wash that in the sink. It won't fit in it for a start.' Lily lifted her heavy hair and let it drop down.

'Tie it up for today,' Gemma said.

Lily doubted whether Gemma would make do with a cat's lick and a scruffy up-do for herself.

Lily balanced inside the shower cubical, standing in a bowl of hot and soapy water and tried to wash herself. It really wasn't very comfortable and every time she bent down she realised that the hangover was still lingering. Without a flannel or sponge – who brings those on holiday when you can have a hot shower – she was struggling to get clean. God knows what her hair would be like when she tried to brush it. Damn Gemma. Selfish Gemma had obviously used copious amounts of hot water on *her* hair.

'There,' said Gemma when Lily appeared in the kitchen twenty minutes later, clean – relatively speaking – and dressed. 'You look quite presentable. And your hair suits you up like that.'

'Thank you, Gemma. I feel just great,' Lily said, loud and slow.

'You're welcome.' Gemma smiled and seemed oblivious to Lily's sarcasm.

Lily's hair was tied tightly up but it wasn't the lovely sleek style she favoured for work, it was a bunch of knots hidden beneath a smoothed and patted down top layer. Her head was already starting to itch and her hand went up and scratched.

'You should probably get a shorter style if you can't cope with it. It is rather long and unruly.'

Lily stood open-mouthed for a second or two and was about to lay into Gemma when Tess caught her eye with an almost imperceptible head-shake. It was a plea, a plea for peace. Lily rolled her eyes and kept her mouth closed.

'I've made a nice pot of tea and taken it out to the

terrace,' Gemma said, impervious to Lily's hostility.

Tess followed Gemma outside and looking back, urged Lily to follow.

The terrace ran the width of the cottage and looked down towards the sea. Between the brilliant blue water and the cottage was rolling green countryside.

'How far is the sea again, Tess?' Lily asked.

'Ten-minute walk, I think.'

'Ten minutes by car, surely,' Gemma corrected.

'No. Walking. Or did it say hiking? Anyway, not by car.'

Gemma scoffed, then restrained herself and poured the tea.

'Gemma brought the tea and milk with her. As well as the breakfast things. Isn't she good?' Tess said.

Lily nodded. If Tess was trying to win her over she was wasting her time; Gemma was an interloper and a bloody bossy one at that. And a hot water hogger.

'Years of travelling with children,' Gemma sighed. 'Always have to be prepared.'

Lily thought of the bag of tricks Gemma had with her; the rollers, the hairdryer, the straighteners, the, ahem, cellulite massager. Yes, Gemma certainly travelled prepared.

They drank their tea in silence, staring out across the vista, inhaling the clean, sweet air and luxuriating in the gentle sunshine, which had crept up the terrace and was now bathing their faces.

Lily pulled her phone from her pocket. 'I haven't got any messages. Not one. Nor emails. Oh, no signal. Have either of you got a signal?'

'*I* haven't checked,' Gemma said, raising her chin and looking away.

'I had to walk up the lane a bit to ring the owners,'

Tess said. 'Coverage isn't very good.'

That would explain the lack of a message from Will then. After she hadn't replied to his last message she did expect him to try again. Surely even Will wouldn't give up that easily. She just hoped he didn't use the *friends* word again.

'It's warming up nicely,' Lily mused, closing her eyes and tilting her head up to the sky.

'The forecast is good. We're going to be lucky with the weather.' Gemma gathered up the cups and teapot and headed inside.

'I don't know if I can stand this,' Lily whispered to Tess when she heard Gemma clattering in the sink. 'Who put her in charge?'

'I'm sorry. I really am. But don't be hard on her; she's a lot more fragile than she appears.'

'Huh. I doubt that. Anyway, what about me? I'm fragile. I've just broken up with the love of my life.'

'Please…' Tess let the word hang in the air. There it was, that pleading face again.

'Okay.'

By the time Lily and Tess joined Gemma she had already washed up and was drying the last few cups.

'You'll need better shoes than those,' Gemma said, wiping her hands dry and staring at Lily's flip flops. 'They've obviously seen better days.'

'I'm happy in these, thanks. They may be old, but they're comfortable.'

'They're really not suitable for Exeter.'

'Exeter?'

'Yes. We've planned the day shopping in Exeter. It's lovely. Have you ever been there?'

'No. And I don't think I want to go today.' Lily glanced around for Tess who was looking at her own, city-shod, feet.

'Well, we've planned it. It's only about sixty miles; it'll only take ninety minutes at most.'

Lily shuddered. The prospect of another five minutes in the back of that car horrified her, never mind an hour and half with her knees permanently under pressure. She shook her head. 'I think I'll give it a miss.'

'But we're having lunch there.' Gemma's voice moved up an octave. 'What will you do all day?'

'I'll manage. Don't worry about me. I think I can feed myself.' Lily laughed, because if she didn't laugh she might shout at Gemma.

'But what *will* you do all day?'

'What's it to you? I'll go to the beach.'

'Well… well. I suppose it'll be all right.' Gemma huffed and picked up her handbag, turned to look at Tess who followed behind her meekly with her head down and avoiding Lily's gaze.

Gemma stood in the doorway and waited for Lily.

'I'm not coming,' Lily repeated.

'I know. That's fine. But I need to lock up. There's only one key.'

'I'll lock up when I go.' Lily sat down on the sofa to make the point.

'But how will that work? Supposing you're not here when we get back? How will we get in?'

'It's more likely that I'll be back before you.'

'What if you're not? I don't want to have to wait. Supposing you get lost on the way back from the beach? What then?' Gemma stood waiting for a reply.

Lily shrugged. She didn't care.

'We can leave the key where we found it yesterday.' Tess spoke quietly. 'Then it doesn't matter who's back first.'

'That's not very secure though, is it? We have all our luggage here, my clothes, my hairdryer.'

'I doubt anyone will want to steal your cellulite massager,' Lily sniggered. 'Do you?'

Gemma pulled her lips into a sharp pout and turned away. 'Just make sure that key is where it should be,' she called back over her shoulder.

After they'd gone Lily wandered around the cottage, running her fingers over surfaces, enjoying the peace. Gemma was a bossy prima donna. Lily didn't know how, or more to the point why, Tess allowed herself to be corralled like that. The only good thing about Gemma's presence and limelight hogging was that Lily hadn't had much time to dwell on Will. In fact, and she was surprised to realise it, she hadn't thought of him half as much as she supposed she should.

What did that say about their relationship?

In the bedroom Lily hauled her suitcase onto Gemma's bed and unzipped it. She opened the two wardrobes along the wall and discovered, as expected, that they were full – mostly with Gemma's clothes. They had, at least, left her the largest drawer in the chest.

A narrow door in the wall revealed another wardrobe, that would be Lily's then, and it would probably suffice. Then she noticed the timer-switch inside. That must be for the hot water. She checked the time. It would come on at four; she'd make sure she was back in time to use all the hot water she needed. She allowed herself a smug little grin.

Once unpacked she stuffed a towel, her bikini and an old, half empty bottle of sun cream into her tote bag, grabbed her sunglasses and a bottle of water – probably

Gemma's – from the fridge and left. Outside she locked the door and placed the key on top of the window ledge, making sure it was several inches along from where it had originally been. That would wind Gemma up if she was back first.

Lily set off down the lane in her flip flops looking for an obvious route towards the sea. Obligingly it presented itself a few minutes later. The faded green sign showed a walker and pointed the way.

The path was across grass that had been beaten flat by the passage of many feet. Lily walked along enjoying the sunshine, the calling of seagulls, the faint aroma of ozone from the sea. It was lovely and all topped off by the ocean glistening in the distance.

Bliss.

Twenty minutes later and the bliss was wearing off. The sun still shone, the gulls still called – although it now sounded as though they were laughing at her – the glistening sea wasn't getting any nearer and she was sweating, profusely.

She hadn't seen another soul on the entire journey. Was she lost? Had she gone the wrong way? Was she actually going around in circles? Would that explain how the sea never got any nearer? No. Of course not. The sea was always in front of her; she *was* heading in the right direction. She got her phone out to see if she could pull up a map. Still no signal.

She looked behind her, examining the path she had taken, it just seemed to go on for miles. She *must* have travelled miles. Ahead of her more of the same, except the path seemed to be heading into a wood. She felt a little tinge of alarm. She told herself to stop panicking and get on with it.

Five more minutes and she was in amongst increasingly dense trees. Wasn't it supposed to be just a ten-minute walk, or even a hike, but only ten minutes?

The path forked. Lily stopped in her tracks. Which way? Both paths looked worn and beaten down, but which led to the sea? Or was it both?

Ahead of her she glimpsed movement. She squinted, took off her sunglasses and used her hand to shade her eyes from the sharp shards of sun sneaking through the branches above. There was definitely someone there.

It could be an axe murderer. Just hanging about on the off chance that she'd be passing.

Don't be ridiculous.

Behind her there were just trees and acres of fields. Where was a noisy family with several children and a large dog when you needed them? She looked ahead – nothing. Just her imagination.

But which way?

She stared left; she stared right.

Movement. Definitely movement to the right. Someone *was* there. And he was coming towards her. She squinted into the wood. Could she run back fast enough to outrun him? Or should she take the left path? Would he be able to cross over and head her off? She stood rooted to the spot, their jokes from the previous night about the cottage being secluded running through her mind.

She breathed a sigh of relief as the figure came closer and stopped. He was rotund and white haired, he reminded her of Josh from work.

Hang on a minute, it was, it was Josh.

Lily laughed and called his name. 'I'm looking for

the sea,' she shouted.

He waved then beckoned her towards him, pointed down the path then turned back the way he'd come and walked on. Lily quickened her pace to catch up with him.

But she never did. My, that Josh could walk fast; always in her sight but never quite close enough. She thought about running, but the combination of walking for so long over uneven ground and sweating had made the flip flops rub her feet, blisters were forming with every step. Perhaps Gemma had been right about suitable foot attire.

Suddenly Josh stopped. He turned, smiled and waved. Lily raised her hand to wave back, then stood on something squelchy, looked down to see she'd trodden in animal poo – she didn't even want to think about which animal – then looked back to Josh. He'd gone. She wiped her foot as much as she could and carried on. When she reached the spot where she'd last seen Josh she could see the sea again. A narrow meandering path led straight down to the beach.

'Thank God,' Lily said aloud, looking around to see where Josh could have gone. But all she could see were trees and beach.

Lily stepped out of the flip flops once she hit the soft sand, her feet sank. It was cool, almost luxurious; the sand soothed her sore feet and soaked up the sweat. She examined the flip flops' soles but the gravely path down to the beach had worn off the animal poo. She wriggled her toes; the sand felt so good and the sun-sparkled sea looked so inviting.

The beach was wide; the tide was out so the sea was a hundred metres or more away. A surf shack, nestled well above the tide line, was doing brisk business; its colourful boards laid out in the sunshine, assorted wetsuits flapping in the breeze. Even with her sunglasses back on Lily had to shade her eyes to look out to sea. It looked rough, the perfect surfers' sea.

She walked past the surf shack – maybe she'd have a go later, she wondered if she had enough money with her. She bought a Devon clotted cream ice cream from the van parked on the firm wet sand below the tide line, then wandered back onto the dry sand to choose her spot.

Lily perched on a grey rock to finish the ice cream; it was already running down the cone and onto her fingers. She pulled her bottled water from her bag and used it to clean her hands before taking a generous swig; she was glad she'd brought it with her, it would save the hike back up towards the café she could see beyond the surf shack.

She spread her towel out and made herself comfortable. It was hot, much hotter than she had expected. After ten minutes she looked around for toilets, or anywhere she could use to change into her bikini, but she could see nowhere close and she wasn't going all the way up to the café. So she began the tug of war that is changing on a beach while trying to maintain decorum and modesty. Ten minutes later following a quick slathering of sun cream she was settled. She lay back, closed her eyes and slept.

Bliss.

When she awoke – and she had no idea how long she'd been asleep – her hangover headache was starting to creep back. Or maybe it was the sun. She sat up; the beach had filled with families and surfer groups spreading across the sand. The tide had turned and the sea was closer. It looked even more inviting than before. Lily drank what was left of her water, checked the time on her phone, calculated she'd been asleep for at least two hours, and wondered how cold the sea would be.

She stuffed her belongings inside her bag, then pushed the bag under the top of her towel so it looked like a pillow. She called over to a family with a baby and asked if they would watch her stuff. The mother nodded her yawning agreement.

Lily was surprised at how hot the sand now was, she stepped back into her flip flops for the walk down to the sea, she could leave them at the water's edge. She was aware of the sun's strength as it hit her back. Oh well, it would match the front eventually; despite the sun cream she had slopped on herself she could feel the familiar tingle of sunburn.

She left her flip flops well above the tide line and walked on the cool, wet sand. It felt so good. She screamed as the sea lapped at her toes; a little boy swimming in his water wings, giggled at her distress. She laughed back to him.

It was cold. So cold it made her feet ache. How could she think it would be otherwise? This wasn't Spain or Florida. Florida? Was Will going there? No.

She braved a few more steps, went in deeper, then stood and shivered. She heard the little boy giggle again, she turned, he was swimming away, almost completely immersed. If he could do it, she could. She took the plunge and waded in deeper. As the water slapped against her thighs the cold took her breath away. The only way to cope with it would be to dunk herself up to her shoulders. She squealed as her chin hit the water, she immediately jumped back up, but lowering herself a second time wasn't nearly so bad. She smiled over at the little boy; he waved back at her before swimming back towards the shore.

Lily floated on her back, her arms and legs spread like a starfish, she closed her eyes and let the waves lull her. The water was soothing and now her teeth had stopped chattering she was luxuriating in the soft ebb and flow of the lapping water. This was what holidays were for – forgetting your worries, chilling out. The sea rocked her, its rhythm soporific.

She heard the long roar before she realised what it was. The wave that hit her tossed her about like the flotsam she was. She struggled to breath, she couldn't see. The salt water stung her eyes and forced its way up her nose, down her throat, into her lungs.

She struggled to get her head out of the water; she didn't know which way was up. She stopped herself from breathing, from inhaling any more water. How far had she drifted? She scrabbled around trying to reach the ocean floor but felt nothing. Was it already too late? Was this the end? Was she drowning?

There was silence.

There was darkness.

There was nothing.

There was peace.

'You're okay. Just breathe. Just breathe.' The voice was male and reassuring.

Lily coughed and spluttered, her arms flailing.

'Keep your chin up. Breathe. Breathe.' A firm hand was supporting her chin, saving her life.

She opened her eyes as she coughed water into the face of her rescuer. His bright blue eyes showed concern.

'Okay?' he asked.

Lily blinked her agreement, she couldn't speak, her throat was sore, her lungs ached. She would have cried if that were possible. She'd nearly died. Nearly drowned. Floated out of her depth and taken by a wave because she wasn't paying attention. She wondered how far she'd floated out.

'Okay?' the voice asked again.

Lily managed a nod.

'Let's get you up,' he said, grabbing her arms and pulling her.

Her feet scrabbled around, panic set in. What was he doing? She was going to drown again. She flapped her arms, trying to shake him off, but he was strong, much stronger than her and he pulled her upright.

'See, you're okay.'

Lily stood up, her feet firmly planted on the sandy sea bed.

The water lapped gently against her thighs.

Five

'You're shivering,' he said, as they waded out of the sea.

Lily nodded. She wanted to speak but her throat was so sore she didn't even try. With difficulty, she attempted to swallow. It would have been very easy to cry, but she most certainly wasn't going to humiliate herself further.

'Let's get a towel around you.' He guided her up the beach back to her towel and bag.

How did he know where she'd been sitting?

He bent down, whipped her towel from the sand, shook it and wrapped it around her; he pulled it tight and rubbed her arms. She winced.

'Sunburn? Sorry.' He stopped rubbing and just held the towel tight. 'It's shock as well as cold,' he said as her teeth chattered. *His* teeth shone white against his bronzed skin. She noted his bright blue eyes again, or was that also an optical illusion caused by the tan? 'I'm Jackson, by the way,' he said.

'Lily,' she croaked. 'Thanks for helping me. I'm okay now.'

'You're getting there,' he gave a soft laugh.

She wished he would leave, go away, leave her alone with her embarrassment, but he showed no signs of doing that. He still held the towel tightly around her body, still appraising and assessing her condition.

'I think you need a hot drink.' He spoke with authority and bent down to pick up her bag. She held her hand out for it; he gave her a sharp look that said he wasn't stealing it even if she thought he was. 'Come on. I know just the place.'

He guided her up the beach and past the surf shack where a guy polishing a board nodded and grinned at him. Lily felt uncomfortable, but she also felt shaky and ill.

'Here we are,' he said, showing her into the Sunset Cove beach café and sitting her at a table in the window.

While he went to the counter, she dabbed herself as dry as she could and fished in her bag for her dress, hastily pulling it on. Her hair had unravelled from its up-do and hung in wavy rats' tails around her shoulders. She dabbed at it with her wet towel then pushed it back behind her ears.

Jackson had a quick word with the two women serving, then came back with cutlery and napkins which he laid on the table. He sat opposite her and smiled. She offered a quick smile back. He was being kind, she shouldn't be so grumpy but her throat still hurt and her eyes were smarting and she felt stupid and humiliated.

'This will help,' he said, as the waitress put a jug of iced water and glasses down. 'It'll help clear the salt from your throat. It's hell when you drink half the ocean.' He smiled again, his eyes crinkling at the sides. 'I've done it enough times myself.' He poured her a glass of water and waited while she drank.

It soothed, it lubricated, it washed away the vile taste. She poured herself another glass and downed that one as quickly as the first.

'Thank you,' she said, her voice sounding more normal.

'You were probably dehydrated too. Ah perfect, thank you, Marnie,' he said as the waitress put bowls of soup and hunks of bread in front of them both.

It smelled delicious. Lily peered at it, inhaled its soothing vapours.

'It's chicken,' he said. 'Best cure for everything.' He laughed, then his tone changed to one of alarm. 'You're not veggie, are you?'

Lily shook her head. 'No. And thank you.' She picked up her spoon and began to eat. It tasted so good. Her stomach rumbled its appreciation.

Smiling, he ripped off a piece of bread and dunked it, and Lily did the same. She savoured every mouthful, every morsel; she hadn't realised she was quite so hungry. Eating soup on a hot day was so wrong, and yet it felt so right.

'Thank you. I feel much better now,' she said when they'd finished. 'How much do I owe you?' She fumbled for her bag.

'Nothing. Really nothing. My treat.'

She opened her mouth to argue, saw the look in his eyes and instead said, 'Thank you, you're very kind.' She turned away, uncomfortable, embarrassed, and looked out to sea. She could see surfers standing on their boards, riding the waves. 'It's quite rough,' she said, musing, almost to herself.

'Yeah, that's why it's so popular with surfers.'

'It seemed so calm when I went in. I got that wrong, didn't I? Good job you were on hand.' She gave him a shy smile.

'You were in the wrong lane. I was coming to get you anyway.'

'Wrong lane. What do you mean?'

'The beach is sectioned off. Between the black and white chequered flags it's surfers only, between the yellow flags it's swimmers. You were in the surfers' section. Though the red flags will go up soon because it's getting too rough now, and that means no going in the sea for anyone.' He stopped speaking and looked away. 'Of course those who think they can handle the waves will still go in.'

Lily felt her face colour up, not only had she nearly drowned, she hadn't even noticed the flags. 'Sorry,' she mumbled.

'You were lucky a surfboard didn't knock you unconscious. These beaches look idyllic, and they are, but the sea can be treacherous at times. There are several drownings every summer. If only people would pay attention to the flag system.'

'Are you the lifeguard or something?' Lily was tiring of the lecture. She'd nearly drowned, wasn't that punishment enough? She wouldn't do it again.

'No. Just spend a lot of time here.' He looked out of the window, far out to sea; he was miles away, a forlorn look on his face. 'I help out at the surf shack too.'

Lily nodded. That explained the smirk from his mate when they'd walked past.

'Devonshire cream tea?' he asked, suddenly shaking himself back to the present and smiling over at Marnie. She came scuttling over.

Lily gave a nod and smile to the offer; she was tired and couldn't be bothered to disagree. Anyway, why not?

The teapot was a big Brown Betty, Lily guessed it

would hold six cups. The teacups were bone china and came with saucers and matching plates. The scones were still warm, the cream clotted, the jam strawberry. Lily took her scone and cut it in half. Then reached for the jam.

'Whoa,' Jackson said, laughing. 'You're in Devon now, it's cream first, then jam.'

'Okay, if it matters that much.' She shook her head and allowed herself to laugh before taking a generous dollop of cream while Jackson poured tea.

They ate their cream teas in silence.

'Where are you staying?' he asked as he wiped his mouth and hands with a napkin.

Lily hesitated for a moment. 'To be honest, I'm not sure what the address is. All I know is it's up a path behind the beach and then miles of tromping through fields. I almost got lost getting here.' The thought of the hike made her shudder; thank God Josh had pointed the way. 'It's a little cottage with a terrace overlooking the sea, but I think it's miles away, took me ages.'

'Pub at the end of the lane?'

'Yeah.'

'Key left on the top of the window ledge for you?'

'Y-e-a-h,' Lily said, dragging out the word.

'I know that place. I also know a better way back. I'll give you directions. It's no more than a ten-minute walk.'

'Thank you,' Lily said, feeling humbled. 'Am I so obviously on holiday?'

He laughed. 'Yeah,' he said, sipping his tea and looking at her over the rim of the cup with those damn startling eyes.

'What about you? Let me guess.' It was her turn to

appraise him now, to make him feel uncomfortable, but he didn't seem bothered as she scrutinised his face, ran her eyes up and down his body. He was tall, but not too tall, certainly not as tall as Will. He was muscular, probably from swimming and surfing, where Will was gym built. He was clean-shaven; Will favoured the designer-stubble look. His hair fair and straw-like, burnt by the sun and far too long, almost touched his shoulders; Will's hair was dark and definitely on trend. He wore beads around his neck and wrists; Will would never wear beads. Beneath the beads on his left wrist Lily could see a tattoo poking out. She frowned as she stared at it, trying to make it out.

'Well?' Jackson smiled.

'I was wondering about your tattoo.'

'My mermaid.' He pulled the beads aside and showed her the tattoo. 'Had it done in Ibiza when I was a teenager. It's not that good really.'

Lily leaned over to get a closer look, the tail flicked to one side, the hair spread across his wrist. It looked amateurish.

Seeing her face he said, 'A large enough watch covers most of it if I need to hide it.' He pushed the beads back into place.

'Why a mermaid?'

He shrugged. 'When I was a kid I thought I saw one.' He half laughed. 'Every kid who lives near the sea thinks they see a mermaid. Anyway, you were analysing me.'

'You're a surfer-type,' Lily said. 'I expect you bum around the world chasing the waves.' She sounded dismissive. 'I bet you've been to Oz and Hawaii and all those other places. Summer here, winter there.' She waved her hand about.

'You've got me pegged,' he laughed. 'You're right, I've been here since April, before that I was in Oz and New Zealand.'

'There you go,' Lily laughed.

'In my defence,' he said, leaning in. 'I was born here, grew up here and still have family here.' He nodded at Marnie. 'My aunt,' he said.

'Lucky you. Growing up here, I mean.'

'Yep.' He smiled. 'What about you? Let me guess. You live in a city, in a penthouse flat. You don't have a boyfriend because your career is too important. You meet with the girls for glasses of wine and a meal out once a month. You're studying to be an accountant.' He sat back and grinned.

'Ha, ha,' Lily said. 'I don't live in a penthouse flat, I live in a house, a small one. My career is important but not too important. I am an accountant, but I finished studying quite some time ago.'

'Whoa,' he said. 'Well done, you.'

Lily narrowed her eyes, was he patronising her or taking the piss?

'I mean it. I'm impressed.'

'Thanks very much,' she said, not meaning thank you at all.

'I didn't mean…' his voice trailed away. 'I thought we were playing a game. I didn't mean to offend you. If I have, I apologise. I'm sorry, Lily.'

When he said her name it was as though a shot of lightning coursed through her body. She shook herself and sat upright.

'Are you okay?' His eyes narrowed in concern.

'I'm fine. Really.' She fished her phone out of her bag and checked the time. 'I need to get back,' she said, thinking of the hot water that should be awaiting her.

'My friends will be back soon. They'll wonder where I am.'

'Of course.' He stood up. 'I'll show you that quick way back.' He waved at Marnie, she laughed back at him and shook her head.

As they stepped outside the sea breeze caught her hair and blew it wildly about. She grabbed it with both hands, pulling it up and away from her head. 'Damn, messy hair,' she cussed. It felt like gritty, dry rope.

'Mermaid hair,' he said and she could feel his breath on her neck; she hadn't realised he was so close.

'What?' She spun round, frowning.

'Your hair, it's like mermaid hair.' He laughed. 'Come on, I'll show you that path.'

Had he been flirting with her?

They started to walk across the beach but instead of taking the rough path she had come by he guided her to a neat tarmac lane. 'Up there, straight on, then take the right fork. You'll come out just behind your cottage. Ten minutes tops.'

'Thank you. I'm so glad I won't have to tramp over those fields again.'

'You should probably put your shoes on to walk up there,' he said, looking down at her bare feet.

Lily's hand went up to her mouth. 'My flip flops,' she said. 'I left them near the water's edge.'

'Before you went in the sea?' Jackson glanced towards the shoreline and shook his head. 'We can go and look but…' His voice trailed away.

'The sand was so hot,' Lily said, trotting behind him as he strode down to the water. The sand had cooled off now making her explanation sound silly.

'Whereabouts?' He called, marching on ahead of her.

Lily glanced at where she'd been sunbathing then

pointed to where she guessed she'd left them. Jackson strode on. Lily almost cantering behind him – most undignified.

'Here?' he said, standing on the wet sand.

Lily looked up and down the beach. 'I think so.'

'Okay. Let's split up. You go that way as far as the rocks. Don't go beyond the rocks, it's dangerous. I'll go this way.'

Lily nodded and started her search by heading for the rocks, which were more like mini-mountains. There was no sign of the flip flops and, annoyed with herself, she headed back towards the spot where they'd started. Jackson was still marching across to the other side of the beach, scanning the water's edge, his hand shading his eyes. When he reached the farthest point he turned back. Lily met him half way.

'Nothing?' he asked.

Lily shook her head. She was feeling idiotic, foolish; she'd nearly drowned in a metre of water and now she was shoeless.

'Never mind,' he said, grabbing her hand as though she were a child and pacing back up the beach towards the surf shack. 'Let's see if we can find you something.'

Lily trailed up the beach behind him, feeling the warmth of his hand around hers, feeling how smooth and strong it was.

At the surf shack he was greeted with a sly grin by the guy who had hardly moved from earlier. He was still polishing a surf board, the same one as earlier, Lily thought.

'You still got those old shoes?' Jackson asked, bustling past and disappearing into the back of the shack.

'Yep.'

'Have a look through here.' Jackson put a grey, wooden crate onto the sand in front of Lily; it was filled with assorted shoes, trainers and flip flops.

She bent down to look through them, the smell of decaying rubber and mouldy cheese catapulted up to her nose. She recoiled and made a face.

'Bit ripe?' The guy laughed.

'Where did you get them?'

'People leave 'em behind on the beach.' The guy shrugged. 'Some I fish out the sea.' He carried on polishing the board as he spoke, in fact, Lily thought he was still polishing the same small area; it was as though he were stroking a pet.

'Let me,' Jackson said, bending down and rifling through the crate. 'Try these,' he said, holding up a pair of murky brown trainers. They looked enormous. Lily made a face and Jackson dropped them on the sand. 'Foot,' he said, caressing her ankle and urging it up. 'Let me gauge your size.'

'Five,' Lily said balancing precariously on one foot. The sand was giving way and she grabbed Jackson's shoulder to steady herself. 'Sorry,' she said as he looked up and smiled. It was a knowing, cheeky smile. She let go immediately and regained her balance.

'These might be better,' he said, pulling out a pair of black trainers; they looked enormous. He slipped one onto her foot. 'Not too bad,' he said.

'But they're slopping about.'

'They're the smallest I can find. Best we can do.'

'Okay, thank you,' Lily said, feeling sheepish and putting the other trainer on when Jackson had let go of her foot. 'I suppose they're better than nothing.'

'They were once good ones,' surfer guy said. 'Designer, I'd guess.'

'Do I owe you anything for them?' She felt obliged to ask, even though they were only one step up from disgusting.

For a moment Lily could see that he was considering asking for money – she could see the glint in his eye. Out of the corner of her own eye she saw Jackson shake his head.

'No, you have 'em. Gift from me,' he added, grinning.

'Thank you.' Lily turned away and looked towards the lane Jackson had shown her. 'I'd better go now.'

She started to walk away but Jackson kept pace with her. At the start of the lane Lily stopped and held out her hand to Jackson. 'Thank you for everything,' she said. 'For saving me from drowning and for lunch, I can't thank you enough. Oh, and for the shoes.'

Jackson took her hand and shook it, smiling all the while. 'Well, I'm here most days if you need saving again.'

'Okay,' she said, feeling herself start to blush. 'Thanks again.'

Only when she reached a bend in the lane did she dare look back. He was still standing there, still watching her.

The lane was smooth and level and the incline gentle, it would have been a very pleasant walk if only the trainers hadn't kept slopping about on her feet. Every step was tiring and her feet were sweating inside them, the movement rubbing against the blisters her flip flops had already caused. But it didn't take long to get back to the cottage; Jackson had been right – ten minutes tops.

♥ ♥ ♥

She beat Tess and Gemma back to the cottage, located the key, kicked off the hideous trainers, left them on the path outside and let herself in. She ran into the bathroom, ran the taps and squealed with delight when steaming hot water gushed obligingly into the bath. She soaked for twenty minutes before using the bath hand shower attachment to wash her hair. It felt so good to be clean.

As she combed her wet hair through, teasing out the tangles she thought of Jackson. Mermaid hair, he'd called it. Will oscillated between loving it and hating it, calling it sexy-lady hair or a damn nuisance.

'We're back,' Tess called from the doorway just as Lily finished getting dressed; she'd pulled on cosy leggings and a soft top. She'd get changed again when they went to the pub for dinner. She pulled on a pair of cosy socks, so soft against the blisters, and padded out to the kitchen.

'Good day's shopping?' Lily asked. Gemma was loading the fridge as Tess splayed her naked feet out on the cool slate floor.

'This one,' said Tess, pointing at Gemma, 'can shop for England. I'm exhausted.'

'And this one,' Gemma laughed, closing the fridge door, 'has no stamina.' Gemma looked Lily up and down. 'Are you alone?'

'Yes. Why wouldn't I be?'

'When we saw the stinking clodhoppers outside we assumed you'd picked up some man.' Gemma gave a little shudder and turned away as Lily raised her eyebrows at Tess.

'Sorry,' Tess mouthed.

'Just as well you haven't because I don't think we've got enough food to feed a man. I've just bought three of everything.'

'What?' Lily said, still working on a suitable response to Gemma's insult about picking up a man.

'We popped into M&S and picked up some treats, well, since you couldn't join us for the lunch we'd planned, it seemed a shame. So we just had a light lunch and brought this instead. I'm just heating up this geriatric oven before I put our dinner in.' Gemma paused. 'I need a bath before dinner. I hope you haven't used all the hot water.'

'What, like you did this morning?'

Lily saw Tess tense.

Gemma frowned and stomped off to the bathroom.

'Why is she so rude?' Lily said as they heard Gemma bolt the door.

'Just ignore her. That's what I do.'

'You let her walk all over you.' Lily opened the fridge. 'Is there wine?'

'That was good even if I say so myself,' Gemma leaned back in her chair and smiled to herself.

'Yes, you can heat up a good ready meal,' Lily said, smiling too, probably a bit too much.

'Yes, but I chose it. And the wine.'

'I have to agree the food was good, and the wine excellent. So good, I'm on my third glass.'

'Your fourth actually,' Gemma said, 'but who's counting?' She topped their glasses up.

Gemma and Tess had rosy pink cheeks and Lily couldn't help commenting on it.

'Only our cheeks?' Tess teased.

'What?' Lily watched the smirks spread across Tess's

and Gemma's faces.

'Have you looked in the mirror lately?'

Lily ran into the bathroom.

Well, it doesn't hurt,' she said on her return. 'Just feels a bit warm, that's all.' She pressed her cool knuckles into her now flaming cheeks. 'Wine always does that to me,' she said, reassuring herself.

'You do look a little like a tomato,' Tess said, as Gemma snorted into her wine glass.

'Did you wear sunscreen?' Gemma sounded so superior.

Lily shrugged. Had she? On her face? She couldn't remember.

'You can use my moisturiser before bed. It'll help. It's the good stuff.' Gemma patted Lily on the shoulder. 'And I've got a really good sunscreen you can use, factor fifty, apply once a day. It's expensive, of course, but you get what you pay for. You won't see me with a face like a burnt pumpkin.' She chuckled to herself.

'Maybe I'll give the beach a miss tomorrow,' Lily said, thinking about the cringe-making horror of nearly drowning in a metre of water, and the kindness of Jackson. Did she want to see him again? Probably not, and definitely not with a big red face.

'Oh no, you can't. It's all booked.' Gemma giggled, it made her sound like a school girl; it didn't suit her image. 'And paid for,' she added.

'What is?'

'Shush,' Gemma said. 'You'll wake Tess. I think she might be drunk.'

She's not the only one, thought Lily, only now noticing that Tess had fallen asleep with her head on the table.

'But what's booked?' Lily persisted.

'Our lessons.'

Lily sighed. Tess was unconscious and Gemma was incoherent.

'What lessons?' But even as she asked the question she had a horrible feeling.

'Surf lessons. I've booked us onto a course.'

'What? No.'

'Don't worry,' Gemma leaned over and patted Lily on the arm; she was patting a bit too often this evening. 'It's all paid for. My treat to make up for gate-crashing your holiday.'

'How far is it?' Lily sighed. 'The prospect of squashing into the back of the car reared its ugly head again.

'Not far, apparently.' Gemma burped. 'Excuse me,' she said. 'I don't know where that came from.'

'Well, where is it?'

'Where is what?'

This was becoming tedious. 'The surfing.'

Gemma tilted her head at an awkward angle and retrieved her handbag from the floor. 'We stopped off at the pub and booked it. I noticed it when we were in there last night. You can book all sorts from that pub. Here.' Gemma thrust the tickets at Lily. 'See for yourself.'

Lily's hands trembled as she unfolded the tickets. 'Sunset Cove Surfing School,' she read aloud. And groaned.

Six

'You were snoring away like an old man,' Lily said, as Tess rubbed her eyes and sat up in bed.

'Sorry.' Tess looked down on Lily in her camp bed. 'I was exhausted. Food and wine just finished me off. No more shopping for me.'

'It's surfing today.' Lily gave Tess a quick mock grin and waited for her to respond.

'Yeah, sorry about that. It was done before I had time to object.'

'Really?'

'Well, you did say you wanted to learn to surf.' Tess gave Lily a sheepish grin. 'It's a freebie for you and me.' She got out of bed and padded to the door. 'Is Gem in the bathroom?'

'Where else?' Lily got up and followed Tess out of the bedroom. Tess was right, Lily had wanted to learn but now, after yesterday's drowning debacle she was definitely having second thoughts. Not least because Jackson would be there, watching her with those blue eyes.

'Morning,' Gemma said, her voice as bright as her

teeth as she breezed out of the bathroom trailing steamy vapour, and with her hair wrapped in a towel. 'Our lesson isn't until noon so we can chill out. I'm so looking forward to it.' Gemma paused and stared at Lily's face. 'Is that sore?'

'My face? Lily ran to the bathroom to look in the mirror. 'No,' she called back. 'But it certainly looks it.'

'Never mind, use some more of my moisturiser, it's on the shelf. I'm sure it'll calm down by noon.'

But it didn't.

♥ ♥ ♥

Gemma stood at the front door, her bag in hand and her lips pursed. Lily looked over and smiled as she laced up her trainers.

'What's Gemma got on her head?' Lily whispered to Tess as they both took a surreptitious glance at Gemma's headgear – a large multicoloured scarf tied securely under her chin, tucked in tightly all around and not a wisp of hair daring to sneak out from beneath it.

Tess shook her head. 'Keeps her hair in place.'

'Believe me; nothing will keep her hair in place in that sea. Nothing. I speak from experience.'

'Mmm. You'd be surprised.'

'They're still here,' Gemma said as she finally locked the door behind them and put the key in her bag.

'Who are?'

'Stinking clod hoppers.' Gemma turned her nose up at the trainers Lily had worn back from the beach. 'I'd have thought the owner might have reclaimed them.'

'No.' Lily shook her head. 'I wore them back from the beach.'

'Urgh,' Gemma and Tess chorused.

'Why?' Tess asked.

'Because I lost my flip flops. Okay.'

Gemma and Tess exchanged disgusted looks but didn't comment further.

'You're a bit unlucky with shoes sometimes, aren't you?' Tess whispered in Lily's ear.

Ignoring the remark, Lily led the way to the beach and felt as though she was wearing a mask; she'd applied a liberal amount of Gemma's sun block, which seemed to be setting hard on her face.

'It's not gone white, has it?' she asked Tess as they meandered down the lane.

Tess grimaced but it was Gemma who answered. 'Of course it has, but it's hardly noticeable. Would you prefer to look like a tomato? Would you prefer first degree burns?'

'I'd prefer to stay in and keep out of the sun. I'd prefer to read a book in the shade,' Lily snapped.

'Oh don't be such a bore, Lily. All the surfers wear opaque sun block. You'll fit right in.' Gemma quickened her pace, Tess obligingly matched it and Lily trailed a little behind, seething, but still with them.

♥ ♥ ♥

'Hey again.' Surfer guy leered at Lily as they approached the shack. 'That looks sore. You need to be careful. But I see you got it well covered.' He sniggered.

'Thanks.'

'Anytime, baby.' He grinned.

'Quite,' Gemma said, immediately silencing him as she began to explain why they were there. His attitude changed as soon as he realised they were paying customers. He became less suggestive, more deferential, but Lily had noticed that most people soon deferred to Gemma, herself included.

'I'm Davey,' he said. 'Not Dave or David, just so we have that clear, wouldn't want you mixing me up with them.' He chuckled to himself, enjoying a joke only he understood, then turned back to Lily, looked at her feet now clad in her own trainers. 'You can bring them shoes back if you don't want 'em.'

Lily gave him a quick nod but she was more interested in scanning the beach for Jackson. No sign; she breathed a sigh of relief.

'Wetsuits is extra,' Davey said. 'Unless you got your own?'

'Well,' said Gemma. 'Would we need surf lessons if we had our own wetsuits? It's unlikely isn't it? And it never said anything about extras in your advert, or on the tickets. You'll be telling us the boards are extra next.' Gemma stood with her hands on her hips and waited.

'You can go in without wet suits,' Davey said, turning away.

'The water's too cold and too rough,' Lily said, remembering the previous day.

Davey turned back to them, but Gemma still stood with her hands on her hips, her head wobbling with annoyance, an action exaggerated by her giant headgear. She raised an enquiring eyebrow.

Davey sighed. 'Okay, you can have the wetsuits for free, but only for today. Probably best, don't want you ladies getting friction burns, do we?' He allowed a grin to spread from ear to ear.

'Certainly not,' said Gemma striding towards the wetsuit rack.

'Not those ones,' Davey snapped. 'They're for those

who pay.'

Lily shuddered; he probably had another crate just like the shoe one, but full of disgusting, discarded wetsuits.

Davey bobbed into the surf shack then reappeared with three wetsuits and dropped them onto the sand. 'There you go,' he said. 'Get 'em on.'

'And where do we change?' Gemma's voice was starting to rise in pitch.

'What? Just pull 'em on. Unless you've got a handy Range Rover you can climb into the back of.' He chortled to himself, evidently enjoying another joke that only he understood.

Gemma took the biggest wetsuit, despite being the slimmest, she declared she was the tallest. Tess took the middle size one and Lily was left with the smallest.

'Well you are the shortest,' Gemma retorted when she saw the expression on Lily's face.

'I think it's a child's size,' Lily said, holding it up for inspection. 'I'll never get my thighs in that.'

'It's supposed to be tight,' Davey said as he dragged three large boards out onto the sand.

And it was. Very tight. So tight that Lily struggled to breathe. The effort of getting into the wetsuits was exhausting for all three; pulling, pushing, and in Lily's case stuffing, themselves into the stiff neoprene.

'Very slimming,' Gemma said, giving Lily an appraising nod after zipping her up.

'I'm gasping for oxygen.' Lily pulled at the neck of the wetsuit and took dramatic gulps of air.

'Nonsense, that's just the effort of pulling it on. We all feel like that, don't we?'

Tess nodded and smiled, but *her* wetsuit was bagging around her thighs even if it was tight around her waist.

'Put these on.' Davey threw t-shirts at them.

'Yellow,' Gemma said. 'Like a canary. I won't, thank you. And it will clash with my Hermes.' She pronounced it Er-mez and handed the t-shirt back.

'Your what?' Davey frowned.

'My Hermes.' She tutted when he continued to frown. 'My scarf.'

'Oh. Doesn't matter. You have to wear them. It's not a fashion statement, it's health and safety. Makes you easy to spot in the water.'

'And advertises your business,' Gemma said, pulling it on, flapping it around (it was far too big for her) before tying a jaunty knot in the side. *Davey's Surf School* bunched and distorted across her trim chest.

It splayed across Lily's.

Gemma stood on her board and took a surfing stance. Davey told her to get off immediately.

'Just need to go through a few things first,' he said. 'We need to ensure everyone stays safe in the water.'

Lily cringed and hoped he wouldn't bring up her near drowning. She thanked God Jackson wasn't about.

Ten minutes later and with only the enrolment forms completed Lily thought she might pass out in the heat. The combination of sunshine and sweaty rubber was just too much. She noticed that Davey only had the bottom half of his wetsuit on, the top half swung loosely around his waist, showing off his muscled torso, and allowing the sea breeze to cool his dark-bronzed skin.

'Can we get in the water soon please?' She flapped her hand in front of her face to create a breeze as

Davey droned on through the safety instructions.

'Not unless you want to nearly drown again,' a voice said from behind her.

Jackson.

Oh God. How long had he'd been there?

'Again?' Gemma queried.

Lily shook her head and scowled at Jackson who smiled and moved inside the surf shack and out of sight. Or, at least, Lily couldn't see *him*; he could be watching *her*, she supposed.

Davey droned on and on before finally it was time to get in the water. They attempted to pick up their boards, realised they were too heavy and were instructed by Davey to double up and carry each board down to the water's edge between them. Davey smirked, watching as they moved back and forth; he didn't offer to help.

He showed them the correct way to get in and out of the water with the board, then how to catch the waves while lying down – he called it riding prone. Soon they were having a go. Although apprehensive Lily was starting to enjoy herself, she'd only swallowed the sea once and it was nothing compared to yesterday's quantity. She hadn't seen any more of Jackson, so that was a blessing too.

'Why are we getting out?' Lily asked Tess as they hauled their boards back onto the beach, but Davey answered before Tess had a chance.

'Okay. You all seem to have the hang of that. Now we're going to try popping up.'

'I feel as if I am already popping in this wetsuit,' Lily quipped and even Gemma sniggered.

Davey showed them how to stand up in one go on the surfboard from a prone position – that was why it was called a pop up – you just popped up. But only Gemma was able to do it in one go, Lily and Tess had to get onto their knees first and even that proved difficult for Lily in the thigh-busting wetsuit. After a few more attempts they were ready to try it out in the water.

They waded out once more and lay on the surfboards, then attempted to pop up. Even Gemma couldn't do it in the water. All three fell off. Tess and Gemma saw the funny side; Lily was a little guarded about laughing especially if it meant opening her mouth to the sea.

Valiantly all three climbed back onto the surfboards and tried to pop up again. They all fell off. Again.

On the next go Gemma managed to stand up, even if only for two seconds. Tess fell off immediately without ever popping up, and Lily was now struggling just to get on the board, never mind pop up. Then a wave took Lily's board and flung it at her. Donk. Donk. The board on slapped on her head. It hurt. She did her best not to panic, reminding herself that it wasn't deep, that she wouldn't drown – probably. She heard a squeal in the waves as she came up. Tess's head bobbed on the surface as she gasped for breath.

'Sorry. Did my board hit you?' Lily shouted above the waves.

'No. Mine did.' Was Tess crying?

They retrieved their boards and clung onto them. Lily's arms were aching with the effort of getting on and off the board while fighting the sea's swell. Seconds later her board bucked and threw her off and donked her on the head again. And she was drinking seawater now, lots of it – it could have been worse, she could have been inhaling it.

She gave it one more go, climbing onto the board and clinging on desperately. The board flipped and she fell off, but she kept her mouth shut, her eyes shut and exhaled through her nose to prevent the water getting in. She rose to the surface and gasped; her board was almost airborne but it soon came down again and this time donked Gemma on the head.

Lily screamed before Gemma did.

'I'm so sorry, so sorry,' Lily yelled above the waves. 'Are you all right?'

Gemma stood up to her full height in the water and shook herself. 'I'm fine,' she called. 'My hair and my Hermes saved me.' The scarf was still resolutely in place.

'Good job you had your helmet on,' Davey shouted, laughing.

Even amid the waves Gemma managed to silence Davey with a single, poisonous look.

'I need a rest,' Tess said, grappling with her board.

'Me too,' Lily agreed, grabbing her own board.

They hauled the boards back through the water, dropped them on the beach then flopped down on the sand.

'I hated that,' Tess said, her voice a mixture of whispers and crying.

'Me too. And look at her.'

They both watched Gemma standing triumphant on the board as it glided into the shallows where she stepped off, jumped back on in the prone position and paddled back out to deeper water.

'And I've got another headache,' Lily whinged.

'I feel sick from drinking so much salt water.' Tess sniffed, then cuffed her nose with the back of her hand. 'Sorry,' she said, when she realised Lily had seen her. 'I haven't got a tissue, and anyway, I'm past caring.'

'And me.' Lily wiped her eyes with her knuckles.

Neither went back into the sea.

'Wasn't that fun!' Gemma declared as, lesson over, they carried the boards back up the beach. 'Exhilarating.'

'Exhausting.' Tess put on a brave face. 'But yes, it was mostly fun.'

'Not including the crying,' Lily said quietly into Tess's ear. 'And my face is really stinging,' she added.

'While I remember,' Davey said, waving squares of blue paper about. 'There's a beach party tonight. Make sure you bring your appetites. There's a barbeque and drink is provided, though you can bring your own if preferred.' He pushed an invitation at each of them.

'Sounds fun.' Gemma studied the wording before putting it into her bag.

Davey inspected the boards and racked them, while Gemma, Tess and Lily began to extricate themselves from the wetsuits. Once she'd got her shoulders out Gemma's came away quite easily. Once Tess unzipped hers it was easy to peel off. Lily couldn't even reach to pull her zip down and had to wait for Gemma to help.

As the zip went down she felt herself expand. She clawed at the neck and pulled the wetsuit down to her shoulders. She felt the grip of its suction on her skin as she struggled to pull it down. Minutes seemed to pass, both Gemma and Tess had already pulled on their sun dresses but Lily continued to struggle with her wetsuit.

'Let me help you again,' Gemma said, taking control of the situation.

'Ouch, you're taking my skin off,' Lily screeched.

'You're worse than Pixie-Bella,' Gemma muttered as she yanked the wetsuit down. It came away with a long gloopy slurp as it snaked its way down her thighs, the force of it made Lily bend over involuntarily.

'Ooowee, ooowee,' Davey yelled, 'flesh alert.'

Gemma marched towards him and as Lily watched from her bent position she thought Gemma was going to hit him. Gemma stopped in front of his face. 'Better. Wet. Suits. Next time,' she enunciated.

'Whoa. Okay. Back off, lady.'

Lily felt a towel wrap around her body. She straightened up and turned sharply. Jackson was face to face with her, his blue eyes staring directly into hers.

'Protect your modesty,' he said quietly.

Only as Lily felt the softness of the towel rub against her bare buttocks did she realise what had happened.

Seven

'You're looking glum.' Tess sat down on the sofa next to Lily.

'Mmm.' Lily sighed.

Gemma joined them, reeking of expensive perfume and fully made up. She wore a sequin boob-tube and her long, slender legs were clad in skin tight, satin Lycra. 'Not still sulking about the beach incident?'

'Ha. Ha.' Lily didn't even bother smiling.

'I'm sure no one was watching you.' Gemma flicked through her phone and smiled to herself.

'Not when they could watch you and your *Hermeese* helmet,' Lily said, knowing how snide that sounded.

'Hermes, Hermes, rhymes with fez,' Gemma corrected without a hint of irony. 'Anyway, your own personal surf bum came to the rescue.'

Gemma giggled and out of the corner of her eye Lily could see Tess fighting off a smile.

'Glad everyone's so amused.' Lily got up and fished out her phone from her handbag. She slumped back down on the sofa and looked at her friends, both absorbed in their own phones. She watched a secret smile play over Tess's face as the screen reflected in her eyes. 'You're getting messages then?' Lily asked.

'Yeah,' Tess said, smiling and putting her phone down. 'Not here, the signal is rubbish here, but they download when I get up the lane a bit. Aren't you?' She didn't wait for an answer. 'Must be your network. Which one are you on?'

'Same as you,' Lily said, flicking through her phone again.

'Could be your settings,' Gemma offered.

'Haven't changed them and I got a message a few days ago.'

'So, nothing from Will?' Tess offered a sympathetic smile. 'Not even a Facebook post?'

'No.'

'Take it out with you tonight. Maybe some will download. Or trot up the lane now. We've got time before we go.'

'He's obviously not posting. Probably him who can't get the signal.' Anyway, Lily told herself, she didn't care what Will was up to.

'I took myself off Facebook last year,' Gemma announced. 'It became so tiresome. People were constantly posting pictures of themselves out drinking, or with hangovers. Urgh.'

'What's wrong? Weren't your selfies getting enough likes?' Lily said, sounding as catty as she felt. 'Or maybe you've just grown out of it.' Deep down she blamed Gemma for the wetsuit arse-exposure.

'I'm not that old.' Gemma's neck grew longer as her head raised itself. 'Probably only a year or two older than you.'

'Don't think so,' Lily said, knowing she'd hit a nerve. She could see Tess squirming.

'Are you going up the lane to check for messages?' Tess tried to divert the conversation, relieve the pressure.

'No. Not much point.' Lily sighed and noticed how flushed Gemma's face was. Was that anger or embarrassment? 'What time do we have to go to this thing?'

'Starts at seven.' Tess smiled.

'I don't know if I fancy it.' Lily oscillated between wanting to see Jackson again and not. Would he even be there?

'Aren't you going to dress up a bit?' Gemma ran her hands down her trouser legs, smoothing imaginary creases.

'No, Gemma. It's a beach bonfire, we're not going clubbing.' Lily paused. 'Or are we? Is that what you've planned?'

'Not at all. I just like to look my best.'

'How did your hair get on in the sea?' Lily was curious about Gemma's hair, it was always perfect. No one had perfect hair on a beach holiday.

'It was fine.' Gemma got up to fetch a jumper from the bedroom. 'My Hermes kept the salt off,' she called, over her shoulder.

'Not on its own it didn't,' Lily sniggered to Tess. 'What did she have on underneath that scarf?'

'Shower cap,' Tess mouthed, careful to keep her voice low.

'Why bother? Look at my hair. Mermaid hair,' she said, recalling Jackson's words. 'I'm on holiday. I don't care. And my face has calmed down; I'm not even wearing makeup.'

'I have standards,' Gemma said, coming back into the room.

Behind Gemma's back Tess grimaced at Lily and put her finger up to her lips indicating that Lily should be quiet.

Lily complied. For now.

The sun was low in the sky as they approached the beach and a cool offshore breeze made Lily glad she had worn a jumper. She glanced over at the boob-tubed Gemma and waited for her to pull hers out of her bag; but Gemma seemed determined to get the full value out of her sequined top.

'Lot of people here,' Tess said as Lily scanned the faces looking for Jackson. Davey spotted them and gave them the benefit of a leering grin.

'There's a hog roast. Well, I hope they've cooked it properly.' Gemma strode towards it, whether to inspect it or soak up the heat it cast off, Lily wasn't sure.

'I've just got a load of messages,' Tess said, thumbing through her phone. 'You should check yours, Lily. Oh look, I've got one from my mum; it's a picture of Pixie-Bella and Rafe. I'll see if Gemma's got it too. I know she's missing the children.'

Lily wondered if that was true; Gemma had hardly mentioned them, or at least not to her. Once alone she got her own phone out, if there was nothing from Will she didn't want an audience.

Four messages. Lily's heart suddenly beat heavily in her chest. She felt nervous and excited. Were they from Will? Two were. She breathed a sigh of relief.

One, a bad selfie, showed him sitting on his bike posing beside a road sign. It was out of focus and she couldn't read the sign. Underneath he had written *Road trip, USA.* He was wearing the bin-retrieved leathers, the sun was shining and he looked hot. Sweaty hot. She sighed before thumbing through to the next message. It simply said: *Really missing you babe. Hope you're okay. xx*

She wondered what the time was where he was. Wondered exactly where he was. Her fingers hovered over the screen. Should she reply straight away? She flicked back up to the photo – the message was fifteen minutes old. She hit reply, typed: *Looks like you're having fun. I'm on holiday in Devon. Learning to surf.* Her finger hovered over send.

She wiped the message off.

Then retyped it and pressed send.

She waited for him to reply, imagined him sitting astride the motorbike reading her response. She stared at her phone willing him to reply. What would he say? At least he hadn't used the *friends* word again.

'Hey there, Lily.' The voice came from behind her. She didn't need to turn around to know who it was.

'Hey, Jackson,' she said, affecting nonchalance over her shoulder. Her heart fluttered – still recovering from Will's messages? She pushed her phone back into her bag.

'Have you got a drink?'

'Gemma brought some wine.'

'No, I mean have *you* got a drink? To drink? I can recommend the local cider.'

'And its accompanying hangover.' Lily heard herself laugh. She heard Jackson join in.

'There's truth in that,' he said. His voice was low and seductive. 'Are you okay?'

Lily turned and stared at him. 'Fine,' she said, frowning.

'Good. I wouldn't want you not to be.'

'Why wouldn't I be?' She stopped. 'Oh. You mean… yeah, that was embarrassing.'

'No one saw.'

'You saw.' She blushed. 'I'll have that drink if it's still on offer.'

He smiled over his shoulder at her as he walked away. He was wearing soft, sun-bleached jeans, a white shirt. His body moved with fluidity, his legs were long, but not as long as Will's. She shook her head and looked away.

'There you go,' he said, handing her a bottle on his return. 'Have you eaten yet?'

She shook her head. 'Have you?'

'No. We could go now. It's a hog roast.'

'Yes, I saw. That's a bit fancy. I'd expected a barbeque.'

'No one wants burnt burgers with raw insides. Or food poisoning. It's better to get the professionals in.'

'But who pays for it? Do we need to pay someone?'

'No, all the local businesses club together. It's good PR,' he said, smiling and looking out to sea. Lily followed his gaze; there was nothing, just murky water under a dark grey sky. 'Rain's on its way,' he mused.

'Ah, don't say that.' She had visions of being trapped indoors with Gemma; or worse still, hauled around every indoor shopping mall Gemma could locate – no matter what the distance – and cramped in the back of Tess's car.

'It'll be fine tomorrow. Come on.' He grabbed her hand and a little tingle ran up her spine.

Gemma and Tess had obviously been on the local cider too, they were sitting on a rock giggling to each other. Tess gave Lily an exaggerated wave and Gemma let out a hoot – most unGemma-like.

'Your friends seem to be enjoying themselves,' Jackson said. 'Are you going on somewhere later?'

Lily wondered if it was an invitation. 'No,' she said. 'I don't think so. But we're open to offers.' She laughed then cringed as she saw the look on his face. She wasn't sure if it was disgust or shock.

'I only ask because your friend is so dressed up.' He turned his face out to sea again.

'Oh. Yeah, Gem does like to dress up.'

'And you don't?' he said, turning back towards her, his eyes sweeping up and down her body. Was he mocking her? She shuddered under his gaze then realised they were still holding hands. She let her hand go limp until he got the message and let go.

They queued for hog roast and salad. Jackson hadn't exaggerated when he'd said they'd brought in professionals, the meat was carved and served to them; everything kept under cover until it was on their china plates.

'Don't have the chilli dip,' he said as her hand hovered over a dish of deep red relish. 'It's misleadingly cool but has a lethal after-kick.' Lily moved away from the dip.

He found them a vacant rock and they sat down, staring out to sea and eating their food.

'This is very civilised.'

'Yes. Even at the beach.'

'I didn't mean…'

He laughed. 'I know you didn't. I'm teasing you. Eat up and enjoy it.'

They ate in silence, enjoying the food and each engrossed in their own thoughts. Lily wondered where Will was, wondered what he was doing. Was he alone? Or was he, like her, sitting with an attractive stranger on some distance shore? No, she reminded herself, he was inland, coast-to-coast, not on the coast. Jackson, when he wasn't concentrating on his food, stared out to sea.

'Penny for them?' Lily said, licking her fingers.

'What's that?' He turned back to face her, his mouth smiling broadly, his eyes echoing sadness.

'You're looking out to sea a lot; I just wondered what you were thinking?'

'There's a storm brewing. The sea can be an evil beast.' He stood up, took her empty plate and marched back towards the hog roast.

Evil beast. That sounded ominous and melodramatic, Lily thought as she waited for him to return.

'We have an ice cream van, if you'd like something sweet.' He sat down on the rock again. A sudden, sharp blast of wind blew his hair across his face; he swiped it back just as sharply. Will did that.

'I'll just let my hog roast digest first,' Lily said. She sounded pompous and old fashioned. 'It's getting dark early tonight,' she added, twirling her own windblown hair around her fingers in an attempt to restrain it. Jackson leaned over and caught an errant spiral, tucked it softly behind her ear.

'Clouds.' Jackson's voice was full of melancholy. He seemed to be breathing deeply or was he sighing?

In the distance, far out to sea the horizon lit up, then faded into darkness.

Jackson took her hand again. 'Let's get that ice cream before it's too late.'

They walked back up the beach, past Tess and Gemma who were still giggling on their rock with the debris of their hog roast scattered around them. Lily turned to speak to them but Jackson urged her on.

The ice cream van was parked on the tarmac path, the driver joking with Jackson that he wasn't chancing the sand tonight. Lily chose strawberry ice cream; Jackson chose vanilla. They walked along the sand venturing into a second cove that Lily hadn't noticed before. She looked back and could still see the fire from the hog roast, groups of people standing or sitting, the occasional peal of laughter wafted towards her.

'They'll be packing up soon,' Jackson said, sitting down on a grey stone wall.

Lily watched him, his tongue darting in and out of his mouth as he licked his ice cream. He looked up and caught her eye; she looked away and concentrated on her own ice cream. And when she dared another glance, he was watching her. He didn't look away embarrassed as she had, just smiled before biting into his cone.

A loud rumble made her jump. Squeals came from the party; people were getting up, moving quickly up the beach. The hog roast fire had already been extinguished.

Lily finished her cone and began licking her hands clean. 'It's melted all over me,' she said as Jackson watched her. 'I'm all sticky.' She waved her hands around like a child.

'Mmm,' he said, taking her hand and running his tongue over her fingers.

Common sense told her he shouldn't be doing that, told her she shouldn't let him, that she shouldn't be enjoying it. But something else let a slow moan escape her lips.

He stopped, smiled, placed her hand carefully on her lap.

'Better?'

'Yes. Thank you.' She sounded prim.

The first drop of rain was big and fat and splattered on her spread hand; the one Jackson had just licked clean. She looked up to the sky; the second splat hit her full in the eye. She shrieked. Jumped up.

There were no intervals between the raindrops now, they fell fast and heavy.

Her hand was in his and they were running.

'In here,' he said, pulling her into a doorway, closing it behind them and leaning against it. Lily could see only darkness.

'I'm soaked.' Her clothes were sticking to her, clammy and cold.

'Me too. But at least we're out of the lightening.' As if to prove his point a sudden flash illuminated the beach hut and, momentarily via tiny gaps, its interior.

'I can't see a thing now,' Lily said, her eyes temporarily blinded. She shivered.

'I have lights.' He fumbled in the darkness then two small bulbs screwed into the walls glowed and flickered. 'Sorry, it's a bit weak, battery needs charging.'

'Is that a bed?' Why did she say that?

'Yes. Sometimes I sleep here.'

As her eyes grew accustomed to the dim light, Lily absorbed the details of the hut. Walls painted blue and white, drawers and cupboards beneath a double bed which spanned the width of the room. A soft blue duvet and four pillows. A tiny table, two chairs.

She shivered.

'You're cold,' Jackson said. 'I'll light the stove.' He bent down to an ancient potbellied stove, struck matches and lit kindling. 'Soon be warm.'

Lily folded her arms across her body; her jumper, which had previously been so cosy, was sodden.

'Take it off,' Jackson said. 'Hang it on the chair.' She

let him help her pull it over her head, watched him spread it carefully over the chair back. He rubbed her arms before hugging her tightly, pulling her into his chest. 'Warmer? Better?'

'What are we doing here?' she asked.

Jackson exhaled a laugh through his nostrils. 'Sheltering from the storm.'

'No, I mean what are *we* doing here?'

'Nothing you don't want to do,' he said, loosening his grip.

Lily thought of Will, thought of how he had arranged a special dinner to tell her he was buggering off on holiday for a month without her. Wondered what he was doing now. Right now. This very moment. Then she stopped thinking about Will.

She concentrated on Jackson.

'That's okay then. Just so we're clear.' She wrapped her arms around his waist and pulled him closer. What had Tess recommended? A holiday romance. Was that the answer? Was this it? Or was it just a quick fumble in a beach hut? Did it matter? Did she care? She tilted her head up towards his; their eyes met.

He kissed her and she kissed him back and it felt good. Unfamiliar. No expectations. No disappointments. No history.

'Okay?' he asked.

'Okay.' Whether he was seeking approval or permission she didn't know or care. 'Safe sex?'

'Of course.'

Lily followed his eyes to a drawer beneath the bed. Well prepared then. He probably did this every week – a different girl, a different storm or some other excuse.

This time, she kissed him first.

And when he kissed her back her knees almost buckled.

Eight

Tess grinned then raised her eyebrows in question as she let Lily into the cottage the next morning. 'Everything okay?' she asked, quietly.

'Great,' Lily replied. 'Is there any hot water left?'

'Yes, plenty I would think. Gemma's not been in the bathroom yet.' Tess kept her voice low and nodded towards the sofa where Lily could see Gemma sitting with a towel-wrapped ice pack pressed to her face.

'Hangover?' Lily whispered.

'I'm not deaf. And, no it's not,' Gemma snapped. She pulled the ice pack away and turned to face Lily.

Lily caught sight of Gemma. 'Oh my God, what happened to you? Did you have an accident or get into a fight?' She had visions of Gemma doling out her insults to someone who was less indulgent than she and Tess were.

'No, I didn't.' Gemma pressed the ice pack against her lips, wincing audibly as she did so. She had tears in her eyes.

Lily actually felt sorry for her. 'What happened?'

'Nothing. Nothing happened. I woke up like this.'

'Let me see.' Lily prized the ice pack away from Gemma's lips. They looked like a pair of giant, bruised plums.

'Happy now?' Gemma snapped before covering her mouth again.

'I think it's something she ate,' Tess said. 'An allergy or something.'

'You ate the chilli dip? Didn't you?'

Gemma shook her head. 'It wasn't that. It wasn't even hot'. Her voice was muffled by the ice pack.

'You didn't have it, did you Tess?'

'No. Can't stand the stuff.'

'I think what you've got,' Lily said, trying not to laugh. 'Is a chilli trout pout.'

'What?'

'Apparently that chilli dip is deceptive and packs a belated punch.'

'Says who?' Gemma said, getting up to fetch a fresh ice pack from the freezer. 'Oh, your surf bum, did he tell you that?'

'Warned me off it.'

'Ha. We wondered where you were all night.' Gemma flumped back onto the sofa with her fresh ice. 'You might have messaged, Lily. We were worried about you.'

Lily's eyes flicked between Tess and Gemma's faces. Tess raised her eyebrows, Gemma's eyes bored into Lily's.

'Don't worry, I was fine,' Lily said, dismissively. Better than fine. Amazing. But she wasn't saying that out loud, especially not to Gemma.

'Did you manage to get under cover before the storm broke?' It seemed Gemma wouldn't be put off.

'Yes. I did.'

'Where did you go? Because we got soaked. I was freezing.'

'You should have worn more clothes.' Lily sounded as catty as she felt.

'Says the dirty stop-out.'

'Gemma,' admonished Tess.

'Well, just saying. Next time Lily, let us know if you're not coming back. We waited until very late before we locked the door. You could have been kidnapped or drowned or anything.'

Maybe Gemma had a point. 'Okay,' Lily said. 'If there is a next time, I will.' She then reminded Gemma that she was an adult who didn't need Gemma's permission and could come and go as she pleased.

'Please yourself,' Gemma snapped, adjusting her ice pack. 'Just concerned for your welfare, that's all.'

'I'll have a bath if no one's using the bathroom,' Lily said, throwing down the gauntlet. 'We're not surfing today are we? Only I need to wash my hair after getting caught in the storm last night, but I won't bother if we're surfing.'

'No. Tomorrow. Thank God. I could hardly go like this.' Gemma whisked the ice pack away from her lips again to emphasise the point.

'Oh, I don't know, salt water might be just the thing.' Lily dodged the cushion Gemma threw at her, but only just. At least Gemma wouldn't be planning any shopping trips today, which was just as well because Lily had plans of her own.

Jackson had wanted to escort her to the cottage door, having walked her up the lane from the beach hut, but she hadn't let him. The last thing she wanted was him being interrogated by Gemma – even with her chilli trout pout.

'I love your hair,' Jackson said much later when Lily joined him on the path just out of sight of the cottage. He too had showered and changed. 'It's very glossy.'

Lily had been about to tell him how she'd just washed and conditioned it with Gemma's very expensive hair products, but hadn't had time to blow dry and straighten it properly so it wasn't as glossy as it could be, but she decided to spare him the details. 'Thank you.' She laughed, striding out in front of him, keen to get away from the cottage in case Gemma came out to interrogate him with her big, puce lips.

'And it smells rather nice.'

Lily turned back just in time to see her hair, caught by the breeze, wafting over his face. 'Sorry,' she said, grabbing hold of it and twisting it into a fat roll at the nape of her neck. 'I've got a hair clasp in my bag; I'll tie it up.'

'I'm not complaining.' He laughed. 'Come here.'

Lily glanced back towards the cottage – the trees were now providing enough cover to prevent any prying eyes from seeing them. She stopped and turned towards Jackson.

He kissed her.

'Everything okay?'

'Fine.'

'Only you seem,' he paused and frowned. 'On edge.'

'Just Gemma. I don't want her spying on us.'

'Really? She's the one with the…' he paused, 'hair, um head dress.' He made a shape like a helmet around his own head.

'Yes, that's right. She was wearing her surfing

Hermes headgear yesterday. She's a bit… how shall I put it? Nosey. And she thinks she's in charge. I've just had to remind her that she's not my mum and I'm old enough to look after myself.'

'She doesn't look that old.' Jackson grabbed Lily's hand as they walked along.

'She's not. But she is a mother. She's sort of appointed herself as our leader. Don't know why. She shouldn't even be here.'

'Why's that?' Jackson slowed Lily's pace, put his arm around her shoulder. She wrapped her arm around his waist. It felt so comfortable; she imagined they looked like a couple of love-struck teenagers. Somewhere deep inside a tiny spark of guilt flared up, then immediately died down.

'She's Tess's sister-in-law and came along last minute.'

'Why?'

'Don't know,' Lily lied, suddenly feeling disloyal to Gemma, so much so she decided she wasn't going to mention the chilli trout pout either – tempting as it was.

'I hope you're hungry,' Jackson said when they reached the car park just before the beach. 'I've booked us into a lovely restaurant for lunch.'

'Oh, um, yes. That'd be great. I haven't had anything to eat.' Between Gemma's lips and wrestling with her hair there had been no time for food. 'I just assumed we would go to the café on the beach.'

'We can go there anytime.' Jackson laughed. 'Anyway, the beach is windswept and the sea fierce today so I think the café might be busy with holidaymakers looking for a safe bolthole.'

'I thought you said it would be lovely today.'

'And it is up here; sunny and warm. It's just the sea

really. It can be evil.' His face took on a wistful, faraway look and when he became aware that Lily was looking at him, he suddenly snapped back to the present and smiled. 'There's no surf school today.'

'We weren't going anyway. Our next lesson is tomorrow. Not that I'm looking forward to it.'

'You did okay.'

'Gemma did okay. After the boards donked us on the head and body several times, I had to comfort Tess quite a bit.'

'I noticed you sitting it out along the shoreline for quite a while? I thought you were crying.'

'Crying? No. Well maybe. Tess was a bit upset, that's all. We were fine. Really. Anyway, were you watching us?'

'Not watching. No. I just noticed.'

'Like you noticed my exposure in that awful wetsuit.' Lily smiled and waited for his reaction.

'I've seen rather more of you than your lovely backside now,' he laughed, pulling her in close and kissing her again.

'Ditto,' she said eventually. 'I think I'm going to pay and hire a better wetsuit tomorrow.

'I probably have a wetsuit you can borrow.'

Lily stood back and looked Jackson up and down. He was tall, okay, not as tall as Will, but considerably taller than Lily.

'I don't think it would fit,' she laughed. 'I'd be going from one extreme to the other.'

'It's not mine. It's my sister's. You're about the same size.'

'Won't she mind?'

'No. She'd be pleased.'

'Okay. Thank you.' Lily felt humbled and obliged.

She just hoped his estimation was correct – though she doubted that his sister had thunder thighs.

His car was a silver-grey, hard top convertible. He unlocked the doors as they approached.

'Lovely car.'

'Also my sister's. Do you think it's warm enough to have the top down?' he asked as they got into the car.

The sun was out and shining on the car and inside it felt hot, too hot.

'Yeah, why not.' Lily fished in her handbag for the hair clasp – it would definitely be needed now.

'Let me know if you don't like it,' he said, starting the engine and pressing the button which allowed the roof to fold away.

Lily pulled on her sunglasses, buckled up her belt and settled into the reassuringly comfortable and luxurious seat.

He drove them along the coastal road, then into a sweeping valley before veering down a narrow lane. They rattled across a cobbled car park and pulled up outside a large thatched building, its multi-layer roofs undulating in the sunshine; a sign hanging from the eaves said *The Watermill Restaurant*. Jackson turned off the engine and they listened and watched the water tinkling over the mill wheel in front of them.

'Wow,' Lily said.

'Don't be fooled; it's ornamental.'

'Still lovely, though.'

'It is. I just wished they'd sort the car park out.' He laughed. 'Might spoil the look though.'

'Yes. It does look idyllic.' Lily put her hand on the car door to open it but Jackson leaned over and stopped her by placing his hand over hers.'

'And the food is amazing.' He stopped speaking and

looked into her eyes. 'Lily, there's something I need to say.'

This sounded ominous. Was this the part where he told her he had a wife and three kids down the road; was actually gay – no couldn't be that if last night was anything to go by – or had an incurable illness?

'Lily,' Jackson said, pulling her back from her musing.

'Sorry.'

'Look. I don't know how to put this without sounding…' his voice trailed away. 'Insensitive,' he added finally.

Lily definitely didn't like the sound of this. She stared straight ahead and waited for his pronouncement.

'It's just that, well, I don't know what you're expecting from me.'

Lily turned and frowned, then quipped, 'Lunch?'

He smiled. 'Yeah, and I'm more than happy to treat you to lunch.'

'But?'

'Well. Umm. Look, the truth is I'm not in a position to pursue a relationship.'

Lily laughed out loud; he sounded so prim, so proper.

'I'm glad you're amused.' He gripped the steering wheel and now, he too, stared straight ahead. 'I just want to be honest, not lead you on.'

'You mean you only want a holiday romance?' Lily whispered, sounding sad and pathetic. 'A quickie in your beach hut.'

'Yes. Well no, not the last part. Look, I'm sorry if you are expecting anything further; I'm not in a position to offer it.'

'Good,' Lily said. 'Cos I'm not in a position to offer it either. I have to get back to work at the end of next week.' She slapped her hand on his thigh. He jumped. 'I'm not expecting anything from you. You don't need to worry. I like you and I'm enjoying your company and if you buy me lunch then that's a bonus. Though, I must tell you, I can afford to buy my own lunch, and yours too if necessary. Just so we're clear, I'm not a freeloader.'

'I never thought you were.' He looked indignant, affronted. 'I'm sorry if you even suspect that I think that.'

'I didn't. I don't. I was just being honest…' Lily let her voice trail away and smiled at him before opening the car door. 'I'm starving. Come on, my treat.'

The interior of the restaurant matched the exterior – oak beams and the working parts of the watermill hidden behind glass. Lily flounced in and chose a table while Jackson spoke to the waitress and ordered drinks. Lily positioned herself at their table so that she could see and hear the millpond that fed the millstream through the open window.

'This is lovely,' she said, as Jackson took his place opposite her. 'Is this all authentic or ornamental?' She giggled.

'Authentic but the watermill doesn't grind flour any longer. And it's all been gentrified and cleaned up, of course. So, it's authentic and ornamental.'

'Okay.'

Jackson leaned towards Lily. 'I hope I haven't offended you by saying what I said.' He had a pained look on his face.

'Not at all.' Lily gave him a reassuringly dazzling smile.

He nodded slowly but didn't seem convinced, opened his mouth to speak then closed it as the waitress approached.

They sat in silence as they looked through the menus. There was a palpable air of awkwardness. After a while Lily felt compelled to speak.

'Look,' she began.

Jackson looked up from his menu.

'To be blunt…' Lily fanned herself with her menu. 'I've just come out of a tricky relationship and the last thing I need is anything complicated or heavy.'

'Okay.'

Lily was aware of Jackson's shoulders slowly coming down, of him visibly relaxing, but the look of angst on his face hadn't completely disappeared.

'While we're being honest and, to use your word, blunt,' he said.

Lily leaned in.

'I'll be leaving before you do. I have to move on.'

'Oh.' That was a slap in the face.

'It was already planned before I met you. It's been planned for while actually. It's…' he stalled, then added, 'family business.'

Lily narrowed her eyes. Did she want to know about his family business?

'Not children or ex-wives or anything like that,' he said, reading her expression. He smiled, his eyes crinkling at the sides. 'And one more thing. I *am* paying for lunch. This was my idea and it's my treat.'

Lily looked at him for a long moment. 'Okay, and I'm going to let you pay,' she said decisively. 'And, I'm going to enjoy every morsel.'

After lunch they drove back towards the beach, parked the car and walked along the shoreline. Lily felt liberated; she loosened her hair and let it blow behind her in the wind and the breeze filled her lungs with its salty tang. The beach, despite the sunshine, was not very busy. The sea, however, was full of surfers.

'That's Davey,' Lily said, watching him expertly weaving his way through the waves. 'Looks as though he's enjoying himself. Just as well we weren't having a lesson today or he wouldn't be able to do that – he'd be too busy exercising his patience with us.'

'He'd have cancelled you. These waves are too dangerous for any novice and too good to waste for any serious surfer.'

'Aren't you a serious surfer?'

Jackson laughed. 'Apparently not,' he said, grabbing her hand. 'Let's run. I love to see your hair streaming behind you in the wind.'

'Yeah, until I have to turn around, then we'll both get whiplashed by it,' Lily panted out as he pulled her along.

But she never did turn around; once they reached the far end of the beach they climbed up onto the coastal path and took a slow arcing walk until they came back to the car.

Jackson opened the door for Lily to get in.

'Oh,' she said, 'I thought we might be going back to your beach hut.'

'No. It was okay when we got caught in the rain last night, but no.' He shook his head, pulled a pained expression. 'No,' he said again.

Lily got into the car and felt saddened. Her memory of the previous night was warm and cosy with a considerate lover and a lot of affection. Somehow, with just a few words Jackson had soured that memory, cheapened it.

He started the car and they drove on in silence, away from the beach and along tiny, bisecting country lanes, but always the sea was visible on the horizon, its azure lure ever present.

They pulled up outside a large whitewashed cottage, nestling beneath a dark slate roof; a pretty garden wrapped itself around the building, a meandering slate path curved to the front door.

'This is me,' he said, almost to himself as he switched off the engine.

'Ah.'

'Come on; let's see if we can find that wetsuit.'

Ah, Lily thought. So he shared this place with his sister. And, probably some of that family he'd mentioned.

Half way down the path Lily stopped, caught her breath.

'Okay?' Jackson's concerned voice asked.

'Wow, wow…' Lily's voice trailed away.

Jackson smiled and followed her eyes to the panoramic view of the beach and bay below, the soft white sand framing the turquoise sea. 'Yes, it is rather breath taking.'

'It is,' Lily felt inexplicably flustered. 'And it looks so calm from here.'

'It probably is. It's a very sheltered bay and the wind doesn't whip the sea up here like it does on the main beach.'

'You'll be telling me you own it next,' Lily laughed.

'No. No.' He laughed. 'I wish. But it's not accessible by car, so it is a bit of a hidden gem, though people still find it.' He opened the front door and stepped aside to let Lily into the hallway; elegant wooden banisters ran up the stairs in front of them. 'Let's check that wetsuit out before we forget.'

Jackson led the way through the hall, out through a beautiful kitchen, past a utility room with shower and finally came to a purpose-built outhouse. Lily blinked at the array of wetsuits hanging on a rail – it would put Davey's sad display to shame, as would the number of boards racked against the wall.

'Um,' she said, quickly followed by, 'Wow. Do you run a surf school too?'

'Another wish,' Jackson laughed. 'No, we've just accumulated a lot of gear. 'This one.' He pulled a wetsuit down and held it against Lily. 'I think this will be perfect.' The wetsuit was blue and sleek and obviously not a nasty cheap thing like the one Davey had inflicted on her.

Lily eyed it dubiously. It looked long, it looked lean. Too lean on the thigh area.

'Is your sister tall?'

Jackson shrugged. 'Your height?'

'Really?'

He shrugged again.

Lily didn't trust his sizing judgement. She forced a smile. She'd hate another embarrassing arse-exposure moment.

'Can I try it on?'

'Sure. Let's go upstairs.'

Lily laughed, embarrassed. Then felt embarrassed for feeling embarrassed. How stupid. After what they had done last night under beach hut battery-lights, how could she be coy?

'I meant you go upstairs, to see if it fits,' Jackson said, looking away from her and apparently embarrassed too. Or was he feeling her embarrassment?

Lily felt flustered as Jackson led the way. Despite their closeness last night, they were still strangers who each knew little about the other.

'Use the bathroom; the mirror's good in there.' Jackson opened the bathroom door and ushered Lily inside, carefully closing the door behind her.

Cringing, Lily stripped off to her underwear and held the wetsuit up. She could feel its quality, its newness. That was good; it wasn't skanky. She stepped into it and began to haul it up her legs. It was stretchy and forgiving, allowing her to manoeuvre her thighs comfortably into it. She smiled happily then caught sight of herself in the mirror. She shrieked. Rather too loudly.

'You okay?' Jackson burst in through the bathroom door.

'Um, yes.' Lily's voice was quiet and sheepish. He hadn't been joking when he'd said the mirror was good, it showed every lump and bump in the lower half of the wetsuit and a ring of fat hanging over the waist.

'Only you…' his voice stopped. 'Called out,' he said eventually.

'I'm fine,' she said, flapping her hands at him, hoping he would get the message and push off. She felt hot and she knew her face was pinking up a treat, especially because she could see it in the *good* mirror. 'I caught myself in the zip.' The lie tripped off her tongue too easily.

'Ah, easily done.' Jackson's voice oozed sympathy

and understanding. 'Here let me help.' He stepped forward and grabbed the wetsuit hanging around her waist and hauled it up.

The smile on Lily's face was rictus, the air in her lungs exhaled; she pulled in her stomach and closed her eyes.

'Point your fingers as you put your arms in,' Jackson said as he held the wetsuit in front of her. Deftly he nipped around to her back and pulled the neoprene over her shoulders.

Lily's fingers clenched.

He gathered her hair into a thick ponytail then scooped it up on the top of her head. Lily shivered; her reaction to the speed of the zip going up to her neck and the warmth of his fingers on her skin.

'There,' he said, pleased with himself. 'You couldn't have done that on your own.'

'I probably could.'

'Not with all this lovely hair.' Jackson let it tumble down her back. 'It would tangle.'

'Thank you.' Lily stepped away from him.

'Perfect fit.' Jackson ran his hands over her hips and thighs. Lily couldn't bring herself to look in the mirror again. 'Open your eyes,' he said. 'Look.'

She'd have to now.

'Oh. Wow,' she said, her surprise as genuine as her delight. 'It does look good.'

'There's a hood too, I think. It zips onto the neck. Beth said it saves your hair from taking such a beating. But, I'm not sure you'll get all yours into it. We could try.'

During his absence Lily studied her reflection; she looked amazing, she hardly recognised herself. The wetsuit acted like a *Spanx* bodysuit, sculpting her curves and creating a tiny waist. Even her legs looked good, the earlier lumps and bumps now smoothed out.

'Found it,' Jackson said, returning. He stretched the hood out and held it over her head. 'Mmm, might not fit,' he said.

'Well, I can try. I'll need to plait my hair tight, but I'll give it a go. I'm feeling hot in this now.' Lily pulled at the neckline to let some cool air in.

'Let me help you.' Jackson scooped her hair up again, and began to pull on the zip. As it travelled down her back the neoprene bounced off her shoulders. Jackson, still holding her hair aloft, leaned forward and kissed the nape of her neck.

Lily shivered.

'Do you live here alone?' she asked, hoping that his sister or parents wouldn't suddenly turn up.

'Yes.' He turned her around, stroked her hair away from her face grazed her lips with his.

♥ ♥ ♥

Several hours passed before they returned to the bathroom to pick up their discarded clothes. The wetsuit lay in a crumpled heap on the floor. Lily grabbed it and gave it a shake.

'I haven't even worn it and I'm treating it badly,' she said, folding and smoothing it into a neat parcel and setting it on the toilet lid. She retrieved the hood from inside the bath where Jackson had thrown it and placed it on top. 'What would your sister think?'

'She wouldn't mind.' Jackson's voice was soft. He pulled on his shirt. 'Anyway, do you think the sea treats it kindly?'

'I suppose not.' Lily pulled on her jeans and zipped

them up. Her stomach rumbled.

'Someone's hungry,' Jackson laughed.

'Hard to believe isn't it, after that lovely lunch.'

'Not really. I'm starving and we have been,' he paused and grinned. 'Busy.'

Lily swiped up her top from the floor and playfully pushed past Jackson.

'You forgot this,' he said, handing her the wetsuit and hood.

Remembering the previous surf lesson and suddenly aware that the next one was less that twenty-four hours away, Lily wasn't sure she was looking forward to it. Good wetsuit or not.

'Scrambled eggs, smoked salmon and thick buttered toast?' Jackson grabbed her hand and pulled her down the stairs.

'And a large mug of tea please.'

They ate on the veranda overlooking the bay. The sun had gone in and the sea was grey instead of its earlier turquoise, but it was still warm.

'Do you think the weather will be okay for our surfing lesson tomorrow?' Lily hoped Jackson would say no.

'Oh yes.'

'How do you know? Do you have a surfer's expert weather nose or something?'

'No. I have a weather app on my phone. Don't you?'

'Oh yeah,' she laughed, wondering where her handbag was. She got up to find it.

The signal in Jackson's cottage was better than where Lily was staying and she immediately saw a message.

She flicked through, it was Tess, asking if everything was okay – Gemma was getting stressed about Lily's continued absence and no word.

Lily messaged back: *Everything's fine. Don't worry about me. Just been busy. :)*

She smiled at the memory of busy. Would that be the word they used? Their euphemism?

She added another message: *Might not be back tonight. Will let you know by 11pm so you can lock up xx*

She watched as the message app told her that Tess was typing. Immediately Tess's reply came back: *Have fun xx*

Lily's thumb hovered over her phone momentarily before she found herself unable to resist. She flicked onto Will's icon. He was online. Online. But he wasn't messaging Lily. And he owed her a reply. At least it confirmed he was still alive. Would anyone know or think to inform her if he had an accident? Did these friends of friends even know she existed?

'Everything okay?' Jackson called as he carried their dirty plates into the kitchen.

'Yeah. Fine.' Lily dropped her phone back into her bag.

'Only you looked a bit worried.'

'Oh, no. It was just Tess asking when I would be back tonight.'

'What did you say?'

'I said I'd let her know later.'

'Good. Because I wondered if you'd like to go for a moonlit walk along the beach later.'

Lily smiled her agreement. Well, who wouldn't?

Jackson's fleece swamped Lily but at least it would keep her warm.

'You'll need this,' Jackson said, handing over a head torch.

'Are we going down a mine?'

'Just dark tracks.' Jackson pulled his own torch on and positioned it in the centre of his forehead.

Lily followed suit after clipping her hair back.

As they set off down the steps leading from Jackson's back garden she understood why they needed the head torches – much of the pathway was shaded by trees which, even the moonlight, couldn't penetrate.

After two flights of steps they were on a slowly descending path to the bay. Jackson took Lily's hand and swung it as they walked.

'What are you thinking?'

'I'm wondering what I'm doing out in the middle of nowhere with a stranger in the dark.'

'Are you really thinking that?' Jackson stopped, faced Lily and looked straight into her eyes. Their head torches clanged together.

They jumped apart.

'Seriously?'

'What?' Lily frowned, rubbing her head.

'What you just said about being out with a stranger.'

'Well,' Lily shrugged. 'You know.'

'Not really. No. Is that how you see me? A stranger? I thought we were friends. At the very least, I thought we were friends.'

Lily angled her head torch so that she could see his face; he looked affronted.

'I've got enough friends,' she said, immediately thinking of Will and trying not to. 'I don't need any more.' She forced a laugh.

'That's charming.'

'Are we having a row? Our first row in our non-relationship?' She forced another laugh.

'I wish I'd never asked.' Jackson pushed his hands into his pockets and marched on.

'Asked what?' Lily trailed alongside him. Was he sulking?

'All I asked was what you were thinking. I thought you might say something about this being your first moonlit walk on a secret beach. Instead you imply I'm a murderer or something.'

'I…I wasn't implying that.' She sighed. 'I wish you'd never asked too.'

They walked on in uneasy silence. No more hand holding. The pace quickened.

They reached the beach. The moonlight bounced off the inky-black ocean. The air was surprisingly warm and still and perfumed with something sweet and sickly.

'Ask me what I'm thinking now,' Lily whispered.

'Do tell me.' Did Lily detect a sarcastic tone in his voice?

'It's breath taking,' she said. 'Absolutely stunning.' She inhaled the aroma that seemed to be all around them. 'And beautiful,' she added. 'Just like you.'

'Is that an apology?' Jackson gave a half-laugh as though daring her to say no.

'Yes.'

'Accepted.' He grabbed her hand and headed towards the shoreline.

'What's that smell?' Lily asked, inhaling it again.

'Honeysuckle. It grows up the lane, but when the breeze is right it scents the beach.'

'Delicious. It's quite magical down here.'

'Yes.' He paused. 'Lily, your point about us being

strangers – I do understand what you're saying. We know nothing about each other.'

'I thought that was the deal. A quick, no commitment, holiday romance. Isn't that what you want? What we both want? You're leaving before me. Remember?'

'Yes. I suppose.' He stopped, looked out to sea; he had that wistful look in his eyes again. He switched off his head torch then leaned over and switched off Lily's. Without the tree shadows, the moonlight reflecting off the sea was illumination enough.

Side by side they looked out across the ocean, listening to the waves as they swept up the sand and ebbed away. She didn't know what to say.

'You know how you asked me if I ran a surf school when you saw my wetsuits?'

'Yes.'

'It was, still is, a dream of mine. I would like to do that.'

'What's stopping you?'

He exhaled through his nostrils then grabbed Lily's hand and started to walk again.

'Family business,' he said. 'Commitments. You know how it is.'

'Not really. My family leaves me to my own devices where work is concerned. Don't get me wrong, they do care, they just don't interfere.'

'That's good,' Jackson said.

'What is the family business? I thought you just followed the surf around the world.'

'I have done, this past year or more. But now…' his voice trailed away, or maybe it was the sea breeze that carried his words away. 'It's complicated.' His words had an air of finality about them; Lily decided not to press him further but squeezed his hand instead.

'What about you?' he said, in response to her hand squeeze. 'What's your dream?'

Should she tell him how Will had let her down? Should she tell him how she'd spent the last ten years loving Will more than he loved her? 'There's a job I'm after at work. If I get it, it'll be a big promotion.'

'Good luck to you. I hope you're successful.'

'We'll see. I think I'm in with a good chance.' The conversation was getting a bit too real, too serious, too close to home. 'Do you think the water's too cold for a paddle?'

He laughed. And, after they'd taken off their shoes, ventured in and Lily had run out screaming, he'd given her a piggy-back before plonking her down on a rock, so she wouldn't have to stand on the sand with wet feet.

He knelt in front of her and rubbed her feet until they were dry.

'I feel like Cinderella.' Lily allowed Jackson to push her shoes onto her feet.

'That must make me Prince Charming then.' He put out his hand to help her off the rock, then wrapped his arm around her shoulder at the same time as he switched on her head torch, then his own.

'What's the time?'

Jackson pulled his phone out of his pocket. 'Just after eleven.'

'I need to message Tess. Tell her what I'm doing. We'd better hurry back.'

'Why don't you do it now?'

'I didn't bring my phone, didn't want to have to carry my bag.'

'Ah. You can use mine.'

Lily laughed. 'Like I've memorised her number. Come on; get me back up there quickly.'

They dashed up the beach and up the path and tumbled into his cottage. Lily found her phone, read Tess's message asking if she was okay, if she was coming back.

Lily couldn't reply. She didn't know what she was doing. All she knew was that either way Jackson had control because Lily had no idea where she was or how to get back without Jackson.

'Tess wants to know when I'll be back,' she said, keeping her back to Jackson and pretending to flick through her endless messages – of which there was only the one from Tess.

'Whenever you like,' he tossed back casually. He'd gone into the kitchen and put the kettle on.

'Right.' Now what? Was that an invitation to stay or to go? They'd spent the afternoon in bed but did that mean he wanted her to stay overnight? Or not? And what did she want to do?

She could hear him clattering in the kitchen; the kettle boiled, he opened a drawer. As she stood waiting, wondering, another message popped up; probably Tess pressing for a reply. Lily had visions of Gemma's chilli trout pout lips wanting an early night and the door locked.

But it wasn't from Tess. It was from Will; he'd sent a picture of himself on a motorbike – nothing new there then. Only this time he was bare-chested, the biking leathers pulled down to his waist. The picture was reminiscent of Lily in the wetsuit earlier, but there was no roll of fat hanging over the top, just Will's gym-toned, and now tanned, torso. He'd captioned it, 'Hey Babe, how cool is this?'

'I've put milk in your coffee, that is right isn't it?' Jackson's appearance made her jump.

'Yes. Thank you.'

'What did you tell your friend?'

'Umm? What?' Had he seen Will's photo?

'What I mean is… I'd love you to stay the night.' He stopped and offered her a smile; it was almost shy. 'But no pressure.'

Lily thought of their passionate afternoon, their beach hut adventure. She thought of Will.

'I'd love to,' she said, immediately flicking back on her phone to inform Tess.

She didn't reply to Will's message, even though he was still online and could see that she was too.

Nine

'Dirty stop out – day two,' Gemma snipped as she opened the door to Lily. 'We were wondering if you would make it in time for our surf lesson.' Gemma was already wearing her Hermes helmet in readiness.

'Don't worry about me, Gemma,' Lily said. 'I'm a big girl now.'

'Mmm.' Gemma looked Lily up and down.

'How are your lips? Has your chilli trout pout subsided?'

Gemma turned on her heels and stomped away.

'Oh hi,' Tess said, when Lily entered the bedroom. 'Did you have a good time?'

'Yes. Thank you. I hope Gemma hasn't been giving you a hard time on my account. Not that she has a right to.'

'Don't worry. Water off a duck's back.' Tess zipped her top up and picked up her bag. 'We're leaving in about ten minutes, is that enough time for you?'

'Yeah, won't take me long to change and tie my hair down.'

♥ ♥ ♥

On the beach it was hot and sunny again. And crowded. Davey nodded to the trio then looked pointedly at the wetsuits hanging on the rack.

'Don't worry, we'll pay today.' Gemma strode towards the rack. 'Extortionist,' she muttered, barely under her breath. 'Here, Lily, this one should fit you.' She held up a bright orange wetsuit – with wide legs.

'Don't worry. I've got my own.' Lily pulled Jackson's sister's wetsuit from her bag.

'Oh. When did you buy that? Was it expensive? It looks expensive? Bit of waste for a few days.' Gemma tutted to herself while Lily exchanged looks with Tess.

'Don't worry yourself about it, Gemma. I've borrowed it.'

'I suppose that's all right then.'

Lily opened her mouth to speak but Tess caught her eye with a pleading look in her own. Lily shut her mouth.

Once Gemma and Tess had selected their wetsuits – and paid for them – all three pulled them on.

'Well, that's better than a bodycon dress,' Gemma said to Lily. 'I hardly recognise you from the back.'

'Thanks. I think.' Lily began to pull the hood on over her carefully plaited hair.

'That's a bit excessive,' Gemma scoffed but Lily chose to ignore her. How Mrs Hermes Helmet could make such a comment defied belief.

'You do look amazing,' Tess said as they picked up the boards and began the walk to the sea.

As they reached the water's edge and Davey began shouting instructions to them, Jackson appeared. He smiled a hello to everyone but beamed at Lily. Davey nodded at him and shouted only at Tess and Gemma while Jackson led Lily further along the beach.

It took seconds for Gemma to realise Lily wasn't staying with them. 'So that's how it is,' she called loud enough for Lily to hear even above the noise of the waves.

Lily raised her hand and waved. Tess waved back. Gemma looked the other way.

'She's quite angry your friend, isn't she? How do you cope with it?'

'I try to just smile sweetly,' Lily said, which was not entirely true.

The surf lesson with Jackson was much more successful than it had been with Davey, though it probably helped that Jackson had taken her to a less busy part of the sea. But – as he pointed out – still in the designated surfing area. Lily didn't manage to stand up on the board, Jackson explained that few people were able to do that on their second lesson. But it appeared that Gemma could, for when Lily looked towards her friends, she was definitely riding a wave again, albeit a shallow one.

'Your angry friend has amazing balance,' Jackson said, eyeing Gemma admirably.

'Does she?'

'Yes, she must have terrific core strength. Does she go to the gym a lot?'

'I don't know,' Lily said, pulling her own stomach muscles in. 'She's a stay at home mum and both her kids are at school so she probably has time to.'

Jackson gave Lily a quick look but didn't comment. Lily read it as reproachful; maybe that last comment was a bit bitchy.

When the lesson was over they met up at the surf shack again, peeled off their wetsuits – with no arse exposure this time – and wandered up to the beach café. Gemma was still wearing her Hermes helmet and despite double-takes from some customers, none of the group commented; they were becoming used to it now, Gemma's headgear was almost normal.

Lily, Tess and Jackson had a Devon cream tea while Gemma picked at a salad.

'You were impressive on that board today,' Jackson said to Gemma.

'Thank you.' Gemma simpered.

'Yeah, Jackson wondered if you go to the gym a lot,' Lily chipped in, determined not to be left out of the conversation, or let Gemma dominate it, even if it was about her.

'No. I'm not that sort.' Another simper. 'I usually just do a bit of yoga every day and my Pilates class once a week, of course.'

Tess's eyes rolled up to the ceiling and she smirked briefly at Lily without Gemma seeing.

'It works,' Jackson said and he sounded genuinely impressed. 'You have amazing core strength and balance. Not many people stand up on the board so quickly. Or have you surfed before?'

'Oh no. This is my first time, though I have always wanted to learn. Not too bad for a mum of two.' Gemma patted her perfectly smooth and flat stomach and glowed with self-satisfaction.

Both Lily and Tess glanced down at their own stomachs, and Lily attempted to tighten her muscles. Again.

'What are you doing this evening, Jackson?' Gemma

asked, continuing before he could answer, 'Only us girls are popping along to the pub for dinner. Maybe you'd like to join us.'

Lily felt her shoulders and her hackles rise. How dare Gemma try to muscle in?

'That's kind of you. But I have plans.'

Oh. Did he? Lily obviously wasn't included; so it would be dinner at the pub with the girls then. Lily's shoulders drooped.

'Oh really? Shame you can't join us. You could have given me some surfing tips. Lily seems to be doing much better with you than with Davey.' Gemma smiled her best, wide-mouthed grin.

What a shame her chilli trout pout has deflated, Lily thought, not feeling at all mean.

'Yes. Lily and I are driving down the coast for dinner with some friends of mine.' Jackson took Lily's hand and squeezed it. Now it was Lily's turn to smile broadly.

'That sounds very nice.' Gemma's tone was clipped. She stood up. 'Well, I need to be getting back. I need to take this scarf off my head and get the salt water out of my hair. I'll expect you'll need to do your mop, Lily.'

'No. I think the hood has done its job.' Lily touched her hair, it was soft and dry; the hood had actually performed its task well.

'Was that true?' Lily asked Jackson as they strolled behind Gemma and Tess up the path to the holiday cottage. Gemma had flounced on like a woman on a mission, urging Tess – in a sharp schoolteacher tone – to keep up.

Jackson stopped and looked Lily in the eye. 'No,' he

said. 'Am I a complete arse for lying?'

'God no.' Lily grabbed his hair with both hands and pulled his face down to hers; she gave him a long, lingering kiss. 'Best lie I ever heard.'

'I'm glad you think so. No offence to your friend but she is bit full on.'

'No offence taken on my part.' Lily took a breath, almost afraid of the answer to her next question. 'So what *are* you doing this evening?'

'Well, to paraphrase my fellow surfers in Oz, I thought I'd fire up the barbie and throw on a couple of steaks. Are you up for that?'

'Oh, yes please.'

Jackson sat on the terrace in the late afternoon sunshine while Lily showered and changed. Gemma had very graciously allowed Lily in the bathroom first – provided that she was being truthful about not washing her hair and promised not to use all the hot water.

'You could have showered at my place if it's such a big deal,' Jackson said as they sauntered back down the path to the beach car park.

'It's fine,' Lily said, swinging her bag – packed with overnight essentials and a change of clothes for the morning – over her shoulder.

'Let me take that, it looks heavy.' Jackson reached for the bag.

'No. It's fine.' Lily didn't want him thinking she was making assumptions.

'Give it here,' he said, lifting it off her shoulder. 'Whoa, that's heavy. What have you got in there?'

'Just stuff.' Lily made a grab for the bag, but he

dodged out of her way and laughed.

'I hope the reason it's heavy is because the *just stuff* is overnight stuff.'

Lily looked down. Was he mocking her?

He stopped walking, grabbed her arm and lifted her chin. 'I've been thinking,' he said, his voice soft. 'If this is a full on, no strings attached, holiday romance we're having…' He waited.

'Yes.'

'Why don't you move in with me until I have to leave? My bed is a lot more comfortable than that camp bed you're sleeping on.'

'How do you know about the camp bed?'

He laughed. 'Gemma gave me a tour while you were in the bathroom. She said you'd volunteered to sleep on it because you were the shortest.'

Lily blinked back her excitement. Part of her felt disloyal to Will, but who knew what he was up to? And anyway, she reminded herself, they had broken up. Oh, the irony of Jackson asking her to move in, albeit temporarily, when that's all she'd ever wanted from Will. Part of her felt it was wrong, but a bigger part of her wanted to punch the air and shout yes. 'Okay. That would be nice. Thank you.' She worked hard to keep her tone level and restrained.

'Great. We can pick up more of your stuff tomorrow.' They'd reached his car and he opened the boot and dropped Lily's bag in. 'And, you can wash your hair as often, or not, as you like. There is no restriction on hot water.'

Lily felt excited as they drove off down the country lanes, the top down, the sea always part of the vista. Excited and scared. What was she doing? They hardly knew each other. She glanced over at him, his surfer hair, too long, brittle and bleached, waving in the wind. His tanned-skin, much softer than it looked. His sharp blue eyes, now covered by sunglasses, but the long, dark lashes clearly visible from the side. His hands on the wheel, his muscular forearms – the mermaid's tail flicking around his wrist, his muscular thighs.

'What the hell,' she said, not meaning to say it out loud.

'What's that?' Jackson turned briefly and smiled at her showing his teeth. She'd forgotten his teeth, straight and white against his tan.

'Oh, nothing.'

When they got to Jackson's he lit the barbecue before taking a shower while Lily sat in the garden soaking up the last rays of the day and sipping chilled, white wine. When Jackson reappeared, he smelt delicious. Lily inhaled his lovely odour.

'Mmm. What's that?'

Jackson frowned.

'That lovely smell. I mean, it's you. But what is it?'

'Shower gel and shampoo.' He shrugged.

'Is that all? It smells lovely. You smell lovely.'

'God, what did I smell like before?'

'Stinky,' Lily said, laughing. But he hadn't.

After he'd checked the barbecue he produced the steaks and laid them on the grill before disappearing into the kitchen. Lily followed him, with her wine glass still in her hand she offered to help.

'No, you sit down. You're on holiday. I'll be out in a minute anyway; I don't want our steaks to burn.'

Lily didn't argue with him. Why would she?

The meal was simple and delightful. Because it was so warm they sat out in the garden eating, drinking and laughing, until the sky was black and the stars came out.

Jackson had given Lily his fleece again when she'd shivered but was reluctant to go inside. From the garden they could hear the sea below gently brushing against the sand with each lapping wave.

'This is idyllic.'

'I always think so when I'm here.'

'I don't know how you can bear to leave it.' She stopped. 'Do you own this place? Or is it rented?' Was she being too nosey?

'It's mine. It was a bit derelict when I bought it early last year, but I had some work done on it and…' His voice trailed away and he looked to the dark horizon, a wistful look in his eyes.

'Then you went off surfing in faraway lands,' Lily said in an attempt to lighten the mood.

'Yeah. Something like that. Another wine? I could open a new bottle.'

Lily shook her head; she'd had enough, not too much, just enough. 'Tea would be nice.'

Jackson got up. 'I'll make a pot.'

While he clattered in the kitchen Lily collected up their plates and glasses and took them inside. They stacked the dishwasher together before sitting down on the sofa to drink their tea.

'I'm already enjoying having you here,' Jackson said, stroking Lily's hair away from her eyes.

'Me too.' She closed her eyes and enjoyed his attention.

'Did I tell you I love your hair? I love the way it waves and curls.'

'You won't say that when I have to wash it and you see me fighting it into submission.'

He lifted her hair up and watched it fall. 'It reminds me of mermaids.' He laughed.

'You said that before. Do you see a lot of mermaids in Devon?'

'Thousands.'

'My hair's okay here, on holiday I mean, but it's a right pain every day for work. I keep meaning to get it cut much shorter. But, part of me likes having long hair.'

'It would be a shame to cut it short.' His voice was quiet as he leaned in and held a tendril of Lily's hair to his nose. 'It even smells nice.'

'God knows how.' Lily laughed. She felt self-conscious.

Jackson took her hand and put it up to his lips, kissed the back of it.

'Bed time?'

There was only one answer to that.

'You're back sooner than expected,' Gemma said as she let Lily into the cottage the next morning. 'How was dinner with Jackson's friends?'

'Great. Thanks.' Lily manoeuvred her way around Gemma and headed for the bedroom to find the curtains closed and Tess still in bed. 'You okay?' she asked her friend.

'Headache,' Tess said.

'Hanging?'

'Maybe. Just a little bit.'

'Did you drink more of that cider in the pub?'

'Yep.' Tess pulled herself up, it was a slow, exaggerated movement which ended with her sinking slowly back onto her pillows. 'What are you up to?' Tess asked, as Lily started rifling through drawers and pulling out her clothes.

'I'm going to bunk in with Jackson. Only for a week or so; he has to leave middle of next week.'

'Oh. Oh?'

Lily slumped down on her friend's bed, realising that this might be a kick in the teeth for Tess. 'I'm sorry if I'm abandoning you with…' Lily jerked her head in the direction of the closed door to the living room.

'I can handle Gem. I'm more concerned about you.'

Lily stood up and started stuffing clothes into her suitcase.

'Lily?'

'I'm just doing what you said. I'm having a holiday romance,' she muttered into her packing.

'You're moving in with him. That's not quite the same, is it?'

'Only for a week or so, then I'll be back on that lovely camp bed.'

'If it's about the camp bed, I'll swap with you.'

Lily turned to Tess and raised an eyebrow. 'With your hangover?' she said. 'Anyway, it's not about the camp bed.'

'But you hardly know him and you're locking yourself away somewhere with him. Actually, where is his place?'

'I'm not locking myself anywhere. I'll see you most days down on the beach or in the sea for our surf lessons. How many more have we got?'

'Don't change the subject, Lily. What's his address?' Tess pulled her phone out from under her pillow. 'And his phone number.'

'I don't know his address. Here's his number.' She swiped through her phone before tossing it to Tess who put Jackson's number into her own phone.

'So where does he live?'

'It's near the beach; well, down some country lanes. You can see the sea.'

'That narrows it down.' Tess's tone was sarcasm dipped in concern. 'Is he here waiting for you?'

'No. I'm meeting him down the lane.'

'When you meet up with him can you message me his address? Just to put my mind at rest.'

'I thought Gemma was the mum among us.' Lily zipped up her suitcase and stood it on its wheels; she put her hand on the door.

'I'm your best friend, Lily. Aren't I allowed to be concerned?'

Lily stopped, let go of the door handle. 'Sorry. Of course you are. You're right. It's better to be safe. I'll message you. You sure you're okay? Do you want me to get you some headache tablets?'

'No need. Gemma is cooking me a fry up. That'll sort me out.'

Lily laughed. Tess joined in as much as her hangover would allow. 'That's good of her.'

'Yeah, she even went down to the village and bought the bacon and eggs. Well, it is her fault. We only drank that stuff at her insistence.'

'Didn't she have a hangover too?'

Tess shrugged. 'Not as bad as mine. Apparently. Anyway, she's more preoccupied with a rash she's developed on her legs.'

'Rash? What's caused that?'

'I don't know. I could hardly see it when she showed me this morning. Mind you, I could hardly see anything.' Tess rolled her eyes and smiled briefly.

'I'm going now. If you're okay?' Lily said, feeling a little bit guilty.

'I'm fine. Have fun. Be safe. Message me.'

'I will, I will.' Lily kissed Tess on her hot and sticky forehead. 'I'll see you later for surf school.'

'Urgh.'

'Do you mind if I don't tell Gemma? Only I don't want a lecture from her.'

'As well as me.' Tess managed a low laugh. 'No. You go. I'll tell her. Not that it's any of her business.'

'That's my girl.' Lily laughed. 'You should be more like that with her.'

'Don't worry about me. You go now.'

Jackson was waiting at the beach car park entrance; he smiled broadly when Lily came into view, then stepped forward and grabbed the case.

'I could have come with you. I could have carried this.'

'It's fine. I'm strong. Anyway I wheeled it here.' Lily got her phone out of her bag – almost as heavy as her case with the wetsuit in it. 'What's your address?'

'What?'

'I have to let Tess know where you live; just in case you plan to murder me or something.' Lily forced a little laugh, and realised how that comment didn't sound at all funny.

Jackson didn't laugh either as he told her his address.

They walked in silence down to the beach. Lily felt stupid. She imagined Jackson felt insulted but he just looked sad.

'I'm sorry,' she said as they stepped down onto the sand.

'About what?'

'The murder joke.'

'Oh. That's okay. I know it was a joke.' But he wasn't laughing. 'Do you fancy sunbathing round by my beach hut until it's surfing time? I can make tea and coffee too. And there might even be a cake in the tin.'

'That'd be great.' Lily gave him her best, grateful smile, then grabbed his hand as they walked along. 'Who made the cake?' She imagined him covered in flour.

'It comes from the café, of course.'

Jackson brought out sun loungers that were hanging from the wall of the beach hut. Lily hadn't noticed them before when they'd spent the night during the storm, but then it had been in weak battery light and she had been rather preoccupied.

Because it was already too hot for tea or coffee, they sat in the sunshine sipping lemonade from cans that Jackson kept in a cool box. Lily closed her eyes and enjoyed the sensation of the sun on her skin.

'It's lovely here,' she said. 'I almost wish I could live here. It must be so nice; by the sea, on the beach every day.'

'Yeah. It is.'

'Oh well,' Lily said, feeling slightly morose. 'Let's enjoy it before I have to go back to horrible reality and you have to go wherever you're going.' Lily suddenly felt self-conscious; she hoped he didn't think she was fishing.

'Yeah, let's,' he said, giving her hand a gentle squeeze.

Lily was dozing when Jackson nudged her awake to tell

her it was time for the surf lesson.

'Oh, must I?'

'Yes, you were really getting the hang of it yesterday.' Jackson stood up and went inside the beach hut to retrieve his wetsuit. He began to pull it on. 'You should get changed here,' he said, as Lily heaved herself up from her sun lounger.

They sauntered down the beach towards the surf shack, both with their wetsuits hanging down around their waists; it was just too hot to put them on properly until they hit the cool water.

Tess and Gemma were already there, Tess still looked hung-over and Gemma had a face like thunder. 'I'm telling you it was your wetsuit,' she shouted at Davey.

'What's going on?' Lily asked, as Tess cringed.

'Gemma's rash; she's blaming Davey.'

'What rash?' Jackson asked.

'This rash, this rash.' Gemma pointed at her legs, which looked suspiciously smooth and tanned beneath her shorts.

Both Lily and Jackson leaned in for a closer look. Tess looked away.

Jackson shook his head. 'I can't see anything wrong,' he said. 'Far from it.'

'Are you wearing tights on the beach?' Lily bent down to get a better look. 'Are they flesh-coloured opaque? I didn't even know you could get those.'

'Nude. The colour is nude. They're my yoga and Pilates tights.'

'Why are you wearing them on the beach?' Why had she even brought them with her?

Gemma glared at Lily. Jackson had a look of puzzlement on his face. Tess struggled to suppress a smirk and Lily shook her head.

'Because. Of. The. Rash.' Gemma narrowed her eyes. 'Caused by his festering wetsuit.'

'Whoa.' Davey put up his hands. 'The ones you wore yesterday were the good ones, not the skank…' He stopped speaking.

'Were you going to say skanky ones? Like the ones we wore on the first day?'

Davey shrugged. 'There's nothing wrong with the one you wore yesterday. And your friends are okay, aren't they?'

'Lily didn't wear yours yesterday. And I have a rash, irrespective of whether anyone else does.' Gemma put her hands on her hips, stood astride and waited for Davey's response.

Davey, knowing when he was beaten, nodded. 'Okay. You can have them for nothing.'

'For the rest of our lessons?'

Davey exhaled slowly through his nostrils. 'Yes, okay.'

'All right.' Gemma stomped towards the wetsuit rack. 'Not,' she called over, 'that that helps my rash. Does it? I'll be choosing a different one today.'

Davey didn't reply. Lily, Tess and Jackson exchanged glances. No one spoke as Gemma flung a wetsuit at Tess and proceeded to choose one for herself.

Jackson and Lily pulled up their wetsuits and did each other's zip up.

'How cute,' Gemma said, almost, but not quite, under her breath.

Lily, remembering what she'd said to Jackson, smiled sweetly. Sickly sweetly.

They waddled with their boards down to the sea and Davey gave everyone the obligatory safety reminders. It was only when Lily and Jackson started to move further down the beach that Gemma called after them, her voice not quite drowned out by the waves. Lily turned around and frowned.

'I said,' Gemma called again. 'That I don't know why you even go through the pretence of joining us when you just sidle off at the first opportunity.'

'Okay, bye. See you later.' Lily pretended she had misheard what Gemma had said. Inside she seethed.

'She has a point,' Jackson said. 'We can surf any time we like. I'm teaching you. Davey doesn't mind; after all he's been paid.'

'Gemma minds. But I'm not letting that influence me. Yes. Let's please ourselves.'

Later, Lily couldn't help taking guilty pleasure in Gemma's sudden inability to stay on her board, especially as Lily, and even Tess, were starting to get the hang of it now.

'Your friend's not so good today,' Jackson said, noticing Gemma too.

'Mmm.'

'Is she still wearing those tights? I mean, under her wetsuit?'

'Oh yes.'

'Do they have feet? That would account for it.'

'I don't know. I doubt it; she said she wears them for yoga.'

Jackson frowned. 'Maybe she's just losing her grip, then.'

'Yes. I think that's it.' Lily bit her lip to prevent a snigger escaping; she wasn't sure if Jackson had intended to make a joke.

Ten

'What are your hopes and dreams for the future?' Jackson asked as he twirled Lily's hair around his finger while they lay on their sun loungers outside his beach hut.

Lily sat up and looked at him. 'I thought we weren't having any serious conversations. Remember we're just having a holiday fling. No past and no future.'

'I know. Okay. Let me rephrase. If you could do anything in the world what would it be?'

'I'm quite enjoying lying here soaking up the sun, listening to the gulls, inhaling the sea air.' She wasn't going to tell him that what she really wanted, or at least had thought she wanted, was a commitment of some sort from Will. That would be divulging just too much.

'Me too,' Jackson said, dropping her hair so it fell around her shoulders. 'I'd be happy staying here.' His voice had that pensive tone again.

'I suppose we all have our mortgages and bills to pay.' Lily sighed and got up to get herself a drink from his cool box.

'The money isn't really my driver.' Jackson's voice

was quiet, so quiet that Lily only just caught it. He smiled at her, then jumped up. 'Fancy another surf lesson?'

'But we were out there this morning.'

'There are no limits to the sea. You're not bound by the rules of surf school.'

'The what?'

'You can surf whenever you like, weather permitting. Since you have decoupled yourself from your fiery friend, Gemma, you can please yourself. Now would be good; the sea is frisky enough but not too violent.'

'Ha. You use some funny terms to describe the sea. Okay, come on then. But after that I want a decent meal, all this surfing makes me hungry.'

Lily's surf lessons were going well. With Jackson's careful schooling Lily was not only mastering the techniques, but actually enjoying it. He'd taught her how to recover if she lost her board, how to ensure she didn't drown – he'd spent a laborious amount of time on that, but after the pseudo-drowning incident on their first acquaintance, perhaps he had a point. Lily could stand up and ride a wave like a pro. Well no, not like a pro, but not like an idiot either. So good, she thought, that she probably didn't need him to accompany her. He'd then spent another laborious amount of time telling her that only a fool surfed alone, that it was the equivalent of setting out for the South Pole without telling anyone and he made her promise she would never do it.

They spent their days surfing, swimming, sunbathing – the weather was very generous and kind – eating, drinking and most importantly making love. They were very *busy*. Although Lily kept telling herself it was sex, not love. This was a holiday fling, not a great romance. This was a no-strings affair. They were just having fun. Jackson's attentiveness was the bonus she deserved after Will's neglect. He was lovely to look at, full of interesting facts about the sea and his adventures – with the odd hint at another life, which she never questioned him about – and a generous lover.

Everywhere they went, people knew Jackson. They patted him on the back and asked how he was now – so much so, that Lily began to wonder if he'd been seriously ill. But, as they'd agreed to never discuss their past, she stopped herself from asking him.

There were times when Lily almost forgot about Will. But only almost. He had, after all, dominated her life for the past ten years, even when he hadn't actually been in her life. She had taken to sending him daily messages with selfies of her on a surfboard, lying on the sun lounger, sipping wine with a fabulous sunset behind her. In the pictures she was always alone; she didn't want to give Will any ideas, not that it was any of his business. Occasionally he replied with a 'cool' or 'hot' depending on the picture, but some days he didn't reply at all, even though Lily could see that he was online, or had been recently. He sent two pictures of himself during that time, both taken by someone else. Lily spent a lot of time scrutinising them for hints of what he was up to, then chiding herself for wasting that time. She took a few sly shots of Jackson when he wasn't looking. She'd delete them if she got back together with Will. And if not, they'd be a nice memento.

If Jackson noticed what she was doing he never asked about it. They'd reached a happy place where nothing mattered except the present. Lily's tan grew deeper, she felt rested and relaxed. She forced herself not to think about Will too much, she stopped herself from fretting about work and from worrying and wondering if she would get the finance director job – which she felt she rightly deserved. She'd been told they wouldn't make a decision until after her return anyway, so there was no point in dwelling on it. In truth, she didn't know what she'd do if she didn't get it; because it would mean that either she or Damon would have to leave. There could only be one head of finance, not two. She had deliberately not brought her work phone with her, so had no idea what was going on – well wasn't that the whole point of a holiday?

Lily saw Tess and Gemma every day and was happy to hear that Gemma's rash had cleared up and that Tess had finally managed to stand up on the board, even if it was only for four seconds. Tess's worries about Jackson and his murderous intentions had evaporated, especially after he'd invited her and Gemma to his place for a lunchtime barbecue. The date was set for the day before he left – secretly Lily wished he hadn't invited them, but it seemed to set Tess's mind at rest. It also endeared Jackson to not just Tess, but also Gemma.

'Are either of your friends vegetarians?' Jackson said as they lay in bed on the morning of the barbecue. 'Only I'm going to the butcher's to pick up some nice cuts.'

'No. They both eat meat, though Gemma does like a lot of salad with hers.' Lily allowed herself a little snigger. 'But don't offer that chilli dip.'

'Ah. Did they have some before? I hope it didn't cause them any problems.'

'Only Gemma.' Lily smirked, remembering chill

trout pout. She untwined Jackson's arm from around her shoulders and got out of bed, then padded into his bathroom and enjoyed the luxury of his power shower as she washed her hair; it would probably be the last time she washed it at his place. Tonight would be their last night together. Again, Lily wished that her friends weren't coming for lunch – she wanted Jackson all to herself. Their time together had gone so quickly.

Of course, in the butcher's everyone knew Jackson. It was one of those family run shops that had long since disappeared from the town Lily lived in. The butcher's wife, tall and wiry and called Mags, came out to see him, asked how he felt about leaving before telling him he shouldn't go, that he should just say no. He'd looked away with sadness in his eyes, then muttered something about doing his duty and about obligations.

'Can't you talk some sense into him?' the butcher's wife said, staring straight at Lily.

'Me? Oh. No.' Lily shook her head. The last thing she had expected from this woman – clad in a bloody, striped apron and wearing white wellies – was a question like that, put in such a way that it sounded like an accusation. The woman shook her head and disappeared into the back of the shop.

'Sorry about that,' Jackson said, once they were outside.

'It's okay,' Lily said. 'At least the butcher didn't round on me too.'

'Yes. She did. Mags *is* the butcher. Her husband serves behind the counter.'

'Oh. Oops. How very sexist of me.' Lily laughed, but also felt embarrassed for stereotyping. 'The bloody apron sort of gave it away, I suppose.'

'Sort of.' Jackson laughed, put his arm around Lily,

hugged her and kissed the top of her head.

It felt so good, so reassuring.

'I don't suppose there'd be any point in trying to persuade you not to go wherever you're going?' Lily ventured. 'Wherever that is. Not that it's any of my business,' she added hastily.

'Obligations.' Jackson let go of Lily and strode towards his car. She hastened her step to catch up with him.

Foot in mouth, Lily thought, wishing she'd kept it shut.

The barbecue was lit and up to temperature, the food was waiting but there was no sign of Tess and Gemma.

'It is today, isn't it?' Lily said, checking the time on her phone.

'Yes. Absolutely.'

They were now fifteen minutes late.

'This is so unlike Tess.' Lily was starting to worry.

'What about Gemma?'

'I don't really know what her timekeeping's like.' Lily thought for a moment. 'No, I don't think she's usually the late type.' Too uptight for that.

Lily messaged Tess and waited for a response, hoping that the signal was strong enough.

'Tess hasn't replied.' They were now twenty-five minutes late. 'I hope they haven't had an accident. Should we go out and look for them?'

'Probably just lost,' Jackson said. 'They'll turn up in a minute. Don't worry.' But his words didn't match his own concerned face.

'Tess is probably driving, so she won't answer her

phone. Don't you think?' Was Lily clutching at straws?

'Yes, of course.'

Ten minutes later – by which time Lily and Jackson had been down to the end of the lane and back – they turned up.

'Where have you been?' Lily tried hard not to sound angry.

Tess, who *was* driving, raised her eyebrows. 'Someone put the wrong postcode in the sat nav.'

'Don't look at me,' Gemma snapped. 'I was just following instructions, helping out, to make sure we got here on time.'

'Well, we didn't,' snapped Tess, which wasn't like Tess at all.

'Never mind, you're here now. I hope you've brought your appetites with you.' Jackson ushered the party through the house and out towards the barbecue.

'Well,' Gemma said, putting her hands on her hips and surveying the terrace, garden and the sweeping views of the bay. 'You never said it was this magnificent, Lily.'

Lily didn't respond, but began to pour the drinks while Jackson attended to the food.

After they'd eaten a meal, (which even Gemma declared to be the best barbecue she'd ever had, and she was not one for barbecues at all,) Lily followed it up with a baked cheesecake which she had made in Jackson's kitchen. It was her speciality, the dish she always made for special occasions.

'Good as it always is,' Tess declared. 'My favourite.'

Lily quickly took a photo of it and sent it to Will, it was his favourite too. She could see he was online, but he didn't reply.

'Well, aren't we the lucky ones. All this sunshine and

sitting in this lovely spot.' Gemma leaned towards Jackson. 'You really do have a lovely place here. Sea, sea everywhere.' She stood up and waved her arms around.

Lily exchanged a glance with Tess, both wondering just how much Gemma had drunk.

'You seem very fond of Lily's hair,' Gemma said as she watched Jackson absently playing with it.

He stopped, letting the strand he had been twirling drop. 'I love Lily's hair.'

Lily felt her heart squeeze.

'I suppose it is quite attractive in its way,' Gemma continued. 'If you like really curly hair. I prefer mine smooth.' She ran her hand over her sleek jumbo bob. 'Of course it does rather rule her life, doesn't it, Lily? Constantly battling to get the frizz under control, using all the hot water up. I can tell you since you've not been at the cottage we haven't run out of hot water once, have we Tess?'

'Well…' Tess began but Gemma cut across her.

'Not once. So there. It was you and your hair all along.'

If Jackson hadn't been there Lily would have called Gemma a bitch, instead she smiled sweetly but Jackson - a distant look in his eyes – didn't even notice.

By seven in the evening Lily wished her friends would go, but they seemed to have settled into Jackson's garden, enjoying the view. In the end, Lily sent out unsubtle hints; she cleared plates and glasses, stacked the dishwasher and offered everyone coffee instead of alcohol. No one seemed to notice.

'What time are you leaving tomorrow, Jackson?' Lily said, deciding direct action needed to be taken.

'Before noon,' he said, sounding morose.

'And you haven't packed yet, have you?'

Jackson shook his head; it was a slow, deliberate action.

'I'm an expert packer,' Gemma piped up. 'If you want any help or hints, just say the word.' She was simpering Gemma again. 'I've become so good because of the children. Have you noticed how the airlines keep reducing the baggage weight? You need to take so much with small children and Joseph won't pay for extra. You know what he's like, Tess. So, I've developed ways of reducing and redefining packing.' Gemma sat up straight and waited for congratulations, when none came she slumped back down in her seat.

Tess got up to use the loo and Lily grasped her opportunity, hovering for her when she came out.

'Do you think you could take Gemma back to the cottage now?' Lily asked. 'Only this is mine and Jackson's last night together.'

'Oh God, yeah, sorry. What is the time?'

'Nearly eight.'

'Oh. No. I'm so sorry, Lily. I hadn't realised.' Tess marched out onto the terrace and informed a reluctant Gemma it was time to leave.

'But we haven't finished the wine,' Gemma protested.

'Please, take it with you,' Jackson smiled and thrust the bottle into her hand.

'Oh, well, all right.'

After they'd gone and Jackson had finished cleaning the barbecue, he joined a wistful Lily on the lawn, where she had moved their chairs so that they could enjoy the sun going down across the bay. He stood in front of her, his arms behind his back.

'So, this is our last night together.'

Lily nodded, then managed a big smile, not that she

felt like smiling.

'In the spirit of fun, no past, no future, no strings and let's not forget more fun, let's make it a good one.' He pulled a bottle of champagne and two flutes from behind his back. He grinned. And so did Lily.

Lily awoke the next morning to find herself alone in Jackson's bed. She could hear him moving around in another room; hear the soft closing of drawers and cupboards, as though he was trying to keep the noise to a minimum. She got out of bed, pulled on his discarded t-shirt and used the bathroom before padding around the bedrooms until she found him. He had two cases open and was speedily packing them; he looked up and saw her.

'Sorry, I was trying not to wake you.'

'That's okay. Shall I make breakfast?'

He flipped the lid of one suitcase down and closed the zip. 'Yes,' he said, coming towards her and hugging her close. 'Let's have a hearty breakfast.'

'You're not a condemned man,' she laughed and when he didn't join in she realised she'd touched a nerve. Maybe there was something wrong with him. No past, no future, she reminded herself.

'Scrambled eggs? I need to use them up before I leave.' He took a bowl out of the cupboard, broke the eggs and started whisking them.

'I can take anything you've got left when I leave. I suppose I should be going soon. I feel awful for asking for a lift but I expect you'll be glad to have me gone so you can get on with your packing. Lily felt awkward, in the way.

'No.' He laid down the whisk and came towards her, grabbed her face playfully between his hands and kissed her hard on the mouth. Lily enjoyed it, but wondered what he thought; she hadn't even brushed her teeth while he smelt squeaky clean and delicious. 'I'll drop you off when I leave; it's almost on my way, only a slight detour.'

'Okay. If you're sure I won't be in your way.' She wrapped her arms around his waist and laid her head on his chest. An image of Will's broad chest flashed through her mind, then vanished just as quickly. She could hear Jackson's heart beating fast as he pulled her in closer and kissed the top of her head.

'I'll miss this.' His voice was husky as he gathered her hair into a pony tail.

'Me too,' she said, gripping him tighter.

'Breakfast.' He let her go, returned to his whisking.

They were getting into the car before she dared say anything. It had been playing on her mind, nagging at her.

She cleared her throat. 'I've been thinking…' she began.

He waited.

'We should delete each other's phone numbers from our phones. That way we can ensure that this was just a lovely holiday romance.' She paused. 'Like we agreed.'

'Okay.' His voice sounded cautious. He started the car without speaking, manoeuvred it into the lane and finally, his thinking evidently done, he spoke. 'That was the deal. You're right. We should delete those numbers.'

'Great,' Lily said, not feeling great at all. 'And we're not likely to see each other ever again, are we?'

'You don't think you'll come here for another holiday?'

Lily shrugged. She tried to imagine Will on a holiday like this. 'No, I doubt it.' Would she be with Will in the future? Would he want to get back together? Would she have him back?

'Shame, because you've done so well at surfing. You should keep it up.'

'We'll delete those numbers together, when you drop me off.' Lily took a deep breath. 'Anyway, you won't be here will you?'

'Probably not, if things pan out. Although I might pop back for the odd holiday.'

'So what will you do with your place?'

'I've put it with a letting agency. The cleaners go in tomorrow and it'll be a holiday let after that.'

'So if you pop back you'll have nowhere to stay.' She laughed. 'Except your beach hut.'

'Wouldn't be the first time I've slept in it.' Now he laughed. But, Lily noticed, he didn't sound any jollier than she felt.

'No,' she mused, remembering that night, their first night together.

He pulled up outside her holiday cottage and switched off the engine. He reached into his pocket for his phone.

'Ready?' Jackson waved his phone at Lily.

She pulled his number up on her phone and, holding the phones side by side, they pressed delete. Then laughed, though to Lily's ears both their laughs sounded hollow.

'Let's hope neither of us needs to get in touch with the other, eh Lily?'

'Why should we? Anyway, if we're meant to meet again, fate will engineer it. I'm a great believer in fate.'

'Fate. Yeah.' Jackson jumped out of the car and pulled Lily's case from the boot. He waited for her.

'Let's say goodbye here,' Lily said. 'I don't want any of Gemma's smart remarks today.'

'Thanks for a great time, Lily. Thanks for making the last few weeks of my freedom such fun. Thanks for the best no strings, no past, no future nine days of my life. Thanks for having mermaid hair.' He kissed her – a passionate kiss to remember. Her knees almost buckled, she felt a tingle run up and down her spine.

'Same here,' Lily said, recovering enough to grab her case and walk away. She inhaled deeply, half turned and waved over her shoulder. She couldn't look at him, couldn't watch him drive away, couldn't let their fun time mean any more that it was supposed to. It was over. Holiday romance: done.

She heard his car roar away up the lane, wiped tears from her eyes and opened the cottage door to find Gemma standing by the window. Had she been watching? Did it matter?

'Hi Gemma.' Lily forced a sweet smile.

The following days dragged. Without Jackson there was no point for Lily; she might as well go back home, back to her life, decide if she wanted Will back – if he wanted to come back. Staying here, lying on the beach, popping into the café, being served by Jackson's relatives, all seemed wrong. She didn't venture into the sea again, neither to surf – her excuse was that she no longer had a decent wetsuit, even though he had offered to let her keep it – nor to swim.

Friday evening saw the trio sitting in the pub, studiously avoiding the local cider and looking glum.

'We've been lucky with the weather, but it's supposed to break tomorrow.' Gemma let out a long sigh before getting up and going to the bar.

'Gem wants to go home,' Tess confided. 'She's missing the children.'

'Is she? She never mentions them.' Was that as spiteful as it sounded.

'Don't be fooled; she is missing them and my brother.'

Gemma came back and plonked three glasses of white wine on their table. 'Let's drink to us and our last full day tomorrow.' Her voice conveyed no enthusiasm.

'Thanks Gem. I've been thinking if we've only got one more day and the weather is turning, why don't we go home tomorrow instead of Sunday? I've got a lot to do before I go back to work on Monday. Tess too.'

'Oh. Well. If you really want to.' Gemma's head rocked on her shoulders. 'I'm quite happy to go with the majority.'

It was raining heavily as they packed the next morning. The weather had definitely turned. The cottage was dark and instead of the lovely coolness they'd enjoyed when it was hot, it now felt damp. Lily rooted through her clothes for something warm to wear.

'Oh no. This is Jackson's fleece. I must have taken it when I grabbed my stuff yesterday.' She held it up to her face and inhaled his sweet odour.

'I suppose we could take a detour via his place and drop it off on the way home.' Tess was saying the right words but her face didn't look happy.

'Naw. He had several.' She wanted it. She wanted to keep it. How bad was that? She pulled it on and zipped it up. It felt so good; it was far too long and she needed to roll up the sleeves but that made it even better. 'Anyway, he's not there and it's all locked up.'

Tess's lips formed a relieved smile.

When they were ready to load up the car Lily opened the cottage door to be confronted by a howling wind. But at least the rain had stopped. They started hauling their cases and stuffing them into Tess's tiny car. Even with Lily supervising the packing, there still wasn't much room, especially in the back. Lily shuddered at the prospect of the long journey cramped in the back of the car.

'This is the last one,' Gemma said, dragging yet another stuffed case towards the car, at the same time fighting against the wind.

'I don't know where we're going to fit that,' Lily muttered to Tess just as Gemma let out an almighty scream.

Lily and Tess watched as Gemma's jumbo bob rolled up the lane like tumbleweed. Lily looked back at Gemma, then back at the hair. A wig. Gemma's amazing hair was a wig, not extensions. Gemma's real hair was thin, wispy, patchy, and very short.

Tess ran to comfort a now hysterical Gemma. Lily chased after the hair as it gained momentum and rolled faster along the lane. When it was within her reach she pounced, but a rogue gust blew it sideways. She made another lunge.

'Got it,' she yelled.

Gemma's yowling – carried by the wind – hit her like a shockwave.

Lily offered the hair to Gemma as though it were a precious pet. Gemma snatched it and ran inside, still bawling. Tess followed Gemma and Lily stayed outside and finished stuffing the car before finally entering the cottage to find a red-eyed Gemma sipping water while a sympathetic Tess patted her hand. The wig was now firmly back in place on her head; had Lily not just chased it up the lane she could have sworn the hair was real.

'So. Now. You. Know,' Gemma managed between sobs. 'I bet you'll have a good laugh about it with your friends.'

'I'm sorry that happened,' Lily said. 'And I won't be discussing it with anyone. I promise.'

'There,' Tess said. 'I told you.'

Gemma sniffed. 'Yes. Well. Good.'

'And Lily did run up the lane and get it back for you.'

'Yes. Thank you, Lily.' Gemma blew her nose. 'It's alopecia, in case you're wondering.'

Lily nodded. She had wondered but would never have asked.

'It happened after I had Pixie-Bella. And that's why I won't have any more. Can you imagine? I'd be completely bald, I'd look like a boiled egg.'

'Eek,' Lily mouthed to Tess behind Gemma's back.

'And your brother wants me to have another one. What do you think of that?' Gemma said to Tess, then turned back to Lily. 'What do *you* think of that?'

Lily, wide-eyed and speechless, looked at Tess.

Tess sighed. 'Gem, all he said was that if you weren't having any more children maybe you should think about getting a part-time job.'

'Is that what he told you?'

'Isn't it true?'

'His version I suppose.' Gemma shook herself before standing up. 'Shall we get going then?' she said, as if the delay had nothing to do with her.

The journey in the back of the car was just as torturous as Lily expected. By the time they arrived at Gemma's – she insisted on being dropped off first – Lily could hardly heave herself out of the car. With aching knees, she helped decant Gemma's vast amount of luggage onto the pavement where it sat until Joe came out to meet them. He hugged Gemma, genuinely pleased she was back. Rafe and Pixie-Bella hugged her too, chanting 'mummy, mummy, did you bring us a present.' Of course, Gemma had.

Back in the car and on their way to Lily's she sat in the front of the car and stretched her legs.

'That's better.'

'Sorry about Gemma being so demanding. I know she needs a lot of airtime. Only I had to let her come.'

'It's okay. I can see that her life isn't as perfect as I thought it was. Will they sort it out? Will it all be okay between them?'

'Yes, I'm sure it will. She has these little tantrums from time to time, she is quite highly-strung, our Gemma.' Tess allowed herself a little snigger. 'The timing was unfortunate; it meant she could latch onto our holiday. Still on the plus side, I suppose if she hadn't been there you wouldn't have been able to go and stay with Jackson. Would you?'

When Lily didn't respond, mainly because the mention of Jackson brought back such bittersweet memories, Tess pressed for an answer.

'No, of course I wouldn't. It was just lucky that I could.'

♥ ♥ ♥

'Well, I know what I'll be doing this evening.' Lily eyed her bags as she and Tess dropped them on the hall floor.

'Washing,' they said in unison, before laughing.

'Actually,' Tess said, leaning in as though telling a secret in a crowded room. 'I'm going out on another date with Gareth.'

'Gareth? What? The same Gareth you met at stained glass classes?'

'Yes. The very same Gareth.'

'I thought you said he was arrogant and rude.'

'He thought the same about me. Seems we both got it wrong. He's really very nice.'

'I can't imagine how anyone could think you were arrogant or rude. You're the sweetest person I know. Let's face it, no one could tolerate Gemma the way you do.'

'Like I said, we both got it wrong.'

'Another date? How many previous dates have there been?'

'This is number six.'

'You've kept that quiet. How long has this been going on?'

'About a month,' she paused. 'Including the two weeks we've been away.'

'That's five dates in two weeks. You are keen.'

'We both are.'

'So he's why you went up the lane to pick up your messages every day. He's the reason you smiled at your phone so often. It all makes sense now.'

Tess smiled. 'Okay, Sherlock, I need to get off now. Have a good rest of your weekend.'

'You too. Urgh back to work on Monday.' Lily mock-shuddered as she hugged Tess goodbye.

Lily had unpacked and already had a load in the washing machine before she checked her phone again. There was a message from Will, a photo no less. He was astride the motorbike – of course – stripped to the waist again, bronzed and wearing sunglasses. God, he looked good. Too good. Lily felt a pang of regret. And yearning. He grinned at the camera. It wasn't a selfie – that much Lily could clearly see – but there was no one else in the picture. She zoomed in to look at Will's gorgeous face – an attempt to forget Jackson's. She probably would take him back, she thought, scanning over the photo. He was so stunningly gorgeous, even if he was a bit inconsiderate at times, and commitment phobic.

'What the hell,' she said out loud, before zooming in closer. Reflected very clearly in his sunglasses was an image of the person who took the photo and it wasn't one of his mates. From what Lily could see, she was tall, leggy, blonde and in a very skimpy one-piece bikini. 'Bastard,' Lily screeched.

Eleven

Lily didn't sleep well the next two nights; she tossed and turned and didn't know quite why she was so annoyed. She'd broken up with Will; *she'd* dumped *him*. He was free to do as he pleased, wasn't that what she'd been doing? So he was with some near naked long-legged lovely. So what? She'd just spent nine days with a tanned surf-Adonis. Nine of the best days of her life, too. How could she possibly object to anything Will did after what she'd done?

And yet she did. She'd dumped him; he should be heart-broken. Maybe he just didn't care. Maybe he never had. He would be away for another two weeks; then it would be crunch time. Either they made a go of it, or never saw each other again.

Was it that simple?

Then there was Jackson. Just the memory of him made her hug herself; she closed her eyes and imagined his strong arms around her. At least there was no decision to make with Jackson; they'd agreed that they would never see each other again.

She spent the rest of the weekend concentrating on

her washing, ironing and getting her hair into some semblance of smooth and professional. Finally, late on Sunday afternoon deciding to check on her work emails – she could at least clear the rubbish ones before Monday – she fished her phone out of the drawer and switched it on, three missed calls from work, but it was the switchboard number so she had no idea who had rung.

'Well, hello Ms Lillian Ward. Look at that fabulous tan. Where *have* you been? And did you have a fab time?' Damon held his arm against hers to compare skin tones.

'Don't call me that,' Lily snapped.

'Oh. Oops.'

'Sorry. Yes. I did have a good time, I went to Devon. I had a great time in fact. Just a bit, you know…' She wasn't telling Damon she was already missing her holiday romance man or that she was seething over Will's behaviour.

'And how's the lovely Will?'

'Yeah, he's good.' She smiled brightly. No need for Damon to know that Will was on the other side of the Atlantic without her.

'So?' Damon waited, expectant.

'Oh no. It was just a nice meal out.' She grimaced, realising he was referring to that fateful meal one Friday, two weeks ago.

Damon, displaying great tactfulness, changed the subject. 'I'm guessing you've heard the news.' Damon lifted his eyes to the sky; an exaggerated movement made all the more dramatic when he kept his head straining upwards for too long.

'No. What news?'

'You must have had an email; they must have sent you an email at the very least, though I think a phone call would be more appropriate.'

'I'm not sure what you're talking about, but I haven't been able to read any emails on my phone, my damn password expired while I was away.'

'Oh well, once you log onto your computer I'm sure you'll be as up to date as the rest of us. I must go; I need to discuss direct debits with The Europeans.' With that Damon strutted back to his own desk and flopped into his chair as though talking to Lily had exhausted him.

Lily logged on, updated her password, and waited for her computer to download over three hundred emails. Her heart sank even though she knew that many of them would be spam, irrelevant, or just out of date. She started at the bottom and began the laborious process of sifting through them. If she was lucky she might get it done in an hour. Maybe that was optimistic, aside from deleting the rubbish ones she'd have to create *action* and *immediate action* folders. Urgh.

'How's it going?' Damon squeezed himself onto the corner of her desk and smiled.

'Still wading through.' Now it was Lily's turn to roll her eyes to the ceiling.

Damon waited as though expecting more and when it didn't come he sighed. 'There is some news that won't be there, I'm afraid.'

'Oh. Not sure I like the sound of that.'

'It's about Josh.'

'Oh. Yes. Have you heard from him? How's he getting on? I saw him down in Devon. Isn't that funny?'

'There's no easy way to say this.' Ignoring Lily's comment, Damon exhaled then took a deep breath before continuing. 'Josh died, Lily.'

'No. How? Why?' Lily's heart was beating so fast she felt faint. She'd chatted to him in the post room on his last day a little over two weeks ago. He'd guided her onto the right path when she'd been lost on her way to the beach. How could he possibly be dead?

'That night. His last day here. He went home, sat in his chair and just popped off. Massive heart attack, or stroke, or something. Anyway, he didn't suffer, just went really quickly.'

'When?'

'His last day here. Friday. Your last day before your hols. Aren't you listening?'

'No, that can't be right. I told you, I saw him in Devon.'

'You couldn't have. He never got there. His son came up to take him down to Devon on the Saturday afternoon and found him dead.' Damon leaned in, his voice a whisper. 'Not very nice, they had to have a post-mortem and everything.'

'Ah, poor Josh.' Lily felt a single tear run down her face. She couldn't understand it. She was certain that she'd seen him on the path in Devon. Absolutely certain it was him. But how could it be?

'When's the funeral? I must go.'

'Last Friday hun, sorry.'

'Did you go?'

'Yes. We had the afternoon off so most of the company went. Remember all those stories about him being a banker and an astronaut. Turned out it was all true. Anyway, our department needed time away from the office, even if it was for a funeral, after the morning's saga.'

'What saga?'

'Haven't you caught up with your emails yet? What have you been doing? You've been at it an hour.'

'Sorting them.' Lily's voice was indignant. 'Appropriately.'

'I suggest you skim through and get to the pertinent ones.' Damon got up. 'Pronto,' he called back at her as he walked away.

The email was marked 'Private and Personal'. How could she have missed that? It was from Heather in HR and started off very formally – the standard 'thank you for applying' letter that they sent to everyone who didn't get the job they'd applied for. It explained that she hadn't been successful and wished her well in her career. Heather had added a personal note on the end explaining that she was so sorry to email this news but hadn't been able to reach Lily by phone. So that explained the missed calls on her work mobile.

Lily's heart sank.

She looked up and saw Damon watching her. He raised his eyebrows and gave her a sardonic sneer.

'I didn't get it,' she mouthed.

'I know,' he said, shrugging.

Lily went to Damon's desk. 'So, who did?'

'Read the emails,' Damon said. 'Just read. Then I'll fill in the juicy details.'

'Can't you just…'

'No,' Damon cut in. 'Just read.'

Back at her desk Lily skimmed through her emails until she reached the one that Damon was obviously referring to. First there was the announcement. It came from the MD, Mr Benson himself. It was the standard, 'We're delighted to announce…' Her eyes glossed over the detail, what did it matter? All she knew was that she hadn't got it. It had gone to some man who'd worked at KPMG and other 'prestigious blue-chip companies'. Oh yes. It was a job for the boys and probably some old boy at that.

Damon caught her eye again. 'Well?'

'I already knew I hadn't got it.'

'There are two emails, have you read them both?'

Lily shook her head and scanned for the final one. And found it. It was from the new finance director. He introduced himself – Cyril Montgomery-Jones. Urgh, even his name made Lily shudder – Montgomery-Jones. She imagined some old stuffed shirt parading around with a fat, red face. He was calling a meeting – that was the meeting Damon had referred to, the one that Lily had missed on Friday morning – where they would discuss how things would be moving forward, blah, blah, blah. Lily couldn't even bring herself to read the rest of it.

'Okay,' she said to Damon when *she* perched on the corner of *his* desk. 'Give me the details.'

'We're going to have our jobs reassessed.'

'Yes. That's hardly news. You and I already know that one of us will be leaving.'

'Not just us. He is going to restructure the whole department and radicalise some of our processes.' Damon folded his arms across his chest.

'And...' Lily was waiting. A restructure was hardly radical; she would have done the same herself.

'The Europeans are absolutely wetting themselves with worry.'

166

Lily glanced over at Urve and Beata, they sat silently side by side in their usual heads-down-working-hard positions. Their jobs were probably the safest in the department.

'What's he like?'

Damon shrugged. 'Okay. If you like that sort of thing.' A little smile played across his face but Lily could see him fighting it back down.

'Fat old toad?'

'Definitely not.' Now Damon allowed the smile to break free before it turned into a quick, shrill laugh. He put his hand over his mouth.

'So? What is he like?'

'Mmm. Very short, dark hair. Expensive suit. Obviously loves his clothes.' Damon smoothed his hands down his own body as if feeling the expensive suit. 'Seemed very pleasant and knowledgeable. We got on very well.'

'And? What else?'

'No wedding ring. No girlfriend. Make of that what you will. And he smells luscious.'

'How do you know he has no girlfriend?'

'I asked him.' Damon smiled again.

'Right. Old? Young?'

'Just right, I'd say.' He turned his attention back to his work.

'Oh.' Lily sauntered back to her desk. Whether Montgomery-Jones turned out to be gay or not, Damon would still lavish his full man-love on him. Which was rather worrying. Damon may have declared he wasn't ambitious, but now she thought about it, he'd never said he wouldn't fight to keep his job. Lily was now at war with Damon. Lovely.

She carried on through her emails, sorting and

deleting as she went. She was on the lookout for a meeting invitation with her new boss because she needed to present herself in a good light the way Damon apparently had. She pinged a quick email to Veronica, his personal assistant. The response was suitably short and curt: 'He's out all this week, meetings etc. I'll try to find some time for you next week.'

The morning dragged on and Lily soon found herself getting back into her work. At least it distracted her from thinking about Will or trying not to daydream about Jackson.

Damon, who could be both sweet and bitchy at the same time, invited her to lunch. He quizzed her about her holiday. She told him she had learnt to surf – she didn't tell him who had taught her. She didn't tell him that Will hadn't been with her, or that she'd gone with Tess and Gemma. Fortunately, Damon, his eyes starting to glaze over, never asked for more detail; maybe she was being a holiday bore.

Back at her desk she allowed herself the luxury of flicking through the photos on her phone. She smiled to herself when she saw the selfies she'd sent to Will. She glowed inwardly when she looked at the few sneaky shots she'd taken of Jackson. She checked Will's online status, flicking through the messages, glancing with annoyance at the sunglasses' reflection shot. Will was online and he must have noticed that Lily was too.

Will: *Hey babe. Back at work yet?*

Lily: *Sadly, yes.*

Will: *Cool.*

Then he went offline.

Cool? What was that supposed to mean?

Irritated, she dropped her phone into her handbag and got on with her work.

By the end of the week she felt as though she hadn't even had a holiday; her tan was fading fast and Jackson was becoming a dim memory. Will still sent the odd photo of himself, but the one he sent on Saturday morning was a shocker: Purple toes poking out from a plaster cast - he'd broken his ankle.

Lily: *OMG. Are you okay? How did that happen? xx*

Will: *Bike fell on it.* He'd added a sad-face emoji.

Lily frowned. Will never, ever used emojis. He had once launched into a tirade about how stupid they were. Lily wondered if someone else was sending his messages now. She imagined the long-legged half naked lovely ministering to Will's needs.

Lily: *So sorry. How are you coping? xx*

Will: *Can't ride anymore. Coming home early. On crutches. Can you pick me up from airport?* He gave her the details.

On Monday morning she asked Damon to cover for if she was late on Tuesday; Will's plane was due in at one in the morning.

'Of course I will,' Damon beamed at her. 'But why? Do tell, Lillian.'

'Don't call me that.' After she had filled him in, and she'd had to tell him about the USA trip that didn't include her, he was suitably sympathetic both to Will for his horrible, holiday shortening injury, and to Lily for being left behind and now expected to pick up the pieces.

'I'll cope,' she said, secretly wishing she didn't have to. She also wondered what Will thought the status of their relationship was? He could have asked any of his mates to pick him up. He could have got a taxi.

'When's your one-to-one?' Damon asked.

'What one-to-one?'

'With the man?' Damon did a super cheesy grin.

'Oh, I haven't heard, yet.'

'Mine's eleven am, tomorrow morning.'

'Oh? Right. But you've already met him.'

'Everyone's having an individual meeting with him.' He dropped his voice and leaned in. 'The whole damn department. Totally unnecessary. The Europeans are damn near shitting themselves.'

Lily glanced over at Urve and Beata, heads down as usual. She gave Beata a reassuring smile when she glanced up with an anxious look on her face.

Back at her desk Lily saw her own meeting request with Montgomery-Jones in her inbox. It was Tuesday morning, at nine-thirty. Lily didn't accept the appointment but went round to discuss rescheduling with Veronica.

Without lifting her hands from her keyboard, Veronica looked over her glasses at Lily. The smile she gave was brief and only served to prove she *could* smile – if necessary.

'Veronica, hi,' Lily said, feeling like a silly kid – which was the affect Veronica had on everyone. Her age was a closely guarded secret but she'd been with Bensons for over thirty years. Lily couldn't help wondering how she would have handled this scary woman if she had become finance director.

'Yes?'

'I've just received my one-to-one appointment with Cyril.'

'That's correct, I've just sent it.' Veronica's eyes

strayed back to her computer screen.

'I was wondering if I could change it?'

Now Veronica had the perfect excuse to give her attention to her computer. Her eyes flickered as she scanned through Cyril's diary.

'Not really,' she said, without looking at Lily. 'He's fully booked.'

'Oh, but. It's just the time you've given me is a bit awkward.'

'Really? Why?'

Picking up her boyfriend, or more correctly exboyfriend, from the airport was hardly a valid reason. 'It clashes with an appointment.'

Veronica turned her full gaze on Lily. 'According to your diary there are no clashing appointments.' She turned back to her computer and started typing. Evidently the conversation was over.

'Well, I hadn't put it in yet. Can I have a different time? Please.'

Veronica sighed. 'Not this week. He has no gaps.' She leaned towards Lily and gave her another brief smile. 'Listen, Lily. A word to the wise. You haven't met him yet, everyone else has. You're already behind schedule because you were on holiday. Rearrange your other appointment.'

'But I can't.'

'Then perhaps one of your colleagues will exchange appointments with you. I suggest you ask around.' This time the conversation was definitely over as Veronica began furiously stabbing at her keyboard.

The one-to-one was for ninety minutes which meant that Damon was straight in after Lily.

'Damon.' Lily sidled up to his desk. 'Would you mind swapping one-to-one times with me tomorrow?'

'Sure, hun,' Damon said, hardly looking up from his work. 'What time's yours?'

'Nine-thirty.'

'Ah. Sorry. No can do. Can't you speak to Scare-a-Von?'

'I already have. She says I can't change it, I have to swap with someone instead. Why can't you change? You'll be here.'

'Yes, but I have do this plan/report thing for him, and frankly I'm struggling even with an eleven am appointment. Really sorry, I really am. But we're all under pressure and scrutiny here.'

'Yeah. I guess. Do you think Urve or Beata might swap?'

'No. Don't ask. Don't put them on the spot. They go in together immediately after me and like I said earlier, they're shitting themselves. They can't go before me because this plan is partly about their jobs. So no. Try someone else. Sorry, hun.' Damon's sympathy was genuine but useless.

'Okay, I'll ask around.'

An hour later and Lily had been around the whole department – ten people – and the only person willing to swap had an eight am appointment. Eight am – who the hell wanted a one-to-one at that time? No wonder they had been happy to exchange.

She was stuck with nine-thirty.

Lily did a quick calculation, if Will's plane landed at one, they should be out of the airport and on their way home by two. She could comfortably be back in her own bed and asleep by three-thirty. That meant four hours' sleep. It was going to be just fine.

♥ ♥ ♥

At eight pm Lily set the alarm for eleven-thirty. That would give her enough time to pull on her clothes and have a quick coffee before setting off. She snuggled down into her bed and closed her eyes. But even with the curtains drawn daylight sneaked in. She wasn't even tired; normally she went to bed at the time she was due to get up. She tossed and turned before eventually sitting up and flicking through a magazine. A full-page article stared up at her – 'Is your body bikini ready?' The body of the girl in the accompanying picture was definitely bikini ready. She posed in skimpy red, her skin smooth and buffed; behind her a beach and surf shack. Lily felt her heartstrings tug. She wondered where Jackson was now, wondered how he was getting on with his family obligations – whatever they were.

It was dark before she fell asleep and it seemed just as she closed her eyes the alarm went off. She dressed in jeans and t-shirt, went downstairs, made herself a coffee, collected her handbag, phone and car keys and just before she stepped outside, she grabbed Jackson's fleece from the coat hook in the hall. It might be summer but it was the middle of the night and it was nippy. She zipped it up and inhaled Jackson's aroma; she doubted Will would notice it wasn't hers.

The roads to the airport were clear and she made good time, parked the car and found herself waiting in arrivals – with a lot of male taxi drivers – just before one am. She glanced at the arrivals board and grinned to herself when she saw that his plane was on time. She was on schedule to be back in her bed and grabbing her four hours sleep. Hurray.

She heard a collective groan go around her fellow drivers, then looked at the arrivals board. She groaned – albeit belatedly. The plane was delayed an hour. An hour. How annoying that it was such short notice; she could have had another hour in bed.

Okay, so now she'd be back in her bed by four-thirty. Still three hours sleep. That would be okay.

Along with everyone else Lily headed for the limited seating and was lucky enough to find a seat, even if it was wedged between two burly taxi drivers who seemed to feel the need to fan themselves with their passenger name cards.

The hour dragged and when Lily eyes closed she didn't attempt to fight the ensuing sleep, which ended abruptly when her neighbours both jumped up and Lily flopped like a wilting flower.

The plane had landed; the baggage was in the reclaim hall.

Lily hustled and bustled her way to the front of the arrivals cluster, almost crushed against the Perspex barrier she scanned the passengers who wheeled their luggage past her.

Drivers collected their passengers and disappeared into the night; Lily began to worry that Will had marched – no hobbled – straight past her and she hadn't noticed.

She glanced at the time – ten to three.

Eventually she was the only driver left. She pulled out her phone and checked Will's original message, checked the flight number, the date, the airport. Phew, she was definitely in the right place; he should have been on that flight and there was no message to say he wasn't.

Lily looked around her, hoping to find someone to ask if all the passengers were off the plane yet – but there was no one.

She sent Will a message – but he wasn't online.

What now?

She recognised Will's deep, gravelly laughter long before she saw him. Her hackles rose, it was three in the morning and he was laughing.

He was in a wheelchair, a pair of crutches wedged between his knees. Was it really that bad?

'Oh my God,' Lily said, though not so loud that Will could hear. Or his companion. She was tall and had impossibly smooth, slender legs that were on full display beneath her short, flappy skirt. She giggled as Will delivered utterances too low for Lily to hear, even in the empty arrivals hall. The woman was alternately pushing Will's wheelchair and dragging a trolley full of luggage.

Finally, he disengaged from charming his companion and looked at Lily, his grin spread from ear to ear. 'Babe,' he called out. 'You came.'

'Of course I did. You told me to.' Lily didn't attempt to hide her tetchiness.

'Babe,' he drawled. 'Meet Giselle. She's been helping me.'

Had he been drinking? Stupid question.

Giselle said 'hi' in a sharp American accent, her immense teeth on display.

'Hello. I'm Lily,' Lily said, in case Giselle thought her name was actually *Babe*.

With Giselle pushing Will and dragging his luggage and Lily on the other side of the barrier they walked the length of the hall. Finally Will stopped and held his arms open to Lily. 'Have you missed me, babe?' He belched into her ear as she bent down to receive his hug.

'No more than you've missed me.' She could smell whisky in his belch. She recoiled.

'Hey. Don't be like that. I'm back now and I'm real glad to see you.'

'Real glad,' Lily echoed.

'Help Giselle, Lily.' Will waved his arms around as Giselle let go of the luggage trolley and gripped the wheelchair handles.

'I think I'd rather push the wheelchair.' Lily forced a tight smile at Giselle.

'Give Giselle a break, babe. She's dragged that all the way from the baggage hall, and she had to get those cases off the carousel. You in the short stay car park?'

'Yes.' Lily examined the luggage, most of it pink or leopard skin. Most of it definitely not Will's. She turned to remonstrate but Will had already urged Giselle on, urged her out into the night towards the car park.

Lily glanced at her watch. It was three-fifteen am. She could still fit in two hours and forty-five minutes of sleep.

As she stumbled towards the car park, the trolley veering off at angles as and when it pleased, she seethed at the ease with which the wheelchair seemed to travel. Will didn't know exactly where her car was, and Lily reached it first after shouting herself hoarse to get his attention.

'Okay, babe,' he shouted as Giselle pushed him back. 'Let's not get bad tempered.'

Lily heard Giselle giggle. 'Bitch,' she muttered as she pulled Will's three bags from the trolley and hurled them into the boot.

'Hey Lily, we need to get Giselle's stuff in there too.' Will used the crutches to haul himself out of the wheelchair. 'And this wheelchair needs to go back; there's a deposit on it.

'I'll do it.' Giselle grabbed the wheelchair and

marched back towards the airport building.

Will hobbled towards the car's rear door.

'Just a minute. What's going on?'

'Babe, I said we'd drop Giselle off. It's the least I could do.' He flung the rear door open. 'I'll have to sit across the whole seat, got to get this ankle up.'

'Where the hell does Giselle live? It's the middle of the night. I've got work in the morning.'

'Just a little detour. It's only twenty minutes. She's been so helpful. It would be mean to abandon her now. Get her luggage in, then we can get off as soon as she returns.'

Ten minutes later, after wedging Giselle's cases in the boot and relocating Will's bags forcibly into the rear foot-wells, Lily slumped into the driver's seat. 'Where the hell is she?'

It was three-thirty am. Two-and-a-half hours sleep.

'Probably having trouble getting the deposit back.' Will half laughed, then yawned. Lily knew that by the time they got to the car park exit he would be nodding off.

Lily started the engine, put the car in reverse.

'Hey, babe, what are you doing?'

'I'm just turning the car around, just getting ready so we can go when your friend finally comes back.'

Another five minutes passed. Lily seethed. Will gave a loud snore and woke himself up.

'Hi,' Giselle said, throwing the passenger door open and smiling in at Lily. 'Sorry about that. I had to go all the way over to the far desk. Took a while.'

Liar. Giselle had reapplied her make-up, brushed her hair and sprayed on so much cloying perfume that it made Lily first sneeze, then gag.

'Okay, where to?' Lily heard herself say, sounding

like a taxi driver.

Will was right; it was a mere twenty-minute detour. Twenty minutes of freezing with the window down because Lily could hardly breathe for Giselle's perfume. Another five minutes as Will and Giselle exchanged phone numbers and fond farewells. Then ten minutes to help Giselle unload and carry her luggage to her building door. Giselle even expected Lily to help her get the luggage to her first floor flat, but Lily gave an emphatic no to that. Enough was enough.

'Thanks so much for the ride,' Giselle drawled as she fumbled in her purse. She passed Lily a ten dollar note.

'No thanks,' Lily snapped. 'I'm not a bloody taxi.'

'You Brits. I've lived here for ten months and I still don't get your sense of humour.' She cackled before lifting the first of her suitcases inside the building door.

'That's cos it's not bloody funny,' Lily muttered, walking away.

'Great girl, that Giselle. So helpful,' Will said when Lily climbed back into her seat.

She slammed her door and started the car up. She didn't speak.

'Don't be like that, babe,' Will said. 'We'll soon be home. Your place or mine?'

Was he fucking joking?

Lily checked the time. It was ten past four. Another hour or so before they reached Will's. Ten minutes to get him inside. Ten minutes home. She could still be in her bed by five-thirty, still get two hours' sleep.

She turned the radio on, not only to keep herself awake but also to prevent a screaming row with Will while she was driving.

'Ah, home.' Will woke from his deep sleep as Lily pulled onto his drive.

She dragged his bags from the rear foot-well, careful, despite her anger and tiredness, not to knock his ankle. She picked the crutches up from the floor and handed them to him.

'Give me the keys and I'll open the door.' She waited while Will fumbled about in his pockets.

If he didn't have the keys she'd kill him.

Fortunately for them both he found them.

Twelve

Lily jerked awake when the alarm went off. She squinted at her phone; apparently she'd been asleep for over two hours. It felt like five minutes. Damn Will. They weren't even supposed to be together anymore and he had her running around after him. He'd been such a selfish bastard. And she'd been such a fool.

Then he'd kissed her. And her knees had melted.

A goodnight kiss, a thank you kiss. That was how he'd described it after she'd helped him up the stairs and out of his trousers. He'd fallen asleep immediately and she closed his bedroom door behind her quietly as she left.

That was the trouble with Will, it was what had kept her enthralled for ten years. He could be so self-centred then redeem himself with a kiss or a simple little gesture. He was good in bed too, maybe too good – practised and perfected.

With guilt creeping into her heart she thought of Jackson. She pictured his tanned face, his crinkled blue eyes, his sun-bleached hair, his odour – as sweet as a warm, sea-scented breeze. She really must not think about him. Thiers was a nine-day fling, nothing more. Why did he keep cropping up in her thoughts? Still, it was nice to dream of his face, enjoy the memory of their romance. She really would have to stop thinking about Jackson, decide if she wanted to pick up where she'd left off with Will and, most importantly today, focus on work.

She jumped awake again. She'd dozed off; a whole hour had passed.

'Aargh,' she cried. Now she would be late. Late for the meeting with Cyril. The man who had stolen her job.

She jumped in the shower, even cleaned her teeth while standing under the water – a dirty trick she'd seen Will perform many times. He also peed in the shower, but Lily drew the line at that disgusting habit.

She'd had the foresight to choose and lay out her clothes before she'd gone to bed early the previous night. Just as well given how long she'd spent ferrying Will and his American friend around.

The dress was smart and navy with a finishing touch of pink, very business-like but it also managed to convey young and professional without a hint of irony. The last thing Lily wanted was for anyone, especially stuffy Cyril, not to take her seriously. She slipped it on and admired herself in the mirror; she felt confident. Her hair only required its normal, well-practiced manoeuvre with several pins to secure it, a quick slick of soft pink lip gloss – thanks to her tan she didn't need any more makeup – and she was done. She slipped on her jacket and stepped into *the* shoes.

Those navy and pink shoes. She wondered fleetingly whether wearing the shoes was a good idea. So far, they hadn't brought her much luck, quite the opposite; and she had vowed she wouldn't wear them again. Then she caught sight of herself in the mirror and the decision was made. They looked amazing, gave her the required height to add to her confidence – with a bit of luck, old Cyril might even be shorter than her now, allowing her to look down on him. Plus, they were a perfect match to the dress.

She felt good. And she'd even managed to make up for lost time and, providing the traffic was kind, she wouldn't even be late.

And the traffic was kind: no holdups, no breakdowns, no road works. On the journey she considered what she wanted from the meeting, even though it was Cyril who had called it.

She wanted to assert herself – she may not have got the role she rightly deserved but she was still a valuable member of the team. She definitely wanted to stay in her current role at Bensons. Or, if a restructure was taking place she definitely wanted a new role in that structure. Conversely, she didn't want Damon ousted. He was a valuable member of the team too. She wondered whether Damon had defended her? Or, was it really every man and woman for themselves? If a restructure was inevitable – of course it was – she wanted to be part of it, she wanted to influence it, she wanted to save every member of the team.

She pulled into the car park with nearly ten minutes to spare. Just enough time to get to her desk, fire up her computer, take a few deep breaths and compose herself. She smiled as she picked up her bag and marched with purpose and confidence across the car park towards the building entrance. The sun was shining, the birds were singing, the air was fresh but warm; it was a good day. She felt strong and empowered.

Her left foot went down, jarring her right knee and her back in the process. She knew without even looking what had happened – it wasn't even the first time. Where the hell did these drains come from? Did they wait for her approach? Did they follow her around? How could she be so damn, bloody, bloody stupid? Again.

She pulled her foot up, but the shoe didn't give way. Balancing on one foot she bent over and yanked it but it did not budge. There wasn't time for this. No time at all. Why had she worn the damn shoes? She knew they came with bad luck. Why hadn't she learned?

She took the other shoe off and because the car park surface was painfully gritty, she tip-toed back to her car as fast as she could, wincing and yelping out loud as she did so. She threw the remaining shoe into the car boot and foraged in her gym bag for her trainers. She slipped them onto her feet. Dirty white, with pink and green stripes, elegant they were not but they were, at least, comfortable.

♥ ♥ ♥

'You're cutting it fine, Lillian. Scare-a-von has just been looking for you.' Damon nodded at Veronica's retreating form.

'I know. And don't call me that.' Lily dumped her bag and grabbed a notepad and pen from her desk.

'You can borrow my spare shoes,' Urve said, her voice almost a whisper as Lily clomped past her. Using her foot Urve slid a pair of neat, low heeled black courts out from under her desk. Urve was the epitome of discreet. And sweet.

'Thank you,' Lily whispered back. Kicking off the trainers and pushing her left foot into a shoe. 'Oh, maybe not,' she said as the shoe refused her less than tiny hoof. 'Thanks anyway.' Lily stuffed her feet back into the trainers and all but sprinted to her meeting.

Veronica stood at her desk wearing a steel smile and a deep frown. She glanced down at Lily's feet and shuddered. 'So that *was* you in the car park.' She turned her back to lead the way into the director's office.

'You saw me?'

'Yes, we were at the window at what could be deemed an opportune moment.' Was that a snigger?

'Who's we?' But she already knew the answer.

'Mr Montgomery-Jones and I.' Veronica allowed a smile to fully fill her face. 'I'm sure he'll understand why you're wearing *those*.' She nodded at the trainers then shook her head.

To hell with Veronica; to hell with Cyril Montgomery-Jones. Lily didn't care if the pompous old toad understood why she was wearing trainers or not. What was he – a fashion expert? In her experience few financial directors were the epitome of sartorial elegance. Anyway, this was Bensons Wholesale Electricals, not a catwalk in London Fashion week.

Just before Lily entered the office she smoothed down her dress, took a deep breath, put her shoulders back and lifted her head. She was confident, good at her job and would not be cowed by either Scare-a-von or stuffy Cyril.

Lily glanced around the office – the office that she once imagined would be her own. The desk was across the middle of the room, creating a barrier between the director and any visitor. If the job had been Lily's she would have immediately moved that desk, brought in a round table and made the whole room friendlier. The walls were a sombre dark grey, the carpet dull; it's only saving grace was that the office faced east so was sunny in the mornings – if it wasn't raining. There were rumours that the last finance director had had a mini-breakdown in this room. Not that anyone had witnessed it. Veronica was commendably tight-lipped and admonished anyone who asked. Lily would have repainted the room, in something bright and cheery. She wondered, as she looked at him, if Cyril had any such plans.

He was still standing and looking out of the window from which he'd had a good view of Lily and the shoe incident. His dark form was silhouetted in the morning sunshine. Damon was right; he definitely wasn't a fat toad. She could tell, even from the back, that the suit was expensive and it hung well on an athletic frame – he was probably one of those fanatics who spent two hours in the gym before starting work at seven am. Even Will, who loved his gym, didn't do that. His dark hair was closely cropped and his shoulders were just the right side of wide.

From the back there was something inherently attractive about him. Lily pushed the feeling down. He was her rival, her bitter rival; the man who had stolen her job. How dare he be even vaguely appealing, even from the back? She told herself that he would probably have a face like a frog when he turned around. And he was probably much older from the front. Just because he was gym obsessed didn't mean his face wouldn't be a wrinkly old mess. She'd met his sort on her rare visits to the gym, reclaiming their youth during a sad midlife crisis. She allowed a wicked smile to flick across her face before she regained control and forced a deadpan face. Remember, she told herself, you're a professional.

He didn't move until Veronica gave a little, fake cough. He turned and smiled a neat, professional smile.

And Lily's heart stopped.

What? What? Her heart started to beat again in time to the fast ticking thoughts that were running through her brain like a runaway train. She could feel her pulse throbbing in her neck. Could he see it? Could Veronica? It beat so hard and fast she could hear the blood rushing through her ears. Could they hear it?

She gulped air. Had she actually stopped breathing?

What was going on?

Oh, he was attractive.

Far too attractive. The suit looked even better on his body now he was facing her; the cloth clung in all the right places. He wore a blue shirt and no tie, exposing an Adam's apple that bobbed as he slowly swallowed.

He was definitely not wrinkly. He was young.

Her bitter rival was drop dead gorgeous.

And frighteningly familiar.

Thirteen

This man, this Cyril Montgomery-Jones was Jackson's twin – same eyes, same build, same face, even the faint remnants of a tan. Could it be possible? The hair and clothes were very different, but… Lily racked her brain trying to remember if Jackson had mentioned a twin or even a brother. She struggled to remember Jackson's surname, wondered if she had even known it. Montgomery-Jones was distinctive; she would certainly have remembered that.

'Sit down, Lily,' Veronica stage whispered.

'Um?' Lily shook herself to find Cyril and Veronica already seated, their expectant eyes focused on her. What had happened? When had they sat down?

'Veronica, perhaps you could get,' Cyril glanced down at his paperwork, 'Lillian, a glass of water.'

'Of course.' Veronica stood up, her lips pursed, and trotted across the office to pour Lily a drink. She set it down without a word.

'Thank you.'

'So, Lillian,' Cyril began.

'I prefer Lily.'

'Yes,' he said and Lily watched him blink several times. She saw him swallow. Did that mean anything? Had he heard of her? From his twin? If such a person existed? Or was she imagining it? 'Veronica is going to sit in on this one and take a few notes. Is that all right with you?'

'Sure.' Lily forced a brief smile that felt like a grimace and wondered what the tone of the meeting was going to be. Why did Veronica need to be there to take notes? Was this a dismissal meeting? It had all the hallmarks.

Lily felt flustered, confused.

What was going on?

Who was this man sitting in front of her?

'So, as you're aware I had a meeting with the whole team to discuss the future.' He looked up, expectant.

'Yes,' Lily said. 'When I was on holiday.' She wondered if he would ask her where she'd been. He didn't.

'I'm also very aware,' he glanced away, then looked back. 'That you applied for this position.'

'That's right.' Lily stared into his eyes, eyes so very like Jackson's. Perhaps not quite so blue. She continued to stare; she would not be cowed. He looked down.

'I hope that isn't going to cause any problems between us.' He smiled and his face lit up for just a second. He looked so like Jackson, so like him that it made her heart skip again.

'So do I,' she muttered into her chest.

He coughed softly before continuing. 'I'm looking at the work we do, at how the team is structured. I think there are some procedures that we need to modernise, streamline. I expect you would have made changes.' He stopped, waited. He was expecting her to speak.

'Probably.'

'I hope that we can work collaboratively, together, make the whole department more efficient.' He stopped again and focussed an intense stare on her.

'Do you think there will be redundancies?' She blurted, feeling angry and aggressive.

He looked shocked at her directness. 'I think it's too soon to even consider that.'

'What about Damon? What about me? We were told that we both cannot continue as joint heads of finance, that there could be only one.'

'I've never said that.'

'It was said before you arrived.'

Veronica coughed, then stood up. 'Shall I bring us tea or coffee?'

'No thanks,' they both chorused, too quickly, too sharply.

Veronica flopped back down onto her chair with a thud.

'Do you think one of us will have to leave? How will you choose?'

'I think it's too soon…'

'You said that earlier,' she cut across him. She was angry, angrier than she'd been in a long time. Even angrier than she'd been with Will when he'd told her he was sodding off to America.

Why was she so angry? This was just work, just business. If she had to leave she would find another job, she was well qualified and experienced.

She stared hard at Cyril, trying desperately to banish the memory of Jackson from her mind, but how could she when his double, his doppelganger was sitting three feet across the desk from her.

'Are you all right, Lily?' Veronica asked. 'You've

gone very pale.'

Lily turned to look at Veronica whose face appeared fuzzy. Was she all right?

'Do you need more water?' Cyril asked, leaning across the desk, his eyes full of concern.

'I'm fine.' Despite her apparent paleness Lily felt hot. 'I just need air.' She stood up. Without socks the trainers were beginning to rub, she winced.

'Are you sure you're all right?' Cyril stood up and came round to Lily's side of the desk.

'Fine. I'm fine. It's just very hot in here.' She could feel beads of sweat forming around her hairline. She staggered towards the door.

Veronica gave Lily an alarmed look, her mouth forming a small oh, as though Lily were committing the ultimate *faux pas*. Lily shrugged. Did it matter? Did any of it matter? A man who was her erstwhile lover's double had stolen her job; it was unlikely he would keep her on, who would? No one wanted their rival as their deputy.

'Can we continue this another time?' Lily's hand was on the door handle.

'Of course. Veronica will reschedule. Are you sure you're all right? Can I do anything?'

'No thanks,' Lily said, escaping from the room and closing the door behind her.

In the ladies she splashed cold water onto her face, took deep breaths and wondered what the hell was going on. Was she participating in some kind of waking nightmare? Or was she still asleep? Either way if felt surreal.

'Well, that was quick,' Damon announced as Lily stumbled back to her desk. 'I hope he's not going to call me in sooner. I'm not ready. How was it anyway? What did you think of our man?'

Lily's phone buzzed in her handbag and she picked it up without answering Damon's question. What could she say? He's the double of my gorgeous holiday lover, but he's the bastard who stole my job.

She flicked through her phone; a message from Will popped up: *Feeling woozy, babe. Think I might have overdone the painkillers. Help needed.*

The message was thirty minutes old and he was no longer online. She rang him immediately but he didn't answer.

'I have to go.' Lily stood up. 'Medical emergency.'

Alarmed, The Europeans looked up.

'Not life and death,' Lily said, grabbing her things and stomping out, the trainers slipping and slopping on her feet. Or, at least, she hoped not.

'What shall I tell our man?' Damon called after her but Lily didn't care.

When she reached her car, she found that someone had retrieved her shoe from the drain grate and propped it up on her windscreen. The heel was intact, and without so much as a scratch.

'Oh babe, you came,' Will said as he opened the door to Lily. 'So good of you, I know you don't like leaving work early.' If she'd had a key it would have saved him the journey from his kitchen, as well as the painful hobble back with Lily following behind him. He launched himself onto the long, black leather sofa that looked out over the garden via tri-fold glass doors.

Lily took in the debris in the kitchen; not that calling it a kitchen did it justice. It was a giant room that incorporated kitchen, dining room, sitting room and games room – he had a bar billiards table at one end. Next door was what Will called his grown-up sitting room and another room downstairs was home to his computer and gaming machines; he played online and, according to him, was a grand master at something or other.

Lily used to imagine this room filled with family, filled with toddler toys and high chairs. Now, she struggled to even imagine it tidy.

'Cleaner comes tomorrow,' Will said, seeing the look of mild disgust on her face.

Lily moved towards the dirty breakfast dishes and began stacking them in the dishwasher. She picked up a dishcloth, sniffed it, threw it in the bin and pulled a new one from the drawer. Will watched her and said nothing as she cleared and cleaned.

He flicked the TV on.

Finally, she came round and sat opposite him on an Eames chair he'd picked up for nothing – he had a flair for that. He'd bought the house cheaply too when the area was less affluent then extended and modernised it; it was worth a fortune now. Lily sometimes wondered if she loved Will's house more than she loved Will.

And she wasn't even sure she loved him anymore.

'How are you feeling?'

'Oh, it aches a bit.' He shrugged.

'You said you thought you'd overdosed.'

'Did I?'

'Yes. That's why I rushed over here. I left work to get here. But when I arrive you don't even mention it. I think you just wanted someone to clear up after you.'

'Oh. Sorry. I think I'm probably just jetlagged. Not thinking straight.' He shrugged before flicking the TV to another channel, a programme about building cars from scrap spread across the giant screen.

'So,' Lily said. 'Other than to clean up your mess you don't need me.' She stood up and glanced around for her handbag.

'Don't be like that, babe. Of course I need you. In fact, I want you so much that I've got something for you?'

'Yeah?' Lily didn't sit down again. She waited, imagining some tacky bit of weird he'd picked up on his unfinished jaunt across the US, or, more likely, knowing Will, something he'd grabbed in a hurry at the airport.

'Here.' He pulled open a drawer in the coffee table between them and pulled out a neat jewellery box. He slid it across the table towards her.

Lily studied it. It was probably earrings. What else could it be?

She pulled the box closer and picked it up. It was heavier than expected. Too heavy for earrings?

'Open it.' Will's voice sounded eager.

'What is it?' Lily's face lit up in anticipation.

'Just open it, babe.'

She flicked the lid open. 'Oh. It's a key.'

'*The* key. Key to this house. I meant to give it to you before I went away. I had it with me at dinner. But it all got a bit confused.'

'You mean you were going to give this to me then?'

'Yeah, that's what I just said, babe.'

'Wow, Will. I don't know what to say.' In her mind Lily was already rearranging the room, moving the bar billiards table out to the garage, changing the black leather sofa for something lighter and softer. She imagined how some of her own furniture, elegant and feminine, would fit.

'Yeah, I wanted you to look in while I was away.' He started surfing the TV channels, his eyes flicking up and down as he waited for something to catch his fancy.

So he didn't want her to move in. 'Oh. Well, it's a bit late for that.' She placed the key, still in its box, back on the coffee table.

'No, take it, babe. I want you to have it.'

Lily looked up, her spirits lifted. She grabbed the box again.

'Yeah, it'll save me having to limp to the front door when you come round. This cast weighs a ton and it's a bloody nuisance.'

Lily left the box on the table and stood up.

'It's not even a full cast,' Will continued, obliviously. 'I have to get this temporary thing removed and get a proper one on. I've managed to get an appointment at two. Can you run me up to the hospital?'

'But I'm supposed to be at work.'

'It won't take long. Anyway, you're the boss now.' Will laughed. 'Aren't you?'

'No. I didn't get the job.'

'What. Are they mad? Who got it?'

'External candidate,' Lily muttered, thinking about the doppelganger Cyril.

'Man?'

Lily nodded.

'Typical.'

'Yeah.' She sighed. Was it? Was that why she hadn't got it? No one would ever admit it if it was the case.

'What about you? What's going to happen to you?' He looked genuinely concerned. Lily felt touched.

'I don't know. I love working at Bensons. But…' She turned away. She could feel a lump in her throat and her eyes starting to tear up. What was going on? She never cried at work or about work. Never. It was part of the code: dress code, hair code, crying code.

'What's with the dirty trainers?' Will asked.

'Shoe got stuck in the drain again.' Lily let out a long sob. The floodgates were now open.

'Oh babe, not those stupid black and red things again?' Will fought back a snigger.

'Navy and pink,' Lily managed between sobs. 'Not black. Or red.'

Will struggled to get off the sofa then hobbled towards Lily and hugged her.

It felt good to be wrapped in his arms, it felt familiar and comforting. She sobbed on his shoulder for thirty seconds as he patted her back, before pulling herself together. She sniffed.

'You stink,' she said, without thinking.

'Yeah. I know. Do you think you could help me have a shower before we go to the hospital?'

♥ ♥ ♥

Once Lily had found a strong plastic bag – a Sainsbury's bag for life – she hunted through Will's kitchen drawers until she found the electrician's tape that every man has in at least one kitchen drawer. She wrapped his cast and followed him as he hobbled up the stairs.

'I think you can manage without me now,' she said, setting the shower for him and testing the temperature with her fingers.

'Yeah. But can you hang around up here, just in case

I fall, or something.'

'Don't fall. I won't be able to pick you up.'

Will pulled his T-shirt off and flung it on the floor. His tan was impressive, so were his muscles.

'Did you go to the gym while you were away?' Lily said and was immediately annoyed with herself for asking.

'No. Not really.' Will smiled, but not at her, it was a reminiscing smile. 'Could you help with these?' Will yanked at his jeans, wobbling in a way that suggested he would fall if she didn't.

She pulled them down to find he wasn't wearing underpants; her face was level with his hairy backside. Normally she found his body so attractive, but now she recoiled.

'There you go.' She picked up his dirty clothes and pulled out a few more from the top of his still packed bags and took them downstairs while he hobbled into the bathroom.

'I thought you were going to stay up here in case I need you.'

'I'll be back,' she called up the stairs as she headed for the utility room where Will kept his washing machine.

When she came back he was sitting on the unmade bed, a towel wrapped around his waist. His hair, tousled and damp, clung to his head.

'You've had a shave,' Lily said, smiling encouragement at him.

'Thought I'd better make the effort. Can you help get this plastic bag off now? I've had a go but the tape is stuck.' Will swung both legs onto the bed and lay down while Lily attempted to remove the black tape.

'It's going to pull,' she warned him.

And it did, as Lily yanked the tape off and Will howled like a mad dog, she found herself almost enjoying his discomfort.

'Jeez, did you have to stick it so hard to my legs. You're yanking all the hairs out. You've no idea how much that hurts.'

'Yes, I do. What do you think waxing feels like?'

'Not the same,' Will muttered before howling again as Lily pulled a particularly wide piece of tape off his leg.

'You'll have to man up.' She had finished and stood up. 'You've got weeks of this.'

'Oh God. There's got to be a better way.'

While they waited until it was time for Will to go to his hospital appointment, Lily made them both lunch. Will ate his with gusto, Lily nibbled at her own.

She sent Damon a message to let him know she wouldn't be back, then sent an email to Veronica giving sketchy details about a non-fatal hospital emergency and asking if she would pass on the message to Cyril. Veronica came back straight away asking if Lily would be back the next day. Lily sent a reply saying that yes, of course she would.

Why would Veronica even ask that? Maybe the doppelganger had hoped she wouldn't return.

At the hospital Will limped along on his crutches, he managed to look both sexy and vulnerable at the same time. Lily noticed the female heads turning as he made his way along hospital corridors and into waiting rooms as they travelled between fracture clinic and x-ray and back again.

He told the story of how it had happened; the bike, its full weight falling against his leg. Everyone listened with rapt attention as though Will were recounting a journey to the moon, not a road trip with his mates. Yet Will charmed them with his tale, he charmed the women, and the men too, it was what he did, what he was. Lily could see the admiration in their eyes; he was tall and muscular and good-looking. The women wanted him and the men wanted to be him.

He'd charmed Lily since the moment she'd first set eyes on him at university, which was three years before they finally got together at the graduation party. She'd seen him on the campus, in the bars and clubs. He never seemed to notice her until that party. Even the next morning when they woke up side by side, their heads rubbing together on the same pillow, Will had struggled to remember Lily's name. Sometimes she wondered if he even remembered it now. Was that why he called her babe?

'Babe,' Will called as he click-clacked towards her on his crutches. 'Look what the lovely nurse gave me.' He waved a soft, oversized plastic sock at her. 'It's got a drawstring. See. No more black tape.'

Lily glanced at the floppy plastic. 'Good, you won't need me to run around after you.'

'Babe, don't be like that.'

'Why did you choose pink?' Lily stared at the fibre glass cast, its colour particularly garish in the sharp hospital lights.

'I didn't. I just told them to surprise me. It's a bit of fun.' He laughed. 'Anyway, it's only for a few weeks, then I have to come back and they'll put one on with a heel so I can walk a bit.'

Will ordered takeaway when they arrived back at his place.

'I've just downloaded a chick flick for you,' he called over as Lily found plates and cutlery in the kitchen. 'A little reward for you after looking after me today and taking me to the hospital.'

'Thanks,' Lily called as she dished out their Chinese meal. Lily didn't really like Chinese but it was Will's favourite and he'd ordered it online while Lily was sorting out his washing.

Later, as they lay slumped on the sofa full of monosodium glutamate and flat lemonade – a bottle Lily had found at the bottom of Will's fridge – he asked her to stay the night. She refused and he accepted her explanation – a bit too quickly Lily thought – that she couldn't possible sleep in the same bed as his cast. If he kicked out in the night *her* ankle would be broken too. Then what would they do? Will saw the sense in that, but he did persuade her to take the key to his house.

Back home, Lily opened the box, took the key out and examined it. It was brass coloured, new and shiny; it caught the light as she turned it. Now it was hers, the very thing she had spent so long desiring. Now she didn't even know if she wanted it.

Be careful what you wish for.

Fourteen

'Medical emergency over?' Damon whispered. 'Everything okay?'

'Yeah, thanks. It was Will.' Lily rolled her eyes. 'Though it did include a hospital visit. Everything okay here?'

'Fine. Just fine. I covered for you.' Damon chortled to himself, though Lily was struggling to find anything funny at the moment.

'Everything go okay in your meeting with…' Lily winced before saying his name, 'Cyril?'

'Yes, he liked my ideas. And, he didn't even ask where you were. I don't think he noticed you'd gone. One of the advantages of his office being around the corner and out of sight. Mind you, Scare-a-von has eyes like a hawk, but even she didn't say anything. I quite like him, don't you? I think I could work for him, don't you?'

Lily forced a tight smile; she could imagine Damon giving Cyril full-on man love. She didn't want to be drawn into a popularity contest with Damon over Cyril. 'How did it go for your team?'

'Oh, The Europeans? Let's just say that their minds have been set at rest. I've come up with a plan that ensures their jobs are safe and Cyril was very receptive.'

'That's good.' Lily glanced over at The Europeans, beavering away as usual. It would be grossly unfair if either of them lost their jobs.

But life could be like that – unfair. She thought about Will's key now on her key ring. The much-coveted key that wasn't quite so desirable now she had it in her possession. It came with obligations, and they seemed to be those of a domestic slave to an injured Will. She wondered if he would want the key back once he was on his feet. Both feet, that is.

'I could share it with you if you like. And perhaps, you could share yours?'

'What's that?' Lily asked, realising that Damon had been speaking and she hadn't been listening.

'Our plans. For the future. You know, *saving our jobs* plans.'

'Oh. No. I don't have a plan.'

'God. Were you so sure you'd get the job?'

Had she been? She'd hoped she would get it, but had she been convinced she would? Had she been over-confident?

'Not really.' She shrugged. 'Maybe.' Sighing, she stood up. What she needed more than anything was a good strong cup of coffee. 'Anyway, I was on holiday and didn't really have time to formulate a plan.'

'You mean you didn't have one up your sleeve just in case? Lily, you're slipping.'

'I'm going for coffee. Want to join me?'

'Better not,' Damon glanced in the direction of Cyril's office, even though Cyril couldn't see them – as Damon himself had just pointed out.

Lily shrugged. Surely a finance director had better things to do than check on coffee breaks.

She wandered down the office and headed for the miniscule kitchen that held the coffee percolator. It was always full of fresh coffee, no matter what time of day she went. Lily didn't know who kept it going, but she was grateful they did.

'Well hello, Cinderella,' Oliver Banstead's voice oozed over her from behind as she poured a coffee.

She pretended she hadn't heard him.

'That was your shoe, wasn't it? I did put it on the right car, didn't I?'

'Yes. Thanks,' she said, turning around and attempting to pass him.

'That's what I thought when I saw it wedged in the drain. I thought, that shoe is so dainty, so stylish, it must belong to little Lily. And I was right.' He gave her breasts a big grin.

'Thank you,' she said, giving him a weary smile at the same time as being relieved that she was wearing a high neck top. Even so, he still managed to make her feel uncomfortable. She stuck her elbow out, in the hope that he would get the message and move his bulging belly aside and let her pass.

'I'd love to see you in those shoes,' he said. 'Both of them, I mean.'

That was it. No more. 'Would you? Would you indeed? Do you think that's appropriate behaviour? Do you think a remark like that is suitable office conversation?' She stepped forward but Oliver Banstead continued to bar her way.

'I'm just being friendly. After all I did retrieve your shoe for you.'

'Well you needn't have bothered.'

'So ungrateful. Are you annoyed because you didn't get the job? Don't take it out on me, darling. If it's any consolation we all thought you were a shoo-in.' He laughed. 'If you'll excuse the pun. Shoe-in. Get it.' He laughed again.

'Will you excuse me please?' Lily said, her lips tight with rage and indignation. How dare he?

Oliver Banstead still didn't budge.

'Will you please move out of the way?' Lily's voice was loud and firm.

'Make me,' he grinned as he looked down on her, his eyes focusing on her chest again.

Lily couldn't believe the cheek of the man, the brazenness of his actions. She felt her manners slipping away, her politeness giving way to anger.

'Do you know what everyone here calls you? Do you?'

'Stud Muffin,' Oliver Banstead said, preening and laughing.

'Stud Muffin? Muffin top more like.' She glanced at his belly-bulge. 'Oily Bastard. That's what your nickname is. Oily Bastard.'

Oliver Banstead blinked several times and let his mouth drop in shock. Then he stepped aside and let Lily pass, his mouth still gaping.

'You all right?' Damon called over as Lily slipped into her desk. 'Only you look a bit…' he paused before mouthing, 'flushed,' and waved his hands over his face in a fanlike motion.

'I've just had a run in with Oily Bastard.'

'Urgh. He is disgusting. He was ogling my *moobage* again yesterday and I think he was checking me out in the trouser department. The man has no morals and no discernibility.'

'I've had enough. He gets away with murder, has done for years. I'm going to report him to HR this time.'

'Not today. HR Heather is on holiday.' Damon turned back to his work.

'Tomorrow then,' Lily said to herself. 'Definitely tomorrow.'

'Hello, hun.' Lily stood at Tess's front door waving a bottle of Pinot at her.

'Hi, stranger. How are you?' Tess opened the door and welcomed Lily in.

'Been better. Have you got any glasses? It's five-thirty so not too early.'

'Err, sure.'

Lily followed Tess through to the dining room where the table was set for two. Tess swiped the glasses from the table and set them down in front of Lily.

'You're expecting someone?' Lily said, mentally kicking herself for assuming that Tess just sat around waiting to hear what Lily was up to. 'I should have messaged.'

'It's okay. Gareth is coming round later, he's bringing a takeaway. Don't worry, we've got an hour.' Tess smiled at Lily. 'Shall I pour?' She took the bottle and twisted the screw top before giving them each a large glass. 'So, what's new? What's going on that makes this a bottle of Pinot conversation?'

'I don't know where to start.' Lily sighed then took a large gulp of wine. 'That's good. I got this at the Co-op at the end of your road. Very reasonable and straight out of the fridge. Try it. What do you think?'

'I don't think you came here for a wine tasting session. You would have arranged it first.' Tess gave a little smile that turned into a faux laugh. 'Come on, I can tell by your face things aren't good. Tell me all about it.'

'I *really* don't know where to start.' Lily's eyes flickered from left to right as she tried to get everything in order. 'First off, I didn't get the job.'

'What? I can't believe they'd find anyone more suitable or able or more loyal than you.'

'Thanks, hun, that's the right answer.' Lily took another gulp of wine. 'Then Will persuaded me to pick him up from the airport in the middle of the night, which turned into me being a taxi service for some woman he met on the plane.'

Tess grimaced. 'Eugh. He's so clever at that, and you're not even together anymore, are you?' Lily loved that about Tess – fiercely loyal, she would always be on Lily's side and say all the right, soothing things.

'Not really.' Lily wasn't at all sure what the status of her relationship with Will was. 'Then I was almost late for my meeting with the man – of course it was a man – who got my job. Got my shoe stuck in the drain. Again.'

'You weren't wearing those shoes again… not to work?'

'They went with my dress. I looked really smart and business-like. And tall. Anyway, I managed to get there on time, without the shoes, but, well this is the shocker, he looks like Jackson. Except for the hair and suit and stuff, but his eyes – not quite as blue. He's like his… his evil twin. It took my breath away.'

'You mean they look similar?' Now Tess took her first taste of wine. 'Mmm, that is good.'

'Yeah. Your Co-op,' Lily said, before continuing. 'Not just similar. More like a double. You know, a doppelganger. But evil.'

'Are you sure you're not just…' Tess's voice trailed away.

'What?'

'Well, you know, sort of… fantasising? You know, to make it better because he got the job and you didn't?'

Lily paused for a moment. Had she done that? Had she? No. 'How would that make it better?'

When Tess spoke her voice was quiet and her tone considered. 'I don't know. But it's rather odd. Don't you think? It's quite a coincidence. What are the chances?'

'Well, that's what I thought. How could I have spent the best part of two weeks with someone I really fancied then meet his evil double at work the following week? It's just stupid.'

'Are you sure he's his double and you're not just, you know, projecting Jackson's face onto this man?'

'No. No. Why would I do that?'

'I don't know.' Tess took another sip of wine while Lily took another large gulp. 'Maybe you're missing Jackson,' she said tentatively.

'No. No. It was just a holiday romance. That's all it was ever going to be, even before it started. It was you who said I should have a holiday romance. Remember?'

Tess nodded.

'Anyway, that's all it was. We agreed. I knew that. Why would I… Oh, nothing makes sense.'

'No.'

'And Will's given me the key to his house.'

'What? You saved the best news until last. That's

amazing. It's what you've always wanted. Congratulations.' Tess leaned in and hugged Lily, who sat rigid and unresponsive. 'What's wrong?'

'He had it with him that night at the restaurant. He says he was going to give it to me then, but when I got angry about him sodding off on holiday on his own, it killed the moment.'

'And you dumped him.'

'Yeah, and that.'

'It's good he's given it to you though, isn't it? Even if it's later than he planned.'

'It came in a little box. Like a ring box.'

'Oooh.'

'Yes, for a moment I thought…'

'It's still good,' Tess hugged Lily again and this time Lily hugged her back.

It was good. It was. Even if it did come with strings attached. Even if it did mean that Lily was Will's domestic slave and nurse. That's what you did for the man you loved. Didn't you? You looked after him.

'So, when are you moving in? Have you decided yet? What will you do with your place?'

Lily poured another glass of wine. Was this her third? 'I don't think we've got to that stage quite yet.' Nothing had been said about moving in. Nothing at all. In fact, the more Lily thought about it, the more she realised that nothing had been said about the future. The key had just been slid over. It was more a convenience for Will than an offer to Lily. It would save him getting up to answer the door, that was what he had said. 'Early days,' Lily said, tossing back the wine in her glass and laughing.

'Still fab news. It's a real leap forward in your relationship. Congratulations.'

Lily noticed Tess give the clock on the wall a furtive glance. Was their hour up already?

'I'd better go before Gareth arrives.' Lily stood up and snatched at her bag, but she was too late. She heard a key in the door and seconds later Gareth burst into the room, all beaming face and take-away carrier bags.

So, *he* had a key.

Tess made introductions; Gareth smiled at Lily and shook her hand firmly while all the time staring at Tess with adoring puppy-dog eyes, totally besotted.

'I'm just leaving,' Lily said, waving her handbag.

'Why don't you stay? There's plenty,' Gareth called as he made his way to the kitchen.

'Love to. But I have to get round to Will's and sort him out. Broken ankle. Ha.' She laughed as she headed for the front door with Tess close behind.

'Stay,' Tess said. 'Join us. I'd love you to get to know Gareth.'

'I'm not playing gooseberry. Anyway, I really do have to get to Will's. That's why he's given me the key.'

'Okay. Another time. Maybe we could go out on a double date.'

'Yeah. That would be nice.'

'Lily, about that work thing, the Jackson doppelganger. Have a think about it. Maybe you're just, you know…' Tess's voice trailed away.

'Projecting. Yeah. I know. You're probably right.' Lily hiccupped and giggled.

'Where's your car? You're not driving, are you?'

'It's in the Co-op car park. I probably shouldn't drive, should I?'

'Come back in, I'll call you a taxi.'

That had been embarrassing, sitting at the dining table with Tess and Gareth, watching them eat while she waited for a taxi. Then arguing with Tess about seeing her off when it arrived because Lily felt she had already disturbed their evening enough. Joggling about in the back of the taxi and realising that drinking on an empty stomach wasn't the best of ideas either.

'Hi,' Lily called as she let herself into Will's house.

When there was no reply she assumed he was asleep upstairs. She glanced around the kitchen, dishes and debris stacking up. She rolled up her sleeves and began clearing up – a very sobering task. Twenty minutes later and she had finished, the kitchen looked good and she'd tidied the sofa and picked up the discarded motorcycling magazines and tidied them into a neat stack on the coffee table.

Upstairs there was still no sign of him. The bed hadn't been slept in, unless he'd smoothed it out afterwards – highly unlikely. She wandered from room to room looking for him. He couldn't have gone out. Could he?

Idly she glanced out of the window and down into his garden. There he was. Or, at least, there his foot was, propped up on a garden chair; the rest of him was out of sight.

'Hi,' Lily called again as she went out into the garden. She could hear Will laughing and assumed he was on the phone.

But he wasn't.

'Hey there, Lucy,' the voice said as Lily appeared in the garden. 'Good to see you again. How you doing?'

Giselle sat up on her sun lounger and beamed at Lily.

'It's Lily,' Lily corrected. 'I'm fine. How are you?' Why was she even participating in this pretence?

'I'm good. Great, in fact. I've had a swell afternoon with Will here and we've just laughed non-stop.'

'Great,' Lily said, trying not to sound peevish. 'Will, I've cleared up the mess in the kitchen.' Once she'd said it she could have kicked herself. With one stupid little sentence she'd managed to consign herself to the role of cleaning lady. And a martyred one too.

'Thanks, babe. What would I do without you?'

'You seem to be managing okay.' Lily turned to walk away before she said something too spiteful, too bitchy.

She heard Giselle's voice say, 'Oh, oh,' just as she reached the kitchen door. Bitch.

Lily turned around to face her. 'Will, I won't stay over tonight, I've got such a lot on at work tomorrow and you know how you keep me up all night,' she called, with the biggest, most fake grin on her face.

'Sure babe,' Will called back. 'I'll see you tomorrow.' His next words were not audible but Giselle's cackling laughter was. Lily seethed all the way out of his house – spectacular front door slam included – and up the drive to where her car would have been parked if only she had brought it. She felt so sober now that she probably could have driven it.

Will's message arrived just as she'd wasted another ten pounds on the taxi ride home.

Hey, babe. Sorry about that. Giselle just turned up unannounced. You okay?

Well, that wasn't getting an answer. Lily threw her

phone onto the hall table, slammed her own front door, stomped through to the kitchen, yanked a new bottle of Pinot out of the fridge door, poured a glass, and marched through to her sitting room. She flopped down on the sofa and put her feet up. She heard a series of messages pinging away on her phone. Just turned up unannounced - how stupid did he think she was? Giselle couldn't just turn up without Will giving her the address. Will could get lost; he would not be getting any replies tonight. He could stew in it.

She flipped the TV onto a loud music channel – that would drown out his pathetic message pleadings.

After her second glass of wine her stomach rumbled, reminding her that she still hadn't eaten. She reached into the drawer beneath her coffee table and fished out a tube of Pringles. Okay, so they'd been there since Christmas, but what the hell.

Another glass of wine washed down the Pringles – the whole tube – and Lily's eyes were feeling heavy. She had no idea what the time was or how long she'd been sitting on the sofa, but it was dark outside when she woke up.

Maybe she should just go to bed now. She had work in the morning and she really didn't want to be late.

She picked her phone up from the hall table on her way upstairs – three messages. Three. Was that all? He had soon given up. She wasn't going to reply but where was the harm in reading them?

She flicked through the messages; it wasn't Will's face that appeared, but Tess's.

OMG I can't believe it xx

The next message was accompanied by a photo of an elegant, large solitaire diamond ring nestling comfortably on Tess's finger.

Gareth just proposed xxx

It had been sent an hour and a half earlier.

Lily hurriedly messaged back: *OMG hun. Congrats! Congrats! So happy for you xxx*

As she walked up the stairs she swallowed the bile of jealously back down. Lily knew it was too mean to begrudge Tess her happiness, and yet she did. They'd been together for mere weeks, no more than two months.

She'd been with Will for most of the last ten years.

Fifteen

'It's never a good idea to drink on a school night, Lily.' Damon smirked at her across the office.

She mouthed, 'Shush,' and put her finger to her lips before turning her computer on and taking a sip of the cold water she'd poured herself before reaching her desk. How she needed that water, her mouth had felt dry and sore all the way in – in yet another taxi. She'd have to retrieve her car from the Co-op car park at lunchtime.

Damon did have a point though. What had she been thinking? She had drunk the best part of two bottles of wine. And all before she'd even known about Tess's engagement. Well, that had been a shock – a whirlwind romance and probably doomed. Lily shook herself and made a mental note not to feel jealous; easier said than done.

'You cold?' Damon frowned at her.

'No. Why?'

'You just shuddered. Or is it the…' he didn't finish the sentence but mimed knocking a drink back.

'Shush, don't tell everyone.' She put her finger to her

lips again, then turned away to watch her emails loading up. There was one from HR Heather, a request to see Lily urgently. She clicked to open it.

Lily's mouth dropped open and her eyes became saucer-like as she read the email. Damon, ever alert, was suddenly perching himself on her desk.

'What's wrong? You've gone quite white. You're not,' his voice dropped to a whisper. 'Hungover?'

'Stop it,' she snapped. 'I don't do that to you when you've been out on the lash on a Thursday night, do I?'

'Suppose not,' he said turning away.

'Damon, come back. HR Heather says a complaint has been made against me and I'm to pop in at my earliest convenience.'

'What sort of complaint?'

'Doesn't say.'

'That's a bit mean, just putting that in an email.'

'Apparently she tried to ring me, but my phone was on voicemail.' They both glanced at Lily's desk phone, which was flashing rapidly indicating that messages were waiting.

Lily stood up and, sighing as well as feeling weary, headed for HR, which unfortunately was right next door to Cyril's office.

'Cyril's not in today, if you're expecting to see him,' Veronica snapped without looking up.

'I'm going to HR.' Lily felt irritated at having to explain herself to Veronica.

'Someone in there. Take a seat.' Veronica waved her hand at the row of three chairs which constituted a waiting area.

'I'll come back later.'

'I think you should wait; Heather needs to see you urgently.'

Lily slumped down onto a chair and wondered if nosy Veronica knew what the complaint was. Could it be that she had made it? Lily couldn't think of any reason why Veronica would make a complaint, but who knew? Lately Lily's world had gone so mad anything was possible.

Ten minutes passed and the door to HR remained firmly closed. Lily wished she'd brought her cold water with her.

'Just getting a drink,' she said, rising.

Veronica stopped working and looked over her glasses, her lips pursed and two deep frown lines appeared on her disapproving brow.

'Cheeky bitch,' Lily said once she was out of Veronica's earshot.

'Who is?'

'Damon. Where were you lurking?'

'Just getting a drink, same as you.' He followed Lily into the office kitchen. 'So, spill.'

'Nothing to spill.' Lily filled the kettle.

'What did HR Heather want?'

'I don't know. I haven't seen her yet.'

'What have you been doing all this time? Don't tell me; Scare-a-von made you wait.'

'Mmm.' Lily made herself a large cup of tea.

'She did that to me once, when I needed to see Heather. Started interrogating me. You're so right, she is a cheeky bitch.' Damon giggled but Lily didn't.

'Well, she hasn't interrogated me, which suggests she knows all about it, whatever *it* is.'

Lily plonked herself back down in Veronica's waiting

area and sipped her tea, marvelling at its restorative qualities. Finally finished, she stood up.

'I'm not waiting any longer,' she said, just as the door to HR burst open. Veronica arched an eyebrow and gave Lily a knowing look before dropping her attention back to her work.

Oliver Banstead slithered past them, a full width grin spread from ear to ear and his chest puffed out almost as far as his belly. He nodded to Lily as he passed and managed to fit in a quick pervy-peek down her cleavage.

Heather followed him out, a sense of urgency propelling her.

'Hi, Lily. Just need to pop to the ladies. Do you want to wait for me in the office?'

'Not really,' Lily whispered to herself, as a startled Veronica lifted her head and her eyebrows.

The minutes ticked by while Lily waited for Heather in the tiny HR office that smelt of Oily Bastard's stale fags tinged with rank, male sweat. Lily wished the windows opened; instead the air-con would circulate his stench around the entire building for everyone to enjoy.

'Sorry about the wait.' Heather came into the room, breathless and carrying a steaming cup of coffee. 'Been in here for over an hour. I was gasping.'

Lily forced a smile as Heather sat down, and Heather returned it. Both knew they were faking for the sake of politeness.

'I'm sorry about the email; I did try to leave a message.'

'That's okay.' Another fake smile.

'There's been a complaint.' Heather stalled, she looked awkward.

'So you said in your email.'

'It's quite a serious complaint.'

Lily waited to hear it.

'It's quite difficult for me to explain it. Or understand it.' Heather paused again.

'Perhaps if you tell me what the complaint is, I'll be able to help.'

'Yes, quite. There's been a complaint made against you saying you used offensive and sexist language.'

'Really?'

'I'm afraid so.'

'I know exactly who's made that complaint and not just because he smirked and leered at me on his way out of here. That's just hilarious.'

'It's not. It's very serious. It's a serious complaint. He says you called him,' Heather glanced down at her notes, 'an oily bastard.'

'Did he tell you what he said to me? I was actually coming to see you today – well, it would have been yesterday if you'd been here – to make a complaint against him. Did he tell you he leered at me and focused on my chest while making a lewd suggestion about my shoes and barring my way?'

'No. Do you have a witness?' Heather sat forward in her chair.

'Of course not. Does he?' Lily felt confident he didn't.

'Yes, he does.'

'Who?'

'I can't say.'

'No doubt one of his lying cronies.'

'We can't assume his witness is a liar.' Heather's eyebrows rose up in indignation. 'Oliver was very hurt by your comment.'

Lily laughed.

'This really is no laughing matter. What you said was offensive.'

'What he does is offensive. I only said it once; he leers and makes suggestive comments and innuendo all the time. He must have done it to you.'

'No. He hasn't.' Heather shook her head and Lily wondered whether Heather was offended that Oily Bastard hadn't leered at her.

'He's a cunning one.' He was too clever to have his leering witnessed, God knows, he'd had enough practice.

'He wanted to take it to the top. To the board. Can you imagine how old Mr Benson would react if he heard that his best salesman has been subjected to such an insult? As Oliver has just reminded me himself, we do have to remember who brings the money in.'

Lily sighed and crossed her arms, a defensive action, she knew.

'Fortunately, I've persuaded him – and it took quite some time – to accept an apology from you.'

'I'm not apologising.'

'If you apologise, he will drop it.'

'I'm not apologising. Let's take it to the top. I'll tell them all about him and his disgusting behaviour. I can't be the only woman to have complained.'

'But Lily,' Heather leaned towards Lily. 'You could lose your job. What you said was offensive.'

'I won't apologise. What I said is true. Heather, even you must know that everyone calls him Oily Bastard.'

'I… I don't.'

'Take it to the top. Let's do it.'

Now it was Heather's turn to sigh. 'If you're sure. Absolutely sure. Who knows how this will turn out? And you haven't even denied it. It could end badly for you.'

'I'm not denying it. And I am sure.' What the hell.

'The first step is to see Mr Montgomery-Jones. I'll get Veronica to check his schedule.'

It would be him; it would be that damn doppelganger.

Lily suppressed a sigh and shrugged. 'Okay.'

Lily really didn't want to have this conversation with Cyril, even though there was no reason to suppose that he would be on Oliver Banstead's side. Or was there? Hadn't Heather just pointed out that he was the top salesman and wouldn't any financial director value that? Would she have if she'd now been the finance director? It could be the answer to Cyril's dilemma when choosing between her and Damon. It could be a decider. Maybe she should just apologise.

No.

She wouldn't.

Someone had to stand up to him. Someone had to speak up for all the women who had to put up with Oily Bastard's daily leering. He'd got away with it for far too long.

'It's the twenty-first century, for God's sake,' Lily said out loud as she went back to her desk.

'What is?' Damon asked.

'Oh, nothing.'

'Did you see her? What a turn up eh?'

'Nothing surprises me anymore.' Lily felt tired. What with Will's antics with Giselle, Tess's surprise announcement, and now this? 'Anyway, how did you know? I've only just finished my meeting?'

But Damon wasn't listening to Lily, he was chattering away at her. 'I mean, she's very attractive. Stunning actually. And I say that as a man who doesn't really like that sort of thing. If you know what I mean.' He giggled.

'Heather? I've never really thought about it.'

'Not Heather. No. Not Heather.'

'Oh. I thought you were talking about me and Oily Bastard. He's made a complaint. Against me.'

'Yes. I know. Everyone knows.'

'How?'

Damon shrugged. 'Old news,' he said. 'No, I was talking about The French Lady.'

'Who?'

'The French Lady, Mrs Montgomery-Jones.' He dropped his voice as The Europeans' heads both bobbed up, their eyes focusing on Damon. 'Cyril's wife.'

'Oh,' Lily said. 'Right. No, I didn't see her. I thought you said he wasn't married.'

Damon arched his eyebrows. 'Seems I got that wrong. Oh well.'

'Never mind,' Lily said, in her best sympathetic voice. She didn't really care whether Cyril was married or not. What the hell difference did it make to her? It might end one of Damon's little fantasies, but he had so many, she felt sure he'd get over it. And, like she'd just said to Damon, nothing surprised her anymore. There was just a nasty little bitter feeling deep inside, but she kicked it away.

A quick email from Veronica required Lily to pop round immediately to sort out a date for her hearing – that was how Veronica described it – with Cyril.

Typically, Veronica was on the phone when Lily

arrived so she sat down in the waiting area, yet again. It seemed she was spending half the morning sitting in these seats. She sat looking at her fingers and thinking how much she needed a manicure; the last time she'd applied nail varnish was when Will had covered it in furry scarf.

'Ah, bonjour,' the voice said as Lily looked up to see the owner, a concoction of all things chic. Her clothes were Audrey Hepburn a la Breakfast at Tiffany's. Indeed, Lily even glanced at *her* perfectly manicured hands – black nail varnish never looked so good – Lily half expecting to see a cigarette holder. Her hair was a classic full-fringed bob, jet black and glossy – it would have made Gemma's helmet wig look untidy. She drifted past Lily and sat down, wafting clouds of luscious, expensive perfume.

'Mireille Montgomery-Jones,' she said, offering her hand to Lily. Damon's French Lady.

'Lily Ward.'

'You work with my 'usband, *Ceerill*?' Mireille asked, her accent thick.

'Yes. Well, *for* him really.' Lily wondered how much longer that would last. Mireille crossed her legs, displaying snap-thin ankles and black patent leather courts, which were, rather surprisingly, almost flat.

'I have the day wrong,' Mireille said with a tittering laugh. 'C'est la vie.' She shrugged her shoulders and raised her hands, a gesture which looked both elegant and ridiculous.

Lily nodded politely.

'Veronique is going to synch our diaries. Oui, Veronique?' But Veronica was still on the phone, her head down and listening intently. 'I have no head for the dates. They go in, then *pfff*, they go out. I thought

221

the lunch it was today, but…' she splayed her elegant hands and looked up to the ceiling as though searching for inspiration.

Lily smiled to acknowledge Mireille's comment before closing her hands into fists to hide her own tatty nails.

'You have worked here many years?'

'Yes, many.' Would there be many more?

'You like it? Of course?'

'Well, you know…'

Suddenly, Veronica came off the phone and dropped the handset down onto its cradle with a clank.

Mireille jumped up and presented herself at Veronica's desk, blocking Lily's access.

'Mrs Montgomery-Jones,' Veronica began.

'Mireille, please, Veronique.'

'Mireille,' Veronica said, the name rattling in her mouth. 'Do you mind if I speak to Lily first?'

'*Mais, oui*.' Mireille stepped aside and waved Lily towards Veronica. It was only as Lily stood next to her that she realised why Mireille wore such low heels; she towered above Lily; it made Lily wish she was wearing the navy and pink shoes with their leg-lengthening heels rather than her usual office flats.

'The earliest he can see you is Friday at four-thirty.'

'That's late in the day.'

'He's very busy,' Veronica said with a sigh.

'I'm not in any hurry, fit me in another day.'

Veronica stared over her glasses at Lily and smiled the smile of cat waiting to pounce on a mouse. 'He says it must be this week. Four-thirty, then. I'll email you a meeting invitation.'

'Thanks.'

'*Au revoir, Leely*,' Mireille called as Lily walked away.

Lily turned round to say goodbye and saw Veronica visibly shrink as Mireille turned her full attention to her with a loud, 'Veronique.'

'Are those the dulcet tones of The French Lady I can hear?' Damon sniggered as Lily returned.

'Yes.'

'*Très chic*. Don't you think?'

'She looks chic. Yes. And I think Veronica has met her match there.'

'They must make a handsome couple, Mr and Mrs Montgomery-Jones. Both tall, both beautiful in their own way. Him so English, her so very French.'

'Yeah,' Lily said, watching Damon as he smiled to himself. God knows what sort of fantasy was playing out in his head now, and Lily wasn't about to ask. Anyway, she had work to do, she'd done virtually nothing all morning.

'Apparently she's made rather a fuss about dates being mixed up,' continued Damon.

'Damon. What now?' He had pulled his chair up close to Lily's and was speaking in a whisper.

'That's why she had to be shown around the office and the warehouse. Absolutely insisted on it. Poor old Veronica had to trot around all those grubby electrical components and all those butch men with The French Lady in tow. Can you imagine?'

'Oh dear.' Lily kept her eyes on her computer.

'And, it's made everyone nervous, especially with everything that's going on.'

Lily turned to see Damon's grinning, expectant face looming closer.

'What's going on? What do you know? You spill.'

'Well, you know how Cyril's had us checking all the numbers, sales, invoices, payments, everything? And

223

he's had me compiling a full list on all our transactions.'

'No, I didn't really realise.' Why didn't she know? Why was Damon in the know? 'What report are you compiling?'

'About all our financial transactions,' he reiterated. 'I thought you knew.'

Liar. He knew she didn't. What worried her was why she didn't. 'How long have you been doing that?'

'Right from day one. He called me into his office and told me what he wanted.'

'You never said.' Lily tried not to sound peevish.

'He told me not to. He said it was hush, hush.' Damon put his finger to his lips.

'So why are you telling me now?'

'Because it appears it's common knowledge, everyone is talking about it. Some are even saying that The French Lady's parade around was part of assessing Bensons suitability for sale.'

'But Bensons has just been sold, and bought. We were taken over. Remember?'

'But what if the new owners are just asset strippers?'

'You're just speculating, aren't you?' Lily narrowed her eyes at Damon. 'Aren't you?'

'Maybe. But so is everyone else. You need to shake off your post-holiday stupor and get with the programme, Lily. In case you've forgotten we've already had redundancies – even if we didn't call them that. We processed the payoffs, so…' Without getting off his seat Damon wheeled it back across the office.

Was he serious? Was there any truth in what he'd said? Was it possible that Bensons was being asset stripped? Surely not. Rumours about the place going under had been circulating for years; it was an old-world business in a new world economy. Customers could buy direct from China if they wanted to, but that wasn't new. What bothered Lily more was that Damon was in on the investigation.

Cyril Montgomery-Jones had him working on the numbers. Why wasn't Lily involved? Not a word had been said to her. Nothing. She'd been blissfully unaware. What was wrong with her? Normally she was the one leading the race, Damon usually trailing behind. Had the decision already been made? Had Damon already won? Would Lily be the next one for the chop? Would they call it redundancy or something else? She thought about poor old Josh putting on such a brave face on his last day.

Josh, who she thought had guided her to the beach that day, except of course, it wasn't, because Josh had already died by then. Poor Josh.

Damon was deep into his own work now; he was getting closer and closer to his screen and frowning. Maybe he was working on more secret numbers for Cyril. Lily pinged him an email asking if he could give her a lift to pick up her car at lunchtime.

'Why did you leave it here?' Damon said as they pulled into the Co-op car park.

'Because I went in the shop. Tess lives just around the corner.'

'Yes, but why did you leave it here?'

'Because I'd had too many wines, as you well know.' Lily got out of the car but before closing the door she leaned back in. 'Thanks for the lift. Really appreciate it.'

'Any time, hun, is the plonk cheap here?' Smirk, smirk.

'Do you really think Bensons could be in trouble?' she asked.

'Anything's possible.' Well, that wiped the smirk off Damon's face. Not that it was much consolation to Lily.

She pulled her car keys out of her bag, climbed into her car and had already switched on the engine before she noticed it.

'Oh for...' she screeched to herself.

A very large bird, no, probably a flock of birds, had crapped all over her windscreen. A giant white ghost spread across her line of vision. She yanked on the screen washer lever and waited for it to clear, but the sun had set it quite solid and all the wipers did was smear gunk everywhere. No amount of windscreen washer would budge it. She got out of the car and slammed the door.

'You need to wipe that off first,' a helpful man said, as he climbed into his car – an ugly black four-by-four the size of a bus.

'Do you think?'

She went into the Co-op, found the kitchen roll then headed up the water aisle, her eyes scanning for the still water. A big gap presented itself.

'Excuse me; do you have any still water?'

'No love. Waiting on a delivery.' The assistant looked weary and bored.

'None at all? You mean you have none?'

'Yes love. Try flavoured water.' Lily's gaze followed a pointing finger and when she looked back the woman assistant had gone.

For one mad moment Lily considered it, but really, adding sticky to the bird crap, was that a good idea? She made her way to the till.

'Hi there,' she said. 'Do you have a bucket or something I could use to get some tap water?'

The assistant – a spotty boy this time – looked at her as though she were speaking a foreign language.

'Only my car's in your car park and birds have decorated my windscreen.'

Spotty boy blinked at her.

'So that's yours.' The woman assistant reappeared from behind. 'We wondered whose it was. You can't use this as a public car park. Didn't you see the signs? You can't leave your car here overnight.'

'No. Sorry. It was an emergency.' A too much wine emergency. 'I'll take it out of your way now, but I need to clean the bird poo off first. I can't see to drive. That's what this is for.' She waved the kitchen roll at them. 'But I need some water.'

Suddenly spotty boy woke up, pointed into the distance and said, 'Aisle five.'

'Yes, but you don't have any still water. Or, at least, not just plain water.'

'Oh,' he said, his eyes straying back to the till.

'So,' Lily tried again. 'Have you got a bucket I could borrow and some tap water?'

'No love. Sorry we don't. You'll have to buy some.' The female assistant sounded too gleeful.

Lily looked from one blank face to another. She wondered if they were having a joke at her expense. She wasn't finding it funny. The three of them stood in a tableau of dumb stupidity.

'Okay.' Lily stomped back up to the water aisle and picked up two bottles of sparkling water. Four litres should be enough. Co-op own brand – at least it was cheap.

She poured the water onto the bird crap and watched it fizz. And fizz. The white crap seemed to be spreading further and further, bubbling its way across her entire windscreen and down onto the paintwork. She kept pouring.

The four-by-four driver was back, she could see him sniggering out of the corner of her eye. She turned. He grinned.

'Push off,' she muttered under her breath.

Two bottles of water and half a kitchen roll later, the screen was clear enough to use the windscreen washer again. Lily looked around for somewhere to dispose of the empty bottles and crappy paper. She spied a giant wheelie bin.

'You can't put that in there,' the female assistant shouted from the open shop door as the spotty boy hovered behind her, his mouth open in an expression of abject gawkiness.

'Why not?'

'That's for commercial waste.' The woman folded her arms.

'It won't do any harm.'

'No. No. The Council will fine us.'

'No, they won't.' Lily lifted the lid of the bin.

'You can't put that in there. You're on CCTV.' She nodded at the camera perched on the side of the building. It was pointing directly at the wheelie bin.

'So what can I do with it?'

'Take it home with you.'

Lily glanced at her car, thought about having the crappy paper in it and shuddered. The woman smiled, she was reading Lily's mind.

'You can have a carrier bag to put it in.' Both assistants turned and headed back inside the shop. The woman reappeared and waved a plastic carrier at Lily.

'Thank you, thank you so much.' Lily was genuinely grateful. It wasn't the perfect solution, but it was better than nothing.

'That'll be 10p.'

'What?'

'Government tax. We don't get the money.' A well-practised line.

After Lily had stomped over to her car, holding the bird poo paper aloft, extracted 10p from her purse and paid the charge, the woman held the bag open as Lily stuffed it full.

'Thank you,' Lily said, taking the bag and knotting the handles.

'You're welcome. This is for you.' A small piece of paper was pushed at Lily.

'Thanks. What is it?'

'Parking penalty ticket. You can't park overnight.'

Damon laughed hard when she told him about it later, but not as hard as Will did that evening.

Sixteen

The rest of the week was a 'heads down' week. Since Damon had pointed it out Lily began noticing that people were very nervous. If there were going to be job losses, no one wanted to be a loser. Rumours were whispered, nods and knowing looks exchanged. The words 'irregularities' and 'financial' were mentioned in the same sentence. Lily started to feel paranoid. How had she never noticed any issues?

Had Damon been so astute or had he only noticed when it was pointed out to him? She thought about their respective roles, about their areas of responsibility. Damon handled the sales ledger; he knew how much money came in. Lily handled purchases and payroll processing. They collaborated and discussed things but she now realised that neither of them had a complete overview. Until his sudden, early retirement, that had been the responsibility of the financial director.

Now Cyril Montgomery-Jones was in that position.

And he'd seemingly managed to get that overview overnight. Lily felt angry and humiliated. No wonder she hadn't got the finance director job – she wasn't up to it. She felt a fool for ever thinking she had been. She felt an idiot for applying.

♥ ♥ ♥

Tess messaged her to invite her over on Friday night after work – just us girls, she said, making it clear that Gareth wouldn't be there. Lily made a mental note to pick up a nice engagement card and a bottle of champagne, not that she would be drinking it; she'd had enough wine for one week. Lily hoped that a girly evening would be the perfect antidote after the meeting about Oily Bastard with Cyril Doppelganger.

As the meeting approached she began to feel nervous and she had no idea why. She was in the right. Oliver Banstead *was* an oily bastard. He had letched over women left, right and centre. He didn't even attempt to conceal it, but he was cunning enough to ensure there were never any witnesses. Just because he was the top salesman with the best car and biggest bonus in the company and always had been, didn't mean he could behave like that. There was no excuse. There were old rumours about incidents in locked stationery cupboards, a liaison in the warehouse after hours, there was even something supposed to have happened in the basement boiler room.

Lily reminded herself that none of this was evidence, it was just hearsay. But there was too much hearsay, too many rumours. What worried her was that although people were more than willing to joke about Oily Bastard's nickname, when it came to stepping forward and giving evidence, faces were blank and voices were silent. Was Oliver Banstead really so protected?

Lily took a deep breath as she approached Cyril

Doppelganger's office door; it was closed. Heather was already there, sitting opposite Cyril and wearing her serious face. She jumped up as Lily peered in through the door porthole.

Cyril Doppelganger was also wearing a serious face, and, if Lily read him correctly, an angry one. He didn't even bother smiling when Lily came in, just nodded and muttered, 'Thanks for coming.' Then he stood up and removed his suit jacket revealing a fitted shirt that showed off his physique. Lily's treacherous stomach flipped involuntarily.

They hadn't even started the meeting, had barely sat down, when Veronica bustled in with a tray of coffees in cardboard cups. She'd been over the road to the Costa. There were muffins too.

'I hope you like coffee,' Cyril said, a brief smile flickered across his face. 'I find by this time of day I'm flagging and need the caffeine hit.'

'Me too,' Heather said, grabbing her cup. 'And I certainly need that muffin.'

Lily wondered if Oliver had also complained about her calling him a muffin top.

They spent the next five minutes politely eating and wittering on about muffins and coffee. No sooner had they finished than Veronica bustled in again, this time with a jug of water and three glasses.

Lily wondered when they were actually going to discuss Oily Bastard. Oliver Banstead she mentally corrected; that's his name, stick with it.

Finally, Veronica was gone, the water was poured and it was nearly five pm.

Cyril cleared his throat, took a sip of water and looked Lily full in the eye. It gave her an involuntary shudder as it brought back memories of Jackson and that first night in the beach hut. No. No, she said to herself then flicked a quick glance at Heather to ensure she hadn't said it out loud.

'So,' Cyril began. 'I understand that Oliver Banstead has made a complaint against you and you are counter-complaining.

'I suppose I am.' She hadn't thought of it like that, but what the hell.

'According to his complaint you used offensive language.' Was that a hint of a smirk on Cyril's face? 'And you told him that Oily Bastard was his company nickname.'

'I did. I'm not denying it.' Because all of it is true.

'The question for me is why you felt the need to say that.'

'I said it because he leered at me and made suggestions about my shoes. Also, it's true. Everyone does call him that.'

'Your shoes? Ah yes, he does mention your shoes. He says he rescued one from the drain and gave it back to you.' Now Cyril was definitely smirking; he had, after all, witnessed the shoe stuck in drain fiasco from this very office. 'He also says that you weren't particularly grateful.'

'Did he tell you that he would like to see me in those shoes?'

'Well that doesn't sound particularly offensive,' Heather chipped in.

Lily watched a momentary frown play across Cyril's brow.

'Well you weren't there, Heather. It was the way it was said. He was salivating. And he barred my way, he barred by way.'

'Shame you don't have a witness. Unlike our Mr

Banstead who apparently does.' Cyril was flicking through the papers before him, he reminded Lily of a judge.

He reminded Lily of Jackson.

Stop looking at him, she chided herself. Damon's comment popped into her head: they made a handsome couple – Cyril and his French wife. There was no doubting that.

'Oliver is clever like that,' Lily said detecting, if not exactly sympathy, then certainly not antipathy towards her. 'That's why there have never been complaints in the past.'

'Oh, but there have.'

Heather sat up straight. A line had been crossed; Cyril had spoken out of turn. Heather sounded flustered when she spoke. 'None were upheld.'

'No, but as Lily has just pointed out, Oliver is clever. Heather, how thoroughly were these old complaints investigated? Some go back ten years.'

'I don't know; that's before my time.'

'This latest one is only, let me see…' Cyril thumbed back through his papers again. 'Six months ago. Mmm, again no witnesses.'

'I don't think we should be discussing this in front of Lily. It might prejudice her case.'

'I'm not taking the complaint against Lily seriously,' Cyril said dismissively.

Lily sat observing the exchange between Cyril and Heather and wondered what the hell was going on.

'I…I…I don't think this conversation is appropriate.' Heather almost choked before swallowing hard. Maybe she had a piece of muffin stuck in her throat; Lily was just considering hitting her on the back when she blurted out, 'Perhaps Lily should leave if we are to discuss other complaints.'

'I don't think so,' Cyril said, without looking up from the papers. 'Lily you implied that he has a reputation for this sort of thing, what else have you heard?'

Heather's eyes widened like saucers, her chin came out and she gulped again. 'This really isn't appropriate,' she said, standing up.

'Sit down, Heather. This is off the record.' He leaned over and poured her another glass of water and passed it to her. 'Take another sip and stop worrying.'

Heather picked up the glass and took several large gulps. Her neck was covered in red blotches and her cheeks were pink and prominent. Lily had never seen her looking so anxious.

'From what I can see complaints against Mr Banstead are bordering on regular, at least three times a year. And, it looks to me as though this has been going on for years. Who investigated the last one? And don't say it was before your time.'

'Not me.' Heather now looked angry, affronted. 'I take the complaint and pass it on. Your predecessor or Mr Benson made the decisions.'

'Did they interview the complainants?'

'I don't know. I don't get involved.'

'Does it ever go to the board?'

'I've just said I don't know.' Heather sounded defensive.

Cyril glanced at Heather and smiled. Lily felt her stomach flip, her heart race a little. Why did he have to be so like Jackson? Get that image out of your head, she told herself. Stop thinking about Jackson. Start thinking about Mireille, The French Lady, Cyril's wife. Even if you wanted to, which you don't, how could you compete with her?

'Heather, what I'd like you to do is to give Veronica a list of all the complainants so she can arrange for me to see them all.'

'Even the ones who've left?' Heather's face was very pink now, pink and angry.

'Not yet.' Cyril gave Heather a sharp sardonic smile and he seemed to enjoy her discomfort.

Inside Lily winced; he's horrible, she thought, not at all like Jackson. Thank God.

'Right. Good. I'm not about much next week, so it will probably be Thursday or Friday before I get back to this. Lily,' Cyril said, focussing his attention on her, his blue eyes delving into her soul. 'In the meantime, I know that you won't be discussing any of this with anyone else. I need this to be confidential.'

'Of course,' Lily said, annoyed that he had felt the need to mention it. She felt her face heat up, her irritation now almost matching Heather's.

'Well, I think we're done here,' Cyril said, barely suppressing a sigh.

'Is it me or is it warm in here?' Heather said, taking another gulp of water. 'I'll be glad to get outside and get some fresh air.' She stood up.

'It is warm. The air-con in this building isn't very affective, is it?' Cyril unbuttoned his right cuff and rolled his shirt sleeve up a little. His forearm was strong and tanned. He unbuttoned his left sleeve and began to roll it up.

Lily gasped.

Cyril clamped his hand over his wrist, but not before Lily saw it. Not before she saw the mermaid tattoo peeking out from beneath his Tag Heuer watch.

Their eyes met for the briefest of moments. A

sudden flash and then Lily ran out of the office. She was back at her desk, hyperventilating and grateful that the meeting had run over and everyone else had gone home. Grateful that there was no one around to witness her shock. Or horror.

Was he Jackson? Could two men have the same tattoo and look so alike? Why hadn't he declared himself on their first meeting?

Why hadn't she?

'So you just ran out of his office without saying anything?' Tess shook her head in disbelief.

'Yes. I didn't know what to do.'

'Are you absolutely sure it's him and are you absolutely sure that he knows you now know? People pick their tattoos out of books; it's like choosing from a catalogue. Dozens of people could have that tattoo.'

'It was in exactly the same place as Jackson's, we'd even joked about it.'

'Definitely him?'

'No doubt. Our eyes met and in that moment a thousand words were spoken without us saying anything.' Had it really been like that? Or was Lily imagining it? No, she was convinced he now knew she had recognised him.

'What I don't understand,' Tess said, 'is why he didn't say anything at your first meeting? Why the pretence?'

Lily sighed. Hadn't she been over this a thousand times in her own head on the way over? Hadn't she examined the problem from all angles? She'd even scrutinized the sneaky photos she'd taken of Jackson, zooming in to get a good look at his face.

'Because he's a fraud. He even uses a fake name. He's a lying bastard. Oh, and did I mention that he's married?'

'What? No.'

'Oh yes. I've met Mireille. She's chic, tall, wafer thin, and very French. They make a handsome couple, that's what Damon said. And he's right.' And with those snap thin ankles she'd never have a problem squeezing her thighs into a wetsuit; though Mireille didn't seem the type to launch herself onto a surfboard. 'She came into the office to meet him for lunch, but they'd got their dates confused. She swanned around as if she owned the place according to Damon.'

'I don't know what to say. He seemed so genuine on holiday. That lovely barbecue he threw for us; that lovely house, him teaching you to surf.'

'All part of the charade. He probably doesn't own that house.' Had he actually said he did? She couldn't remember. Lily wondered how many lies he'd told her. 'Not that I would be any the wiser or care if he hadn't turned up in my real life. It was only supposed to be a holiday romance. I never expected anything else. I've got my own life too. And he's invading it.' No past, no present and no strings – that's what they'd agreed. Was it him? Was it? Even now, even with the tattoo evidence she was beginning to doubt herself. Maybe Tess was right; maybe those mermaid tattoos on wrists were a fashion that many men had, and women too, probably.

'Did you say his hair was dark? Because Jackson had fair hair.'

'Yes. But it's short now, close cropped. I think his hair was just bleached and brittle before.'

'Yes,' Tess agreed, nodding. She picked up her phone. 'Let's ring him. Let's get to the bottom of this.'

'No. Anyway, I don't have his number.' Lily remembered the sadness she'd felt when they had deleted phone numbers together.

'I do.' Tess pulled it up on her screen, put speaker on and dialled. They both listened as a message told them the phone was switched off.

'Anyway,' Lily said, summoning her resolve and putting on a cheery voice. 'I didn't come here to moan about work, or Cyril-Jackson-Montgomery-Fake or whatever his stupid name is. I came to see your ring and say congratulations.' Lily grabbed Tess's left hand and pulled it to her. The ring was beautiful, understated and classic. Just like Tess really. 'It's lovely. It so suits you.'

'Thank you.' Tess smiled shyly while looking at the ring; her face lit up, her eyes softened.

'So you're a sly one, I didn't see that coming.'

'Neither did I, but when Gareth asked, it seemed like the most natural, normal and wonderful thing in the world. I know it might seem rushed to other people, but really, we feel as though we've known each other all our lives. Can you imagine that?'

'Sort of, I've known Will for most of my life.' Well, better part of ten years anyway but there'd been no mention of rings or commitments. Even the giving of the key had housekeeper and nurse duties attached. 'I have champagne for you and Gareth and a card.' She handed over the glitzy bag she'd bought especially. 'You make a lovely couple, he seems like a lovely guy and you deserve to have a lovely life.'

'Ahh, thank you. It does feel so right. I've met his parents already.'

'Has he met yours?'

'Tomorrow. We're going out for dinner with them.'

'Has he met Gemma yet?'

'No,' Tess laughed. 'But I have warned him.' She looked wistful. 'But he's so nice that I don't think that even Gemma can object to him.'

'Not like she does to me, eh?' Lily laughed now. 'How is she?'

'Oh, you won't have heard. She's got herself a job. It's two days a week at a PR and advertising agency.'

'What does she do?' Lily imagined Gemma calling the tune and bossing everyone around.

'Creative Detailer is her job title.'

'What does that mean?'

'I don't really know. I think she has ideas.' Tess giggled.

'Yes, I can imagine. Well, good for her. What made her decide to do that? I mean, she was ranting about having another baby, or not.'

'Well, I find it best not to ask or get involved. My brother is as good at managing Gemma as she thinks she is at managing him. They're quite well matched.' Tess smiled, a wistful look in her eye. 'I'll be happy if my marriage is as successful as Gemma and Joe's, despite how it looks from the outside.'

'Have you set a date yet?' Lily anticipated a white wedding two years in the future, several bridesmaids, including Pixie-Bella and, of course, Lily as maid of honour.

'Soon as we can arrange it. Probably three to four months.'

'Did you just say three to four months?' Lily was incredulous.

'Yes. We don't want to wait. We don't want anything extravagant. It's about us, not the ceremony. We've waited a long time to meet each other; we don't want to waste another moment.'

'I'm really happy for you. Congratulations.' Lily hoped Tess wasn't rushing into this, but she was right, she had waited a long time to meet the right man. It had been their little joke that Tess was just too fussy, too exacting. She'd had few boyfriends and none of them serious.

As Lily was leaving Tess's, Will messaged her, asking where she was, wondering if she could pick up a takeaway he'd ordered on her way over. It was nearly ten pm and she didn't relish the prospect of queuing up at the Chinese. She was about to message him back when he rang her.

'Hey babe, don't worry about picking up my dinner, just get yourself over here, they're going to deliver it. I've ordered you Crispy Aromatic Duck; I know how you love that.' She didn't love it at all; it was just the dish she least objected to. He rung off as soon as she voiced a tentative okay.

That was that, she was going to Will's.

The takeaway arrived two minutes after Lily had let herself into Will's house using *the* key. She called out to him, and, as expected, found him lounging on the sofa, remote control in hand. He pressed pause when he heard the delivery driver knock on the door. Lily turned back to answer it. They ate hurriedly, neither speaking as Will watched a car show on TV. She wondered if he realised that the vegetables were mixed into the dishes. She considered telling him.

'You haven't noticed,' he said after Lily had cleared

up.

'Noticed what?' She was too tired for guessing games. After the Jackson-slash-Cyril revelation – unless it was her imagination – and Tess's sudden wedding plans, she really had had enough for one day.

'Look.' Will pointed to his injured foot, which was propped up on a footstool. The cast was bright blue, new and clean.

'Oh. Another cast. Already?'

'Yeah. Look. It's got a heel too. So I can put a bit of weight on it. The other one was rubbing really badly, so I went up this afternoon. They x-rayed and said it was healing so well I could have the heel. Great eh?' He smiled one of his heart-melting smiles and Lily briefly remembered just why she'd loved him for so long.

'How did you get up there?'

'Well, when you weren't available, I got a taxi.' He shrugged.

Lily frowned. 'What do you mean?'

'That Damon guy said you were preparing for a meeting and couldn't be disturbed, so I got a taxi.' He paused, watched her face as she thought about what he was saying. 'I know I've taken you for granted since I came back.' He took her hand and rubbed the back of it. 'I don't mean to. I know I can be a bit of an arse. I'm sorry.'

Lily felt tears prick the back of her eyes. She inhaled through her nose and blinked them away and changed the subject.

'Did I tell you, Tess got engaged to Gareth yesterday?'

'Who? No.'

'Gareth, they've only been together for a few months, weeks really. Funny, eh?'

'Ah.' He pulled her closer to him on the sofa; it meant Lily had to shuffle along. Her skirt rucked up and formed a knot in her back as Will wrapped his arm around her shoulder. 'Is that what you want?'

Was it? She didn't know anymore. She looked at Will, his liquid brown eyes, his thick wavy hair, his chiselled, model-good looks.

He leaned over her and pushed her backwards, his lips were on hers and he was kissing her, deeply, longingly and for the first time since he'd buggered off on his biking holiday. It was a good kiss, but not quite good enough to distract her from the skirt-knot now pressing painfully into her left buttock.

Seventeen

Lily awoke first and for a moment didn't know where she was, then she remembered and wondered if staying overnight with Will had been a good idea. Hadn't she dumped him? Somehow, they had drifted back together without even discussing it.

He dozed beside her, snoring softly; he'd lost weight, or, rather, muscle. Without his regular gym trips his shoulders were already narrower, his pecs less firm; he still looked good though.

'What?' he said, suddenly awake and aware of her scrutiny.

'Nothing.'

'I didn't kick you, did I?' He nodded down at the lurid blue cast perched on the edge of the bed.

'No. It was fine.' Lily patted his stomach, still firm she noticed, and smiled.

He sat up and groaned, stretched his arms above his head. 'Best night's sleep I've had since I got back. Thanks to you.' He grinned and swung his legs onto the floor. 'Could you help me shower?'

'Um. Yes. But what do you do when I'm not here?'

'Struggle,' he said, fishing around on the floor for his crutches.

It wasn't very dignified zipping him into his plastic boot so that the cast wouldn't get wet. She gagged as she pulled it on over his toes; the stench of sour cheese coated her nostrils.

'Sorry,' Will said, very aware of her reaction. 'I can't get that foot wet. The smell was really bad when they took the cast off yesterday. All the skin is flaking too. It's disgusting. And embarrassing.'

'Not for too much longer.' Lily felt sorry for him and guilty for gagging.

He limped into the bathroom where he managed perfectly well to turn on the shower and step inside. But, once inside she could see how difficult it was for him to balance and wash properly. When he'd finished in the bathroom he flopped back onto the bed and waited for Lily to remove the plastic boot. He looked exhausted.

'If you've got a flannel I could wipe your foot over. I won't get the cast wet but it would make it,' she paused, searching for the right word. 'Fresher.'

'Cool,' he said, directing her to his airing cupboard.

She filled the sink with water and bubble bath and ran between the bathroom and bedroom, wiping Will's stinky toes down but still gagging when the sour stench inside the cast drifted towards her.

'That's better,' she said, finally satisfied that it was as good as it was going to be.

'Cool,' he said, whipping his towel away and limping around the room naked. Lily feeling oddly embarrassed, excused herself and disappeared into the bathroom to shower. Afterwards she pulled on yesterday's clothes.

♥ ♥ ♥

'What shall we do today?' Will said as he lay on the sofa, remote control in hand as Lily made breakfast. 'No work for you, so you've got the whole weekend free.' He'd made such a show of clomping down the stairs on his crutches that Lily had forced him out of the kitchen area.

'I need to go home and change my clothes.' She didn't add that she also needed to give her hair a good brush, since despite his own luxuriant locks; Will only possessed one comb which was definitely not up to the task of taming Lily's hair.

'Okay, we can stop off there on the way.'

'Way to where?'

'Anywhere. I don't care. Just out. I've only been to the hospital and back since I came home.'

'What about visitors?' Lily thought of Giselle.

'What visitors? You and that loopy bird off the plane? I'm going a bit stir crazy. I need to get out somewhere else.'

Selfish Lily, she hadn't thought of that. She'd been so wrapped up in her work situation and the lying doppelganger, who probably wasn't a doppelganger after all, that she hadn't given Will's situation enough thought. She couldn't suggest a shopping trip, Will liked shopping for clothes – his own – but she couldn't imagine him stomping around fighting off other Saturday shoppers. Anyway, he could hardly try clothes on, because of the cast he was stuck wearing his one pair of baggy jeans or joggers.

'Okay. What about I drive us up to Liffingdon Hill? We could take a picnic and enjoy the view.'

'Anything is good with me, babe. Anything.'

Two hours later they were finally on their way having stopped off at Lily's for change of clothes and a cool box, and Sainsbury's for picnic fodder and petrol. Will had insisted on clomping around the supermarket, wincing and complaining, eliciting sympathetic glances from men and women alike.

In Lily's car he had pushed the front seat so far back that she couldn't see his face, even out of the corner of her eye, when she was driving. As a consequence, she could hear him clearly when he spoke, but he couldn't hear her unless she shouted. She was hoarse by the time they reached Liffingdon Hill.

The picnic area, nestled beneath tall and ancient oaks in full foliage, was dark and damp despite the sunshine. Lily heaved the cool box out of her boot and was pleased with herself for having a tartan blanket in there too. She pulled it out.

'Shall we sit on the grass?'

Will glanced down at his cast, sighed then looked over at the picnic area where a dog was chasing several children while the parents looked on bored and tired. The only empty picnic table was covered in bird crap.

'Yeah. Why not,' he said, clomping off at an impressive speed while Lily followed with the cool box banging into her shins. 'Here's good.' Will stopped and waited for Lily to spread out the blanket before dropping like a stone into the centre of it, his crutches splayed either side of him.

She stood with her hands on her hips and surveyed the view: miles and miles of rolling green hills undulated into the distance. The soft yellow stone and thatched roofs of Liffingdon Village clustered below them; fluffy white clouds floated across a warm blue sky.

She turned back to look at Will on the blanket just as he realised that she needed space to sit down and shuffled across to give her room.

It was barely noon but they broke the picnic out and began eating. Lily had brought pink lemonade – neither could drink alcohol, Lily was driving and Will was still knocking back super strength painkillers – which they poured into plastic champagne flutes.

'Here's to your friend Tess and whathisname,' Will said, lifting his plastic to Lily's.

'Tess and Gareth.' Lily clinked glasses with Will – a dull plastic thud rather than a sweet, tinkling ring.

'I suppose you and Tess will be talking wedding dresses and bridesmaids for the next year.' Will lay back with his hands behind his head and closed his eyes.

'No. I don't think we will. Tess says they're getting married as soon as they can. Three months, she says.'

'What's the rush? She's not…'

'No. I don't think so. That wouldn't rush her anyway. They're just keen to get on with their life together.'

'Good for them.' Will turned on his side away from her.

Lily gazed across the countryside, listening to birdsong and, quite quickly, Will's soft snoring.

'Sorry about that,' he said an hour later. 'I keep doing that, it's the damn painkillers.'

Lily had packed the remains of the picnic back into the cool box and taken it back to the car while he slept.

'Maybe you should cut down on them. Do you really need them now that your ankle is healing?'

Will sat up; he ran his hands through his hair, freakishly the action reminded Lily of Jackson. 'They're not for my ankle they're for my arms and my armpits. The crutches chafe and it's agony.'

Lily guffawed.

Will's brow furrowed in exasperation.

'Sorry,' she said. 'I know that was mean, but it sounded so funny.'

'Yeah, I know. But it is painful; they rub and make my muscles ache.'

'Sorry,' Lily said again, but a snigger escaped through her nose.

'I need to get up and walk around. I need to practice on this ankle so I can ditch the damn crutches.' Will began to scrabble about on the blanket. 'Did you have to put it on a slope?'

She didn't remind him that he had chosen the spot but instead stood up and put both her arms out to help him up. He grabbed both her hands, his blue cast leg hovered in the air as he attempted to haul himself up, but he was too heavy. They both tumbled back onto the blanket.

Lily laughed and, reluctantly, Will joined in.

They had another go with Will starting on all fours, but that didn't work either. Lily could see the beads of sweat forming around his hairline.

'How do you normally get up?'

'I don't *normally* lie on the ground.'

The dog that had earlier been chasing the children appeared beside them and started barking.

'I fucking hate Jack Russells,' Will spat.

'Just ignore him.'

The dog yapped continuously as they struggled to get Will to his feet. Finally, he stood upright and Lily pushed the crutches under his arms; she thought of the chafing and bit her lip.

Will stood still, acting nonchalant but breathing deeply. 'Fucking cast, fucking ankle,' he muttered under his breath.

Lily waited until his breathing calmed. 'How much longer have you got to have it on?'

'Weeks. By the end all my muscles will have withered and died. God, I miss the gym. I never realised how much I enjoyed it.'

Poor Will, Lily thought, feeling sorry for him.

'I'll have to have physio too when the cast comes off. It'll be ages before I can ride my bike again.' He shook his head. 'I probably won't be able to get my bike boot back on for ages.'

He hobbled back across the picnic area with Lily and the yapping dog following. Will had to fend the dog off with his crutches as it tried to get into the car.

'Be careful,' Lily said. 'Don't let it in.'

'I am being careful. Mind you don't drive over it. It's so intent on coming with us it'll probably lie down in front of the wheels.'

'Hey, what you doing with my dog?' The voice was loud and the owner big.

'Nothing. We're trying to fend it off.'

'Him. Him.' The dog owner corrected as she came close to the car, just as Will shut his door. Up close they could see three teeth standing up in her mouth, alone, like tombstones.

'Start the engine,' he muttered under his breath, which Lily did.

The woman scooped the Jack Russell up in her arms and kissed its head. The dog continued to yap and Lily could still hear it as she drove out of the car park.

It was comical really, great big woman, tiny little dog and both of them aggressive. She wanted to joke with Will about it but his chin was jutting out, his jaw clenched.

'I fucking hate dogs,' Will said.

'Oh, I never realised.' The future Lily had imagined for them had at least one dog in it.

They drove home in cranky silence, only the noise of the engine to keep them company.

Will lounged on the sofa while Lily busied herself emptying out the cool box, cleaning it, putting it back in her car. Eventually, she came to sit next to him.

'Sorry,' he said. 'About earlier. It's just so frustrating.'

'I know.' She patted his leg.

'I've been talking to the office; I'm going to work from home next week, since I can't get there easily.'

Lily hesitated. 'I could take you,' she said. 'If you're really stuck.'

'Maybe occasionally,' Will said, distracted by the TV. He flicked the remote, mindlessly going through the channels. 'There is something else you could do for me,' he said, without looking at her.

'Yeah?'

'Yeah. Got this thing coming up. Charity thing.' He continued to flick through the channels, to stare at the TV.

'Yeah?'

'I signed up at the beginning of the year. I've got a lot of sponsorship, almost two thousand pounds.'

'Wow. You never said.'

'No. It was a work thing. Good isn't it, two grand. Shame it'll all go to waste if I don't do the thing. It's for that children's charity, you know the one where the kids are carers for their parents and they go out for a treat, sometimes even a little holiday.'

Lily did know that charity, knew how important it was to Will because his own sister had been a carer to their mum and had pretty much brought Will up. She could feel the guilt being ladled on.

'What's the thing? When is it?'

'Thursday afternoon.'

'Can't you postpone? Do it another time? Do it when your ankle it better.'

'No. It's all laid on. I wondered if you would do it for me.'

'What is it?'

'I think you'd enjoy it.'

'I'm at work on Thursday.'

'You could take half a day. They'd let you. It's for charity. Two thousand pounds.' He shook his head. 'I'll lose it otherwise. I can't collect if I don't do the thing. Such a waste.'

'What is the thing?' she asked again. The last sponsored event he'd taken part in had been a cycle ride – one hundred miles. He'd trained for months, spent a fortune on a gel seat for his bike and still moaned about arse-ache. 'I haven't done any training. I'm not gym fit like you.'

'I'm not gym fit now either. Amazing how quickly that goes.' He sighed. 'Anyway, this doesn't need any training. They give you a bit of instruction first. It doesn't take long.'

'What is it?' She knew he was stalling.

'Skydiving.'

'What? No.' She shook her head and got up and stomped to the kitchen. 'No way,' she called to him.

'You jump in tandem, not on your own. You don't have to do anything really. Just enjoy the ride.'

'No.'

'You're only in the sky for about five minutes.'

'No.'

'Two thousand pounds. For the children. For charity.'

'Can't one of your mates do it for you?'

'They're already doing it.'

'Well, can't you transfer your sponsorship to one of them?'

'Not really. It doesn't work like that.'

'Well I can't do it.'

'Why not?'

'Because…I don't want to.'

'Why not?'

'I don't like heights.'

'Then you should challenge that fear.'

'It's not a fear. I don't like heights.'

'All the more reason to do it then.' Will gave her one of his devastating smiles, the one he used to get his own way.

'No.'

'Okay.' He sighed. 'But I've already paid for it. That's another two hundred quid lost, on top of the sponsorship money.'

'No.'

'Okay. Shall we watch a film?' He patted the sofa and Lily reluctantly sat next to him. 'You can choose.' He handed her the remote control. 'As long as it's not a girly one.'

♥ ♥ ♥

'I won't stay tonight,' Lily said, getting up after two hours of a thriller that she hadn't particularly enjoyed.

'Why not?'

'I didn't bring any of my things, or clean clothes.'

'Why don't you go and get them and I'll order us a takeaway.'

'Um.' What she wanted to say was no, she didn't want to stay cooped up in his house any longer, but then she realised that for him there weren't many alternatives to being cooped up here. They didn't normally spend every weekend, all weekend, together. Lily often spent Saturday evenings with Tess but that probably wouldn't be happening again soon, not now Tess had Gareth. Will invariably spent Sundays out on his motorbike, sometimes he even persuaded Lily to ride pillion.

She didn't have anything else planned. She felt guilty. She felt mean. 'Okay.' She grabbed her bag and car keys.

♥ ♥ ♥

'Great news,' Will said, when she came back carrying her overnight bag.

'Yeah?' Maybe he'd found someone else to do the skydive.

'Just spoke to Big Lee from work and he says that if you do the skydive the firm will match the sponsorship. So that'll be four grand.'

'But I'm not doing it. I've already said I'm not doing it.'

'Four thousand. For the children. For charity.' Will made a pleading face; he didn't quite put his hands together in prayer.

Lily sat down with a thud. 'What do I have to do?'

'I knew it. I knew it. I said to Big Lee if they matched it you'd do it. You're the best, babe. The best. You are attached by harness to your co-jumper. They do all the work; you don't even have to worry about pulling the rip cord, unless you want to. You'll just be along for the ride. And think of all that cash you'll be raising. I'm so grateful to you Lily. You are the best.'

And the stupidest, Lily thought, fully aware that she had been manipulated. Could it be that bad? She was just jumping out of the plane. How high did he go? Did it matter?

She wasn't afraid of flying.

Just falling.

Eighteen

Monday and there was no sign of the non-doppelganger. Lily was relieved, remembering that he'd said he wouldn't be around until the end of the week. Thank God.

She considered using Cyril's absence as the reason for not being able to get time off work on Thursday afternoon – after all, he was her line manager and he had to approve her holiday. In the end, she sent the request to him and hoped it would disappear. That way, she'd asked, but not been granted time off. Will would understand, sort of.

Veronica approved it. Lily's heart sank when she read the email saying that Veronica was approving holidays with immediate effect and was also keeping a chart.

Bang went Lily's excuse.

Things had certainly changed since Cyril had arrived; old Mr Benson used to approve all holiday – and he did approve *all* holiday, relying on his staff to work out rotas and cover. Now Mr Benson seemed to be less and less involved in the business; no one had seen him for weeks.

When Lily had said as much to Damon he replied that Mr Benson was ancient and it was only to be expected. Did that mean that Cyril Non-doppelganger was taking over? Was that how it worked? The finance director ran the company? Lily didn't know much about Jackson but she knew even less about Cyril. What was his connection to the company that had bought out Bensons? He seemed to have been helicoptered in to save the day – according to Damon that was the rumour circulating around the company.

'Fancy a cup of bitchy coffee and a cinnamon swirl?' Damon waved a paper bag at her.

Sugar, just what she needed.

They were alone in the office kitchen and Damon shut the door behind them.

'Spill,' he said. 'Tell me all about your meeting with the man. I hung around on Friday but you went on too late.'

'Nothing to tell.' Lily filled the kettle.

'Really? Really? Are you getting a warning? Did you get your wrist slapped? I must say I wouldn't mind a wrist slapping from our man.'

At the mention of wrists Lily shuddered at the memory of that mermaid peaking at her. 'Stop it,' she said, shaking her head.

'Well what happened?'

'It's still under investigation.'

'Have *you* made a complaint against Oily Bastard?'

Lily thought about it for a moment, had she? Not officially. Her recollection was that Cyril or Jackson or whatever the hell his name was would be looking at historic complaints, but he'd never really asked for much detail about hers, other than smirking about the shoes. 'I can't talk about it,' she said. 'You understand.'

'Urgh. How boring. No sugar in mine.'

'I know.' But she *had* been about to sugar Damon's coffee.

'Cake is nice, thank you,' Lily said after she'd bitten in to it.

'I thought you might be in need of a sweet treat.' He giggled. 'Especially if you were getting the sack.'

'I'm not. And don't start a rumour like that.'

'As if. Seriously though, is everything all right? You look so glum today.'

'I don't know. Bit of a weird weekend. And I don't know what's going to happen here. Do you? Is one of us going?'

'I asked the man and all I got was a fudgy answer about it being too soon to say. So who knows?'

'Same here. Are we fighting for our jobs?' Lily asked quietly. 'Arc we fighting each other?'

'I hope it won't come to that.' Damon dropped his eyes and his voice. 'I've been job hunting. Have you?'

'Not yet.'

'Since I've been involved in this investigation and report writing into our…' Damon glanced around to make sure the kitchen door was still shut, 'financial irregularities,' he whispered. 'I've started to worry for all our jobs. Keep that to yourself.'

'Keep it to *yourself* too. Are you serious?'

'I don't have the full picture, but things are definitely not as clean and tidy as we thought.'

'In what way?'

Damon smiled briefly at Lily then looked away. 'I can't say. Like you, the man has sealed my lips.'

♥ ♥ ♥

At lunchtime Lily began her job search, but it was the same jobs repeated over and over on different websites. None of them really appealed. Perhaps it was time for a complete change in career. Was she having a confidence crisis? She hadn't spotted any irregularities in Bensons; maybe she didn't have what it took to succeed in finance, to get to the top. Perhaps finance and Lily had run their course. What else could she do? What else did she want to do?

She allowed her mind to drift and found herself thinking of the café on that Devon beach. She shook herself. How clichéd. She wasn't going to work in a beach café, no matter how appealing that might seem. Anyway, the evil non-doppelganger would probably turn up in that café. She needed to go somewhere he could never find her.

She messaged Will to say she could get the afternoon off for the skydive. He sent back a one-word reply: *Great!*

Great. Was that it? What had she let herself in for?

Ten minutes later he sent her another message saying that he had successfully changed the insurance to her name, so she wasn't to worry as she had five million pounds worth of cover.

No.

Then he sent the link to the skydiving website:

"You will exit the aircraft from an altitude of up to 13,000 feet securely strapped to the front of your instructor, who will control the freefall element of your tandem skydiving experience, open the parachute for you at around 5,000 feet, and then steer you both safely back to the landing area for a controlled landing."

Lily swallowed hard. It sounded horrendous. Freefalling for, she did a quick calculation, eight thousand feet. Urgh. She didn't like the prospect of being securely strapped to the front of her instructor either. What if he landed on her? What if he squashed her? What if she squashed him?

'God help us all,' she said.

'What was that?' Damon's ears pricked up.

'Nothing. I was just thinking aloud.'

'Work?'

'No. Not work.' She certainly didn't want to be part of starting any more rumours. She shook her head and turned back to her job search. Same old jobs.

At his insistence Lily spent Tuesday night at Will's. She soon realised why he was so eager for her to stay; he didn't want her to chicken out of the skydive. He spent the entire evening and early morning telling how great she was, how much she would enjoy it and how much money she'd be raising for charity.

'I could still come and cheer from the side lines, babe,' Will said.

'No. It's too much trouble. I'd have to leave work, come all the way over here to get you then drive all the way to the airfield. Work is on the way there. Don't worry.' She didn't want any more of his pep talks and she certainly didn't want him to witness the event.

'But I feel mean. You're doing it on my behalf.'

'Yeah but you couldn't stand up and watch, could you. You'd be in the car. What's the point?'

'I could lean on the car.'

'It's fine, really. I'll message you when it's over.'

She wished he would shut up. He was making her nervous; well, more nervous. As she left his house she wondered if he didn't trust her to turn up. She was beginning to not trust herself to go either. But she definitely didn't want an audience, not Will, not anyone else.

On her way to work she felt sick just thinking about falling out of the sky. When she reached the car park she got out of the car and took several deep gulps of fresh air.

'Well, if it isn't little Lily two shoes.'

She spun round to see Oliver Banstead's overhanging belly pointing in her direction. A wide smile spread across his smug-toad face as he approached.

'I'm surprised to see you here. I would have thought you would at least have been suspended after what you said to me.' His words were directed at her chest.

'You're disgusting,' Lily muttered, turning away from him.

'You think you're so it, don't you? Well you're not.' He shook his head. 'Do you think they'll believe you over me? Do you think they'll side with a little finance administrator against the top salesman in the company?'

Lily shook her head as she walked away. She couldn't say anything to him. Didn't dare. She could still hear him chuckling to himself as she pushed the building door open.

'Today's the day,' Damon said as she came in. 'Excited?' He plonked himself on her desk. 'Or shit scared,' he whispered.

'Scared. Very scared.'

'You'll be just fine. Think of the money you're raising.'

'You sound just like Will. I don't know why I ever agreed to it.'

'What time are you leaving?'

'Twelve. Why?'

'I'm coming with you. A bit of moral support.'

'I'd rather you didn't,' Lily said, a feeling of panic sweeping over her.

'Why not?'

'I don't want anyone who knows me witnessing my humiliation.' She inhaled sharply, stifling the tears that were pricking the back of her eyes. 'I just want to get it over and done with, like going to the dentist.'

'It's not that bad, surely.'

'Yes, it is. I don't want to do it.'

'Then don't, Lily. If you're that scared, don't.'

'I have to. Will's relying on me. There's four grand in sponsorship money at stake. I have no choice.'

'Let me come with you. I can hold your handbag, cheer you on.'

Lily shook her head.

'I've booked the afternoon off. And I'm happy to drive. Let me come.'

Lily shook her head again and Damon wandered back to his desk.

At quarter to twelve Lily went into the toilets to change, she wasn't sure what was appropriate wear for skydiving, but had chosen to wear her gym gear with an extra sweatshirt on top – she reasoned it would be cold at thirteen thousand feet. On her way back to her desk she muttered 'Okay,' to Damon as she passed him.

He beamed his pleasure back at her and winked. 'I'm

driving,' he mouthed which was probably just as well; given the chance Lily might just drive in the opposite direction.

♥ ♥ ♥

'Have we got time for some lunch before we get there?' Damon said, as Lily handed over her keys and he started the engine.

'Maybe. But I can't eat anything. I might be sick mid-air.'

'Really?'

'I'd rather not chance it. We could grab something afterwards if you like. I don't think the ordeal lasts very long.'

'Of course. It'll be over in minutes. I'm going to treat you to a slap-up meal; it'll give you a nice treat to look forward to.'

Afterwards couldn't come soon enough. Just surviving would be a treat.

♥ ♥ ♥

'Thirteen thousand feet,' Damon read from the leaflet after they'd been ushered into the waiting area. He whipped out his phone. 'That's nearly two and a half miles according to Google. Shit, Lily. Did you realise you were going up that high?'

'No. Thanks for that.'

'Lillian Ward,' a voice called. Damon sniggered as Lily went to answer the health and safety questions. When she came back she was strapped into the harness and wearing a vibrant, yellow jumpsuit beneath it, the legs were too long so were rolled up.

'Very fetching.' Damon took a quick photo of her. 'For your Facebook page,' he said, when she scowled at him.

'It's not going on Facebook. Delete it.' She grabbed for the phone but Damon was too tall and kept it out of her reach.

'No. You'll be pleased afterwards.'

'Huh.'

'Just think of the children, think of the charity. Keep focused.'

'Shut up. It's so tight.' Lily pulled at the straps. 'It's cutting me in half.'

'Yes, it's certainly highlighting your assets.'

'Stop it. You sound like Oily Bastard.'

'Sorry. Sorry. Didn't mean it.' He smirked at her and gave her a quick reassuring hug.

The harness was tight across her chest but Lily knew it had to be. The straps between her legs were already starting to chafe; it brought to mind Will and his chafing crutches. Now she knew what it felt like. She really should have gone to the loo before getting all this clobber on. It was just nerves, she told herself. But what if she wet herself mid-air?

A female instructor started circulating around the skydivers, she was checking harnesses and dishing out helmets with integrated cameras.

'You'll need to loosen your hair to get this on,' she said to Lily whose hair was in its normal work configuration – up, tight and lacquered into place.

'But it'll fly everywhere if I take it out.'

'Squash it down or something, the helmet won't fit otherwise.'

Lily loosened her hair making it look like a squashed doughnut and the instructor rammed the helmet on, set the camera and fastened the strap tightly under Lily's chin.

Damon snorted. Lily thumped him.

Across the room several men waved to Lily. Shyly she waved back.

'Ooh, you've made some friends.'

'No. They're Will's mates. The ones he should be jumping with.'

'Should you join them?'

'No. No. It's bad enough that they've seen me.' But it was too late.

'Ooo, a big boy is on his way over.'

Lily glanced in the direction of Damon's admiring gaze. 'Yeah, that's Big Lee.'

'Yes, I can see that.'

'Hey, Lily,' Big Lee shouted as he approached. 'I hardly recognised you with your face… all sort of squashed up like that.' He laughed a big, bellowing laugh that drew everyone's attention.

'Yeah, she does look a bit like a muskrat,' tittered a treacherous Damon. She'd get him back for that later.

'When Will said you were doing this in his place I couldn't quite believe it. I said, little Lily wouldn't jump out of a plane.'

'Hi Lee, I haven't yet, so…' Lily tried to laugh but it came out as a squeak.

'Don't go chickening out up there now, will you? Don't go making a fool of yourself and letting the side down. Good luck.' He slapped her on the back, too hard, and wandered back to his mates.

'Oww. Thanks Lee,' she muttered.

'Jumpers, if you'd like to step forward when your name is called, we'll pair you with your instructors.' It was the helmet woman again, shouting to get attention.

As names were called and instructors greeted their pupils, each pairing went through a series of checks and agreed signals, which seemed to comprise mainly of thumbs up. As well as the helmet cameras each instructor wore a wrist camera; everything was being filmed and would be uploaded to the charity website later. Lily cringed – would there be no anonymity?

Most of the instructors were men, but there were a few women and Lily hoped and prayed that she would get a woman; even if it was helmet-woman. The prospect of having a man, a stranger at that, strapped to her back was appalling. As the entire group stood in twos, Lily's name was last to be called. She stepped forward.

'Sorry about this Lillian.'

'Lily,' she corrected.

'Lily. Yeah. Your instructor's been delayed, he says he should make it, but, I'm afraid we're running out of time so we will have to postpone your jump.'

Lily's heart soared. Hurray, hurray, and it wasn't her fault. She was off the hook and she hadn't chickened out.

'As you know this flight is only for the sponsored jumps and we've contributed a lot of the cost to the charity, but, in the circumstances, we would be able to fit you onto another flight, at no charge. It just might be a while, as we're very busy at this time of year.' Helmet-woman smiled and Lily smiled back, her biggest, brightest smile. With luck, Will would be recovered enough to do it himself. What a reprieve.

'Ah, that's no problem.' Lily started to undo her helmet, desperate to get its choking strap off. Now free, her hair started to escape.

Suddenly helmet-woman was doing thumbs up to

someone in the distance. Then she placed her hand over Lily's.

'Put that helmet back on; it looks as though he's arrived. What great timing. What luck.'

Noooo.

'Okay group, let's go.'

Lily turned to look at Damon; he gave her a thumbs up and smiled, but he looked as worried as Lily felt.

The group went out in twos, like animals to the ark. Lily tagged along, last in line. She hadn't even met her instructor yet but she already hated him. Why couldn't he have arrived five minutes later? Why couldn't he have missed the flight?

Everyone was excited as they piled into the plane, but Lily hung back on the tarmac. Her fellow victims sat in their tandem pairs, the instructors behind, who then clipped themselves to their pupils. Excited voices mixed with nervous laughter as people settled into their places.

'You'll need these,' a male voice said from behind her, thrusting a pair of plastic goggles into Lily's hand. 'Put them on now, so you don't forget. They'll ensure your eyes aren't damaged.'

She pulled the glasses on; they were tight and uncomfortable and distorted her face even more.

'Okay everyone,' helmet-woman was shouting again. 'This is Steve, he'll be filming some of you as you exit the plane and capturing your experience as you dive. Just ignore him.'

Lily looked around the rest of the people on the plane, they looked excited. Maybe she should just calm down and enjoy it.

'Get on, get on,' helmet-woman urged Lily as the plane engines roared.

A shiver ran down her spine.

'Two minutes. We just need to do our safety checks and signals,' Lily's instructor yelled, putting his hands on her shoulders and turning her around to face him. 'Hi, I'm Jackson.'

Nineteen

Before Lily knew what was happening she was bundled onto the plane, found herself wedged between Jackson legs – almost sitting in his lap – and he was busy leaning forward and attaching himself to her.

Could today get any worse?

The only consolation – and she knew it wouldn't last – was that she was sure he hadn't recognised her. Thank God she looked like a muskrat – a goggle-eyed one now.

But there was no doubt in her mind that this was Jackson, or Cyril, or whatever name he was using today. Those piercing blue eyes were just too familiar and they were definitely bluer outside; the light in the office apparently muted their intensity. She'd been so horrified by the whole situation that she had hardly heard a word of the hurried safety checks Jackson had gone through. Too late now to start questioning him especially at the risk of identifying herself.

The plane taxied a short distance then began to hurtle down the runway. The rattling beneath her backside was increasing her need to go to the loo.

Wetting herself – now wouldn't that be nice.

The plane climbed fast and high – nearly two and a half miles Damon had said. Lily felt sick. The doors were open, the wind bellowed in, it was cold, it was noisy; she wanted to get off.

And pretty soon she would be doing just that.

Helmet-woman began giving thumbs up signs and the occupants of the whole plane, except Lily, returned them. Jackson leaned forward and grabbed her hands with his and formed them into a thumbs up.

Lily shivered, an electric sensation running up and down her spine. The last time she'd had skin to skin contact with him… don't even think about it, she chided herself. He's a deceitful, married liar.

They reached the drop zone and cameraman Steve took his position by the door so that he could capture the look of terror on the skydivers' faces; but most of the faces showed excitement, except for Lily's. And Lee's.

The first tandem pair shuffled forwards and rested on the ledge. Then they were gone, launched into the unknown, falling through the sky. The next couple shuffled forward, then the next. They were sending them out really fast; surely they would bump into each other in the sky. Surely not; Lily reminded herself that health and safety was a priority. She calculated that she would be going about half way through the group and that she wouldn't have long to change her mind, to say no, to chicken out.

More pairs shuffled off the plane; then it was Big Lee's turn. He allowed his instructor to push him forward, no mean feat given how large Lee was. But there was no mistaking his reluctance or the look of abject horror on his face. Lily recognised it as a reflection of her own fear.

Big Lee sat in the doorway, his instructor put his thumbs up, but Lee put his thumbs down then gripped onto the handles either side of the door. He wasn't going out. After some urging and pushing – oh my God, would Jackson do that to her – Big Lee and his instructor agreed to abandon the jump and scuttled like a giant awkward crab back into the plane. Lily cast a furtive look in Big Lee's direction; he studiously avoided her glance. She wanted to offer sympathy, but he obviously didn't want it.

He'd chickened out. Never mind, Lily wanted to say to him, I'll soon be joining you.

The next couple went, then the next couple and now it was Lily's turn. She hesitated as they were beckoned over. Jackson leaned in spoke softly in her ear.

'Come on, Lily. I'll look after you. Trust me.'

Oh. My. God. Had he recognised her? Trust him? Trust him? Who the hell was she trusting? Jackson or Cyril? Single or married? Surfer or job stealer?

She found herself gliding smoothly towards the door, the rush of the wind increased as they got closer – it was taking her breath away. Jackson put his arms out in front of her and gave her a thumbs up sign. He didn't wait for her to do the same.

They continued to move forward like a two-headed spider until Lily's legs were dangling out of the plane. Jackson did the thumbs up thing in front of her again and, stupidly, involuntarily, she reciprocated.

Cameraman Steve called her name before thrusting the camera up too close and too personal. She knew that shot would be an unattractive grimacing one with the inside of her nostrils taking centre frame.

Then they were out.

Two and half miles up in the sky and falling, falling, falling. The ground was getting closer, her mouth was forced open and her lips were flapping like a camel's, her mouth filling up with too much air. She tried to put her hand over her mouth but could not defy the falling effect of gravity and gave up, gulping too much air and feeling unable to get it out.

She looked down to see little legs flailing around hopelessly. Were they her legs? Yes, banana-yellow rolled up trousers – of course they were her legs. Close behind her own legs hung Jackson's, managing to convey an air of confidence and safety.

She looked up; sky filled her view. Where was the plane? She could hear its screaming engines but couldn't see it.

They were falling so fast now that she was starting to panic. How much longer before the shoot deployed? Was she supposed to do that? If only she could remember those damn health and safety instructions. What was she supposed to do? Jackson's arms were out in front of her, he made another signal, but she didn't know what it meant.

Then she did. He was pushing the chute pull into her hands, giving her the thumbs up again. She pulled on it hard.

The parachute deployed, yanking them up and slowing their descent. Lily's head was yanked back and she felt the harness chafing her groin and cutting across her chest so tightly that she could hardly breathe.

Then it was bliss. They were gliding. Below them a patchwork of green fields spreading for miles and miles. Jackson was tugging on chords and steering them towards the landing area, in the process giving Lily a panoramic view of the world. It was heavenly.

But she could still hear those screaming plane engines.

The float down to the ground seemed to go on and on. How long? Five minutes? More? Lily felt weightless, featherlike, peaceful and calm, and finally the engine noise stopped. She felt serene, gliding through the air, all cares temporarily abandoned. Everything would be just fine; the world was a better place when you were floating in the sky.

Jackson was pointing out landmarks with one hand and filming her reaction with the other. Yuk. She'd forgotten about the camera on his wrist – and the one on her helmet. She'd make sure she had veto power when she got down, she didn't want any horror shots being posted online – not even for charity.

Jackson began pointing down; they were closing in on the big white cross that denoted the landing area.

'Take it easy, Lily,' he said. 'We'll be just fine.'

Lily looked down and saw the ground approaching. She felt sad; she was enjoying it, she felt at peace with the world and yet also exhilarated.

Jackson was saying something about running, but she was too distracted by the approaching ground, the prospect of hitting it hard, landing on her backside, being so close to him, to fully absorb what he said.

They hit the ground with a thud. Lily's little legs pumped away, running as fast as she could.

Jackson began shouting. 'Up, up.'

How the hell could they go back up? Had he gone mad?

'Stop running, stop running and pull your legs up,' he shouted again.

Lily wished he'd make his mind up, he'd told her to run. Hadn't he? She pulled her knees up into her stomach and wrapped her arms around them. Jackson's legs continued to run.

Was she doing the right thing now? He wasn't shouting anymore, so presumably she was.

Then they stopped moving forward. Lily felt herself being yanked back hard and her head cracked backwards.

They were in a heap on the floor, legs and arms entangled.

They flailed around together trying to disentangle their bodies.

'I said don't run,' Jackson said. 'You should have pulled your feet out of the way.'

'Sorry. I thought you said run.'

'Never mind.' He unclipped them and finally they were separate. Lily exhaled a long sigh of relief.

'Lily, Lily, that was hilarious.' Damon trotted across the landing area. 'Your arms and legs were flapping about all over the place. And was that you screaming all the way down? I got some good pics.' He paused to snigger. 'And what were you doing when you landed? First your little legs were going like the clappers then you turned into a human cannon ball. So funny.'

Lily scowled. She would deal with Damon later.

'Oh, hello Cyril, Mr Montgomery-Jones, sir. What are you doing here?' Damon's mouth dropped in surprise. Then he thrust out his hand to shake Cyril's. 'Well done,' he said as his hand flapped mid-air because Jackson, or Cyril or whoever he was today, was too busy taking his helmet off to shake hands. 'Oh my, how did that happen?' Damon couldn't prevent a little snort escaping as he put his hand over his mouth.

Lily, still in helmet and goggles turned to look at Jackson. 'Oh,' she said.

Jackson's eye was already closing, even without the inevitable bruising that would follow the swelling was developing with speed.

'You need to get some ice on that.' Damon looked around. 'First aid required over here,' he called to no one in particular.

'Did I do that?' Lily's voice was tinged with horror and concern.

'It happens,' Jackson said, shrugging, bending down to scoop up the parachute, gathering it in his arms and striding off towards the aircraft hangar with Damon fast on his heels like a little dog yapping nonsense all the way to the doorway.

Lily followed sedately behind them.

At least she'd raised four thousand pounds for charity.

'Smile,' a voice which she immediately recognised yelled as Lily stepped inside the hangar.

'Gemma?' Gemma? Could the day get any worse? 'What are you doing here?'

'I'm doing the PR for the charity – my new job.' She grinned. 'We're just doing a few post-jump snaps for the website. Come on, say cheese, Lily. Where's your instructor? We need him for this.'

'No. Please. Don't.' Lily turned away but not before Jackson appeared at her side, his right eye now just a slit.

'Jackson?' Gemma frowned. 'Is that you beneath the injury?'

'Hello, Gemma.'

'Who's Jackson?' Damon asked, almost stroking

Jackson's arm.

'Don't tell me Lily did that to you?' Gemma shook her head. 'Tut, tut.'

'Who's Jackson?' Damon asked again.

'Oh shut up all of you.' Lily stumbled away from them, tears in her eyes as she started to yank at the harness, unzip the vile, yellow jumpsuit. So now it was finally, ultimately confirmed. Jackson and Cyril were the same person. Just as she'd always known. Tess had been wrong; Lily hadn't fantasized or projected or whatever it was Tess had suggested she was doing. Jackson and Cyril were Jackson. Or Cyril.

'Probably best not to put you two on the website anyway. It would give the wrong impression; put others off for future charity jumps.' Gemma's loud voice carried across the hangar.

Lily stepped out of the jumpsuit, draped it over a chair, retrieved her bag and ran for her car.

It was only when she drove out through the airfield entrance that she remembered Damon.

'Oh shit!' she called out as she pulled over and let her head slump against the steering wheel.

In her bag her phone was dinging away with incoming messages.

Gemma: *What's Jackson doing here?*

Damon: *Don't come back for me. Going to drive Cyril's car back for him. He can't drive it himself. Lol*

Will: *How did it go, babe? Did you survive?*

Damon: *Why were you calling Cyril, Jackson? What's that about? xx*

She switched her phone to silent, threw it back in her bag, turned the radio up too loud and drove home.

Twenty

Will: *You okay, babe? Saw your pics on the website. Grim. xx*

Lily read the message and seethed. Grim? Grim. How dare he?

Will: *Rung you twice, you're not picking up. x*

Will: *Know you're reading these messages. Ring me.*

He was spying on her the way she had spied on him when he was in America. Now he knew how it felt – to be ignored.

She might ring him when she calmed down; she just didn't know when that might be. For the time being she was slouched on her sofa and licking her wounds.

On her tablet she flicked onto the charity website but couldn't see any reference to the event. So where had Will seen those photos? She tried the skydiving company website and there they were.

Grim.

It was all Will's fault.

Another message came from Will: *Hey babe, answer me. I see Big Lee chickened out. Ha ha. x*

Lily flicked around the website until she found what she was dreading. Video footage. Oh no. How the hell did they get that up so quickly? A panning shot showed everyone sitting in the plane as they approached the drop zone. Big Lee's horror was already evident on his face; it matched Lily's, though as it had turned out, his fear had surpassed hers.

There were still shots of everyone as they clung on for dear life at the doorway. Big Lee was shown scuttling back inside the plane; that was just plain cruel – they could have edited that out. Will was right; grim didn't even begin to describe Lily's face, ashen with her mouth pulled back into a rigid grimace. Behind her Jackson's stunning blue eyes stared into the camera. One of them wasn't quite so lovely now though, thought Lily, with spite and a little sorrow. She hoped he'd recover quickly, she hoped he wasn't in too much pain.

There were shots of retreating backsides as they launched out of the plane. Lily recognised her own thunder thighs wriggling around.

Then came the proper footage. She saw her mouth flapping about; it looked worse than it had felt, her teeth were bared and so were her gums and she was sure her nose hair needed plucking. This was obviously footage from Jackson's wrist-cam. Next came a shot of the ground and her little legs dangly limply – footage from her helmet-cam.

The wind could be heard battering them and there was the overriding scream of the plane engines. Lily winced at the memory. Then winced again. She rewound the movie and watched her own face, the screaming was coming from her mouth, it wasn't the plane at all. So that's what Damon meant. How generous of them to leave it on the soundtrack.

Why did they have to post it? And so quickly too.

At the thought of Damon, she immediately flicked onto Facebook. There it was, a hideous picture of her immediately after landing staring frog-eyed in her goggles into the camera. Behind her a one-eyed Jackson. Damon had entitled the picture 'Lily does it'.

She messaged Damon immediately to take the picture down.

His reply was swift: *Already done, hun. By orders of The Man xx*

She checked Facebook again – it was already gone.

The message she sent to Gemma was more conciliatory, and definitely pleading. She begged Gemma not to publish any pictures of her, or Jackson, and especially not together.

Gemma was another rapid responder: *Have nothing decent of you so not planning anything. Black eyes aren't good for charity fundraising.*

Then in response to Lily's quick thanks Gemma wrote: *So what's with surfer-boy? I thought that was just a holiday romance???*

What could Lily say? She was too confused herself as to what was going on in her life. How could she tell Gemma that he was not only her holiday lover but her boss? In the end she didn't reply.

Next on the list was to tackle the awful video.

The email response from the skydiving company took longer – to be fair she hadn't expected a response until the next day, so at least a two-hour wait was a good sign – but was short and sharp. They would not be removing the video because Lily had 'been fully advised as to what the footage would be used for' and had had 'ample opportunity to refuse to be included,' and had 'given her consent by signing the form.' They suggested that she take it up with their legal advisors should she still wish to pursue her demand; then they reminded her that the jump had been for charity.

Lily slumped back on her sofa. Why was life so complicated? She had no idea what was going on with Jackson-slash-Cyril and his double identity. She was worried about her job, whether she'd still have one soon, whether her colleagues would too. What if the rumours were true? What if Bensons really was going under? Then there was her ability? How had she not noticed these financial irregularities? Was she really so naïve?

And Will. What about Will? Were they together? Properly together? With a future? Or just bumbling along the way they had for the past ten years, or two years, according to Will and Tess? Tess's words rung in her ears, 'It's not as if you've actually been together all that time, is it?' Or was Lily just Will's nurse and domestic servant? For now.

Why was life so complicated?

Why were people so complicated?

She messaged Will to say she was fine but had a headache so wouldn't be over.

Will: *OK.*

Was that the best he could do? OK?

'You look like shit, sweetie,' Damon whispered as Lily sidled past him on her way to her desk the next morning. She was late. Typically sleep had evaded her until five am, when it had taken her into the dark recesses of a slumber-coma.

'And you are one,' she spat in response.

A smirking Damon followed her and took up his

customary perch on her desk. 'Though you don't look as bad as our man did when I left him last night.'

Lily switched her computer on without looking at Damon.

'His eye was colouring up a treat. He'll be black and blue by now.'

Lily felt her throat catch. Poor Jackson. Poor Cyril. Poor whoever he was today. 'I didn't do it on purpose. It was an accident.'

'That's what he said. You'll be glad to know he doesn't hold it against you.'

'Did he say that?'

'Not in so many words, but...' Damon stood up. 'Anyway, you'll be relieved to know he's not in today.'

'Damon,' Lily called after him. 'How's your report going, you know, for him?'

Damon came back, smiling. 'It's finished. I'm just about to email it to our man. I wouldn't mind if you cast your eye over it first, you know, check for typos.'

'That would be great. Thanks.'

'No probs. Um, just one thing you can do for me in return...' He let the words hang in the air.

Lily waited.

'What's all this Jackson thing? Why were you calling Cyril, Jackson?'

Had she really thought she was going to get away with it?

'Shall we go to the kitchen?' she said, sighing.

In the office kitchen with the door shut she told him everything. Recounting it in chronological order helped to get it straight in her own mind, but it didn't help her make sense of it. She'd sworn Damon to secrecy; he'd even gone through the theatrical farce of putting his hand on his heart and promising not to repeat anything.

She knew Damon was a gossip, everyone knew that, but he was also a good mate who wouldn't divulge her secrets, her mess.

She felt a sense of relief once all the words were out. Damon would be more than happy to chew it over with her, to analyse motives and actions. Tess, her best friend and confidante had better things on her mind – and rightly too.

'Gobsmacked,' Damon said when she'd finally recounted everything.

'Yeah. Tell me about it.'

'I can't decide if he's a total shit or a psycho.'

Lily laughed. 'When you put it like that...'

'So he has a double identity, a double life. Why? Are you absolutely sure he is one and the same person?'

'Yes. Well, you took him home; did he pretend not to be Cyril?'

'No. He didn't. We even talked about work. You do know that the company who bought us is owned by his family, don't you?'

'No.' They'd never talked about work; or family, or the past, or the future – it was just a holiday fling. But he had said that he was leaving because of family obligations.

'Yes, it was at their insistence that he came here to oversee the finances. I got the impression,' Damon lowered his voice even though they were alone in the kitchen. 'That he wasn't that keen.'

'Me too,' Lily said, remembering his sad reluctance when he left Devon.

'And he's never identified himself as one and the same person to you? Not even yesterday?'

'He introduced himself as Jackson, but there really wasn't much opportunity for proper conversation when we were flapping about in the air. Anyway, I'm not sure he recognised me at first.' A shiver went down her spine as she remembered how he tried to reassure her in the plane, called her by her name.

'Yes, he did.'

'What?'

'Yes, he said he recognised you from the back, even with, and I quote…' Damon smirked. 'All that lovely hair tucked into your helmet.'

'He said that?' Probably remembered the thunder thighs.

'Oh yes. Just so we're clear, Lily, have you identified yourself to him?'

'No. There's never been a chance. All the meetings we've had have been with other people present. But *I* haven't drastically altered my appearance. I look the same. He doesn't.'

Damon raised an eyebrow. 'Mmm. I think you're as bad as each other. And where does the love of your life, Will, fit in all this?'

Lily shook her head slowly. Where did he fit? Where did anyone fit?

'And then there's The French Lady, his wife, where does she fit?'

'I don't know. It's a mess, isn't it? Maybe none of it fits. Maybe we're all just separate pieces that don't go together. And none of it would matter if I hadn't had a holiday fling with him first. I wish that hadn't happened.'

'Really? When he spoke of you yesterday he had that look in his eyes, well, his one good eye anyway.' Damon tittered.

'What look?'

'Mmm. Let me think. Love. Or it could have been

lust.'

'Ha, ha. Not funny.'

'You need to have this out with him. You need everything out in the open. You need to bury the hatchet, so to speak.' He laughed then opened the kitchen door. 'Come on, I've got work to do, and you've got a report to proof.'

The report was perfect, not one error, not one typo, but she knew that before she even looked at it – this was Damon's way of bringing her up-to-date and making her feel included. She wondered if Jackson-slash-Cyril thought she was involved in the irregularities. Was that why he hadn't involved her in the investigation? The thought made her heart sink.

The report was long and detailed; some of Damon's best work. As Lily absorbed its contents she felt relieved, Damon concluded that there had been no irregularities in their department, no financial errors on their part. He suspected, and had found evidence to support his suspicion, that there were other bank accounts, other transactions that were not going through Bensons' accounts. Selfishly she was grateful that she wasn't a complete dunderhead. But what did it mean for Bensons? What would happen now?

'He has auditors working on tracking the other accounts,' Damon said over lunch in a little café he'd taken Lily to. He was on his second piece of lemon drizzle cake. 'You should try this, it's so good.'

She thought of her thighs. 'Not for me, thanks. Did he already know about other accounts then?'

'I told him my suspicions as soon as I started

looking into it. To be honest once I really started to dig, I don't know how we didn't notice before. Of course, it was cleverly done, so we wouldn't have gone looking. Sort of hidden in plain sight. But Cyril smelled a rat pretty quickly. He's better than us at this.' Damon licked lemon drizzle off his fingers. 'That's why he's never here; he's in London with the auditors, going through stuff from years ago.'

Lily felt sick; so she was a dunderhead. Damon had just said they should have spotted it.

'It's all stopped now. Whatever was going on. All the bank accounts have been frozen, even the ones we didn't know about.'

'Good. That's good, isn't it?' Lily felt anxious.

'Problem is we don't know what will happen now? To Bensons, I mean. We all know how the recession hit the company; we survived, but only just. We know it's been touch and go since, what with China and cheap imports and customers being able to source their own products direct. But when this news gets out, what then? Let's hope our man can pull something out of his bag of tricks.'

'Yeah.'

'From what you've said, he's quite good at deception – is that the right word?' Damon laughed. 'So there's hope for us all.'

'Is there?' Lily doubted that.

'Let's hope. Because the last thing anyone wants is for the company to go out of business. Think of The Europeans, how will they cope?'

'Better than the rest of us, I suspect,' Lily said, getting up.

'We don't want any more going like poor old Josh. Made redundant and dying on the same day.' Damon waved to the waitress as he left cash on the table.

Poor Josh. She still couldn't accept he had died, moreover because she still believed she'd seen him in Devon. 'We'd better get back,' she muttered. 'While we still have jobs to go to.'

She arrived at Will's after work to find him in the kitchen cooking; he had propped himself up on a bar stool and was using it like a Zimmer frame.

'Come in, sit down,' he said, after she'd let herself in with her key. 'I'm making a celebratory meal.'

'What's the occasion?' Did he mean the skydiving?

'You! Raising four grand.' He did mean the skydiving.

'Oh, that. I'm trying to forget that.'

'Why? You did so well. My mates were really impressed you went through with it, especially after Big Lee chickened out.' He laughed. Too much.

'Don't mock Big Lee. I almost didn't do it. It was terrifying.' She didn't tell Will how Big Lee had mocked her. 'Anyway, you don't know how you would have reacted.'

He frowned at her. 'Never mind Big Lee, this is about you.' He pulled a bottle of prosecco from the fridge and poured them both a glass.

'Mmm, not champagne.' She forced a laugh.

'Not on this occasion.' He winked at her. 'To Lily,' he said. 'For her bravery.'

'To me,' she echoed. For my stupidity.

'I was going to cook this last night.' He pushed minced beef around in a frying pan, before adding chopped tomatoes. 'But you didn't come home.' He winked at her again; did he have a twitch?

'I did go home, to my home. Anyway, I told you, I had a headache.' She didn't know if she was in the mood for one of Will's spag bols. She watched him force the spaghetti into a pan of boiling water.

Will fell asleep on the sofa after they'd eaten the meal and finished off the prosecco.

Lily checked the time, it was quarter past nine. Should she stay or should she go?

Then Tess messaged: *Just seen the video and pics. Hilarz xx*

Lily: *Yeah. Very. Lol xx*

Tess: *Gemma said Jackson was there. That you gave him a black eye??*

Lily: *Not on purpose. Hilarz. Long story xx*

Tess: *Well done you – not for the eye, for the jump. Catch up soon xx*

Will started to snore as Lily cleared the kitchen, put the dishwasher on and collected her things. She'd drunk too much to drive home; she would have to stay.

She climbed into Will's bed and, tired from lack of sleep the night before, fell instantly into a deep slumber while Will snored on downstairs.

It was past midnight when she awoke, screaming out in pain.

'Sorry,' Will said, patting her. 'This bloody cast.'

'It's okay.' She rubbed her throbbing shin.

'Sorry I nodded off too. It's the painkillers and the wine. Killer combo.' He kept using that excuse.

Now disturbed and too alert, Lily lay awake listening to Will who was soon snoring again. Eventually she got up, went downstairs and watched TV. But she couldn't concentrate, couldn't think of anything but the mess she was in with Jackson, with Cyril, with work.

Tomorrow, when Jackson was in the office she would confront him; clear the air, put the past behind them. If they were going to work together their relationship had to be professional. If they weren't going to work together she would need a good reference from him.

Either way, they needed clarity. *She* needed clarity.

Twenty-one

'Can you fit me in to see Jackson, err, I mean Cyril, as soon as possible today, please?' Lily stood in front of Veronica's desk.

'He's back-to-back all day,' Veronica said without even looking up.

'But I really need to see him today. It's important. Please.'

Sighing Veronica scanned her computer screen. 'Okay. Four-thirty is the best I can do.'

'Nothing earlier?'

'No. Can't it wait until Monday?'

'No. I'll take four-thirty. Will you tell him I want to see him urgently?'

'Yes. At four-thirty.' Veronica began stabbing the keys on her computer.

'Tell him before four-thirty, if you can. Please.'

'I'll see what I can do.'

'Have you just had a run in with Scare-a-von?' Damon asked as Lily returned to her desk.

'Yeah.'

'Me too. She's obviously in that sort of mood. She

read my report before passing it on to Cyril, but she told me it had a grammatical error in it.'

'Did it? I never noticed.'

'That's because it didn't. We almost had a stand-up row about the apostrophe rule, then she had to admit she was wrong. One-nil to Damon, I think.' He licked a finger and drew an imaginary one in the air. 'Anyway, did you win *your* battle with her?'

'Sort of. It's okay.' She slumped into her seat and turned to her work. 'I'm seeing him later.'

Damon arched his eyebrows.

The day dragged, she popped round several times to find Veronica scowling at people as a steady stream of employees – all female – trouped in and out of Cyril's office. HR Heather emerged on one occasion looking hot and harassed; she gave Lily a tight-lipped smile on her way to get coffee.

Of course, today was the day he was seeing Oliver Banstead's previous victims. If he was back-to-back with appointments, how many were there? Lily wondered if she'd stirred up a real hornets' nest, wondered how it would end. But then she reminded herself that Oliver Banstead had friends on high, otherwise he'd have gone years ago – he'd probably be the one who came out smiling.

At lunchtime she drove into town; she was going to cheer herself up with a new dress to celebrate the skydiving triumph. But she came back empty handed – the truth was her mind just wasn't on the task. As she parked her car back in Bensons' car park and got out she heard a loud cackle behind her.

'So, it's little Lily two shoes again.'

'Oliver,' Lily said, surprised to see him. She tried to keep her face impassive.

'We're making a habit of meeting in this car park.' He cackled again, his belly-bulge wobbling rhythmically.

'It's the company car park, so that will happen.' Lily locked her car.

'Thanks to you I've been given some extra holiday. On top of the extra bonus I'm expecting this month, it's win-win for me. I'm just off now to the races, got complimentary tickets from a customer.'

'Good for you,' Lily said, turning to walk away. 'Have a nice afternoon.'

'Aren't you going to ask why I'm thanking you?'

Lily stood dumbfounded. Should she even be talking to him? Weren't they pitted on opposite sides of a serious complaint?

'Well I'll tell you anyway. I've been given extra leave to get over the trauma of what you called me, and the stress of the complaints process. Like I said, it's all a big win for me.' He grinned.

Lily nodded and smiled and walked away as fast as she could. 'Oily Bastard,' she muttered under her breath.

After lunch she approached Veronica again, but the aggressive raised eyebrows that greeted her request soon told her that no, Cyril would not be available before four-thirty.

At three pm she pulled out her notebook and started making her list. She wanted to ensure that she didn't miss anything in her meeting with Cyril.

First point: is Cyril, in fact, Jackson?

She already knew the answer to that one, but she wanted him to say it. Say it out loud; say it with his own voice, hear the words from his own lips.

Second point: why hadn't he identified himself when they first met in his office?

She thought back to that first meeting, had he actually recognised her then? He must have done, she wasn't the one who'd had a complete makeover and assumed a new identity. Other than tidying her hair, she looked exactly the same. What would he say? Would he use the excuse of Veronica being present? Would he ask her why she hadn't identified herself? Would *she* use the excuse of Veronica being present?

Third point: what was he doing invading her real life?

Fourth point: why hadn't he explained himself at the skydive – before she'd given him a black eye? Why had they been paired together?

He would probably ask why she had gone to such lengths to keep her face hidden when she could easily be identified by her thunder thighs. He wouldn't say that, would he?

She turned back to her work, stopping occasionally to add another question to the list, sometimes to doodle comments – not all of them polite – in the margin. She had plenty to ask Jackson-slash-Cyril and she wanted answers.

'Oh. My. God.' Damon's voice was too high and too loud.

Lily turned and gave him a quizzical frown. What was he squawking about?

Damon's eyes swivelled to his left and he used his head to point in the same direction. 'Look,' he mouthed, as if she needed any more indicators.

At the far end of the office Will hobbled into sight. He was using only one crutch now – Lily thought of the chafing under his arms, at least it would halve his discomfort. In his other arm he gripped a giant bouquet of flowers.

What the hell was he doing?

He clomped down the office, gingerly putting weight on the bright blue cast. Clomp went the cast, click went the crutch, rustle went the flowers.

Clomp, click, rustle.

As he passed desks people stopped what they were doing and stared after him. Little smiles played on some faces, little sneers on others.

Clomp, click, rustle.

It took a long time for him to reach her; the world seemed to be moving in slow motion.

'Hello,' he said. Clomp, click, rustle. He looked nervous, almost shy. He thrust the flowers at her. 'These are for you. You've been so good to me.'

Lily swallowed hard. 'Thank you,' she croaked, turning to lay them on her desk. He could have sent them, she thought, rather than go through this. He could have given them to her at home. Don't be so ungrateful, she chided herself. 'They're beautiful.'

When she turned back Will was on one knee and wobbling around on his cast, still clutching the crutch. 'Oh my God,' she said, worrying about the damage he might be doing to his ankle. What was he playing at?

'Lily,' he began to a hushed office. 'We've been together on and off for a few years now and I know I'm not always the most attentive boyfriend.' A little murmur rippled through the audience that had now assembled and was creeping closer.

Lily gave off a stupid little titter. The realisation of what was about to happen was beginning to dawn on her.

'Lily, babe,' Will said, his voice hoarse. 'Will you marry me?' He proffered a ring box, flipped open and displaying the most exquisite diamond and emerald ring.

This was what she'd always wanted, a commitment from him. Living together would have done the trick, certainly for now, but this, she'd never expected this. Did she want it? Did she want to marry him? She looked across the sea of expectant faces, all silent, all waiting, all holding their breath for her answer.

And there was Jackson. Watching intently, his face blank, his eyes so wide-open and blue. Was she late for her appointment with him? Was it four-thirty already?

'Lily?' Will said, an edge of fear to his voice.

She looked into Will's earnest, handsome face, glanced around the assembled crowd. What would she say? What could she say?

'Yes,' she proclaimed. 'Yes.' She spread the biggest, brightest smile across her face for all to see. Will fumbled the ring out of its box and Lily stepped forward so he could place, well, force, it onto her finger.

'Your fingers are fatter than I thought,' Will mumbled to himself.

Finally, it was on; she held up her hand and smiled.

A loud rumble of laughter followed by clapping and whooping filled the office. Lily watched Jackson blink several times then turn away; he strode back to his office.

'Lily,' Damon said, getting her attention. He wobbled his head around as though trying to say something without using words. He had a hand under Will's elbow, attempting to get him up.

'Oh, right.' Lily laughed as she grabbed Will's other

elbow and together she and Damon hauled Will to his feet.

'Not very dignified that.' Will rammed his arm into the crutch.

'No one noticed,' Lily lied.

'Show me properly.' Damon grabbed Lily's hand and inspected the ring closely. 'Lovely. What a lucky girl.' He pulled Lily into a hug. 'You okay, girl?'

'Sure,' she said, wondering if it had been wise to confess all to Damon. Was he now looking on Will with pity?

'Oh, here comes Scare-a-von.'

'I know, I'm late for my appointment,' Lily said, before Veronica had even opened her mouth.

'Cyril says to forget it; he'll see you on Monday. I've emailed you the time. And he says congratulations. From me too.' Veronica cast a quick glance at Lily's ring, muttered, 'Very nice,' and was gone.

Lily logged her computer off, snatched up her bag and the flowers. 'Just get my jacket.' As she plucked it from the coat rack, she glanced out of the window; Jackson was in the car park, unlocking his car. He turned and gazed at her, an unfathomable look in his eyes. She looked away.

It wasn't a walk of shame, of course it wasn't. She had nothing to be ashamed of. Maybe a walk of embarrassment was a better description, she thought as she and Will clomped, clicked and rustled back up the office.

Will struggled to get into her car then lay back in his seat.

'Phew,' he said. 'I'm knackered after that.'

'I'm still in shock.' Lily started the engine.

'I know it's what you've always wanted.'

'Did you? Really? Then why now?'

'Why not? You've been looking after me so well, I thought, well why not? After you did that skydive, how could I resist?' He laughed and let a satisfied smile spread across his face.

Lily smiled back – her face was beginning to ache from all the forced smiling. Was Will's proposal a reward? That's what it sounded like. Was that how he viewed it?

She concentrated on driving them home. Will's home. Soon to be her home?

It was only as they pulled onto the drive that she realised they hadn't even sealed their engagement with a kiss.

'Maybe we could make it a double wedding with your friend Tess and whatshisname,' Will said, once he was back in his usual position on the sofa.

'Oh. Um.'

'It could work out a lot cheaper and get it all done in one. All your friends are the same, aren't they? Save a lot of fuss.'

'A lot of fuss?' Lily echoed. 'Is that how you see it?'

'Well, you know what I mean. Just being practical, babe. You have whatever you want.'

'Thanks,' Lily said, wondering exactly what she did want.

'What shall we do tonight?' Will asked, but he wasn't even looking at her, he was flicking through the TV channels.

'Haven't you planned something?' Lily affected a laugh.

'We could go to that restaurant. You know, the one you like. As long as you don't stomp out half way through like you did last time and for God's sake don't wear those damn shoes again. You know, the black and red ones that keep breaking.' He laughed to himself.

'Navy and pink,' she corrected, walking away. 'You'll need to book a table.'

'Already did,' he chortled then waited for her to congratulate him.

'Ooo, you were so sure of yourself.' She held her hand out and admired the ring, it was exquisite. The emerald was enormous, even the diamonds around it were large enough to be solitaires in their own right.

'Could always have cancelled.' He narrowed his eyes. 'Come here, you haven't even kissed me properly.'

Lily went home to shower and change – she didn't have the right clothes at Will's. As she pulled on her dress – a soft, pink, floaty creation that had been sitting in her wardrobe waiting for the right moment – she pondered for a second whether she could wear the shoes. They would go so well with this dress too, so well that she wondered if she subconsciously always bought dresses to go with the cursed shoes.

Don't tempt fate.

She found a pair of strappy sandals and pulled them on. They didn't go quite so well, but they still looked good.

She messaged all her friends with her news – it

would be weird if she didn't, wouldn't it?

Tess came back immediately with an OMG. Then she rang.

'Congratulations. I didn't see that coming, did you? How exciting.'

'No, I didn't,' Lily agreed before telling Tess about the whole proposal at work situation.

'That's very public,' Tess said. 'And you've doubted his commitment all these years. He must love you very much to make such a grand gesture and chance you saying no.'

'Yeah. As if I would.' Lily laughed lightly. 'I've got to go, we're dining out.' Of course, she wouldn't have humiliated him like that, no one would. That would have been just too cruel.

'Have a fab evening. I'm so happy for you.'

She parked her car at Will's then let herself into his house. Is this where they would live? There would have to be some changes. The pool table would have to go.

'Babe,' Will called. 'Could have done with you here earlier. Got the damn cast wet in the shower. Look.' Will stood in front of his sofa wearing shorts and a t-shirt, the cast was wrapped in a white towel; blue dye bleeding onto it.

'It's fibreglass, isn't it. Won't that be okay?'

'The cast is okay it's the stuff underneath it, it's all wet and squidgy.'

Lily bent down to look, carefully removing the towel so she could see clearly.

'At least it's not smelly,' she said, trying to make light of it. She used the towel to blot up the excess moisture.

298

'Do you want to cancel?' She wasn't sure if she felt annoyed or relieved at the prospect of not going out.

'No. Can't you dry it off somehow?'

'Hairdryer? We could try that. Where is it?'

'No, I'm more of a wash and go man.' He tossed his hair to make the point. 'Could you go and get yours?'

'Not if we're going to get to the restaurant on time.' They both stared at his cast. 'How did you get it wet? Didn't you put your waterproof sleeve on?'

'Yeah, but I didn't zip it up enough. I thought it would be okay.'

'Fan heater,' Lily said, suddenly inspired. 'I'm sure I've seen one here.'

Ten minutes later, after Lily had rummaged around in the under stairs cupboard, attracting spiders in the process, Will was sitting with his leg propped up and the stench of burnt dust blowing in his face.

'Won't that do?' he moaned for the third time in as many minutes. 'It's burning me.'

Lily inspected the cast and its lining. 'That'll do,' she said, switching the fan off. She didn't tell Will that it had singed the cast lining which had now turned brown, any longer and it would have caught fire.

Lily drove; they had left it too late to wait for a taxi.

Sitting at the table in the restaurant Will looked smart, he wore a crisp cotton shirt and dark linen jacket, beneath the table he was dressed in his baggy jeans. 'Only thing I can get on over the cast, babe,' he'd said when Lily protested. 'These or joggers.'

They were half way through their starters when the people at the next table complained, calling the waiter over and asking if something was on fire in the kitchen.

'Yeah, I can smell burning,' Will chipped in, giving support to his neighbour.

'And me,' offered another diner.

'Me too,' someone else added.

'I can assure you that nothing is burning in the kitchen.' The waiter narrowed his eyes before retreating through the swing door. 'Absolutely no problem in the kitchen,' he said on his return.

'Must be out here then.'

'Yeah,' Will agreed. 'Must be. You can smell it can't you, babe?'

'No, it's you.' Lily concentrated on her plate, pushing the food around with her fork and wishing Will would shut up.

'I can definitely smell burning,' someone said.

'We have smoke detectors, they would go off if there was burning.' The waiter sighed.

'Burning?' someone asked.

'When were they last tested? Your smoke detectors.'

'Recently,' the waiter snapped.

'I don't like it. You hear stories about people getting trapped in public places. You hear stories about batteries being removed.' The people on the neighbouring table, who hadn't ordered, stood up. 'We'll come back another time, when you've sorted out your fire alarms.'

'There is no fire.'

'Fire? Fire? Did someone say fire?' Several diners stood up at once, bustling with their belongings, asking about paying, asking about not paying.

Leaving.

Will pulled his wallet out and left fifteen pounds on the table, then stumbled to his feet, wedging his arm into his crutch. 'Come on, babe. I won't be able to get out in a hurry when the burning starts.'

'There isn't a fire.' Lily said, shaking her head. 'It's fine. It's you. It's your cast. Sit down.'

'I can definitely smell something,' Will said, his voice too loud. 'I'm not chancing it.' He turned to the waiter; thrust a five-pound note in his hand. 'Sorry mate.'

Outside on the pavement, Lily felt shocked. 'That was you,' she said to Will as they shuffled towards her car.

'Me what,' he said, clicking his crutch on the pavement.

'You. The smell was you. It's your cast, actually it's the lining. It got a bit singed by the fan heater.'

'No. It wouldn't smell that strong.'

'It does. And you ruined everyone's evening. And what about the restaurant? You've certainly ruined their evening, maybe even their business.'

'Why didn't you say something when we were in there?'

'I did.'

'I never heard you.'

'No. You never do.'

Twenty-two

'Morning. You're in early, Lily.' Damon was already at his desk, deep into his work.

'Not as early as you.'

'Got a meeting with Cyril in a minute.' Damon started scrabbling around on his desk for a pen.

'Oh, what's that about?' Was there any cause for Lily to be alarmed?

'Don't know, got the request late Friday.' Damon grimaced. 'Anyway, never mind that. How was your weekend? What's it like being newly engaged? Let me see that ring again.' Damon grabbed her hand and pulled it towards him. 'Oh, not wearing it? You getting it resized? I noticed it was a bit of a squeeze.'

Lily pulled her bare hand away. Did she want to tell Damon about her weekend? 'Yeah, that's right.' She blinked back tears and headed for her desk. Thank God Damon was going to a meeting and wouldn't be around to continually ask her questions. He'd want a blow-by-blow account; did they go out; did they celebrate with friends? Would there be a party? When?

There would be nothing, there had been nothing.

Just a major row in the car after they'd left the restaurant. He'd blamed her for singeing his cast; she'd blamed him for getting it wet. It wasn't a good start to their future together.

She'd dropped him off at home and hadn't even followed him in. He left her car with the emerald ring and his front door key pushed into his jacket pocket.

Lily knew that Damon's meeting was scheduled to last an hour because that's when her own meeting with Jackson started, so when Veronica appeared at her desk just as the hour was up, Lily's heart sank.

'He sends his apologies, but he's stuck in a meeting. I'll come and get you when he's free. Heather knows.' Veronica turned on her heels.

'Heather?'

'Heather. HR Heather.' Veronica gave Lily a look that screamed: fool.

So Heather would be in their meeting, yet again. There'd be no opportunity for honesty or frankness. It seemed that the week was beginning the way the weekend had ended. Frustrating.

Tess messaged to see if Lily was all right. Lily lied and replied that all was well.

Thank God for Tess. Her calmness, her level head, her sympathy had all helped to ease Lily's pain after she'd told Will that there was no future for them together. Tess was the person Lily had rushed to in the aftermath.

303

'What really hurt,' Lily said to Tess as they sat in Tess's sitting room with a box of tissues and a large mug of tea. 'Was that he didn't really seem that bothered, or that surprised.'

'I'm sure he was. It's just that some people have a different way of showing it. Especially men.'

'When I gave him back the ring,' Lily said, between sobs. 'He popped it in his pocket and said it was okay, he had it on sale or return anyway.'

'I think he was joking.'

'Not funny.'

'Maybe he said it to save face.'

'I think he meant it. I really do think he had it on sale or return.'

'Can you even do that?'

'If anyone can, Will can.'

'Yeah,' agreed Tess.

'Yeah,' Lily echoed. Will would have no problem persuading a shop to take something back, even an engagement ring. 'Do you think he asked them if he could bring it back if I said no?'

'Does it matter? You have said no, haven't you?'

'I didn't, not at first. I couldn't, could I? I couldn't humiliate him like that, in front of all those people. People I work with, people I will have to face every day, they'll all be looking at me and judging when they find out. But I knew, even as I was saying yes, the voice in my head was screaming, *No! Wait!*.' She didn't tell Tess about the look of sadness on Jackson's face as she'd said yes, didn't mention him at all.

'But you've always wanted him to commit. Isn't that why you broke up with him before we went on holiday?'

'I know. I know. That's what I thought. You know

I've always wanted him, I spent all my twenties pining after him, even when he wasn't interested in me.'

Tess patted Lily's hand. 'Would you like wine? Do you want to stay the night?'

'I would, but what about Gareth?'

'I've messaged him, he's not coming over tonight.'

'That's very tactful of him.' Selfless Lily admired Gareth, Tess has made a good choice; selfish Lily was pleased he was staying away. 'Bring on the wine, then.' She allowed herself a laugh, but it barely left her lips.

'What about Jackson?' Tess asked, after they had consumed a whole bottle of Pinot?

'You mean Jackson-slash-Cyril. That's how I think of him now. Jackson-slash-Cyril. Well, what about him? That's what I want to know? I've got a meeting with him first thing Monday morning and I'm going to have it out with him. Sort out this double identity thing. Get it all out in the open.' Lily banged her empty glass on the coffee table.

'We've run out,' Tess giggled.

'What? How much have we had?'

'A whole bottle.'

'Each?'

'No.' Tess frowned. 'Between us.'

'Right.' Lily scrabbled around on the floor for her handbag, extracted her purse and took out three ten-pound notes. 'You know what this means?'

'No?'

'We'll have to walk down and get some more. I'm just going to have to front it out with those arses who run your Co-op. It should still be open.'

'It's not my Co-op.'

'It's at the end of your street, isn't it? So it's your Co-op.' Lily forced her feet into her sandals. 'And bring a carrier bag; I'm not paying them 10p for one.'

Neither of the arses was in the Co-op; Lily and Tess bought two bottles of Pinot and a large selection of crisps, peanuts and chocolate without any drama and waddled their way back to Tess's home.

'I told you he was married, didn't I?' Lily said, as she scoffed a whole bag of crisps almost without stopping. Not quite the meal at Fabio's she'd been expecting.

'Who, Will?'

'No, Jackson-slash-Cyril. Anyway, what sort of a name is Cyril? If you're going to have an alter ego you wouldn't choose a name like Cyril? It's so…' Lily waved her hands around as though trying to catch the word in the air.

'Old,' Tess said. 'I think my great granddad might have been called Cyril. Or maybe it was Cecil. Or something like that.'

'Yeah. Old. It is old. Old and weird. Just like him.' Except that Lily didn't think he was old, or weird. Was he the real reason she had split up with Will?

'Does Will know about Jackson-slash-Cyril?'

Lily gasped. Trust mind reader Tess to say the unthinkable.

'No. No. There's nothing to know. Nothing at all. Anyway, he's married. Remember? Ours was just a holiday fling.' No past, no present, no strings. 'And Tess, if you remember, it was your idea.'

'And if Jackson-slash-Cyril wasn't married?'

'Well he is. So. There. And believe me, if you could see his wife, you'd know that there is no way I could compete with that. Even if I wanted to… which I don't. Obviously.' Lily snatched up a packet of peanuts and pulled the bag apart, venting her aggression. They both watched the peanuts scatter over Tess's wood floor, skittering into corners and rolling under the sofa.

'Leave 'em, leave 'em.' Tess giggled. 'Gareth will sort them out in the morning.

'Will he? He's a keeper, Tess.' Lily raised her glass to Gareth. 'And I've never seen you looking so happy.' Lily took a long gulp of wine.

'I've never been so happy.' Tess gulped her own wine. 'Or so drunk. I don't normally drink this much.'

'And, I might lose my job.'

'No. You're good at your job. You're always saying so.' Tess, realising what she'd just said, put her hand up to cover her mouth.

Lily swiped at her, but missed. 'Yeah, it's me or Damon and Damon's doing full on man-love with Jackson-slash-Cyril.'

'But Jackson's not…?'

'No. No. Huh, who knows? What do I know? Anyway, it might be all of us, Bensons is…*pfft*.' Lily waved her arms around like a magician.

'What do you mean?'

'Nothing, just ignore me. I'm just being silly.' But it could be true. Couldn't it? It might happen.

In the morning when Lily woke up in Tess's spare room, her head throbbed and her mouth tasted and felt as though it was full of shag pile carpet. She lay in bed listening to the noises downstairs; someone was vacuuming.

Half an hour later, after she'd staggered around the bathroom – should she really have drunk so much shower water – and cleaned her teeth with toothpaste on her finger, she crept downstairs.

Gareth greeted her with a cheery, 'morning.'

Tess waved from her position in the kitchen, still in her pyjamas, propped up on a kitchen barstool, leaning against the worktop and sipping a giant mug of tea.

'I'm doing a fry up,' Gareth said, smiling. He had one of those permanent smiley-faces complete with upturned mouth; the sort of face that no matter how miserable the owner was, they always looked happy. Lily fought an unreasonable urge to slap it. 'Would you like some?'

He put his arm around Tess who, despite her evident hangover, also looked happy. Lily noticed, probably for the first time, that Tess also had a smiley-face. What a pair they made. Lucky pair.

'Yes. Thank you,' Lily heard herself say, even though she just wanted to run and hide and get away from all this happy togetherness.

Gareth piled up Lily's plate with bacon, eggs, mushrooms, baked beans and fried bread. Lily salivated before the first mouthful was even in her mouth. The restorative effects of fried food and three cups of tea should never be underestimated – especially where a hangover is concerned.

After saying her thank yous and goodbyes, Lily made her way home. She was preparing herself to make a difficult phone call, one she didn't want to make, but knew she must.

Act like a grownup she told herself.

She dialled the number and waited, hoping it would go straight to voicemail, fully expecting it to.

'Hi babe,' Will said as though nothing had happened.

'Hi Will. Just wanted to check you were okay?'

'To be honest, I've been better. And you?' His voice was clipped now but he definitely wasn't on the verge of tears, unlike Lily.

'Same here.' She stalled. 'I'm sorry.'

'It's not too late if you want to change your mind.'

Lily couldn't speak, couldn't answer.

'Babe?' Will prompted.

Lily swallowed hard, took a big breath, thanked God that she was at home and Will couldn't see her, forced a smile onto her face – wasn't that supposed to be good phone etiquette, smile and it comes across in your voice – and said, 'I don't think that would work. Do you?'

'No,' Will said, sounding resigned.

'I hope we can still be friends.' As soon as Lily had spoken those fatuous words she wanted to snatch them back. She hated that phrase, the very words that Will had said to her in the message from his American adventure.

'I don't think that would work, babe. Do you?' Now he sounded sombre.

Lily sniffed. She'd promised herself she wasn't going to cry, but the big fat salty drops were already running down her face. 'Suppose not,' she whispered.

'Hey, Will,' a female voice called in the background. 'Shower's running hot now.'

'Who's that?' Lily snapped.

'Oh, Giselle. She came over to help me. And to cheer me up.'

'Oh. When did she come over?'

Will was silent for a beat too long. 'Anyway,' he said. 'I'd better go.'

'Did she come over last night? Did you get her over as soon as I dropped you off?'

Silence again, then, 'I've got to go. Take care, Lily. Remember the good times.' He ended the call.

'Phew,' Damon sat down at his desk with a thump. 'That was a bit full-on.'

Lily jumped up, grabbed her notebook and pen, the half-completed list from Friday still showing. 'You were a long time. What was it about?'

Damon raised his eyebrows and forced his mouth down. 'I can't say,' he said, glancing over at The Europeans, whose alert eyes suggested that their ears were already tuned in.

'Okay. My turn now.' Lily sounded more confident than she felt, whatever this meeting was about she needed to turn it around to fulfil her own needs and ensure that Heather left the room.

Veronica held a hand up as Lily approached. 'I said I'd come and get you when he was free.'

'Oh, but I thought…' Lily's voice trailed away as she glanced into the office and saw a red-faced Heather and a purple-faced Oliver Banstead sitting opposite a jacketless Jackson-slash-Cyril.

'I'll let you know when it's your turn,' Veronica snapped. 'But it'll probably be an hour.'

'Thank you,' Lily said, not at all grateful.

'I don't know why Scare-a-von has to be so damned rude,' Lily said as she and Damon stood in the kitchen munching on biscuits from a packet that definitely didn't belong to either of them.

'Because. She's. A. Bitch,' Damon said between bites.

'That's a bit harsh, but she so is. These are nice

biscuits.'

Damon tittered. 'They're hers.' He snatched another one from the box.

'Oh no. We'll have to replace them.'

'Doubt we can. She brought them back from her hols in Croatia.'

'Oh, then they're for everyone, that's okay then.'

Damon picked up the box. 'Um, no. It says "Veronica's – do not touch" on the box, in her own fair hand, I think.' He grabbed another one and forced it into Lily's hand.

'No. No,' she said, waving it around with a giggle.

'Nice to see you laugh,' Damon said. 'First time today?'

'Put it back in the box,' Lily said, by way of diversion.

'No. Have it. She'll blame me anyway, she always does.' He giggled. 'And she's usually right. Anyway, spill.'

'What?'

'Spill. What's wrong?'

'Never mind me, you spill. What happened in your meeting?' Lily absently bit into the biscuit. 'Look what you've made me do; I wasn't going to eat that one.'

'I can't tell you about my meeting. Cyril is going to tell you himself when he meets with you. He told me not to discuss it.'

'I don't like the sound of that.'

Damon shrugged.

'Or that shrug. I'm going, aren't I? You're staying and I'm losing my job.'

'I don't know. I don't think so.' Damon picked up the biscuit box and shook it. 'Oops. Only two left, we might as well finish them off.' He reached into the box and pulled one out, biting into it with relish.

'Caught red-handed,' Veronica boomed from the doorway. 'I knew it was you.'

'What?' Damon said, displaying his best innocent face, as Lily blinked and wished they'd remembered to shut the kitchen door.

'I knew it was you. All those times you've denied it. And you, Lily, I'd have expected better from you.'

'Sorry,' Lily muttered like a naughty child. She laid her half-eaten biscuit on the worktop and backed away from it.

'Sorry,' Damon echoed, but his voice was high and sing-song. 'Didn't realise they were just for you. We thought they were holiday biscuits you'd brought back for everyone. Oh well, there you go.' He marched past Veronica, rattling the one remaining biscuit in the box and thrust it into her hand. 'Enjoy.'

Back at their desks they giggled like school children.

'It's all right for you; I have to face her again soon.'

Damon pulled his chair up to Lily's desk just as The Europeans got up to go for coffee. 'And, she saved you from telling me what's going on with you!' He raised his eyebrows. 'You've broken it off with Will, haven't you?'

'How did… what?'

'The look on your face when he asked you to marry him. I know that look. How is he?'

'Well, he's just fine.' Lily wondered how quickly he'd rung Giselle.

'Good. More importantly, how are you?'

Lily shrugged. 'Been better. You know.'

'And what about our man?'

'What man?'

'Cyril or Jackson or whatever his name is? Because I saw the look on his face when Will asked you to marry him.'

'What look?' Lily tried to hide the hope in her voice.

'Mmm, let me think.' Damon pressed his finger to his forehead. He shook his head.

'Don't be such a drama queen, just tell me.'

'Devastated,' he whispered before scooting his chair back to his desk.

So it hadn't been her imagination. Lily's mouth dropped open just as her phone rang.

'He'll see you now,' Veronica's clipped voice intoned when Lily answered it.

Twenty-three

Lily stood up and smoothed her clothes down, patted her hair, picked up her notepad again and, raising her eyebrows at Damon as she passed, headed for Jackson-slash-Cyril's office. She glanced down at her list as she approached Veronica.

'They're waiting for you,' Veronica said as though it were Lily who had kept them waiting.

The smell in the office was one hundred percent Oily Bastard; his greasy odour and smug stench hovered in the air. Heather and Jackson-slash-Cyril both stood up as Lily entered. They looked flushed and exhausted.

'Phew, it's warm in here,' Lily said, regretting her lack of tact as she said it, especially when Heather flapped her hands in front of her face and let her shoulders drop.

Then Lily saw Jackson-slash-Cyril's eye. Black, blue, purple, yellow at the edges, still puffy. Had she done that? Should she apologise now?

Jackson acknowledged her shock with a quick, straight-lipped smile. Hardly a smile at all, which Lily took as a signal not to mention it.

They went through the motions of smiling and offering drinks – cold water all round, brought in by a reluctant Veronica who plonked the jug on the desk and left without a word.

'You'll have to excuse Veronica's mood; she thinks she should be in here.' Jackson-slash-Cyril poured them a glass each.

'Why?'

'We'll come to that later. Right, I've called this meeting…' he began before Lily cut in.

'Excuse me, I requested this meeting. It was postponed from Friday.'

'Ah. Yes. Well this takes priority at the moment. I need to bring you up to speed with the situation.'

'Okay,' Lily said slowly. But he wasn't getting away with it, she would have her say, she would get to the bottom of who he was and what the hell he thought he was doing. She had a list and she wouldn't be diverted from it.

'Oliver Banstead has now left Bensons Wholesale Electrical. He resigned today and his resignation is with immediate effect.'

'Oh.' Lily pondered for a moment. 'Good.'

'I've spoken to many of his victims, past and present, and many of them would have been very happy to speak to the police if it had come to that. Fortunately, Oliver has decided to take the honourable way out.' Jackson-slash-Cyril's eyes met briefly with Lily's before he turned to Heather.

'The official line,' Heather added, taking her cue, 'is that he's decided to take early retirement due to ill health. There will be gossip, of course, but we know that you won't be spreading it.' Heather arched her eyebrows at Lily.

'What? He's getting away with it? That's not right. That's not fair.'

'Well, that's what has been decided and agreed.' Jackson sighed. 'Sorry you won't get your pound of flesh.'

'This isn't about me getting revenge, this is about justice. He's a dirty old letch. He'll just go somewhere else and do it again.'

Jackson stood up, he had rolled his sleeves up again and Lily saw the mermaid's tail flicking from beneath his watch; it made her heart clench. 'You're probably correct, but that will be their problem.'

'Well that's not good enough. I think…'

'Sorry, it's not up for discussion,' Jackson cut across her. 'That's how it is.'

'I don't agree with it.'

Jackson let out a long, drawn-out sigh. 'I think that this subject is at an end now. Heather, if you wouldn't mind leaving us, I have some finance matters I need to discuss with Lily.' He smiled as Heather, who, looking relieved to be escaping the stuffy room, gathered up her papers and left in haste.

Was this when he told her she didn't have a job?

Was this when he told her that Damon was the winner?

Was this when she told him to stop playing around and tell her who the hell he really was? She glanced at her notepad. Would she write the answers down?

'I'm sorry about this whole business, Lily,' Jackson began. 'But we had a Mexican standoff situation.'

'A what?'

'We couldn't win, we couldn't take, ahem, Oily Bastard to court,' he allowed a smile to play across his face.

'Why not?'

'In fact,' Jackson continued, ignoring her question. 'If it hadn't been for you and your counter-complaint, we would have been up shit creek without a paddle. You've saved Bensons from financial ruin.'

'Have I? How?' What the hell was he talking about?

'No doubt Damon has shared his report with you. You know about the unofficial bank accounts, the irregularities in Bensons accounting.'

Lily hesitated while Jackson waited for an answer.

'Yes.' Was she getting Damon into trouble by admitting it?

'It appears that my predecessor, Malcolm Block, and our Oily Bastard were effectively running a shadow company alongside Bensons, diverting funds into other bank accounts and, of course, paying themselves handsomely into the bargain. They pulled the wool over old Mr Benson's eyes – not difficult as it turns out – and got away with it for years. It only started to unravel when my predecessor left. Or maybe it was starting to unravel and that was why he left.'

Lily slumped in her seat, swallowing hard before speaking, her voice a sad whisper. 'I didn't know anything about it. I feel such a fool. So must Damon. How could we not have spotted it?'

'Don't blame yourselves, no evidence came your way, the money was creamed off long before it got that far.'

'Can't they be prosecuted? It's theft. They should be made examples of. Everyone here thinks the company is going under, especially after...' Lily's voice trailed away.

'After what?' Jackson looked alarmed.

'After your wife toured the building and put the fear of God into everyone.' She watched for a reaction on his face, but there was none; for him this was strictly business.

Jackson shook his head. 'Is that all? Is that the only reason?'

Lily nodded slowly. 'I think so. Although now people mutter about financial irregularities but I don't think they did before her visit.'

'No one needs to worry about her.'

Of course not, thought Lily. 'But you could prosecute Oily Bastard on both counts – sexual harassment and embezzlement.'

'Much as he and Block deserve it, that's the last thing we want to do. We need Bensons to appear stable and profitable, otherwise it will go under – rumours have killed many a good business. If we go public with this, it will ruin us. We have to front it out, present a confident face to our customers and our suppliers. Banstead was going to go public with the financial fraud if we pursued the sexual harassment.'

'But he was in the wrong on both counts. He'd be putting himself in the firing line.'

'Yes, it's a game of cat and mouse. As I said, we had a standoff. Interestingly, the evidence suggests that he was a pawn in the game, although according to Block, Banstead was a major player, perhaps even *the* major player.' Jackson sighed. 'I spent a hurried weekend in Spain – Block has a beautiful villa overlooking the Med, no doubt funded illegally – trying to get to the bottom of it. Inevitably they each blame the other and each accuses the other of being the mastermind. But it makes no difference; we have to keep this quiet. Your accusation against Banstead gave us a bit of leverage to silence him; even *he* doesn't want to be prosecuted for sexual harassment. Bensons owes you.'

'It's wrong, morally wrong.'

'I agree. Shamefully we've even had to provide a decent reference for him and a payoff. As I've said, it's a standoff. We're buying his silence. And yes, he might go somewhere else and behave like that again, but let's hope that another company has better morals and better checks and balances than this one had.'

'Had? What do you mean?'

'Let's just say that old Mr Benson is no longer running the company – in any capacity. I don't want this repeated, but there is a suspicion that he probably isn't up to it any longer. He probably hasn't been for a long time. Banstead and Block had no problems pulling the wool over his eyes. We'll need to appoint a new MD in due course, but we need to keep that quiet too until we're ready.'

'Poor Mr Benson.'

'Poor Bensons Wholesale Electricals. But the future is brighter now.' Jackson ran his hand through his hair, what little there was of it.

'But we've just lost our best salesman, however despicable he was.' Lily felt despondent; suddenly her own problems seemed less important against the survival of a company that provided so many jobs, so many livelihoods.

'Another myth,' Jackson said. 'He might have been the best officially, that is in the official Benson accounts, but the best salesmen's orders were going through the bogus company. How's that for irony?'

Lily shook her head. It sounded horrendous. 'I feel such a fool,' she said. 'I've been here for years and never suspected; you've been here five minutes….'

'Stop.' Jackson said, holding up his hand. 'We had teams of top accountants on Bensons' books for months before we took it over, that's how we knew something wasn't right. Then there's Veronica; she's insistent she knew nothing about it, yet she worked very closely with them both.'

'Surely you don't think she's involved. I know she can be an old battle axe but she wouldn't do anything illegal.' Lily couldn't quite believe she was defending Scare-a-von, especially when all she really wanted to ask was who the 'we' were that had taken Bensons over. 'She's been here so long, she's like a piece of the furniture and she rules the roost.'

'Thinks she does,' Jackson said. 'But that's another issue.'

'What will you do?'

'Wait and see, but I think we might have to let her go. I don't know. When my father persuaded me to come here I didn't know it was going to be such a headache.'

'Your father?' Lily prompted, seizing her opportunity.

'Yes, we, that is, our family business – which is quite large – bought Bensons out.'

'Hostile takeover,' Lily muttered.

'Not at all. Bensons' directors approached us. Old Mr Benson was making some erratic decisions and things weren't looking good. Ironically none of them suspected what was really going on. Frankly it's a bloody mess. This sort of thing is the reason why I got out of this career in the first place.'

'And went surfing,' Lily added, her tone mocking.

'That's right.'

Lily grasped her opportunity. 'So who the hell are

you? What's with the Jackson-slash-Cyril thing?'

He laughed. Really loud. He looked into her eyes and laughed again. 'Jackson-slash-Cyril?'

'That's what I call you because I don't know who the hell you are.'

'Me neither,' he said softly, slumping back in his chair.

'So?' He was not getting away with it.

'Full name: Cyril Jackson Montgomery-Jones.'

'Yes?' Lily spread her hands inviting more explanation.

'Cyril is a family name, my father is called Cyril, his father was Cyril and so on, going back generations. It's become a tradition. But I've always hated that name. I spent much of my childhood in Devon, along with my sister, Beth. We lived with my maternal grandparents until I was thirteen; they pretty much brought us up while my parents flew around the world on business. In Devon I was Jackson – always have been. That's who I really am.'

'Is it? Then why the subterfuge?'

'What subterfuge?'

'You never identified yourself. You never acknowledged you knew me.'

'I didn't know you. That is, I didn't know who you were until you walked into my office. Until then yours was just a name on a long list of employees. I never guessed that Lillian Ward was the Lily I'd spent nine days in Devon with.'

'And then?'

'And then, apart from there always being someone else with us – and I wasn't having that conversation in front of an audience – you were a suspect.'

'What?' Lily stood up.

'Joint head of finance – of course you were a suspect. As was Damon. Even,' he smirked. 'The Europeans.'

'But we are innocent. How could you think that we, that I, would be involved in anything dodgy?' Lily flopped back into her seat.

'I'm sorry. But, despite my personal feelings, I had to ensure…' He stopped speaking and looked away.

Silence: the air crackled around them.

'Your personal feelings?' she said, her voice croaking.

He turned back to face her and a brief, insincere smile flashed across his face. 'Congratulations on your engagement. I witnessed the romantic proposal.'

'Thank you,' she said. 'I met your wife.'

'Did you?'

'Mireille, isn't it? I know that during our little holiday romance we agreed on no past and no strings, but I think it was duplicitous of you to forget you had a wife.'

'And you a forthcoming fiancé,' he countered.

Lily stood up so she could look down on a seated Jackson, she definitely had the moral high ground on this. How dare he, a wife was far more serious than a recently dumped boyfriend. 'For your information we had broken up. That was why I was on holiday with my friends, to cheer myself up, to get over him. So, I was quite free to do as I please.' She flung the office door open. 'Can you say the same?' She slammed the door behind her and marched back to her desk. 'Going to lunch now,' she said to Damon who jumped when she whistled past him. Lily snatched up her handbag and jacket and made her escape.

How dare he? How dare he throw Will's proposal at her while he had a wife. Who the hell did he think he was? He was a lying, two-faced, smug two-timer. Adulterer. That's what he was, an adulterer. No one could accuse her of that. No one. She had broken up with Will before the holiday. She was single. Cyril Jackson Montgomery-Jones was not single; he had a wife. A former boyfriend did not have the same status as a wife.

A wife. A wife. For God's sake. That made Lily a cheap little bit on the side. She'd had no illusions about the holiday fling, that's all it ever was, all it was meant to be from the beginning, but a wife? A wife! How dare he bring up Will's romantic gesture, how dare he belittle Will? She cringed on Will's behalf, felt mean and spiteful for finishing with him. Poor Will.

She seethed and stomped her way out of the building, strode out to the car park, aggressively pressing the door release on her key fob as she approached her car. She yanked the door open and flung her bag and jacket onto the passenger seat. Then she looked back. Why did she have to look back?

Jackson was standing at his office window, no doubt surveying his domain. She glowered at him but he didn't look away. He stood motionless, his arms behind his back, his legs slightly apart. He looked like a sentinel.

'Arrogant bastard,' she hissed to herself.

She revved the car out of its space, revved it out of the car park and put her foot down hard when she reached the dual carriageway. Where was she going? She hadn't given it any thought; she just wanted to get away.

If Tess had been at home she would have gone there, but Tess was at work. She thought briefly of Will, shook her head and half laughed at herself as she drove.

What would she say to Will? What could she say to Will? Come to that, what could she say to Tess? So much of what had happened couldn't be repeated for fear of jeopardising the future and reputation of Bensons Wholesale Electricals.

Had she really been a suspect? Had he really thought that she and Damon were in on it? But he hadn't suspected Damon for long. Damon had been entrusted with compiling the report. Lily had been a prime suspect.

And why not? He didn't know her? And she didn't know him; that much was obvious.

She found herself at home without even noticing how she'd got there. She scraped the tyres against the curb as she parallel parked.

Inside she filled the kettle, slamming it on to its base as she flicked the power on. A big mug of coffee would help.

Damon messaged to see if she was okay, she messaged back to say she might be late back. Was that true? Was she going back? Was she going to face him again?

Then, as her heart dropped with a sickening thud, she realised she'd left her notepad in his office. He was probably perusing that damning list at this very moment.

Twenty-four

She lay on the sofa, hugging herself and thinking about the list. Not just the questions but the vile comments aggressively scribbled in the margins, even if they were true:

Cyril – sly doppelganger

Jackson – sneaky, lying bastard with a secret wife

Jackson-slash-Cyril- who the hell does he think he is?

Jackson-slash-Cyril – hate him

She cringed. The thought of him reading the list, inspecting every line – urgh. She'd even doodled his name inside a heart. Why? Was she mad? Had she scribbled it out? She thought she had. Now she wasn't sure.

She could never go back to Bensons. Never face him again.

Why had he invaded her real life?

Why did she ever think that she could have a no-strings-attached holiday romance?

Had she been right to dump Will? She felt guilty when she thought of Will, not just because she'd dumped him, but because he took up less room in her thoughts than Jackson did. It never used to be like that, she was – to use Tess's words – obsessed with Will. But now, now her feelings towards him were quickly becoming neutral. She felt more sorry for him than any other emotion. When had that happened?

She sat up and swallowed her guilt down with a large mouthful of coffee. Then reminded herself that Giselle had been summoned to Will's aid almost as soon as Lily had dropped him off home after the fateful conversation in the car. Should she have waited until the morning and had that conversation in the cold light of day? Would it have changed the outcome? She wondered if Giselle now had the coveted key.

Damon messaged her: *What have you done to Cyril, hun? He's stomping around with a thunder face. Scared The Europeans shitless xx*

Lily read the message several times before dropping her phone back on the coffee table. What could she say? Nothing was probably the best response.

She lay back down on the sofa and pulled her knees up to her chest, rocking herself like a baby.

What a mess. It was so depressing, so demoralising. She would have to get a new job; maybe it was time for a change of career. No more finance. Hey, maybe no more offices. A complete change of career. What could she do? What did she want to do?

Damon messaged again: *Where are you, hun? Cyril wants to know what time you will be back.*

Lily: *Not coming back. Ever.*

She switched her phone to silent, closed her eyes and fought back tears.

Her stupid holiday fling with Jackson-slash-Cyril had ruined her life. If she'd never met him on holiday she certainly wouldn't have fallen for him in the office; only fools mixed work with romance, no matter how strong the attraction. But there was no denying that the attraction had been strong. And mutual.

She wouldn't have found it so insulting that he even vaguely suspected her of fraud and embezzlement; she would have seen it for what it was – just business. Everything was spoiled, tainted. Nothing would ever be the same again. It was all such a mess.

She let the tears flow; self-pity, humiliation, sadness. And finally, she cried herself to sleep, waking only to a loud banging on the door and a snot bubble escaping her left nostril.

'All right, all right,' she called out as the banging continued. She snatched a tissue from the box in the hall and wiped her nose on her way to the front door. A quick look in the mirror showed mad bed-hair and panda eyes. She shrugged. Who would care? She didn't anymore.

She opened the door a little and peaked through the gap.

'Jackson?'

'Hello, Lily.'

She stared at him without speaking.

'Can I come in?' he asked.

'Why?'

'We need to talk.'

Lily shrugged but didn't open the door further, didn't step aside to let him in.

'About your list,' he added.

Lily pushed the door shut, but Jackson already had his foot inside preventing the door from closing. She stared hard, challenging him to move. Their eyes met, his startling blue eyes – just as blue as they had been on the beach – one ringed in black and yellow; her panda eyes.

He moved his foot away.

Lily opened the door and stood back to let him in.

What was she doing?

What the hell.

'I recognise this,' he said, touching his fleece hanging on the coat rack in the hall.

'Yeah. Sorry. I didn't realise I had it.' It sounded so pathetic.

In the sitting room she plonked herself back down on the sofa, then, when Jackson didn't sit down, she waved him into the armchair furthest from her. Her aim had been to keep him as far away as possible, but the plan backfired – his distance allowed her to observe his whole body, his chiselled jaw, his muscular frame, his strong arms. He had changed his clothes, now wearing a t-shirt and jeans; he looked more like the Jackson she had met in Devon. He wore no watch – the mermaid tattoo now on full display, ridiculing her.

'I read your list,' he began, pulling a torn off page from his pocket.

She swallowed before speaking. 'Stupid of me to leave it behind.'

'Do you really think I'm a,' he glanced down, 'sneaky, lying bastard with a secret wife?'

'Yes, because you are.'

'And you hate me?'

Lily raised her eyebrows – a sardonic act.

'But you've drawn my name in a heart.'

'And scribbled it out.'

'Not very well.'

'Where are we going with this? Could you just give me that back and sod off. I won't be coming back to

Bensons.' She stood up and grabbed for the paper but he was too fast and tucked it back into his pocket.

'Sit down,' he said, sighing and rubbing his head.

'Don't tell me what to do in my own house.'

'Sit down, please. Let's discuss this.'

'It's pointless.' She put her hands on her hips. 'You know what I think of you; you have my list. And you didn't trust me; you thought I was part of a financial fraud, a thief no less.'

'I never thought that.'

'You said you did.'

'I never believed that of you. I had to play it by the book. I had to,' he stalled, swallowed hard. 'Act like a professional.'

'Really.' Lily tried not to look at him, tried to put the memory of what was beneath that t-shirt, those jeans, out of her head. Tried to forget that night in the beach hut. Tried to forget their wonderful nine days together.

'You didn't trust me, yet you trusted Damon.'

'Not to start off with. I didn't, couldn't, trust anyone. I came to trust Damon after several meetings with him. The reports and plans he presented showed that he was honest.'

'And me? What about me?'

'You applied for the job. That could have implied that you were in on it and prepared to carry on with the fraud.'

'What? No.'

'And you stole my fleece.' He shrugged, implying that was proof enough of dishonesty.

'No. I didn't. I…'

'I was joking. A stupid joke. I know you weren't involved. But you see how it looked. I had to be certain. I had to show I was impartial.'

Lily thought for a moment. That made sense. It was logical, but she wasn't telling him that.

'Please sit down.' He said, his brow furrowed. 'I have so much to say.'

'Bit late, mate,' she said, affecting her best nonchalant air. But she sat back down because standing with her hands on her hips for too long felt ridiculous.

He pulled the list out again.

'Point one: Is Cyril, in fact, Jackson.' He looked up at her and smiled. 'I think we both know the answer to that one now.' He looked back at the list. 'Point two: why didn't I identify myself? As I said earlier in my office, I was as shocked as you; I never expected to see you again. I could ask why you never identified yourself.'

Lily stared at him for a long time, contemplating her response.

'Mmm, let me see. Would it be because you had a different name and a completely different look? I wasn't even sure it was you at first.' Even sitting down, she found herself aggressively folding her arms.

He looked into her eyes and almost smiled. Lily looked away.

'Point three: What am I doing invading your real life? I can't really answer that except to counter it with what are you doing invading my real life?'

'I was here first.' How petulant that sounded.

'I was drafted in by my father to help the family business. It really wasn't a choice for me, more an obligation.'

'How noble,' Lily muttered, but he didn't respond. 'And you've already said that.'

'Yeah. It should have been my sister but...' His voice trailed away, then he coughed and returned to the list. 'Point four: Why was I paired with you for the skydive?' He shook his head. 'Nothing to do with me. I was as horrified as you were. When I saw you in that waiting area and realised we were tandem diving together I tried to change it. But, because I was late, there was no chance to swap.'

'You saw me in the waiting area? I didn't see you.'

'No, you were too busy arguing with a helmet, forcing your hair back into it. That's how I knew it was you – from the back – your hair.' He smiled to himself, his eyes almost glazing over.

Lily took small comfort from the fact that it hadn't been her thunder-thighs that had identified her.

'Point five: Why did I lie about being married? I never lied about being married. We never discussed marriage.' He sighed and screwed up the list, dropped it on the coffee table. 'Look,' he said, leaning forward. 'I'm going to tell you all about myself and you are going to tell me all about yourself, then we'll take it from there. Okay?'

'Yeah. Enlighten me,' Lily said, sighing herself.

He told her about his idyllic childhood in Devon, his grandparents. Explained how at thirteen he and his sister were pulled out of Devon and given a "proper education" – his father's words. He'd left university with a first-class degree and worked hard to become a top chartered accountant; he'd had a succession of great jobs in The City. He spent every holiday he could in Devon, but those holidays were shorter and fewer and farther between.

Then, while on business in Paris, he met Mireille. She was very French, very *Parisienne*. She followed him back to London and within a year they were married.

'How romantic,' Lily heard herself say.

'Yeah,' he said. 'She was the perfect corporate wife. We were the perfect corporate couple. I've no doubt that Mireille's talents furthered my career. Just when I thought we were at the stage to settle down and start a family Mireille had an affair.' His face took on a soft, pained expression.

'I'm sorry,' Lily said.

'It was nothing really, her affair. It was short and certainly not serious; it was, however, indicative of how bored she had become. I forgave her, we moved on. We even had the conversation about children.' He shrugged, his eyes staring into the distance. 'Six months later she did it again. There was no coming back after that.'

'Oh.'

'We divorced. We sold the house and split the proceeds. She'd never worked but as I said earlier, she was the perfect corporate wife and I owed her something for her part in my successful career.'

He stopped speaking, his eyes flicking left and right as he replayed the past.

'Would you like a drink?' Lily asked, getting up, feeling embarrassed for his evident pain.

'If you're having one,' he said.

She made them both coffee and reached for her emergency stash of chocolate biscuits, the ones she kept in a tin on the highest shelf. But try as she might she couldn't reach, she'd have to get a chair – climbing on the chair was part of the emergency procedure, if she couldn't reach them, she wouldn't eat them unless absolutely necessary.

'Let me help,' Jackson said from behind her, reaching up with ease and pulling the tin down. He was too close, far too close. 'Only to be opened in emergencies,' he read from the tin lid. 'Is this an emergency?'

Lily nodded. 'I think so.' She moved away from him, moved away from the heat and scent of his body.

'I left London after the divorce,' he continued once they were back in the sitting room sipping coffee. 'Gave up my job and spent my share of the house sale on the cottage in Devon. We'd done well; property prices had risen much faster in London than anywhere else in the country, so I could buy the cottage outright. I spent what cash I had left doing it up. Oh, and I bought the café where my aunts work – it was going to close down otherwise.'

'And the beach hut?' Lily asked, allowing herself to enjoy the memory.

'I already owned that. Well, strictly speaking my sister, Beth, and I co-owned it; it was left to us by our grandparents. Now it's just mine.' He stopped speaking for a moment, then shook himself, and grabbed his second emergency chocolate biscuit. 'I surfed most days and when winter came I followed the surf around the world. My father kept telling me that if I really didn't want to go back to The City, I should work in the family business. I didn't want to; I really had had enough of all it.'

'Until you came to Bensons,' Lily added, wistfully.

'Yeah. I felt obliged. It should have been Beth who came to Bensons. Beth was my father's number two. She'd been in the business almost since childhood. Worked there every school holiday, every college holiday, during university. She loved it. Always had. She loved working with our dad.' He stopped speaking, the silence in the room seemed to go on for minutes.

'So where is she now?' Lily prompted.

'She died.' His voice was flat, as though he'd practised this line a thousand times.

'I'm sorry.'

'It was stupid. How she died, I mean. There was a storm; she went out and rode fierce waves on her own when I was on the other side of the world. I should have been there. It was a Bank Holiday weekend, we always spent those together surfing. Mireille never liked the beach or the sea, so it was always just me and Beth.

Beth went out on her own early one morning.' He stopped again and Lily could see him swallowing hard. 'I came back immediately, but it was pointless. Losing Beth, I don't think I'll ever recover. Then I went off surfing again,' he added flippantly.

'I'm so sorry about your sister.' Lily didn't know what else to say. She felt so desperately sad on his behalf and it explained why he had been obsessive about safety in the water.

'Yes. So, I came to Bensons in her place, to sort of make it up to my dad. As if. I can't say it's been the happiest time of my life. Though…' He smiled at her, his eyes meeting hers. 'There have been compensations.'

Lily felt herself blush.

'What was your wife doing at Bensons that day she put the fear of God into the workforce?'

'Ex-wife,' he corrected. 'She was trying her luck. She'd heard I was back in, what she calls, a proper job. She was between lovers and bored.'

'Oh. Does she do that often?'

He laughed, a hollow laugh. 'No. First and last time. I've made sure of that. Your turn.' He lay back in his seat and looked relieved that his story was over.

Lily took a deep breath. Where should she start? Her

tale couldn't match the drama or sadness of his. She told him how she'd met Will at university. Told him how she'd worked her way up in Bensons, how much she used to enjoy her job, until the redundancies started, until…

'Until I came and spoiled it,' Jackson added, reading her mind.

'Not your fault, I see that now.'

'My father sent me in to troubleshoot, that's what I've done.' He shrugged. 'You were telling me about your fiancé.'

Lily wondered if she really wanted to divulge the years of wanting Will and his inability to commit to her. Disclosing her obsession was humiliating. But, she supposed, not as humiliating as his disclosure about his wife's affairs.

'Will and I,' she began, feeling sorry for herself and fighting back tears. How stupid. Stop it. She sniffed and took a deep breath. 'Will and I had been together…' her voice trailed away.

'You don't have to tell me if you don't want to. It's none of my business.' He stood up.

Was he leaving?

Lily gestured frantically for him to sit back down and waved her hands in front of her face, fanning back the tears. She realised that she did want to tell him. She actually wanted him to know. She just couldn't get the words out.

He came over and sat next to her, put his arm around her shoulders and pulled her close, then stroked her messy hair away from her face.

'I'm sorry about your eye,' she sniffed.

He smiled. 'These things happen. Don't worry.'

'It's just that I thought you said run, not don't run.'

He laughed. Kissed her on the forehead.

She wished he wouldn't do that. She liked it too much.

'Will and I,' she began again. 'Had been together on and off for ten years, although according to Will it's only about two years really. Anyway, we finished when he decided to go to America on a motorbike holiday with his mates for a month. That's when I went on holiday to Devon with Tess and Gemma.'

'I see.'

'We're not together any longer.'

'I know.'

Lily pulled away from him. 'How do you know?' Had Damon been spilling the beans?

'Well, I guessed. That would be more accurate – I guessed. You're not wearing your engagement ring.'

'It might have been at the jewellers being resized.' Lily felt indignant, irrationally annoyed.

'And you drew my name inside a heart.' He was smirking.

Lily pulled herself from his embrace and stood up, hands on her hips again.

'You're very sure of yourself. You're being arrogant.'

'I am. It's one of my many failings. I'm sorry.' He looked contrite, , although a little smile was playing at the corners of his mouth.

'Well, that's it,' she said.

'What do you mean?' The smile vanished.

'That's it, my story. Not as exciting or dramatic as yours, but that's it.' She realised how dismissive that sounded, she was horrified to belittle his sister's death. 'I'm sorry. I didn't mean…'

'It's okay.' A glimmer of a smile returned to his face.

'So here we are,' Lily said, immediately wishing she

hadn't spoken.

'Yes. Here we are. Fate has brought us together – just as you said it could.' He stood up and took her hands in his. 'Are you coming back to Bensons?'

She shrugged. 'I don't know. Are you?'

He shook his head. 'No, well yes. But only to clear up the mess and set things in order for my replacement.' He pulled her left hand up to his mouth and kissed it.

'Right.'

'That could be you.' He looked into her eyes, his expression earnest. 'If you want it. I would support your application wholeheartedly.'

'I've been there, done that. I wasn't very successful the first time.'

'You were, actually. If it hadn't been for all the irregularities you would have got it.'

'Really? You're not just saying that.'

'Truly. You were by far the best candidate. And they had enough applicants; I know, I saw all the CVs.'

'You're not just sucking up to me, are you? Trying to make me feel better.' Lily couldn't quite believe it. Until now she'd had no feedback from her application or interview.

'Why would I?' He kissed her other hand.

'And where will you be?'

'I'm going back to Devon. My father and I have both agreed that this isn't my calling. He thinks I've done a great job, but he also sees how unhappy this corporate life makes me.'

'He sounds very understanding.'

'He is. And with the money I'll have earned here I'll be able to buy Davey out of his surf-school. He's been looking to sell it for ages.'

'Oh. I see. That sounds great for you.' Lily pulled her hands from his and stepped away from him. 'So I have two options, I can go for the job again, or, if I don't get it, I can take my chances with your replacement and possibly end up out of a job?'.

He stepped towards her, closing the gap she had just created. 'There is a third option.' He put his hands on her hair, smoothed it away from her face, used his thumbs to wipe away her panda eyes. 'Come with me.'

'To Devon?'

'Yes.'

'But…'

'Come here, mermaid hair,' he said, taking her face in his hands and kissing her.

She felt her knees buckle. She felt her head swim. She wrapped her arms around him and pulled him closer.

'You're cheating,' she said, when they finally let go of each other. 'You're trying to influence my decision.'

'You bet I am,' he said and kissed her again.

Later, much later, as Lily sat brushing her hair in front of her dressing table he said, 'Seriously, I don't want to force you into a hasty decision. You take your time. I'm not leaving until everything is sorted out at Bensons anyway.'

'You've changed your mind now?' she laughed.

'No. No. Of course not. I want you to come with me, more than anything.'

'Good.'

'Not that it should influence your decision, but I fell in love with you weeks ago.'

'Me too,' Lily said, feeling shy.

'Yeah, I think it was when I saw your arse hanging out of that skanky wetsuit.'

Lily turned towards him, her eyes narrowing. She attempted to swipe him with the hairbrush but he was too quick and dodged out of the way. She shrieked as she chased him around the bedroom and he laughed when she caught him.

Epilogue

Lily basked in the sun in front of the surf-shack, wriggling her toes in the warm, soft sand. It was late September and few people were to be seen on the beach; the children were back at school and the holidaymakers had gone back to work.

The sea however, fierce and frothy, was full of surfers. She envied them their freedom to ride the waves and feel the spray on their faces.

Her phone pinged as a message arrived from Damon: *How you doing? Any news hun? xx*

Lily couldn't help smiling. Her reply was immediate and short: *Still waiting, lol xx*

Damon: *Loving my new PA, so glad Scare-a-von decided to retire, lol xxx*

Lily replied with a smiley face, she really didn't want to get into a conversation about Veronica. If she was totally honest she was no longer interested in the day-to-day activities of Bensons, she had more important things to focus on.

♥ ♥ ♥

When Jackson had asked her to come with him to Devon she'd never imagined it would take so long to tie up all the loose ends at Bensons, sell her house and move lock, stock and barrel to the coast. They'd now lived in Devon for six glorious months, but it had been a year since they'd made their decision.

At least the delay had given her the opportunity to help with Tess's wedding, which, just as Tess had predicted, took place a mere three months after Gareth had proposed. They had tied the knot in the local Registry Office, then taken all twenty-two of their guests on a vintage bus tour to a chic and tiny boutique hotel in Somerset. Tess had worn a vintage frock which her mother had had stashed in the attic for just such an occasion. 'How lucky was that?' had been Tess's laughing comment when she'd told Lily about it. The reception had been reminiscent of a children's party; balloons and trifle, music played on a 70s turntable and guests able to choose the songs themselves from the hotel's vast collection of vinyl records.

Lily and Jackson had danced the night away and, in the morning, before Lily had even got out of bed and was wondering how bad her hangover would be, Jackson had got down on one knee by her side of the bed and asked her to marry him.

'Don't get carried away by the romance of this wedding,' she laughed, thinking he was joking. 'You really don't have to do this.' Shy and embarrassed, she pulled the covers over her head.

'I don't have to. I want to.' He pulled the duvet back and grabbed her left hand, pulled it to his mouth and kissed her fingers. 'What's your answer?'

Lily didn't hesitate, didn't think about anything other than how much she wanted to be with Jackson.

Forever. Afterwards, whenever she thought about his proposal a warm glow enveloped her. How different it had felt to her reaction to Will's proposal.

'Yes please,' she said, looking into his earnest eyes; so blue, so beautiful.

'Thank you,' he whispered, slipping the diamond solitaire easily onto her finger.

Lily sat up in bed and stared at the ring. 'It's beautiful, but…'

'You don't like it?'

'I love it. Oh, I love it.' She pulled him in and kissed him hard. 'But where did it come from?'

He frowned. 'I brought it with me.'

'But when did you buy it? I mean…' What did she mean? She wasn't sure herself.

Now he laughed and appeared to consider his answer. 'I actually bought it the day after we went skydiving.'

'What? For me? After I'd blacked your eye?'

'Of course for you. Who else? I told you, I fell in love with you on a Devon beach when you were not looking your best.'

She punched him playfully on the arm and pushed him away. 'You were very sure of yourself, you arrogant…'

She never finished the sentence because he wrapped her in his arms and smothered her with kisses as he whispered, 'I've already admitted it's one of my many failings.'

Their wedding followed very quickly. Less vintage than Tess's, it was a winter wedding, held between Christmas and New Year, in a charming little castle near Lily's parents. Her dad had given her away and her mum had sung Jackson's praises after he had charmed his way into her heart. Jackson's parents had flown in by helicopter, landing in the castle grounds.

Tess had been a bridesmaid and, after a lot of hints and lobbying from Gemma, so had Pixie-Bella. Everyone had agreed that she had stolen the show. Gemma had played a pivotal part in the wedding; it was thanks to her that they found such a stunning venue at such short notice. It was Gemma who had located the castle and used her powers of persuasion on the owners to allow it to be used over the Christmas holiday period. It was also Gemma who convinced them that a helicopter landing in their grounds would do no damage to their award-winning landscaped grounds, just as it was Gemma who gave the owners a year's free PR advice as compensation for the damage it did do. Fortunately, Gemma was in a position to offer such advice for free, because despite only working part-time and barely being there five minutes, she now ran the entire PR and advertising company.

'Sure beats having another baby. Who knew work could be such fun?' She had shared this nugget with Lily and Tess the week before the wedding when they met for a combined Christmas drink and hen party. She also had a trendy new hairstyle, but Lily didn't have to courage to ask if her own hair had regrown or if it was a wig.

It had snowed just after the ceremony and Lily and Jackson had toasted their marriage with champagne, while watching giant snowflakes fall past leaded-light windows. It had been the happiest day of Lily's life.

So far.

♥ ♥ ♥

Lily watched Jackson stride up the beach carrying his

surfboard. His hair had grown longer again and was already bleached by the sun and the sea. He dropped the board on the sand and unzipped his wetsuit, letting it fall to his waist. Just the sight of him made her heart flip.

'And how are my girls?' he asked, bending down to Lily and kissing her.

'Well, this girl,' she said, pointing at herself. 'Is tired and rapidly losing patience. And this girl,' she patted her very pregnant bump. 'Is looping the loop and showing no signs of making an appearance.'

Jackson laughed. 'She's only two days overdue. Come on.' He grabbed her hands to pull her up. 'Let's get you home.'

'Oh, and look what I found in the discarded shoe crate.' Lily pushed her feet into her flip-flops.

Jackson looked down. 'Cool,' he said.

'No. They're the ones I lost that day I met you. Remember? I had to borrow those disgusting trainers from Davey.'

'I remember.' Jackson laughed. 'He never said he found yours. What else is back there?'

'Not much. I've thrown a lot of rubbish away.'

Jackson peeled off his wetsuit and hung it up.

'Damon messaged me,' Lily said as they packed up their belongings and closed up the surf-shack.

'He should be well settled into the job now. I think we made the right decision there.'

'So does he.' Lily laughed. Damon, who always professed to not being at all ambitious, had slid into the role of finance director as smoothly as if he had been born to it. 'He says he's loving his new PA.'

'I bet. I'm glad he managed to let Veronica leave in a pleasant way. Though I'm still not convinced she wasn't, if not part of the fraud, certainly aware of it.'

'We'll never know. Anyway, Damon thinks that she left because of him.'

'Because of him?'

'She thought he was too flamboyant, too camp.'

'I'm sure she would never say that.'

'No,' laughed Lily. 'She's not stupid; she's not Oily Bastard.'

Jackson joined in her laughter. 'That reminds me,' he said. 'I had an email from Bensons' lawyers today. Our Oily Bastard should finally receive justice.'

'For what?' Lily rubbed her back as they walked up the beach.

'It appears the company he went to after Bensons weren't quite so tolerant of his behaviour towards women.'

'Did he lose his job?' Lily sighed. 'He'll just talk his way into another one and do it all over again.' It still rankled with her that he'd been able to walk away blemish free from Bensons.

'Oh no,' Jackson smiled. 'They reported him to the police. Opened a can of worms. Apparently, in the distant past, long before he came to Bensons, there had been suggestive remarks and inappropriate touching of a work experience student. Court case and, with luck, a custodial sentence.'

'Serves him right. Justice. Yes. Pity about the poor girl.'

'Nothing we could have done about that. It was before Bensons.'

'I still think we should have prosecuted him.'

'Well, as I said at the time, we had little choice. We had to ensure Bensons' future and we had to safeguard all those jobs. He got his comeuppance in the end.'

'I suppose.'

♥ ♥ ♥

'Will,' Jackson called and whistled.

'I can't get used to that,' Lily said, shaking her head.

'Not our fault, that was already his name.' He bent down, laughing and patting the rescue Jack Russell who jumped around his ankles.

Jackson had to almost haul Lily up the little beach path to the car park.

'I will be glad when our little mermaid is born,' Lily said, rubbing her back again.

'Little mermaid. I like that.'

'Maybe we should call her Ariel.'

'Ariel?'

'The little mermaid. You know, Disney.'

'No.' Jackson shook his head.

'I suppose you didn't spend your childhood watching girly Disney films.' Not like me and Tess, she thought.

'I thought Ariel was a character in a Marvel comic. I think.' He shook his head again.

'I was only joking. I don't really want to call her Ariel, but we do need to decide on a name.'

'Maybe that's why she's taking so long to make her appearance; she won't come until we settle on a name. At least she won't be saddled with the name Cyril. Though if we have another and it's a boy, there will be expectations.'

'Don't even think about it,' Lily said, getting into the car while Jackson loaded the boot. 'This little one hasn't arrived yet and I can't even think about another. Whatever happens in the distant future, we're breaking the Cyril tradition.'

'You'll get no arguments from me on that. And we will need to be careful to make sure there isn't another quickly.' Jackson got into the car and started the engine. 'We didn't expect our little girl to come along so soon, did we?'

'No. But I'm not sorry.' It was such a cliché, a honeymoon baby, but Lily had never felt so happy.

'Me neither.' Jackson squeezed Lily's knee as he drove out of the car park.

Just before they pulled out onto the main road Lily noticed an old man standing on the corner in the distance. He turned and seemed to wave in her direction. He reminded her of Josh, Josh who used to work in Bensons' post room, Josh who died the same day he was made redundant. Josh who Lily was convinced she had seen on her first day on holiday, the day she met Jackson.

'Do you know him?' Lily said, pointing in the old man's direction. 'Only it looks as though he's waving at you.'

Jackson turned and looked where Lily was pointing. 'Who?'

'That old chap,' Lily said, turning and looking again, but he had gone.

'What did he look like?' Jackson pulled out onto the main road.

She described Josh. 'He looks like a guy who used to work at Bensons, in the post room. His name was Josh. But he died.'

'Josh. He hasn't got a son called Ewan, has he? Lives

local.'

'I think he did.'

'I know him.'

'If it's the same guy, then he died.'

'Then it can't be the same guy. I saw him the day I met you. The day I pulled you out of the sea when you were drowning in three feet of water.'

'Ha, ha,' Lily said, smiling.

'Yeah. I hadn't really been watching the sea that closely. Then he pointed you out and I saw that you were in the surf lane. I had noticed you earlier though, baking yourself on the beach.' He smiled to himself.

'Did he speak?'

'No. He just waved and pointed. He was up on the beach path, not on the actual beach; he was too far away for conversation.'

'That's the day I saw him too; he set me on the right path when I got lost on my way to the beach. The thing is, which I found out later, he was already dead.'

'Well, he couldn't have been, could he? Not if we both saw him.'

'No. It must have been someone who looks like him.'

'Yeah,' Jackson agreed.

They drove home in subdued silence; Lily wondering if they had really been brought together by the ghost of Bensons' post room? Fate worked in mysterious ways.

Lily woke in the night; she shook a slumbering Jackson awake. 'I think it's happening.'

'Is your bag packed?'

'Yeah. In the hall cupboard.'

'Is it time to go yet?'

'I think it might be. And she still doesn't have a name.'

Their little mermaid was born three hours later.

'She has the bluest eyes,' Jackson said, staring into them.

'All babies have blue eyes,' the midwife said. 'They can change later.'

'No.' Lily and Jackson chorused.

'I will say this,' the midwife said. 'I don't see hair like that on a baby very often. It's so long, she needs a haircut.' She laughed and left them alone.

'Mermaid hair,' Jackson said, kissing Lily, then the baby on the forehead. 'And look at those lips.'

'They're like ruby rosebuds. So cute.'

'Ruby,' Jackson repeated.

'Beth,' Lily said.

Ruby Beth Montgomery-Jones.

THE END.

Acknowledgements

My special thanks go to the following for their help, support and encouragement during the writing of this book: Amy Mayes, Sophie Mayes, Barbara Fulford, Jenny Tiley, Chloe Dodgson.

Thank you also to Alex McAuley for allowing me to steal some of his phrases, especially *The Europeans,* to Sinead Champ for *chilli trout pout* and to Marie Setterfield for the hair-raising incident which inspired chapter ten.

She just wanted to be alone...

Escape to Christmas Cottage

CJ MORROW

CJ MORROW

Sooo Not ♥ Looking For a Man

And with an attitude like that,
never likely to find one!

Little

Mishaps

& *Big*

Surprises

CJ MORROW

Another delightful
romantic comedy from the
author of best seller
Blame it on the Onesie